THE UNFAITHFUL QUEEN

Also by Carolly Erickson

the
UNFAITHFUL
QUEEN

A Novel Of Henry VIII's Fifth Wife

Carolly Erickson

ST. MARTIN'S PRESS

NEW YORK

THE UNFAITHFUL QUEEN. Copyright © 2012 by Carolly Erickson. All rights reserved. Printed in the United States of America. For information, address St. Martin's Press, 175 Fifth Avenue, New York, N.Y. 10010.

www.stmartins.com

Library of Congress Cataloging-in-Publication Data

Erickson, Carolly, 1943–
    The unfaithful queen : a novel of Henry VIII's fifth wife / Carolly Erickson.
— 1st ed.
      p. cm.
    ISBN 978-0-312-59691-0 (hardcover)
    ISBN 978-1-250-01102-2 (e-book)
  1. Catherine Howard, Queen, consort of Henry VIII, King of England, d. 1542.
2. Great Britain—History—Henry VIII, 1509–1547—Fiction.   3. Queens—
Great Britain—Fiction.   I. Title.
    PS3605.R53U54 2012
    813'.6—dc23

2012026402

First Edition: September 2012

10 9 8 7 6 5 4 3 2 1

To John with love

THE UNFAITHFUL QUEEN

ONE

Tower Green
May 1536

THE new-mown grass smelled sweet as we took our places along the verge on that grey dawn, all of us together, waiting for my cousin Anne to be brought out to die.

Though the spring was well advanced there was a chill in the air, and I shivered under my thin Spanish cloak. I drew nearer to my aunts and my grandmother Agnes, sidling up against her long bony body swathed in a gown of watchet blue under her warm woolen ermine-trimmed mantle. She did not look at me, but stood very still, her back very straight, her crimsoned cheeks wrinkled, her lips widened in a half smile. My grandma had once been handsome, so it was said, but her youth was long past and no finery, no amount of paint on her sallow cheeks, could disguise the marks of age. She was said to be the richest woman in England, and one of the most fearsome.

I drew nearer to her now, as the sun began to rise and the first crimson streaks blazed along the horizon. The hour was nearly at hand. The faces of the relatives all around me were growing tighter, aunts and uncles and cousins, ancient great-aunts whose names I barely knew, aged great-uncles who, I had been told, had fought alongside my late grandfather in the long wars that had brought him fame.

At the center of the crowded nest of relatives was my uncle Thomas, third Duke of Norfolk, the head of our family. He stood slightly apart from the rest of us, feet planted firmly, his dark face with its hooded eyes grim, his mouth set in a firm line. His elaborate padded and slashed doublet of quilted yellow silk made him stand out from among the growing number of spectators gathering to watch the dread spectacle to come.

"Get on with it then," we who were closest to him heard him mutter. "Kill the big whore!"

Birds began twittering and chirping as the sky lightened. They swooped in and out of chinks and crannies in the great blocks of grey stone in the ancient tower walls. I watched them, fluttering and flapping their small wings, glad for a chance to be distracted by something other than the grisly business to come. I tried to forget that my cousin Anne, many years older than I and Queen of England, was to die this morning.

I had never seen anyone die by the sword. I did not want to watch. I shrank back among the others, glad for once that I was so small (at fifteen years old, I was a full head shorter than other girls my age) that I could not see over the heads of those in front of me. I could barely glimpse the raised platform, draped in black, with its thick block of wood, the guardsmen in royal livery who stood around it, the tall halberdiers with their sharp-bladed, long-handled hatchets that glinted in the sunlight.

For what seemed an hour or more we stood, weary of waiting, while the crowd grew larger and larger and the sun rose higher.

"Remember, she is not one of us!" my grandmother hissed. "She has betrayed the family! She has betrayed the Howard name! Take warning from her fate!"

Her words unleashed more accusations. Terrible accusations, from those standing near me. I heard someone say that Anne had had many lovers, that every night when she went to bed she had men lined up, ready to do her bidding. Even her brother George!

How could such things be said, I wondered. How could my cousin have so dishonored our Howard lineage? Unless she was mad, or possessed by a demon.

"Do you think she was possessed by a demon?" I whispered to my cousin Charyn, who stood near me, looking remarkably calm and self-possessed, not a single blond hair out of place under her dark headdress, her cloak lifting in the slight breeze, her gloved hands folded in front of her.

"The demon of lust, most likely," was Charyn's prompt reply.

Charyn was seventeen, much taller than I was and much prettier. Her hair curled naturally and seemed to flow without tangles, even on the windiest day. Her grey eyes were never troubled or filled with confusion, as mine so often were. When she spoke, her words were few and crisp and telling, and she always seemed to know just what to say. She would not believe in demons. She was sensible and practical, not easily led astray by gossip.

"He might have burned her, like a heretic," another soft female voice reached me. "But he couldn't. He still loves her."

There was more hushed talk—of the swordsman brought from Calais many weeks before our cousin Anne's trial and condemnation. The swordsman whose sole purpose was to carry out executions.

"He was planning it all along," I heard a man say. "He wanted to be rid of her. He had tired of her. And she was cursed—she couldn't give him a son. So he hired the French executioner. He hired him months ago. He paid him twenty-three pounds!" There were exclamations at this. Twenty-three pounds was a great deal of money, enough to buy several estates.

"Is it true she sent her gold bracelets to her old nurse and rocker, as a last keepsake?"

"She promised to marry Norris, her favorite lover," one daring voice murmured. "She was going to kill the king and then marry him."

"Don't say such a thing—or you will die too!"

The babble of voices, the tramp of soldiers' boots—then the gasps when Anne was brought out and helped to go up the steps to where the block was waiting.

Her step was brisk, lively. There was no heaviness about her. Once again I thought, she is mad, she has gone mad. She does not feel the pangs of her approaching death. Or is she relieved that she is not to suffer the agonies of death by fire?

I felt Charyn take my hand. She had taken off her glove. Her hand was cold in my warmer one.

Some in the crowd were kneeling. I heard sighs. People were drying their eyes. My uncle the duke was frowning.

"She deserves to die!" he was saying through clenched teeth. "She must suffer for her treasons!" We all knew that he had been the one to preside over the group of peers that had condemned Anne. Anne—the favorite child of his favorite sister Elizabeth.

I could see her clearly now, my view was no longer blocked by the capes and mantles of those in front of me. So many of those around me had begun to kneel—though my grandmother continued to stand rigidly in place, and as far as I could tell, none of my Howard relations appeared to be preparing to kneel. Not a knee was buckling. Charyn was trembling, but she stood.

The Lord Mayor and aldermen, solemn-faced in their black robes, watched impassively as the tall, brawny dark-haired Frenchman, his heavy broadsword drawn from its wide leather scabbard, climbed the steps to stand behind Anne. Compared to him, she looked very small. She kept turning her head to see him, to see what he was doing.

I felt Charyn squeeze my hand, her nails biting into my palm, and for the first time my stomach lurched with fear. I lowered my head. I did not want to see this.

Anne stepped forward. Her voice was strong as she asked for prayers. She did not confess her guilt. Rather she swore, on the host, that she was innocent. I was certain I saw her smile. Was she thinking of her daughter, I wondered, in those last few moments of life left to her? Her one child, Elizabeth, the child who the king had hoped would be a prince. Her legacy.

Once again she looked behind her. The swordsman was waiting. The women in attendance on her unfastened her ermine mantle and waited while she took off her headdress and covered her hair with a linen cap.

Did I only imagine that at that moment a cloud covered the sun and the sky darkened? Afterwards I could not remember clearly. I know that I looked in vain for a chaplain. Was there to be no chaplain, to say a prayer with Anne, or read words of forgiveness from the Bible? Was Anne to be denied these final comforts?

She murmured a few words to each of her attendants, no doubt wishing them well, and all but one received her last words with tearful thanks. Then she knelt. She knelt upright. She had no need to put her head on the block, for the swordsman's blade slashed sideways, not downward.

Charyn fainted. I looked down at her. And at that moment I heard the horrible sound: a swishing in the air, a crunching, cries of fright and alarm. Looking up, I saw Anne's twitching body, a rush of blood staining her grey gown deep red, her attendants wrapping something in a reddening cloth.

I could hardly breathe. I staggered. For a brief time everything around me seemed to blur, then my vision cleared and I began to catch my breath again. I saw that Charyn was being helped to her feet. The sky was lightening—or had it ever really gone dark?

The high grey stone walls still loomed, the birds, heedless of the drama below them, continued to soar and plunge, and then to rise, wings flapping, up into the sunny sky.

Not long after Anne's death my father crept quietly in through a side door of the west wing of Horsham, my grandmother Agnes's great sprawling country house in Sussex. He had sent me a note to say he was coming, and I was waiting for him in an anteroom.

I could tell as soon as I saw him that he was troubled and subdued. His shoulders were hunched, his expression dour. He had never been a robust man, but now that he was beginning to age his physical strength was waning. He sought me out from across the small room, his lined face sagging, his light blue eyes filled with worry. The eyes of a boy, I thought, rather than a man. A boy afraid of his master, like the half-naked scullery boys that scrubbed the huge pots in my grandmother's kitchens. The thin blond hair that poked out from under father's cap gave him a foolish look. His scraggly mop of hair was far different from my own thick auburn mane. I was proud of my hair, people said it was like the rich red-brown curls of my late mother. I resembled her—in vitality and lightness of spirit as well as in my coloring—rather than my ever anxious father.

Wearily he unhooked his cloak and cast it off, throwing himself down on a bench beside the thick wooden table in the anteroom and calling to the nearest groom for a tankard of ale. He sighed heavily and put his head in his hands.

I went to him and knelt. Weakly, almost absentmindedly, he laid his hand on my head to give me his blessing. I got up and joined him at the table.

"Did you have a rough crossing then, father? Were you ill?"

He nodded and pressed one hand to his back.

"The seas were high. And I am tortured with the stone."

Kidney stones were the bane of my father's life. He suffered terribly, and shouted loudly when his suffering was at its worst.

He had come from Calais, the French coastal town held by the English, where he held the office of Controller—by far the highest of the series of low court positions he had held. But I knew from his letters that he was in disgrace with his superiors there; the English governor of the town slighted him and criticized him, he wrote, and the French so disliked him that he was sure that if he left the town, he would never be allowed back in.

He clung to his office, fearing to leave. And as a result he had not been present at my cousin Anne's execution. He had not been there to stand with the rest of us in the Howard clan, to stand beside his brother the duke, who treated him with scorn, or to bow to their stepmother, my grandmother Agnes, who did not disguise the fact that of all her many children and stepchildren, she despised my father the most.

He drained the tankard that was placed before him and called for another.

"The stone, the everlasting stone! It burns me. It stabs me. I tell you, Catherine, there are times when it makes me writhe in agony."

"I'm sorry father. I wish I could help you. Can you get no physick there in Calais? I have heard that the apothecaries of France are superior to our own."

He shrugged.

"I have medicine—but it works over well. It breaks the stone, I void the gravel and then—" he spat into the rushes at his feet "—and then it makes me piss all night long."

I tried not to laugh at his forlorn words. He looked over at me.

"I dare not go home because of Margaret's wrath! She beats me when I piss our bed. I tell you, she beats me! She says, 'Only children piss their beds, not old men!' But I am not old, merely afflicted. I would do anything to rid myself of that damnable pain!"

"They say eating a stork's wing will keep your water from spilling over," I suggested.

"Not true. I have tried it. Margaret laughed at me for trying it."

I had little love for my stepmother Margaret Jennings, my father's blustering, bullying third wife. She had been my stepmother for some three years, and the best thing about her was that she stayed away in the country most of the time, avoiding my father and taking no interest in me. She had married him because he was Lord Edmund Howard, brother of the powerful, wealthy Duke of Norfolk, and for no other reason. He had married her because she had a modest fortune, and now that he had spent that fortune (he had none of his own, being a younger son), he had no further use for her nor she for him. Yet they still shared a hearth—when he was not in Calais—and she continued to mistreat him.

I called for a plate of comfits for my father and turned the conversation to other topics. But there was really only one topic that concerned those of us living in Grandmother Agnes's household: that of our late cousin Anne, and the king's new wife Jane Seymour.

Father shifted on his bench and rubbed his sore back.

"Everyone fears that the new queen will cancel all of Queen Anne's appointments," he said as he picked at the plate in front of him. Father owed his position as Controller of Calais to the benevolence of the late Queen Anne; he had begged her to help him and she had. Now that Anne was dead, Anne who had shown him pity, he was afraid that he would lose his office for sure.

"All we hear from morning to night is Seymour, Seymour, Seymour. I have to tell you, Catherine, I am in dread of losing my office."

"Cannot Uncle Thomas find you another?"

"He can—if he will. There is an Englishman lately condemned whose goods are forfeit. I have written to Thomas to ask for them as a gratuity."

"And has he replied?"

Father shrugged. "He sends me a golden toothpick and some slates for my roof. A golden toothpick! Now what is such a silly bauble worth? A golden toothpick will not keep me out of debtor's prison, nor keep my wife from beating me when I piss my bed!"

He rose to go, and sighed once more.

"I cannot keep mother waiting any longer."

I knew that he dreaded facing her. Yet there was the smallest of smiles on his face as he turned to leave me.

"You will be glad to hear that I am doing well here at Horsham, father," I called out to his retreating figure, and at my words he turned back, eager for the chance to delay his interview with the duchess a bit longer. For the first time he looked at me fixedly, really taking in my appearance.

He nodded. "Yes. You are ripe. You are doing as you're told then? Minding your manners? Staying out of harm's way? Staying out of your grandmother's way?" He chuckled.

"If you mean, am I whipped? I can of a truth say no. I am learning to avoid the rod—and grandmother's wrath."

He continued to scan my face, and it seemed to me that his gaze was more tender than appraising.

"And how do you spend your days then? Does she have you splitting wood, or baking bread, or collecting goose down for her pillows?"

Now it was my turn to chuckle. "Perhaps all that is to come. For now I am taught to dance, and to bow gracefully, and never to wipe my fingers on the curtains the way the servants do when they think grandmother is not watching."

He laughed.

"I practice my stitching, and listen to Father Dawes while he reads to us from the Scriptures, and I practice my letters, and I go with grandmother and my cousins to the farms and villages near here when she gives out her cures."

"Her cures?"

"Her medicines. Her gingerflower water and oil of rosemary and all the other potions and possets she says will cure the poor."

"I wish she had a cure for the stone," my father muttered.

"Ask her for one," I said. "And father—"

"Yes?"

"Until you are recovered, why not stay with Uncle William? He would welcome you I'm sure." My uncle William Cotton, my late mother's half brother, had a large estate in Kent. He was a warm, congenial man, known for his kindness and goodheartedness. I had never heard him speak ill of my father. "No need to go back to stay with Margaret."

Father nodded. "Yes. I'll do that. If only his estate were nearer the court." And with a final pat on my shoulder he went to find grandmother.

I never knew what I might find when I went upstairs, into the room we called the Paradise Chamber, the cold, drafty, barnlike room with the lofty ceiling where we girls spent our days and nights when not attending to our duties or our lessons.

When I first arrived at Horsham it was all I could do not to think of the Paradise Chamber as not a paradise at all but rather a sort of dungeon, a place of no escape where we girls were locked in at night and watched by our jailers. We each had a small bed, with a thin mattress and a blanket, but bedwarmers were few, and my feet were always cold at night. The Paradise Chamber was drafty, and the beds farthest from the single hearth got little heat. At the foot of each bed was a trunk that held our clothing and other possessions. Some of the girls hid things underneath their mattresses but as the mattresses were full of fleas nothing of value could be kept there, except coins, and no one dared to put coins under their mattress because everyone knew that was where they were likely to be hidden.

Nights in the Paradise Chamber were full of discomforts. We were awakened by the barking of the watchdogs in the courtyard, or by the moans and coughs of the sick girls among us, or by the cries of others awakened by nightmares.

Some girls wept. One night not long after I arrived at Horsham I was awakened by the sound of sobbing from a bed near mine. The fire in the hearth had burned low and the few candles in the room gave little light, but when I sat up and looked for the source of the sobbing I quickly realized that it was coming from the bed directly across the room from mine. The bed where Alice Restvold slept. Like nearly all the girls in the room, Alice was a distant relation of mine, a few years older than I was, a red-headed girl with a pinched face and large staring blue eyes.

The noise of her sobbing and sniffing annoyed me, I did not like being awakened. But at the same time I was curious to know what was causing her such distress. I got out of bed and, taking a candle, went to her.

"Alice!" I whispered. "What is it, Alice?"

"He—has—gone away," she managed to say.

"Who has gone away?"

"My John."

"He is—your betrothed?"

"No!"

"Then who is he?"

"My—beloved!"

11

Her beloved, I thought. But not her betrothed. I had never known love, but I had seen it, often. I had seen lovers walking hand in hand, lying together in the warm wet grass on May Day, exchanging glances in church or at table—even embracing in darkened hallways. Father Dawes lectured us sternly about lust, the devil's temptation of the flesh, but young as I was, I knew that love was a thing apart, nobler far than lust. A treasure to be cherished. I did not yet understand how the two can be entangled, how confusing the urges and pleasures of the body can be.

"Why would your beloved ever leave you?" I whispered to Alice.

But my question only made her sob more freely and more loudly. Several of the other girls tossed irritably in their beds and tried to shush her.

"She's at it again!" I heard one of them say. "Why can't she just forget him! He's gone!"

Presently I heard a disturbance behind me and in a moment another girl had come up to Alice's bed. A girl I didn't recognize. In the dim light I could tell only that she had long dark hair, loosely braided, and that she wore around her shoulders a thick woolen shawl embroidered in a pattern of deep blue and sparkling silver.

"Stop that noise, foolish chit!" the newcomer said tartly. "You're keeping us all awake!" She did not bother to keep her own voice low, but barked out her words as she reached swiftly under the blanket and took Alice by the hand.

"Come with me!" she said. "I'll give you something to put you to sleep, so we can all sleep through the night." And pulling the weeping Alice out of bed she fairly dragged her to a door at the opposite end of the long room and, taking a key that she wore around her neck, unlocked the door.

"You may as well come along," she said to me as she pulled Alice through the door after her.

We were in a small chamber furnished with two beds, a chest and a low table. It had a sloping roof and a little barred window, beneath which was a brazier full of red coals. The room smelled of smoke and of something else, something heavy and sweet. A scent I had never smelled before.

"You are both new to this house," the girl with the braid said. "You are Catherine, whose mother no one mentions because she was the king's whore. And you are the sniveling Alice, whose lover has married another."

"What?" The shock of the girl's words made Alice stop crying. "What did you say?"

"I said your lover, John Brockley, the gentleman usher, has married another woman. He never told you he was betrothed, did he."

Alice, her eyes wide, shook her head.

"What other woman?"

The girl with the braid went to the wardrobe and began pouring what looked like wine into a goblet. To this she added powder from a jar and stirred the concoction.

"It matters not. When next you see him, he will have a wife."

She handed the goblet to Alice.

"Here. Drink this."

Alice sniffed the liquid, made a sour face, then looked at us. She flinched, but obeyed and drank the liquid in a single gulp. When she finished she wiped her mouth with the back of her hand—something we were admonished never to do—and handed the goblet back.

I stood watching, somewhat dazed.

"Who are you?" I asked the girl with the braid. "And how dare you speak ill of my mother?"

She regarded me coolly. "I am Joan. My father is William Bulmer, Lord Mannering. And everyone in this household knows about your mother, the ill-famed Lady Jocasta."

Alice was staring at me.

"My mother was beautiful. Others were envious of her beauty, and so they defamed her."

Joan smiled. "If you like," she said. "The truth is known, whatever you may say. And besides, she is long dead."

I needed no reminder that my mother had been laid to rest long before, when I was a very small child, barely old enough to remember her. My memory of her was of a great sadness, of something warm and loving that had suddenly vanished from my life, leaving only sorrow behind.

"You guard your tongue about my mother, Joan Bulmer! Or I will whip you!"

"Indeed? I would not advise it. The last girl who struck me was found much bruised and broken, beside the malt-house door."

The menace in her tone made me wary. I knew little of the workings of my grandmother's large household, but I was aware that every large noble household had its share of ruffians, its cliques, its back-stairs brawls. It had been that way in my father's much smaller establishment. Things went on behind the backs of the stewards—deeds that were never brought to light. Sometimes quite violent deeds. Until I knew more about the ways of my grandmother's establishment I would not provoke this brazen girl further.

But before I could decide how to reply, or what to do, I saw that Alice was slipping down in a faint. To my surprise, Joan reached down and tried to pick her up.

"Help me," she said, and together we lifted Alice onto one of the small room's two beds. She lay there, still and pale, her eyes closed. Frowning, Joan picked up a candle and held it close to Alice's white face.

"Has she been spewing?" she asked me.

"I don't know."

She set the candle back down and felt Alice's stomach and belly, making her moan.

I heard Joan swear under her breath.

"By the bones of Christ, not another one!"

I looked at Joan questioningly, our quarrel and clashing words for the moment forgotten.

"These girls! These rich, protected girls, who know nothing of the world, who come here to this lustpit of a house, and get themselves with child, and then—"

"She's carrying a child? Are you sure?"

Joan gave me a withering look, then slapped Alice's cheek. "Wake up girl!"

Alice protested, pushing Joan away feebly with one hand.

"Don't hurt her!" I objected.

"Hurt her? I'm helping her! I'm going to help her get rid of this unwanted encumbrance! Before we all are whipped till our backs are raw!"

What I was seeing and hearing confused me. This forceful, unsparing girl Joan, with her threats and her slaps and her insult to my mother's memory, seemed to be saying that Alice's disgrace reflected on us all. That we were living in what she called a pit of lust, not a noble household—my grandmother's noble household. How could she say such a thing? And how could she be certain that Alice was carrying a child?

As the night wore on, my confusion lessened. At Joan's insistence ("Do you really want the wrath of the old duchess to come down on all our heads?" she demanded) I stayed on in the small room while Joan administered another drink to the drowsy Alice. This one took longer to make, and smelled so foul that I thought I would retch. The stench of it filled the room.

Poor Alice admitted that she had not had her monthly flux for many weeks and that she had often been sick, that whatever she ate would not stay in her stomach.

"Did no one ever tell you that if you let a man have his pleasure with you there would be a child? Did no one ever show you what to do to make sure no child would be born?"

Alice shook her head.

"Then I will tell you." With a sigh Joan went to the wardrobe and brought out a lemon, which she cut in half.

"Here," she said, handing one of the halves to Alice. "Take this and put it inside you."

Alice, groggy from the drinks she had been given, stared at Joan, incomprehending.

"Stupid girl!" Joan spat out. Then, taking the other half of the lemon, she lifted her skirts, spread her legs, and packed the dripping fruit up into her honeypot.

So quickly did she do this that I hardly had time to be surprised. Alice, after fumbling a bit, managed to imitate her.

"Do this whenever you are with a lover. If you have no lemons, use a bit of sponge. Dip it in vinegar first. Or if you have no vinegar, dip it in sour milk."

"How do you know this? How can you be sure it will work?" I wanted to know. "You are no midwife or wise woman."

"I know," Joan responded, "because I have lain with boys and men since I was younger than you, and I am eighteen now, and I have never yet been with child. I learned what I know from other girls, of course. Older girls. How else?"

She looked over at Alice, who was holding her stomach with both hands.

"She's going to need the chamber pot," Joan told me. "Don't be alarmed. The drink I gave her—the second one—was very strong.

The juice of tansy and pennyroyal. It will cause her to expel her child. The pain will be great, but it will not last long."

Alice was doubled over, grimacing and moaning. She squatted over the chamber pot to relieve herself but could only grunt and emit little shrieks. Her forehead shone with perspiration. She reached for my hand, and when I offered it, she squeezed it so hard it hurt.

"Help me," she whispered, then let out a piteous moan.

What happened over the next hour is best left unrecorded, except to write that when Alice's pain was finally past, she was no longer carrying her lover's child. And I, having witnessed her suffering, and done my best to help her through it with soothing words and encouragement, was left exhausted and in need of rest.

But the lessons of that long night stayed with me. If, as Joan Bulmer said, we were living in a lustpit, then I was determined to avoid its pitfalls. I had no lover, but I vowed that, should a lover come to me, I would keep plenty of lemons nearby, and would be wary and prudent in making use of them. I did not yet know how perilous the ways of love could be, and how even the most prudent of girls could fall prey to its perplexing tangles.

TWO

I did not grow much taller, alas! When I turned sixteen I was no taller than I had been at fifteen, and the clothes I brought with me when I first came to Horsham still fit me many months later. They still fit me—but I had worn them so often that they were full of holes and rips and I had been forced to patch them again and again. I had no money to pay a dressmaker to make me new gowns and petticoats, or to buy stockings and trims from the peddlers who came to my grandmother's estate every few weeks.

How I envied my pretty cousin Charyn, who not only grew taller and more attractive but became more and more sure of her loveliness the older she became. I saw her looking with satisfaction at her own reflection, smiling at herself in the long pier glass in the Paradise Chamber, or gazing into a pond in the garden in search of her own face. She noticed the admiring glances of the household servants and the gentlemen ushers who served my grandmother the duchess. The envious glances of other girls she pretended to ignore, but I could tell that secretly they pleased her.

Knowing that others were admiring her, she carried herself proudly, her head held high on her slender neck, her back straight, a tight smile on her face. Frowns were unbecoming, so she seldom frowned. One of her teeth was crooked—her only visible flaw—but she was careful not to let that tooth show when she smiled. And her manner toward others was reserved, her gestures restrained. She never raised her voice, never appeared to quarrel.

Grandmother Agnes, who was all but impossible to please, gave a slight nod of satisfaction when Charyn passed by, or when she came to our dancing class—something she rarely did—and observed Charyn hopping daintily to the music, never out of step, never disheveled at the end of a long intricate dance.

Though Charyn and I were friends, and had been friends since we were very young, her father's estate being near ours, we could hardly have been less alike, and the older we grew, the more dissimilar we became. I liked to giggle and tell jokes—anything to make the other girls laugh. If I could make them laugh, they might not notice that my nose was too big and my eyes were set too far apart for beauty—flaws Charyn was forever pointing out to me. I liked to romp and play games and go for long walks, even in the rain sometimes. Walking lifted my spirits, though I was often bedraggled by the time I got back to the Paradise Chamber, my torn skirts ever more torn, my petticoats muddy. I was not careful to walk in a certain way or keep a certain expression on my face. And I hardly ever looked in the pier glass. Seeing my appearance made me glum, and reminded me that my nose was too big and long. If I thought about it, I realized that my lack of beauty might keep me from ever marrying.

Charyn was desirable as a wife, because she was a Howard and her father could provide a generous dowry, and because of her youth and beauty. She boasted that discussions were already under way between Grandma Agnes and several highborn, well-to-do men seeking brides. These discussions made my cousin more prideful than ever, and more quick than ever in reminding me that no match might ever be made for me.

"There is a reason why I am soon to be betrothed and you are still a maid, with no suitors for your hand."

"You are two years older than I am," I countered. "I am too young to be betrothed."

"Many girls are married at twelve," Charyn snapped, her usual reserve cast aside, her usually low voice raised.

"Your age is not the reason. The fact is, we are very unalike. I have the fine breeding of a nobleman's daughter, and you do not.

"When a litter of pups is born, one is always the most desirable. The handsomest, with the best and thickest coat, the keenest sense of smell, the most skillful at the hunt. But one or two of the pups are always runts—small, like you. They are inferior whelps, to be discarded. They cannot be allowed to breed. Their inferior sire and dam condemn them.

"You, Catherine, are an inferior whelp and it is time you realized it, as everyone else does. You cannot be allowed to breed. You will never marry."

Charyn's cutting words brought out all my defiance.

"At least I am not going to be sent to a convent, like Margery Pounder." Margery, a sullen girl cursed with a clubfoot and with an unsightly birthmark on her forehead, was ridiculed by the other girls and even more cruelly by the grooms and valets. She had not been at Horsham long before we heard that she was going to be sent to live with the Sisters of Charity. It was understood that she would not marry.

"Not yet," Charyn was saying. "But that may be your fate before long, if you do not grow any taller."

"Perhaps my feet will sprout stumps," I joked. "Or perhaps my head will expand—as yours has."

Charyn gave me one of her rare frowns, then stalked off, her back very straight.

I had deflected her barbs, yet her words worried me. Was I indeed to be sent away if I failed to grow? Would I never know love? Would I be denied the pleasure of a happy marriage, children of my own, all of us living in a fine house with spacious grounds, and perhaps other manors and estates besides?

Could it not happen? I was the niece of the mighty Duke of Norfolk, the granddaughter of the dowager duchess. Why shouldn't I have a wealthy husband, just because I was not very tall?

Inferior whelp indeed!

I was musical and liked to pick out tunes on the virginals. I could play almost any tune I heard, at least I could find the melody easily enough on the wooden keys. There were two virginals kept in one of the upper rooms at Horsham, one quite old with a beautiful case painted with cupids and blue gillyflowers and the other one newer with a plain case but keys that responded more easily to the touch. I sometimes sat playing tunes for an hour or more, making up melodies of my own and amusing myself by singing them.

One afternoon I was startled when my grandmother Agnes came into the room. With her was my uncle William Cotton, benign and pleasant as always. His belly seemed rounder than ever, and his hair thinner and more sparse. He looked as though he had a priest's tonsure. But his face was jolly and smiling, and his eyes were bright with pleasure at the sight of me.

"So that was you banging away on the keys," my grandmother said. "I would hear more."

I thought for a moment, then played "Into the Greenwood Go," a song I had often heard the musicians play at my father's house.

"Good girl," my uncle said. "Clever girl. She has always played well, you know. Ever since she was very small. Catherine dear, can you give us a sacred melody?"

I played a hymn the choir sang at Easter and sang along with my playing, and when I finished I heard my grandmother saying, "Well now, at least she can do *something*!"

"Have you had instruction, Catherine?" my uncle asked. "Did your father provide you with a music teacher?"

"No, Uncle William. His—his means did not permit it."

Grandma Agnes snorted loudly. "His means indeed! What means? He's been living off the rest of us all his life!"

"Doesn't your neighbor George Manox have a son who is a music teacher?" my uncle asked my grandmother.

She nodded.

"Well, could he not come to Horsham and teach Catherine? And perhaps some of the other girls as well?"

She shrugged.

"He could, if he wasn't in disgrace."

"What do you mean?"

She sighed in exasperation. "William, why must you meddle in the affairs of my household? Why must you come and pester me!"

My uncle chuckled. "Because you like my company, that's why!"

And at that the old lady laughed—but only briefly.

"He brought shame on himself," she said at length. "He did something to anger the king, and he brought shame on himself. He was sent away. That's all I know."

"So he taught music at the royal court," I said. "He must have been a fine player and teacher indeed."

Grandma glowered at me.

"Hold your tongue, girl! You know nothing about it!"

For several weeks nothing more was said to me about my uncle's suggestion that a music teacher be found for me. But then, one day, when Alice Restvold and I were listening to Father Dawes lecture us on the purity of womanhood and the virtue of chastity, one of the gentleman ushers came into the room, bringing another man with him.

I had seen the gentleman usher before. He was Joan Bulmer's preferred companion, Edward Waldegrave, a smooth-faced, blond young man who looked well in his livery but lacked dash and manliness. But the man with him, a much older man, with a dark moustache and beard, deep brown eyes and a quick, darting glance—that man I had never seen before. I was sure I would have remembered him. I tried not to stare, but I confess he fascinated me. Who could he be? He was not a member of my grandmother's household, for he was not dressed as a servant or official. He was not a soldier, for he wore no sword at his waist and lacked the swagger I had often seen in soldiers' walk. Could he be a merchant? A townsman visiting from the capital? Or perhaps a foreigner, come from far away on an errand for his masters, and sent by a court official to see Grandmother Agnes? I would know when he spoke.

"I come at the duchess's command," Edward Waldegrave said. "I am to say that Master Manox will be instructing you, Catherine, and you, Alice, in the virginals and lute and that your instruction is to begin this afternoon."

Father Dawes had stopped talking. He closed the book he had before him.

"I was just concluding my own instruction," he said gravely, and bowed slightly to the dark-eyed music master.

"Well then, ladies, let us go up to the music room," Master Manox said to us with a smile and a bow. Alice looked flustered, I was charmed. I was more than charmed, I was excited. Something about this man ignited me, as a burning brand ignites kindling, so that a flame leaps up.

I thought I saw the merest hint in his brown eyes that he too felt some of the same excitement.

I did not stop to think: but he's old. He's so very old.

We made our way to the upper chamber where the two virginals were, escorted by the gentleman usher. Then he left us and Alice and I spent an hour or so with Master Manox.

He played for us, he listened to us play. I played boldly, enjoying the tunes and caring little if I struck a wrong key, as long as the tune was recognizable. Alice confessed that she could hardly play at all, and Master Manox patiently helped her to place her fingers correctly on the keys and strike them in a pleasing order. He spent far more time with Alice than he did with me, but often, as he was teaching her and gently correcting her, he looked over at me.

The hour passed in a blur of happy confusion.

"When shall we have our next lesson?" he asked us when it was over. Alice was silent. She glanced at me, wanting me to make the decision for both of us.

"In a day or two?" I ventured, giving Master Manox a look that frankly said, let it be soon, please.

"Of course," was his swift response.

"I cannot," Alice put in. "I am leaving tomorrow to visit my friend in Exeter."

I knew very well that her "friend in Exeter" was in fact her beloved John, the man who had fathered her child and then abandoned her and was now married to someone else.

Alice could not seem to accept the fact that he had betrayed and mistreated her. She could not let him go. In her mind he was still the man who loved her—and went on loving her, even though he had married someone else. Joan and I both tried to make her see that she was deluded and would only suffer more pain before long. But she would not see reason, and clung to the dream of living with John—even becoming his wife—one day. And he, caring little for the wife his family had arranged for him to marry, was only too content to nourish Alice's hopes. She confided to me that they met in secret from time to time. She had no fear of becoming pregnant again, trusting in Joan's preventive measures and keeping lemons (ripe, unripe, or withered) always at hand.

"Then Catherine will have to take her lesson without you, Alice." The music master's voice held a warmth I had not heard in it until that moment. "Until tomorrow?"

I nodded, then looked over at Alice. Did I see a smile cross her small features? I thought I did.

"Enjoy your lesson," she said to me as she left the room. I began to follow her, but stopped when I felt the music master grasp my arm.

"Catherine," he said urgently.

I turned to look at him, aware that my arm was as if aflame, burning with the heat from his gripping fingers. I did not feel pain, he was not hurting me. Rather it was the burning of flesh igniting flesh, and I was aware of my increasing heartbeat.

"I cannot stay here alone with you," I said bravely, despite my being afraid of offending this much older man, a man sent to me by my all-powerful grandmother.

Manox's reply came with a bow of mock solemnity—a gesture he made often, and that amused him, I noticed.

"I assure you, madam, all the proprieties will be observed."

"They will be observed, because I am leaving now." And I pulled my arm out of his grasp and left the room, half expecting that he might follow me. But he did not, and it took all my resolve not to look back at him as I passed through the open doorway.

The following morning a note was brought to me.

"No music lesson today," it read, and "H. Manox" was scrawled at the bottom.

My disappointment was great. I had slept poorly the night before, kept awake by thoughts of the music master and the memory of his fingers on my arm, the excitement I had felt. Had I offended him? Or was he merely respecting my wishes that we not be alone together?

"I cannot stay here alone with you," I had said. Was he waiting until Alice's return so that he could give us a lesson together?

Either way I had reason to be worried and preoccupied. I was eager to be with him again, yet I knew that it was not seemly for me to be alone with him. Yet I was alone at times with my tutor—a fragile creature, an Oxford master not much older than I was, who was obviously far more interested in the young page boys and the brawny man who brought in our firewood than he was in me. And in truth my actual wishes were unclear, even to me. Somehow being alone with my tutor while I copied out poems or wrote my lessons was beyond criticism.

Days passed and I was tense and uncomfortable, wondering when I might hear from Master Manox again. Something led me to go up into the music room. I sat at the old virginal, the one with the cupids and flowers, and let my fingers drift over the keys. I found that I was playing a fragment of a love song, "Enchantment Sweet She Is to Me," again and again. I tried to sing it as I played but the words would not come to mind. I was stuck.

Then I heard a strong male voice, singing the tune and with the correct words. "Enchantment sweet she is to me, my lady full of courtesy, And fairer far than others be—"

It was the music master. He broke off, and went to sit at the newer virginal. He played the song through, far more expertly than I had, but broke off once again, shaking his head.

"It's no good. I can't remember it."

I paused, then asked, "Was that why you were sent away from the royal court? Because you forgot your tunes?"

The music master burst out laughing.

"No, by the short hairs of the Virgin, of course not."

"Why not?"

"Ah! 'Tis a story not fit for a young girl's ears."

He began to play once again, this time a melancholy tune, almost a dirge. I tried to follow along on my instrument, imitating the notes he played.

"You have a gift, Catherine," he remarked. "Not many young girls can do what you are doing. Or if they can, they hide their skill in order not to seem too forward."

He looked at me for a moment.

"Come and sit beside me," he said, patting the bench he sat on.

Once again I felt a twinge of unease.

"I wish Alice were here."

"But Alice plays poorly, and you play so well.

"Here," he said, reaching for my hand, "let me show you another song."

As soon as he took my hand all my resistance seemed to fall away. I sat down next to him, quite alone—for unless we sat close together I could not reach the keys in front of him, where the melody lay.

"Now then," he went on, his voice soothing, "just relax your hand, and let me press your fingers to the keys."

He cupped my hand under his, in such a way that he could easily push down each of my fingers, and curled his thumb around mine.

The feel of his hand on mine, the warmth of his touch—which was surprisingly gentle—was very pleasurable. He guided my fingers through the song twice, then released my hand.

"Now you try it on your own."

With ease, for it was a simple tune, and quite short, I repeated it, without Master Manox's help.

He nodded when I finished. "Well done. We shall try another."

The afternoon passed in enjoyable music making, with Master Manox teaching me half a dozen tunes, all of which I learned quickly. His gentle guiding of my fingers gave way to a firmer, more directing grip, and every now and then he caressed my hand, fleetingly, and each time he did it I felt a renewed excitement. We did not speak of what was passing between us, but it was understood that we were doing more than merely playing music. And when, our lesson at an end, Master Manox said, "Do we need to wait for Alice to return before we play together again?" I immediately shook my head.

"Good," he said and touched his finger softly to my cheek.

It did not take me long to discover that the Horsham household was very badly run. On some days everything was done as it should be—the food cooked on time and served correctly, the fires laid, the grooms in their places, their liveries brushed, even the laundresses looking neat in their white caps and aprons. But on most days there was disorganization, with no one in charge. The smell of burnt food came to the upper floors from the kitchens, along with the sounds of smashed crockery and shouts and swearing. The rooms were cold and the servants still asleep, or stumbling groggily along the corridors late in the morning, their tasks left undone. Liveries were neglected, laundry left to pile up.

It was whispered that the duchess was showing the effects of her advanced age, becoming forgetful and neglecting to supervise her servants. She relied far too much on one particular servant, her household steward, who snored in the wine cupboard on most afternoons, and on the stout, sour-faced Mistress Phippson, who was in charge of overseeing the female servants and who had shown herself only too eager to be bribed. Mistress Phippson was willing to tolerate all sorts of misbehavior among the servants and also those of us Howards who were living with the duchess. Provided we gave her enough coins, we could flout the rules of the household and do what we liked.

And flout them we did—or rather, Joan did, and the rest of us followed her example. I had already seen the chamber Joan occupied that adjoined the Paradise Chamber, our common dormitory. Joan paid Mistress Phippson a few small coins every month and in return received a key to the room (the key she wore around her neck) and the right to use it, undisturbed by any of the household servants or Mistress Phippson herself.

As to what went on in that room, there were rumors aplenty. Edward Waldegrave spent nights there with Joan, that we observed. Other shadowy figures were seen going in and out of the little chamber in the middle of the night, and from time to time we heard laughter and loud playful talk. I always want to be where there is mirth and merriment, and I hoped that in time Joan might invite me into her chamber to share the jollity. But she did not, though she was perfectly friendly to me.

While I was waiting, hoping for an invitation, we were all shocked one night to see Father Dawes, our religious instructor and the duchess's chaplain, stumble into Joan's small chamber and not stumble out again until morning.

Father Dawes drank too much, and reeked of his drink. There were times when he was instructing us and he lost his train of thought completely. He became confused and had to sit down for a while and recover his wits before going on. At night, when drunk, he wandered. That we knew. But to see him wandering into the Paradise Chamber, and even into Joan's inner chamber: that greatly surprised us all. The following morning Charyn went to Grandma Agnes and told her what we had all seen. The result was a visit to the Paradise Chamber by Grandma Agnes herself—a very rare event.

She and Charyn came in together, Grandma Agnes frowning and carrying a rod in her hand and Charyn looking smug and very pleased with herself. (And very pretty, I have to add.)

"Girls! Girls!" Grandma Agnes said loudly as we all made our reverence to her. We were quite astonished to see her.

"Girls!" she said again, her voice shrill. "I am told that Father Dawes was in this room last night, and stayed among you for hours. Many of you saw him. Yet you said nothing. Only one among you, Charyn here, has come to me to reveal this wickedness. Why have the rest of you kept silent?"

"We were sleeping, grandmother," someone said timidly. This comment led to much muffled laughter.

"Silence! I am told that a number of you were awake. You were overheard whispering about the father, and making jokes about him. Speak up! Which of you saw this, and did nothing? Why did you conceal the truth from me?"

She cracked the rod against a bench, making us all flinch. I was trembling, I was so frightened. I began to cough, as I sometimes did when fearful.

"Who is that coughing?" Grandma Agnes demanded. "Speak up!"

I couldn't very well speak, I could only cough. Someone patted me on the back.

In the next moment I looked up—and there was my grandmother, standing before me, tall and spare and withered—and glowering, the awful rod in her hand.

"Please, grandmother, I—"

But Charyn, who was beside the duchess, interrupted me.

"She was awake. I saw her. She was making the others laugh, as she always does."

I shook my head, but my grandmother raised the rod as if to strike me. Then she looked at me more closely, squinting.

"Ah! Worthless Edmund's daughter! No wonder! Get on down to the scullery then, and wash the pans for a day! Let that be your punishment!"

I scurried out of the room, relieved that I was not going to be beaten.

I grew to resent Charyn more and more after that incident, and I was not the only one. She was hated for being a tattle-tale, and since she was pretty it was being said that she would soon be betrothed, so she was hated all the more.

I thought Charyn cold, cold as marble. Beautiful, like marble, but lacking in feeling. She began putting on airs with me, and boasting that she would indeed (as everyone was saying) soon be betrothed.

But the man she thought would soon ask for her hand, Sir Edward Ringley, was old. And bald. And he had devilish eyes and bushy eyebrows.

"Why would you want to marry a man old enough to be your grandfather? And ugly too," I taunted her. "Are there no handsome young men who desire you?"

"What do his looks matter? Or his age?" she snapped back. "He has four estates! Four fine houses, four fine hunting parks. He is rich!"

"Is that all you care about?"

Charyn bristled. "Wealth is important. I cannot be left without a home, servants, without any place in the world. I cannot be left not knowing where I belong, an old maid living in the closets of others."

No, I thought. You must have high standing in the world, so that you can feel superior to others. Only you will never be superior. Not really.

I wanted to say to her, what good is wealth if there is no love? Is not love the most important thing in marriage? But I knew that if I said this, she would only scoff at me and tell me I was being foolish. Or that I was forgetting all that Father Dawes told us about the importance of remaining pure and chaste. She would think I was speaking, not of the love of the heart, but the lust of the flesh. Of all that is forbidden between a man and a woman—the sort of love that rears its head unwanted, unbidden, and leads to sin and tears.

Of the sort of love I felt (heaven help me!) for Master Manox.

Charyn was shrewd—and well informed. It did not take her long to discover that I was taking lessons on the virginal from Master Manox, the two of us alone in the upper room, sometimes joined by Alice—who was not proving to be a very apt pupil—but more often alone.

"I believe our grandmother will not be at all pleased to hear that you have been letting that man Manox get near you. Far too near, and far too often."

Though shocked by her words, I shrugged, dismissing their obvious meaning.

"He is giving me lessons on the virginals," I said. "He is a very good and patient teacher. Ask Alice. He gives her lessons also."

"It was Alice who told me about the two of you. She knows what is going on."

"Nothing is going on but music instruction. And Master Manox is a very fine player."

Charyn gave me a hard look.

"You might like to know that Master Manox was sent away from the royal court because he dishonored his marriage. He sinned with one of Queen Jane's maids of honor. A girl not much older than you or I. It was a scandal. The girl took music lessons from him—and then had his child. He denied that the child was his, and tried to convince others that the girl was wanton and had been the mistress of other men before he knew her. But everything he said was a lie. He was shamed and sent away."

"I did not know that," I said quickly. Perhaps too quickly, for I saw Charyn lift one eyebrow skeptically.

"You do know he is married?"

"Yes. He told me. He often speaks of his wife, in fact. With affection." This was a lie. Even as I said the words I wondered, why was I lying? Out of guilt? Or fear?

Charyn hooted with laughter.

"They can't stand each other. She hates him because of his deceit. She says he hates her."

"Perhaps she is unworthy of him. He is very gifted."

But Charyn only shook her head slowly.

"Do not let him deceive you, Catherine. Guard your honor. Guard your maidenhead. If you do not, no man will ever want to marry you. And you will burn in hell."

I said nothing.

"Remember Anne," Charyn added after a moment. "She came to grief because of the lust of the flesh. And it was a musician, Mark Smeaton, who caused her ruin."

"Along with several other men who were not musicians," I said. "Besides, grandmother always said Anne was not one of us."

"Take care you do not prove to be like Anne. Not one of us. And stay away from that whore Joan Bulmer," Charyn added, her tone as blunt as her words. "She will surely come to grief."

But I did not agree. I drew further and further away from Charyn, and was more and more drawn to Joan. Joan and Charyn were very much at odds, their enmity worsening after Charyn told our grandmother the duchess about Joan's trysts with Father Dawes. The two girls could not have been less alike, the dark-haired Joan with her air of worldly knowledge, her outspokenness and self-confidence, her contempt for more refined, protected, somewhat unsure girls of higher birth and blond Charyn with her cool aristocratic reserve, her condemnation of bed-sharing and wanton behavior, her talebearing and spying on others.

I thought Joan admirable for her strength and daring, though the truth was I found her to be a little frightening as well. I had the feeling that she would go to any lengths, ignore any warnings and that she might one day, as Charyn warned, come to grief.

Slowly Henry Manox reached into the mouth of a silken bag and drew out a comfit. He lifted it to my lips. I could smell the luscious sugary fruity scent.

"Open," he whispered.

We were in Joan's small chamber, she had lent it to us for an hour.

"Only an hour," she had told me. "Then Edward and I will join you."

What could happen in an hour, I asked myself. Henry and I could share a great deal of pleasure together in an hour's time, but I would not yield to him the ultimate prize of my maidenhead. I would remain intact. Unsullied, as Charyn might have said. Only Charyn would never know. I would make sure of that.

Henry knew of a secret entrance to Joan's chamber—through the sweets closet, which had a false back that could be opened from a storage room on the other side of the wall. He assured me that he could make his way in and out of the small chamber through the sweets closet without being seen by anyone in the Paradise Chamber. Especially not by Charyn.

"And besides, I can bring you comfits that I find there," he said with a smile, dangling the silken bag full of fragrant candies.

I opened my mouth and closed my eyes and let him put the soft jellylike confection on my tongue, leaving his fingers in my mouth for a moment along with it. As he drew his fingers out I bit down on the sweet, but hardly had I swallowed it when I felt his mouth on mine, tasted his tartness and felt myself melt under his caress.

As we kissed his hands began moving over my body, more boldly than ever before, and I pulled back slightly from his embrace. I wanted him to go on doing what he was doing, yet I was only too aware that Master Manox was several times my size—he was a tall, hefty man and I, as I have said, was very small. He was far stronger than I was. I could not but feel some degree of alarm at this.

I freed myself from his probing hands and jumped onto the nearest of the two mattresses in the room. Looking slightly puzzled, Master Manox pursued me, only to meet the barrier of my stiffly outstretched arms. Held back, he snorted.

"What's this? Do you mislike me of a sudden?"

The stirrings of passion turned to playfulness as I jumped on the thin mattress, clumsy in my long skirt, and he tried to follow me, but stumbled.

"Your skirt is a hindrance, madam," he said. "Let me unburden you."

Obediently I allowed him to unfasten my heavy, wide skirt at the waist and pull it off, revealing my petticoat beneath.

"Could we not relieve you of this petticoat as well? You will feel so much lighter and freer without it."

His words seemed so logical, his actions in undressing me so sensible. Before long I stood in my shift, my hair spilling over my shoulder and down my back, my arms and legs bare—even my stockings removed—and Master Manox was gazing at my lightly clad body in admiration.

Rapidly he threw off his doublet and shirt, shoes and stockings and pantaloons, until he wore only the light tunic that covered him from his shoulders to his loins.

I was too fascinated to move. I had never before seen a gentleman in his underclothes, though I had seen servants and village laborers in a near-naked state many times before.

Henry Manox had a broad chest and strong legs, a thick neck with cords that stood out. Black hair covered much of his body that I could see, with wisps of grey mingled with the black. I tried to avert my eyes from his groin, but could not. I saw there what I expected to see, what Joan's knowing talk and descriptions of lovemaking had prepared me to see. The light tunic that shielded his nakedness covered a mound, a lump, a sizable expansion of flesh. Curiosity compelled me to move nearer to him, any sense of alarm I had felt earlier dissolved.

He reached for my hand and pulled it toward him, lowering it to the mound between his legs. I touched it lightly, then quickly pulled my hand away.

"Nothing to fear, Catherine," Master Manox said softly. "It will not bite you."

I giggled, but kept my hand withdrawn. Gently he lifted me in his arms and laid me on the mattress, then lay down beside me. His face loomed over mine, his breath fanned me. Keeping his eyes on mine, he moved his hand upward along my thigh until it approached the cleft between my legs. I shivered, quivered. I burned. And I was afraid.

"Let me touch your sweetness, Catherine," he said.

I was silent—and I knew, keeping my silence, that I was saying yes.

I felt him touch me. I nearly swooned. I turned my head away from him—whether in modesty or shame I could not have said. I could not look at him. But I could not tear myself away from his insistent, steady, intensely pleasurable touch. It was like no other pleasure I had ever known. And when it was over I felt as if I had been carried off into a realm of sensual delight I hadn't known existed.

I had not given him my maidenhead. Rather he had given me a

bodily rapture like no other. I fell into a deep sleep until I heard Joan enter the small chamber, bringing Edward with her, and calling out cheerfully that she had brought wine and cheese and fruit for us all to share.

THREE

THERE was great rejoicing in my grandmother's household at Horsham when Queen Jane was delivered of a son. Prince Edward was the name the king chose for him. Prince Edward, who would one day reign over us, in that future time when King Henry died, as all kings must, and his throne would pass to his successor.

The wait for a prince had been long and tedious. King Henry's first queen, Queen Catherine (a good and gracious lady, but a very unfortunate one in that all her children died but one), had given him only a daughter, the Lady Mary, and his second queen, my cousin Anne, had also been unable to present him with a prince— only a princess, Elizabeth, who people said was never a princess at all because most likely the king was not her father.

But now at long last Queen Jane had had her boy, and he was said to be healthy and strong, and even my grandmother nodded her head and mumbled, yes, yes, a prince at last, and punched her bony fist against her palm.

Our prince had finally arrived—but almost at once our queen was taken from us. Queen Jane, mild and good, had been taken deathly ill as so many women were in childbed and died soon after her boy was born. We mourned her—yet we continued to rejoice over the prince, who grew bigger and stronger and gave his father the king much pleasure and satisfaction.

I was by then in my seventeenth year. I had been at Horsham for many months and had learned much about the ways of a large noble establishment. My one regret was that I had not grown any taller, though my figure had taken on a more pleasing outline and my small waist, generous curves and eager young face were drawing attention and compliments. I was certainly more sensually appealing than Charyn, though her delicate blond beauty was the more highly prized. Charyn would be married before long, just as soon as her parents settled on the right husband for her and came to terms with his family. I, on the other hand, had Henry Manox: not a suitor, not really a lover either (since I was still a virgin), but occupying some role for which I had no name. I had Henry.

I did not know just how I felt about Henry Manox, but my feelings were changing. When we were together I sank into pleasure, I abandoned myself to the warmly passionate sensations he awakened in me. I was determined to guard my virginity—something that irked and offended him—but shared my body freely and affectionately, and let him undress me, hold and touch and kiss me with an ardor that thrilled me.

Though as the months passed, I had to admit that the thrilling sensations were growing duller, and Henry's pleas and demands more tiresome. All the furtiveness, the secrecy, his sly comings and goings through the sweets closet were beginning to seem rather silly. I began to wonder whether Henry was too old for such pranks.

"Could we not meet elsewhere?" I asked him. "Somewhere we

could be alone all night, instead of having to share this stuffy little room with Joan and Edward?"

Joan did allow us to use her private chamber for an hour or so on occasion, but more often, when we were invited to use it, she and Edward were there and sometimes others as well. All of us but Henry were quite young, and we enjoyed not only romping and loving on the beds but doing the things young people did: feasting together at midnight on suckets and sugar-bread, meat pasties and oysters stolen from the kitchens and wine and ale borrowed (Joan's word) from the cellars and malt-house, singing, joking, making fun of Grandma Agnes and Mistress Phippson and the self-important steward and pantler. I told amusing stories and Edward Waldegrave made playing cards disappear and appear again in Joan's corslet. But Henry, because he was so much older and was not a part of the Horsham household, was left out. He sulked. He complained.

Finally Joan complained as well—only to me, not to Henry.

"Your music master is a dullard," she said. "And as you know, you are not the first young girl he has tried to seduce. He is well known for causing scandal."

"Nevertheless I enjoy him. He has given me much pleasure."

"Why not meet him in the duchess's private chapel, behind the altar screen? No one ever goes there. You know how rare it is for milady to attend to her devotions. And as for Father Dawes—" She did not need to say more. The often drunken Father Dawes was hardly ever to be seen inside the chapel. "You and your Henry can have your time together," she went on, "and later, you can come alone to visit us—and we will be spared Henry's moodiness."

I followed Joan's suggestion, and Henry and I began seeking each other out in Grandma Agnes's dim chapel, where no priest presided and only a few candles were left burning in case the duchess should feel a need to say her prayers before the carved wooden altar. The chapel was always empty when we went there, we felt in no danger of being discovered.

At first the shrouded darkness of the narrow space behind the altar, the uncertainty of finding one another there (would one of us be called away, unable to arrive as planned? Would we encounter servants in the corridor outside, or guardsmen, or poor folk from the villages nearby seeking alms, and would we then have to pass on by the chapel door, and forego our meeting?), the mere anticipation of seeing one another was enough to excite us. Later, however, Henry became worried and discontented.

He knew that I continued to visit Joan in her small room off the Paradise Chamber late at night. He demanded that I tell him who I saw there and what I did. When I protested he grew angry, then begged for me to relieve his misery and assure him that he was the one I loved. He and no one else.

Begging and demanding, wheedling and arguing and sulking: it wearied me, and before long I could not help noticing that there were more good-looking, younger, more pleasing men in my grandmother's large household—and in Joan's private chamber.

Then one afternoon, when once again Henry and I were alone in the duchess's chapel, I in my scanty shift and Henry untrousered and bare-buttocked, the chapel doors burst open and I heard a young woman's voice.

"They're in here, grandmother. I saw him go in. He went first, and then she came a little while later."

"Charyn!" I cried.

Henry made a sound I had never before heard him make, between a wail and a screech.

"Where are you?" I heard my grandmother call out angrily. "Come out from there!"

In a moment Charyn had come around behind the altar and was staring at us, one hand held in front of her mouth.

"Here they are! He's got nothing on!" And she began to giggle.

Henry scrambled to cover himself, snatching up the altar cloth and holding it in front of his nakedness. I picked up my skirt and held it at my waist, so that it fell around my legs.

"Come out at once, I say!"

I was trembling. Would grandmother beat me? Would she send me away? I cared nothing for Henry's fate.

I came around from behind the altar, Henry following me. There stood Grandma Agnes, her face tight and frowning, her lips pressed together.

"Please, I beg you, milady, do not tell my wife about this!"

A scornful guffaw from the duchess, more giggling from Charyn.

"Put your breeches back on and get out!"

Henry hesitated.

"If milady pleases, I am still owed payment for music lessons—".

There was cold fury in grandmother's eyes. Henry was silenced. He groped for the rest of his clothes and his boots, then struggled out.

"So! Jocasta's daughter has come to grief! She is a little whore, just as her mother was a great whore!"

A protest rose to my lips but I managed to suppress it. I glared at Charyn, who looked very self-satisfied.

"Traitor!" I hissed at her. "Tattle-tale! Goody-goody! Killjoy!"

Grandmother was pondering, while staring at me coldly. Once again I began to tremble.

"You could send her to the kitchens," Charyn suggested. "To be a turnspit."

I'd like to turn you over the fire, I thought. Miserable traitor! False friend!

"Are you with child by that fellow Manox? Tell me the truth!"

"No, grandmother. I am still a virgin."

"Hah! And I'm the Mother Superior of this convent! I warn

you, girl, don't lie to me or I'll have you beaten until your head is soft as a boiled apple!"

She looked me up and down.

"Drop that skirt!" she ordered. I obeyed. Then, "Take off that shift!"

"But I have on nothing underneath."

"Take it off at once!"

I had not felt embarrassed before, only afraid. Now my modesty rose to hinder me—though why it should, given what had just happened, I couldn't imagine.

"I cannot."

"What did you say?" I had never before seen my fierce, commanding grandmother look incredulous.

"I cannot, for shame."

Her gaze narrowed.

"Are you deformed then?"

"No, grandmother."

"Because if you are deformed, you will be sent to Saint Frideswide's at once."

A girl had come to Horsham only a short time before, a distant Howard relation, and she had suffered from a palsy. She shook and quivered. She was sent at once to the convent of Saint Frideswide's.

"I am not deformed. I am merely shamefaced."

"Except in front of Master Manox."

I thought quickly.

"He forced me to meet him, to allow him liberties. He said that if I did not, he would kill my father."

It was a lie. Henry had never threatened to harm my father, and I had always met him willingly, even eagerly.

"You are a comely enough wench," the duchess said after looking me over. "Though dwarfish. And you have spirit. I should beat it out of you, but at the moment I haven't the strength."

I saw that she looked tired. She was after all very old. No doubt she tired swiftly, as the old do. My fear began to grow less. I was no longer trembling.

The duchess sighed. "I will send my chamberer to dress you. If you let Manox near you again you will be beaten. Should he threaten you, or your father, come to me at once."

She walked to the chapel doorway, then turned back toward me.

"Manox's wife will hear of this. She will beat him senseless."

"Pray, grandmother, for my sake, do not tell her my name, else she will beat me too."

But the duchess only pursed her lips, then turned back toward the door and was gone.

"Guess who they made Controller of Calais!" my father said in wry tones. "You cannot imagine."

"I cannot."

"John Parker! Yeoman of the Wardrobe! A servant! Barely a gentleman's son!"

That his own cherished but forfeited position should pass to a servant of much lower birth was irksome in the extreme to my father. He felt he had been unjustly deprived of the post, and dishonored by the loss of the revenues that went with it. But to be replaced by such a man, a Howard replaced by a nobody—ah, that was a cruel humiliation.

"Was there no compensation for you, father? No other post offered you?"

"Thomas spoke to Lord Cromwell and arranged a loan," father mumbled. "And I will be appointed commissioner of the sewers for Surrey."

"Well, that is something," I said as father sat down, slowly and carefully, on a cushioned bench. I sat nearby.

"Oh, and I am to receive licenses to import Gascon wine and Toulouse wood."

"Trade in Gascon wine must be quite profitable."

He rolled his eyes.

"But the wine trade, Catherine, is for men of low birth. Not for a Howard, whose brother Thomas is Duke of Norfolk, the highest nobleman in the realm."

He shook his head. "At least they did not send me to Sark, or Orkney, or to live among the wild Irish—"

"Father, I must speak to you—"

"But then, the best appointments are sure to be those in the new queen's household." He nodded sagely. "If only she would make me her chancellor, or her emissary to foreign courts, or—"

"Who is to be the new queen, father? I have not heard her name spoken."

"And you will not, until the marriage contracts have been drawn up."

He made a wry face. I knew at once that he was in pain from the stone.

"If you please, father, I have need—"

He raised his hand. "Not now, Catherine. I have too much else on my mind."

But whatever was on his mind, did not find its way to his lips. Not for many minutes. He was lost in his musings. Finally he spoke again.

"Lord Cromwell is dealing with the Clevans, Catherine. Yes. The Clevans. Of all people!"

He paused again. "There is a Clevan woman, Lady Anna. Lord Cromwell wants her to be our next queen."

He looked over at me. "There will be many appointments to her new household. Highborn young women. Good-looking, godfearing, chaste young women. Not young women who disgrace themselves with their music masters—"

"Father, I—"

"Oh yes, mother told me. I know all."

"She forgave me. She understood."

But father merely gave a low chuckle. "You are your mother's daughter," he said quietly. "And besides, the man has a poor history. He has been sent away. We will say no more about it."

"I need clothing, father," I burst out. "My gowns are too small for me. They cannot be let out or patched or re-hemmed any more. Please let me share some of your new loan to pay a dressmaker."

He slapped his knee. "Ask your uncle William, Catherine. He always has coins in his treasure chests. Don't come to me. I am left to go a-begging while others flourish. Don't come to me!"

My need for money was great, and growing greater. I had been borrowing small sums from Alice and Joan, from my cousins Malyn and Catherine Tylney, even from Henry and Edward Waldegrave ever since I first arrived at Horsham, for my father gave me no pocket money and my stepmother Margaret, who I never saw, scarcely acknowledged that I was alive.

I was a poor relation. That needed to end.

In the Horsham household, I noticed, people acted not according to the moral laws in the Bible but according to what chance and opportunity offered. Do what you can, take what you need, act as you must: this was the guiding rule. I was not slow to learn it.

I knew that Grandma Agnes, who was very very rich, had small chests of coins scattered here and there throughout the household.

She was forever taking handfuls of coins from these chests to give in alms, or to pay tradesmen or servants, or to give out to the steward or chamberer to buy provisions. The chests were kept locked, to be sure, but she kept the keys in the pockets of her gowns and I had seen them fall out more than once. I had also noticed that she sometimes forgot to fasten the locks securely.

I began paying closer attention to her goings and comings and taking careful note when she took money from one of her chests. My opportunity came when a commotion arose in the courtyard just as Grandma Agnes was handing a pouch of coins to her head ostler. Two of the grooms were brawling. Others were threatening to join in.

"Stop that at once!" she shouted, and stalked out among the men, heedless of the mud and dirt that was staining her hem and equally heedless of the unlocked chest she had left behind.

I quickly rushed to the table, reached into the chest, snatched a pouch—a rather heavy pouch—of coins and hurriedly put it in my pocket. Then I went outside and joined the others.

Not until after supper did I allow myself to open the pouch and count the money I had taken. It was nearly eight pounds! A fortune!

My first thought was an unkind one: I must not let my father know that I had this money, for he would be sure to try to convince me that he needed it far more than I did and that it was my duty to give it to him. I hid the gleaming coins in a little closet next to the chamber of easement, under a bundle of rags. Each time I visited the chamber I extracted a few coins. Gradually I paid my debts. And I paid the duchess's dressmaker, Master Spiershon, to make me five day gowns and two court gowns, suitable to wear in the presence of the king. For I had decided that I had had enough of Horsham, and was determined to travel to the capital at my earliest opportunity.

• • •

I had been hearing about Grandma Agnes's great house at Lambeth for a long time. It was said to be far larger and more grand than Horsham, with three times as many servants and far more elegant grounds. Most important, Lambeth was just across the Thames and a little ways upstream from the royal court of King Henry and the great capital, London.

The hub of the realm, Henry Manox had called London. The center of the universe. He had often spoken to me of the splendor of the royal court and how he regretted the shortness of his stay there.

Imagine my delight when I heard from Joan that the duchess was going to Lambeth and we were all going with her!

"She wants to place as many Howards as possible in the household of the new queen," Joan announced. "In order to do that, she must be as near the royal court as possible. Lambeth it is."

Everything was packed up and moved—and when we arrived, I glimpsed, for the first time, an immense ducal household with (so my father told me) some seven hundred servants and three hundred horses in the stables and a great hall larger than all the upper chambers at Horsham combined.

Lambeth Great House was an establishment fit for the wealthiest duchess in England—my grandmother Agnes—and for England's premier duke, my uncle Thomas, who was often present in its spacious halls.

I was only too glad to move in to my new and much larger quarters, which I shared with only a dozen other girls. My bed was larger and the mattress much more comfortable, the blankets thicker and warmer, the hearth larger and with more wood kept piled at the side so that we almost never ran out and suffered from cold on chill nights. I had not only a trunk at the foot of my bed to hold my possessions but a wardrobe as well, though I had to share the wardrobe with two other girls. In my new gowns and kirtles, sleeves and petticoats I no longer looked like a poor relation but a privileged, highborn young woman. A true Howard. I was proud in them—even though I could never forget that they had been bought with stolen coins.

Soon after we moved into the large residence Uncle Thomas gave a banquet for the Clevan ambassador in the great hall, with its high ceiling painted in bright blues and reds and greens, its tall gilded columns, its magnificent parquet floor and its wide high doors that opened onto the vast fragrant gardens. Long tables were laid with cream-colored napery and gleaming silver candlesticks, bowls of greenery and fresh flowers, silver and gold plate in abundance.

I had never seen the like, and I marveled at the sight.

But then, I too was in fresh array, and when I entered the great hall in company with some half dozen of my cousins, I was aware that I was much admired.

The new wardrobe made for me by Spiershon the tailor was proving to be of great benefit to me. Master Spiershon had been only too glad to create a wardrobe for a niece of the great Duke of Norfolk, and his gowns were sumptuous: gowns of silk and velvet and Venetian brocade, in flattering colors of ash and lady blush and bear's ear, carnation and dove grey and violet blue. There were light silk petticoats to match (for the season was warm), and full sleeves embroidered in silk ribbon, and stomachers and headdresses and fine woven silk for garters.

"Not too large in the bodice!" Master Spiershon had barked to his assistants as the gowns were being fitted. "She is young. She must appear shapely but maidenly!"

I hoped I did appear maidenly, and youthful, not coarsened by my experience in the duchess's household. When I looked in the pier glass as I was being dressed on the night of my first banquet at Lambeth I saw a fresh-faced, happy, cheerful young woman. Not a knowing, shrewd one like Joan, or a timid, fretful one like Alice, or a superior, self-satisfied one like Charyn. I saw a face lit with anticipation, the eyes filled with jollity and the hope of amusement. The face of a girl who might be chosen to join the household of the new queen.

"Is she going to be here tonight, the king's new wife?" Alice asked me as we took our places at the long banqueting table.

"Hush! No one knows for certain who his wife will be. The king's men of business are merely talking to the ambassador from Cleves."

I felt very superior, knowing what little I did about the talks between the king's chief minister, Thomas Cromwell, and the Clevans. The household was abuzz with rumor; I did not have to listen very long or very hard to gather what was going on. My uncle William Cotton had come to stay at Lambeth and he was well informed. He was fond of me and was usually willing to answer my questions, provided I did not pester him.

I knew that the king needed a new wife, to give him more sons in case the young Prince Edward died. She had to be royal, or from the highest nobility. She could not belong to the Romish church, or owe obedience to the pope; that had been decided when the king married my cousin Anne. No more papists!

The Clevans, it seemed, were not papists. So it was possible our king might marry one of them. But nothing was determined yet.

I noticed Uncle Thomas and Grandma Agnes talking together and looking toward me and my cousins. Grandma Agnes glittered in a gown of gold bawdkin, while Uncle Thomas, his slight upper body covered in an elaborate doublet of quilted green velvet, a cap with a jaunty grey feather on his small dark head, stood out boldly from the handsome younger men around him.

In another moment Uncle Thomas beckoned to us. Obediently my cousins and I rose at once and went to where he was sitting with the duchess. We dipped our knees in reverence. He scrutinized us, taking his time, scanning our bodies, then our faces.

"Which of you is Jocasta's daughter?" he asked.

"I am Lord Edmund's daughter," I answered, speaking up and holding my head high. "My mother was the Lady Jocasta."

"Proud," the duke said. "But fetching." He looked more carefully at my lovely gown, his gaze lingering on the full yet maidenly bodice. He raised one eyebrow critically, then turned to his mother. He was about to speak when she silenced him.

"No," she said. "Not this one."

With a look of sudden anger he turned his face away. He was an ugly man, my uncle Thomas, with small piglike eyes and a nose that curved downward and thin, tightly pursed lips. Yet in that moment he looked uglier than ever. With another wave of his hand he dismissed us and we went back to our places at the long table.

I had never before seen so many good-looking, charming, clever young men as at the banquet that night. Many wore the livery of Uncle Thomas's household or Grandma Agnes's, others the livery of the royal court. Lord Cromwell, Lord Privy Seal, had at least two dozen retainers to escort him, along with a large number of tall, muscular guardsmen. Archbishop Cranmer, Bishop Tunstal and Bishop Gardiner were well attended, as were the many lords and high officials who swept into the great hall with their richly garbed retainers at their heels.

It was as if each great man (and one great lady, my grandmother) was in competition with every other, each vying with the others for the prize of most important, most honored, most wealthy, most powerful. Who would win? The king, I supposed. Surely the king was above every subject. And yet—I had heard Uncle Thomas mutter that the Howards were an older and more distinguished family than the Tudors, and that the Tudors were an upstart dynasty that did not deserve first rank.

He was a haughty man, my uncle Thomas! Disdainful of others. Scornful of their claims to rank and privilege. In his own eyes he was above everyone—even God, the servants joked. And his eye had rested on me. Fortunately Grandma Agnes had said no to him. Though exactly what she had meant, what he might have intended doing or saying had she not interrupted him, I had no idea.

As we dined I watched the table of honor where the dignitaries of highest rank were served. There sat the Clevan ambassador, between Lord Cromwell and Uncle Thomas. He did not look like a man of rank, but more like a stolid villager driving his oxen behind a plough. The expression on his broad, flat face was blank, he paid no attention to those around him or to the beauties of the great hall. He sat impassive, eating plateful after plateful of the delicacies set before him and emptying his goblet again and again. His manners were coarse, he wiped his mouth on his sleeve, on the back of his hand, even, I noticed, on the fine linen tablecloth. He did not make conversation but stared straight ahead, though those around him spoke to him and were clearly attempting to draw him out.

I watched, fascinated. And as I watched, I could not help but notice that behind the ambassador, seated at a table of their own, were a group of women dressed in unattractive foreign garb. Their headdresses did not frame their faces like the headdresses we wore, but spread out to the side like spaniels' ears. The bodices of their gowns were overly full and ill-fitting, the gowns themselves more like capes or mantles, with heavy low-hanging sleeves and drooping skirts. Were there no clever dressmakers in Cleves? For surely, I surmised, these were Clevan ladies. They had the same stolid look about them as the ambassador, the same blank expressions on their broad white faces, the same lack of animation.

Joan would know. I leaned across the table and asked her who the women were, whether they came from Cleves.

She nodded, and made a face.

"The godmother, the sister, the aunts of Anna of Cleves."

Anna, I knew, was the woman who was being considered as a bride for King Henry.

"Of course Anna herself remains at home. It would hardly be seemly for her to show herself here, like a prize mount being put up for auction."

The other girls who were within earshot at our table, overhearing Joan's words, began to laugh.

"I would not bid on any of those mounts, if I were the king," I said, making the girls laugh once again. "They have stuffed themselves with too many oats!"

"Such pockmarked skin," I heard another of the girls say. "Do all the women of Cleves have the pox?"

"Perhaps Anna is the beauty of the family," Charyn put in. "Perhaps she puts these others to shame."

We left it at that, for as Charyn was finishing her thought a young man came up to the table where the Clevan women were sitting, and as soon as they saw him they began to smile and gesture and speak animatedly, giggling like young girls and holding their hands before their mouths coquettishly.

He was a very handsome young man indeed, slender, graceful, light on his feet, and with a most charming smile on his pleasing features. The musicians had begun to play and he led one of the older Clevan ladies in a dance. She was clumsy, her long heavy skirts weighed her down. But the young man adroitly kept her balanced, and I could tell that she was enjoying herself. Soon other partners came forward for the rest of the Clevan ladies, and then for Joan and Alice and the others of my cousins, and for me.

I jumped and twirled and hopped with abandon, enjoying the music and the movement. But I could not wait until the dancing was over, so that I could find out who the handsome young man was, and how I might manage to see him again.

• • •

We were taken to London for the first time on the Feast of St. Sylvanus the Martyr and I could not sleep at all the night before, I was so excited.

We rode in covered coaches, Charyn and I and Malyn and another girl I hardly knew, a very pretty girl named Mary Sidford, all together in one coach and the rest of my numerous cousinage in others. Twenty heralds rode before us, all wearing the brilliantly colored Howard livery, and announced our coming with a loud blare of trumpets and an even louder beating of drums. Dogs barked, horses whinnied in terror, and the people in the crowded streets scattered before us as we passed—or rather, as we attempted to pass, for time and again the narrow roadways were blocked by flocks of sheep and cattle being driven to the markets at Smithfield.

From across the river I had seen the soaring tall spire of St. Paul's, but once we entered the tangled warren of streets and alleyways all I could see were the old wooden buildings on either side of us, many leaning at angles over the street, whose blackened timbers made it plain that fire was an everpresent danger to Londoners.

A great and nauseous stench arose to assault me, growing stronger the deeper into the city we went. We all took out our scented pomanders and held them under our noses, yet the stink was far stronger than their spicy scent. Wide streams of filth ran down the centers of the streets we passed through, I saw people empty waste buckets out of second-story windows onto the heads of passers-by beneath. Mounds of rotting food, dead animals, refuse of all kinds were heaped at street corners, covered with flies and running with sickly-looking liquids. I shuddered at the sight of rats scurrying down the alleys—fat, well-fed rats—in large numbers.

I had coins in my pockets to spend but our coach did not stop at any of the shops or stalls where trims and buttons and stockings, foodstuffs, kerchiefs and trinkets were being offered for sale.

"'Tis worth your life to stop in the streets of London, miss," one of the ostlers called up to me when I asked if we might pause long enough for me to buy a muffin and a pair of doeskin gloves. "The wild rogues that wander about would break your pate in a minute just to steal your purse. And the constables are never nearby to protect you."

His warning seemed more than justified when we felt our coach jolt sharply and lean to one side. Before I could realize what had happened a dirty face peered in, and dirty hands reached towards me. A laborer or a beggar, by the look of him, with filthy hair spilling out from under a ragged cap. I drew back in alarm, but almost at once I heard the crack of a whip and saw that one of the guardsmen had cut the man down. He lay writhing amid the mud of the street. With a lurch the coach moved forward again.

"What happened? Who was that horrible-looking man?" It was Mary Sidford, who until then had said little to the rest of us.

"Some thief," Malyn answered with a shudder. "I want to go back to Lambeth."

But before we went back we were to see many more ragged folk, beggars and peddlers, low servants hurrying on errands for their masters, apprentices with tools hanging from their belts and scowls on their faces, flower-sellers, young and not-so-young women dressed in slatternly finery, strolling past workmen and soldiers as if to say, here I am, look at me, I am for sale.

We paused to let a religious procession pass, black-robed priests carrying large silver crosses and boys singing and chanting, their silvery voices carrying above the hubbub of commerce and the loud grinding of wheels over the cobblestones. Then we came to London Bridge, with its strong towers and ancient drawbridge, and paused to watch the river rushing under the old stone pillars, the grey water clogged with refuse and rotting timbers, dead dogs and cats and masses of floating rubble.

This, then, was the hub of the realm, the center of the universe. Astounding in its size and noise and stench, yes: I had to agree. But almost equally astounding in its urgent vivid life and color. A dangerous, exciting place pulsing with vitality. A place where, I felt, anything could happen.

FOUR

FRANCIS Dereham," he said with a bow.

He was more fair than dark, with thick, light brown wavy hair that brushed his neck and clear, light blue eyes with thick long lashes. His skin was pink and healthy and without the pits or pockmarks that disfigured so many of the men of the household. I wondered whether his skin was smooth and unscarred all over. My hands itched to touch him, to feel the softness of his skin, he was so beautiful.

"I've brought you some partridges, and some custard tarts," he said with a smile. "You do like custard tarts, do you not?"

With a sweep of one liveried arm he indicated a basket from which came the rich aromas of roasted fowl, butter and onion, and sugary desserts. I saw that the basket had been carefully packed with linens and embroidered napery, wax candles and a candelabra to hold them.

"Anything you bring me, Master Dereham, will be most welcome. I see that you have gone to a great deal of trouble."

He had been in my thoughts ever since the night of Uncle Thomas's banquet in honor of the Clevan ambassador, when I had watched him dance with the clumsy foreign woman in the ugly, ill-fitting gown. I had found out his name, and knew that he was one of Grandma Agnes's gentlemen pensioners, and that he was about twenty-four years old (so Joan believed)—much older than I for I had yet to turn eighteen. He was a gentleman's son, Joan said, a Howard relation by marriage. And he was much admired by the women of the Lambeth household, some of whom were thought to be his conquests.

Yet here he was, in the duchess's apartments where I was sitting and talking with Mary Sidford and my cousin Catherine Tylney. And he was approaching me, addressing me. Not the others.

"May I serve you ladies now? Or shall we have a game of primero first?"

"You presume on our leisure—and our desire for your company," was cousin Catherine's rather ungracious reply, almost a reprimand. Cousin Catherine was ill-humored, having never received an offer of marriage (despite possessing a sizeable dowry) and having just learned earlier that morning that Charyn had become betrothed to Lord Morley's son Randall, which was a very good match indeed. Every time Cousin Catherine found out about another girl's betrothal she became glum and out of sorts. Having reached the age of nearly thirty (she would not admit to any of us exactly how old she was, only her sister Malyn knew the truth, and she refused to divulge it), it was unlikely any man would ever offer for her hand.

"You are too hasty, cousin," I hastened to say. "Master Dereham is a delightful companion—and if he is not, his custard tarts certainly will be." Francis Dereham and I exchanged a laugh.

"With your permission, then," he said as he waved two grooms forward into the room, bringing with them a small trestle table. In no time at all Master Dereham had whisked the tablecloth and napkins from the basket and put them deftly in place, set the candles in the candelabra, prepared our places and brought out the delicious-smelling food.

"Ah," Mary sighed as she savored the roast fowl. "This is lovely. A treat."

We fell to eating. The food was indeed delicious. Yet Master Dereham was not eating. He was looking at me. We sought each other's eyes, and did not look away. His was a look that conveyed friendly invitation. Mine, I'm sure, conveyed frank admiration of his beauty and the grace of his movements. His soft skin. His lithe body. Everything about him.

"We were talking earlier of our cousin Charyn's betrothal, just announced today," I said at length, wanting to fill the silence.

"Yes," he said. "Randall Morley. He is heir to his father's lands and title. And until he inherits, he enjoys a substantial fortune. Most likely he will be appointed under-chamberer to the new queen, whoever she may be," he added.

"My father hopes for an appointment to the new queen's household," I remarked with a sigh. "Though he seldom manages to get what he hopes for." I bit into a custard tart.

"What a disloyal thing to say!" Cousin Catherine put in.

"Not disloyal, I hope," I responded wistfully, "only truthful. I love my father and wish he could have everything he wants."

Master Dereham smiled.

"Very kind I'm sure. Not all children are as forgiving toward their parents, I've noticed."

"We rarely see our father," Malyn said. "He is always off to the wars."

"Off somewhere, at any rate," Catherine added. "Mother hardly ever knows where he is."

"And what of your mother and father, Master Dereham?" I wanted to know. "Clearly they have done well by you, to obtain a place for you in the duchess's household."

I saw the faintest hint of a grimace cross his bow-shaped pink lips.

"I was left without parents at a very young age, Mistress Catherine, and obtained my place by—"

"By knowing several wealthy married ladies better than their husbands know them," was Cousin Catherine's unkind rejoinder.

Master Dereham bristled, stood, and drew himself up to his full height.

"Perhaps I have overstayed my welcome," he said, and prepared to leave.

"No, wait," Mary pleaded. "I have not yet finished my sweet. Please stay."

"Yes, please stay," I said and reached out to touch his sleeve.

He looked down at my hand, then back at me.

Cousin Catherine sniffed loudly, stood, and left us without another word. I drew Master Dereham back to the table. And in that moment I thought, he and I, he and I—

He recovered his former geniality, and sat contentedly while Mary and I finished our meal, a smile of satisfaction on his face, as if he had accomplished what he had come for. Presently Joan came in, and Alice with her, and Master Dereham bowed and took his leave. When he was gone, Joan looked over at me. A knowing look.

"Well," she said after a long silence, "so that's how it is then. Mistress Catherine and the handsome Master Dereham."

She knew, even then, she knew far better than I, that I was already lost to love.

•   •   •

He did not need to woo me, I was already his. Every time I saw Francis Dereham standing with the other gentlemen pensioners in attendance on the duchess, lithe and slim and graceful in his red and black livery, every time I observed him escorting visitors newly arrived at Lambeth, whenever I watched him doing some small service for Uncle Thomas or answering the command of some other dignitary, every time I saw him standing behind the chair of a nobleman who was dining at my grandmother's table, I felt again the desire to touch his smooth unblemished skin and look into his light blue eyes with their fringe of long lashes.

He was kept very busy from early morning until late at night. When he came looking for me, as he did from time to time, he would greet me with the greatest politeness, often bringing gifts or food or pretty trinkets or tokens of affection. But he could never stay with me long.

"Sweetheart, I must away to the duchess's antechamber in a quarter of an hour," he would say, or "Dearest Catherine, I must leave you soon, but I will stay with you as long as I can."

My longing for him grew, and I struggled not to lose patience. My eagerness for his company increased. During our times together he would take my hand, stroke my cheek, draw me into a secluded alcove and kiss me—but never for long enough to do more than tantalize me, and leave me counting the hours—or more often, the days and sleepless nights—until our next meeting.

I grew anxious, pale, edgy with worry. What was I to make of his infrequent appearances in my life (for they seemed infrequent to me)? Was it just that he was being given more and more responsibilities by my grandmother and Uncle Thomas—who seemed to spend a great deal of time at Lambeth—or was he keeping company with another girl or woman? Or several others?

There seemed to be no way to find out, though I tried and tried. Meanwhile the household was distracted by more talk of the king's forthcoming marriage. Lord Cromwell was said to be very satisfied with the bargaining over Anna of Cleves's dowry. The lady herself was not nearly as important as the benefits the marriage would bring to England. I heard much talk of how English trade would flourish anew, how sturdy, warlike Clevan soldiers would join our English trained bands. Of how all the North German lands and the flat lowland countries would join with our King Henry against the Spanish Emperor Charles, weakening his overweening might and making us safer.

Now and then, to be sure, I heard someone scoff.

"Cleves! Where is this little Cleves? A land of windmills and floods!"

And there was muffled laughter about the woman no one at court had seen, Anna. The woman Lord Cromwell wanted to make our queen.

"She's an old maid! She's nearly twenty-five!"

"She was betrothed once, but for some reason they didn't marry. Why?"

No one seemed to know why.

"Could it be that she didn't like the man? Or that he was old and poor, and she wanted someone young and rich?"

We knew that a portrait of the Lady Anna had been sent to the palace, for the king to see and approve.

"German women are all big, striding, yellow-haired fishwives," I heard Uncle Thomas say. Uncle Thomas did not spare his words! But I doubted whether he had seen the portrait of the Lady Anna, and my father told me that Uncle Thomas was opposed to the marriage because it was Lord Cromwell's idea, and he hated Lord Cromwell.

I found all the talk and wrangling wearisome—and besides, there was only one thing, or rather one man, on my mind just then: Francis Dereham.

One afternoon he surprised me with a visit. He was not wearing his livery. For an instant I was worried: had he lost his position as gentleman pensioner? Had he done something to anger Grandma Agnes?

But he quickly reassured me. He was not wearing his livery because he was not needed that afternoon. Grandma Agnes had gone to Greenwich and taken only a few members of her household with her. He was not among them.

He kissed me lightly on the cheek.

"I thought we might go into the orchard and have a picnic," he said, his smile charming as always. "I don't need to return until after vespers."

I brightened at once. We set off with a basket of food and a blanket. I took my cloak in case of rain.

The orchard that adjoined Lambeth Great House was large and thickly wooded. Rabbits and deer foraged in the grass beneath the tall trees, the cherries just beginning to put forth their unripe fruit, the apple trees still in flower.

I was happy, walking along with Francis, enjoying the feeling that, for once, there was no urgency about our time together, no need to rush. The sun was warm, the grass smelled sweet beneath our feet as we went along. We were quiet, at peace together. I felt my desire for him rise. Impulsively I took the blanket from under his arm and spread it on the fragrant grass. I lay down and reached for him.

He came into my arms and kissed me, a long unhurried kiss, then another. I expected him to begin to undress me, as Henry Manox had, eager to reveal all of me to his excited gaze. But he did not. And after a time he stopped kissing me as well.

"What is it?" I asked, full of fear. "Do you find me wanting?"

"No indeed," came the answer. "But I cannot dishonor you, Catherine, as some would surely try to do were they fortunate enough to be here with you. Lovemaking must take place within a bond of trust."

"I trust you, Francis." There was a catch in my voice as I said the words.

"I refer to the trust between a husband and wife."

A silence fell between us. I did not know what to say. I sat up on the blanket. Francis leaned comfortably on one elbow.

"There must be a future in view," he said presently.

Once again I did not know what to say, for I could not tell what he meant. Was he hinting that he wanted us to marry? Even if that was not what he meant, surely he was honoring me by protecting my virginity. Why then did I feel so bereft, cheated of the pleasure I wanted so badly, kept waiting in uncertainty and suffering while I waited? Why did I feel unwanted?

He got to his feet and, when I stood as well, feeling crestfallen, he began to fold the blanket into a neat square.

"We have not eaten our picnic," he said blandly. "Are you hungry?"

I shook my head.

"Then let us go back. I may be needed. I like to be ready, on call, in case my services are required."

"I am being considered," my father told me somewhat lugubriously, "for second under-cellarer to the new queen."

"That's wonderful, father! But only considered? Not actually appointed?"

"Not as yet."

He sighed. "Others have already received appointments. I have been overlooked, it would seem."

So he had been disappointed once again.

"Have you spoken to Grandma Agnes about it?"

He rolled his eyes, as if to say, she cares nothing for my welfare, and thinks poorly of me. It would do no good whatever to talk to her. Knowing that he was probably right, I let the question hang in the air, unanswered.

"I hope that a place may be found for you, however, Catherine, and for your cousin Charyn, among the new queen's women. And perhaps, once you are well established there, and the king's new bride becomes fond of you, you can tell her that your father would be well qualified and eager to serve her."

"I would of course do as you ask, father."

"Good girl. Good loyal girl." He nodded his head, and reaching for my hand, he patted it. I could see that there were tears in his eyes.

"Ah, there is one thing more," he added. "Francis Dereham, the gentleman pensioner, came to see me."

My heart leapt.

"About me?"

"Indeed. He asked me if anyone had yet asked for your hand."

I held my breath.

"I told him no one, not as yet." He frowned. "Perhaps I should have lied, to make him think you have been much in demand."

I could not believe what I was hearing. So this was what Francis meant when he said there must be a future in view before we loved one another in the flesh. What was it he had said? Lovemaking must take place within a bond of trust. The trust between a husband and a wife.

"He wants to marry me then, does he father?" I could not keep the excitement from my voice.

"Assuredly, Catherine, he wants to marry you, or someone like you. He would value a Howard bride. He has already asked for several of your cousins, and even for the widow of your great-uncle Richard. But no one has accepted him."

"But he is so very handsome, father," I burst out, ignoring what I had just heard. "And so much a gentleman. He speaks so well, and with such perfect courtesy, and dances so gracefully."

"He does indeed. But he has no money, or title, and though he is distantly related to our family, he is an orphan, with no parents to speak for him or aid him in his suit."

My hopes fell, I could hear the disapproval in my father's voice. "Yes. He told me."

"And there is another thing. He is Irish, on his father's side."

"Oh."

My Francis had Irish blood! That came as a blow. If I married him, our children too would possess the taint of Irishness. No one wanted that. But a thought came to me.

"Is it not true, father, that our king has Welsh blood? Yet no one looks on him as unfit to reign."

Father looked at me balefully, then grew exasperated.

"Must you always argue, Catherine? Can you not be womanly and silent? Especially about things that do not concern you? Francis Dereham is not a meet husband for a Howard! And there's an end to it!"

I hung my head.

"But I love him, father," I murmured.

He got to his feet and began pacing, one hand held to his lower back.

"When will you understand! Love doesn't enter in, Catherine. Love is just a silly girl's fancy. And it passes as quickly as a dream."

He winced, then sat down again, his hand still pressed to his back, his forehead creased. I knew he was in pain, the familiar pain of a kidney stone.

"I loved your mother once. But the king took her from me. She disappeared, into that brothel of his. The Maidens' Bower. Maidens, hah! The Whores' Chamber, more likely!"

I had never before heard my father speak of my mother, and why she had vanished from our lives. I knew that my Howard relatives had nothing but contempt for her, and that she had died, but how and why remained a mystery.

On an impulse I got down on my knees.

"Please, father, I beg you. Tell me how mother died. No one will ever speak of it."

"Hush, child! Hush!" He looked around, quickly and furtively, to see whether my words had been overheard. But no one was nearby.

He swore then, and got to his feet, and left me. I knew it would do no good to follow him, for when the pain of the stone attacked him his mood grew sour and there was no approaching him. I watched him go, feeling let down, discouraged. I had been on the brink of discovering what had happened to my mother, but then, as always, I had failed to find out the answer.

I was happy to know that Francis had chosen me as the girl he wanted to marry, yet at the same time upset that father thought so little of him as a potential husband for me.

I wanted him. Oh, how I wanted him! What was I to do?

Francis was persistent—and clever. My father would not agree to a betrothal, but he did not shout at Francis and send him away either. For once Francis discovered my father's weakness—his constant shortage of money, and his worries about never having any more of it in the future—it was easy enough for him to use that knowledge to his advantage.

He began bringing father gifts, shirts of fine linen, costly boots, a handsome gold belt buckle. He offered to bring an Italian moneylender to Lambeth who, he said, would put an end to father's seemingly endless cycle of worsening debt. He boasted of having a rich relation in Ireland who, he was assured, was growing richer all the time, and was sending him larger and larger sums. ("Perhaps the wild Irish are not so bad as we think," father remarked to me after one of Francis's visits.)

At the same time, Francis was wooing me with greater fervor, ending my longing to see more of him and promising me that his heart was mine and only mine. He presented me with lengths of fine satin and velvet to be made into gowns, a quilted cap of silver sarcenet, coils of gold and silver braid, French gloves of the softest doeskin. He brought minstrels to sing to me, he gave me a small whimpering lapdog whose collar was a golden love knot bearing our initials. Each day brought new proofs of his devotion, until finally, one evening, he showed me two silver rings and said that they were meant for us.

"One day, dear Catherine, when you are willing, we will don these rings and promise ourselves to one another. Then I will call you wife and you will call me husband. No one will ever be able to separate us, for we will be handfasted, pledged and promised in the eyes of God."

I knew about handfasting, the ancient way of marriage that had been known since before churches existed. I was touched that Francis had bought the rings and imagined us vowing our love in the old way.

There was no Mistress Phippson at Lambeth, and no Paradise Chamber. But Grandma Agnes did have a special chamberer, Mary Lascelles, who oversaw the unmarried girls of the household, and who, in return for a generous money gift, would unlock special rooms she called her cupboards.

The cupboards were small but comfortable, with rushes on the stone floors and soft mattresses and pillowed benches. Mary knew well enough who entered and left the cupboards and when, but she did not tell Grandma Agnes or anyone else (at least she promised not to tell) and we felt safe and private there.

Joan and Edward Waldegrave, Francis and I took our pleasure in the privacy of these cupboards, just as Henry and I and the others had at Horsham, and before long Francis and I put on the silver rings he had bought for us and promised to love each other for the rest of our lives.

It was as solemn, as beautiful a pledge as I had ever made, and I meant the words I spoke with all my heart. I had no doubt that Francis was equally sincere in promising himself to me, and when he took his vow, I saw such love in his beautiful eyes that it made me cry.

At last I knew what it was to be a wife, for once we were pledged, I gladly offered Francis my body, my maidenhead, my greatest treasure. He loved me tenderly, and very gently, eager not to hurt me, and with none of the huffing and puffing I had grown accustomed to with Henry. But then, I had denied Henry the ultimate pleasure, while with Francis I opened myself fully to his rather quick glance and entry.

I felt him inside me, I felt an odd unfamiliar mixture of pain and pleasure. But what I did not feel—and this puzzled me greatly— was excitement. The warmth of passion. The passion I had felt so strongly with Henry that I almost burst. The strong tide of desire— desire thwarted, with Henry, but now unleashed, with the man who was my husband. Where was desire?

Perhaps, I thought, when one is married to one's true love, romance and affection take the place of that heated craving Henry had brought out in me. I prayed that this was true, but had no way to find out.

Besides, I did not want anyone to know of our secret pledge. I did not want to reveal the fact that I, a Howard, had married a distant relation with no living parents and Irish blood.

At least I could be sure that there would be no child to give our secret away. I remembered well what Joan had taught Alice about how to make certain she would not become pregnant. I used my knowledge and felt certain I would not be a mother any time soon.

And in fact, Francis and I did not share a bed very often. On many nights he was kept busy until long past midnight, in attendance on Grandma Agnes at banquets or other evening entertainments, accompanying her when she visited Horsham, escorting her to the royal palace at Hampton Court or Greenwich or across the river at Cardinal Wolsey's old palace of York Place, now renamed Whitehall.

When at Lambeth Francis slept in quarters with the other gentlemen pensioners, I in the wing with the other unmarried young women (for of course no one knew of our handfasted vows) who served the duchess. Only on occasion did Francis pay Mary Lascelles to let us use one of the cupboards where we could be together undisturbed. Even less often we shared a cupboard with Joan and Edward, who had their own duties and obligations and seemed less and less available for carefree nights and midnight feasting.

Francis continued to be an affectionate partner and lover, embracing me tenderly when we met, exchanging stolen kisses in the duchess's apartments when no one was near to see us, giving me gifts and calling me wife.

"Catherine, my dear wife," he would often say, relishing the words. "My own dear wife Catherine Howard Dereham."

Unlike Henry, Francis never sulked, he was not jealous, he seemed always to maintain a pleasant, calm manner. He was exceptionally courteous. Younger, more handsome men (there were few at Lambeth who were more handsome than he was) did not make him envious. In fact he seemed to take a particular pleasure in the company of good-looking men—men such as my slim, boyish, fair-haired tutor. He never became demanding, as Henry often had, and did not insist that I tell him everyone I saw and how I spent my time.

His talk, when we were together, was nearly always of the new queen's establishment: how many people were to be appointed to her household, which appointments had been made and which were still undecided, who was in favor with the king and who was not. According to Francis, Lord Cromwell was still the most powerful man at the royal court. It was entirely his idea that King Henry should marry the Lady Anna of Cleves, though the king was said to be nervous and uncertain about marrying a woman he had never met. Opposed to Lord Cromwell was my uncle Thomas and my grandmother and any among the nobility who thought an obscure German princess with a very small dowry was not a suitable wife for our king.

It wearied me to hear about the endless wrangles over offices and fees and favors, whose position took precedence, who had the ear of the Lord Privy Seal and who he disliked. It wearied me, not only because I would have preferred hearing words of love and concern from my new husband, but because I had to hear about matters of court offices and conflicts from my father as well as from Francis. Father was still waiting in great discontent to hear whether or not he was to be made under-cellarer to the next queen. Between Francis and my father, I had more than my fill of dull and (to me) trivial matters.

But then came a change. Suddenly I myself was drawn into the swirling fog of intrigue, and before I knew it the things I had been hearing about from others began to concern me, very immediately and vitally. In fact, they began to concern me in ways that changed my life from then on.

An order was sent to Lambeth, to Uncle Thomas, by King Henry himself. "Assemble eight of the fairest young women from among your relations," it read. "Have them attend me at Whitehall so that I may make their acquaintance." A date and time was set forth. It only remained for my uncle to make his choices.

"Which of us do you think he will choose?" Malyn asked, her deep blue eyes bright, clearly anxious to be among the favored few.

"I've heard he wants Charyn to be there. But she's already betrothed."

"Betrothals can be broken," Joan put in thoughtfully. "At the king's command."

"Mary Sidford," was my comment. She was certainly very lovely, among the loveliest among us—blond, pink-cheeked, dimpled and with a generously ripe figure.

"Does this mean he isn't going to marry the old maid from Cleves?" Alice asked tentatively. "I thought it was all arranged."

"Nothing is arranged until all the official papers have been drawn up," Joan told us. As usual, she was the best informed of us all. "Lord Cromwell has not been able to persuade the king to agree. So nothing is settled. Edward told me that he heard from one of the king's chamber gentlemen that the marriage documents have not been written yet, much less signed."

Edward Waldegrave, Joan's lover, went back and forth between Lambeth and the royal palace often, on Grandma Agnes's business. He was on familiar terms with the king's chamber gentlemen and passed on to Joan the most recent news from court and even the newest bawdy jokes.

"Edward says King Henry asked the French to send their prettiest girls to Calais for him to look over. And do you know what they said? They said, 'What next, do you want to lie with them all too?' He says the king actually got red in the face when he heard that."

The request from the palace caused a great stir at Lambeth. It indicated that King Henry was openly shopping for a bride—and that the power of Lord Cromwell was waning, since the choice of the Lady Anna of Cleves had been his and not the king's.

We heard that all sorts and conditions of girls and women were being delivered to Whitehall for the king's perusal.

"He'll love that," was the comment of my bitter cousin Catherine Tylney. "He can't get enough of women."

"At least we know *you* won't be sent to Whitehall," Joan retorted. "King Henry likes gentle, softspoken women, not shrews. Oh, and they must also be young and sweet, not old and sour."

Francis told me that my uncle Thomas could not have been happier at Lord Cromwell's loss of influence over the king. Now he himself could rise, his own views on the choice of a bride might yet prevail. He began, Francis said, by tempting King Henry with one of his former favorites, Margaret Shelton. He went on to offer the king another girl, barely fourteen years old, who had been a maid of honor at the Flemish court, and another—his own ward—who was not yet twelve.

"If you are among the girls chosen to appear before the king, Catherine, you will have an advantage," Francis said. "You are quite young. Therein lies your advantage."

"But Francis!" I burst out, "We are married! We are handfasted. I cannot even be considered by the king."

Francis looked thoughtful. "It would not be a bad thing if he were to choose you. Think of what it would mean for us both: wealth, lands, the title of queen for you, no doubt a position as chief bedchamber gentleman for me, if not something even higher—" The gleam in his eyes told me all; he would gladly give me to the king, if only it meant that his dream of riches and high status could come true.

"But what of our vows? What of our pledge to love and honor one another?"

Francis shrugged. "If we were lucky enough that the king showed you favor, either as his mistress or his wife, we would still continue to belong to each other. You would simply belong to the king as well."

I shook my head in disbelief. Francis, my husband, was telling me he would be willing to share me with the king in return for money and a high position. To sell me, in effect. To barter my honor, my future, my reputation, in exchange for a few coins and a title in the royal household.

Francis smiled down at me and stroked my cheek.

"Remember Mary Boleyn," he said. "Wife and royal mistress both—and much much happier than her sister Anne."

"Mary Boleyn was a whore. Everyone says so. Cast out by her relations, dishonored by everyone."

But Francis only laughed. "She had her reward. You must learn, my dear wife, to adapt yourself to the ways of those around you. Be supple, be wise!"

Uncle Thomas made his choices. There were to be eight of us sent to the king: Charyn (despite her betrothal), Mary Sidford, Alice Restvold, my cousins Malyn Tylney, Dorothy Baskerville and Margaret Benet, and me. Yes, me. And there was one other, Uncle Thomas's mistress Elizabeth Holland. Like Francis, Uncle Thomas was apparently willing to share his lover with the king. Elizabeth Holland was much older than the rest of us, sensuous and alluring, with lustrous chestnut brown hair and a sly smile. I wondered if she was too old to bear the king children.

But I had no time for such speculations, for the eight of us were far too busy preparing ourselves to meet the king. We had to look our best, our garments and behavior had to show us to greatest advantage, that was obvious. Grandma Agnes brought in seamstresses and tailors, lengths of gleaming satin and sarcenet, cut Genoa velvet and shimmering bawdkin in dozens of colors, from the London warehouses, lengths of lace and ribbon and jeweled trim. As our gowns were cut and sewn and fitted she inspected each of us, noting where a stomacher could be tightened, a bodice lowered, a petticoat made more flirtatiously full.

As my gown was taking shape she stood back and looked at me with a very critical eye.

"Can that girl not be made taller?" she asked. "Her mother was taller, was she not?"

My mother! I looked over at grandma, but she was directing her question to the tailor.

"I did not know the lady," he said. "I cannot say. But the shoemaker can easily add to the heels of Mistress Catherine's slippers, to make her appear taller."

"Tell him to do so. And see that her headdress is raised up as well."

At last we were ready, our gowns and petticoats fluffed and glimmering, our hair neatly and modestly—and most becomingly—arranged beneath our headdresses, our eyes brightened with a drop of belladonna and our cheeks delicately pinked with red ochre. Together the eight of us set off in two coaches for the royal court at Whitehall, our hearts in our mouths, our hopes soaring.

For I too was caught up in the excitement of being shown off to the king. I loved Francis and cherished our bond and pledge—but if fate should lead me to a higher destiny, who was I to refuse it, especially since Francis was more than willing to share me with King Henry?

"Seek the king's fantasy, all of you!" Uncle Thomas called out to us as our coaches rumbled out of the courtyard of Lambeth. "Remember who you are, and make our family proud!"

His words echoed in my ears as we left the precincts of the great house and set out along the crowded high road toward the river and the capital. And I remembered too what Francis so often said, though the memory was chilling: Do what you can, take what you need, act as you must. I vowed to make this motto my watchword in the days to come.

FIVE

I will never forget, not if I live to be a hundred, my first sight of King Henry. We were shown into the grand, high-ceilinged presence chamber, the eight of us, and the king was leaning casually against a large cabinet of polished wood. Half a dozen men were near him, one of them writing on a scroll, another handing him papers, another standing back, surveying the scene, others waiting to do his bidding.

As we approached I heard the king say, his voice warm and resonant, "At my age, better a soft bed than a hard harlot." The others laughed—not the polite, feigned laughter of flatterers but the genuine, hearty laughter of companions.

He was much taller than the others, and much more stout, though his beard was still thick and red-gold and there was little of the old man about him despite his age. He was quite old, nearly fifty. He wore a coat such as I had never seen before, so rich a coat that I can hardly describe it, braided all over in glimmering gold and set with clusters of large orient pearls and sparkling emeralds and diamonds, among them other gems in colors new to me, pale yellow and blood red and bluish purple, with enormous diamonds for buttons. Oh, how he gleamed! The slightest movement he made set the gold braid dancing, and the jewels flashing.

As we came closer I saw that his swordgirdle and sword were studded with large emeralds, and his bonnet too was heavy with gleaming stones and shining golden aglets. He was dressed with such magnificence, yet there was not the least formality about his manner. He continued to joke and laugh with the others, all the while glancing at the papers handed to him and reaching for a pen to sign one or two of them.

I heard him say something about artichokes, then he glanced up at us, and—I could swear that he looked right at me.

He looked at me, his broad, handsome face pleasant and wearing a smile of welcome—and then, the merest instant later, full of shock. I thought I heard a sharp intake of breath, certainly there was a brief moment of absolute silence. Then he looked away and was his relaxed, carefree self again, coming toward us to greet us.

"Ladies, beautiful young ladies," he said in a joyful tone, rubbing his hands together, "won't you join me for a light collation? Come, sit down, all of you, and tell me all about yourselves. I have seen your beautiful persons, now I must hear your beautiful voices."

We joined him around a table laid with linens and gold trenchers and goblets and a great round Suffolk cheese. He encouraged us to put all ceremony aside and in fact his manner was quite disarming. He waved away the men of business and ordered food to be brought in. As we were being served we each said a few words, with the king's eager encouragement. Charyn was cool and reserved, Mary Sidford intelligent and soft-spoken, Alice nervous and jittery, overwhelmed by her surroundings. My cousins Dorothy and Margaret looked pretty but lacked charm and sparkle, I thought. Malyn's words were clever, but her tone detached. Elizabeth Holland, self-assured and very sensual in her dress and manner, was evidently not to the king's taste and he turned aside as she was speaking. It was an awkward moment; she knew he was spurning her and was offended.

When my turn came I was very conscious that many pairs of eyes were on me. I rose to my full height—actually to higher than my full height, thanks to my new slippers—and thanked the king for his gracious invitation to visit the palace and added, with a smile, that I wondered how he knew I was fond of artichokes and haggis and Suffolk cheese. At this he burst into laughter and the others at the table tittered dutifully—all but Elizabeth Holland, who gave me a scornful look. I noticed that Malyn narrowed her eyes and looked me up and down, no doubt wondering whether I was being artless or conniving. I looked back at her with amusement.

"My physician Dr. Chambers tells me," the king began, "that I am of a sanguine temperament, cheerful, gamesome, insouciant and overly fond of women and drink." He winked at us. "On such an afternoon as this, surrounded as I am with so much beauty and charm, I am inclined to think he is right."

He took a long draught from his goblet.

Listening to him, and watching the gems on his remarkable coat flash with fire whenever he moved, it was difficult for me to remember that it was King Henry who had ordered cousin Anne Boleyn to her death—that gruesome, ghastly death I had been forced to watch—and in recent months had ordered more than a dozen of his other relations to die as well, assuming my father's count was correct. How could one man be so amicable and pleasing and at the same time so dangerous and cruel? According to my father, some of the relatives King Henry committed to the Tower were small children, rumored to have been strangled by their guards or left to starve on the king's orders.

But then, he was said to be a man of quicksilver moods, genial one moment and furious the next. And he had recently been very ill, deathly ill, and all of us at Lambeth had been summoned to Grandma Agnes's chapel to pray for him.

His legs gave him great pain, and his surgeons had to bleed him and purge him to tame the fatal humors that threatened to end his life. Right before Grandma Agnes moved her household from Horsham to Lambeth his legs swelled and tormented him yet again. Only this time no amount of bleeding or purging, no medicines prepared by the royal apothecaries could bring him back to health.

We prayed for him. Processions were held, holy relics brought to his bedside. But he only grew worse, full of fever and choking and gasping for breath. The crass serving boys wagered with one another, guessing when he would die. Uncle Thomas went to the palace in hopes that the dying king would name him regent for the baby Prince Edward, but he was not allowed to see the king. Lord Cromwell forbade it.

For twelve days we gathered to pray, morning and evening, wondering whether the baby prince would become our new king, with Lord Cromwell as his regent and guardian, or whether Princess Mary would rally her supporters and seize the throne.

We grew tired of waiting. But in the end the king recovered, though his legs still pained him, and we felt greatly relieved. Since that anxious time he had not had any further serious illnesses. But there were those who said that his changeable temperament had grown more unpredictable, his moods more extreme.

"Would it amuse you ladies to see some of the gifts I've received in recent days?" the king was asking as the table was being cleared. He drank deeply from his goblet and a servant refilled it.

We could hardly refuse—and besides, the array of objects being carried in by valets and grooms looked very intriguing. There were velvet purses and hawks' hoods of silver and gold, paintings and other art works of many kinds, books with covers stamped with filigree gold work, jeweled coffers and a long leather scabbard with an edge of thick gold braid. Most intriguing to me was a small monkey in a gilded cage, its tiny hands grasping the bars, its piteous little face peering out at us, as if to plead for its freedom.

"What if I told you that each of you may choose a gift of your own from among these things here arrayed?"

Several of my cousins gave cries of delight at this, and Bess Holland's face lit up in pleasure, a gleam of avarice in her hard grey eyes.

"There is only one thing I ask of you," King Henry added, raising one finger in caution. "You must explain the reason for your choice."

We set about examining the beautiful, precious objects and before long we had each chosen one we wanted to keep. Charyn decided on a gold dog collar studded with pearls.

"For your future husband to wear, perhaps?" King Henry remarked.

Mary Sidford chose a carved chest full of embroidered shirts.

"For my future husband to wear," she said gently, echoing the king and earning his nod of approval.

Alice chose a long knife with a silver hilt, chased with elaborate Spanish work.

"To do away with your future husband, perhaps?" was the king's darkly teasing query—which caused the uneasy Alice to burst into tears.

My cousin Dorothy chose a painting of a forest scene, with hunters and their dogs pursuing fleeing nymphs. Margaret's choice was a small but lovely Turkey carpet.

"To decorate your palaces," was all the king said—and all he needed to say. Neither of my duller cousins had captivated him, that much was plain.

Malyn took one of the purses of coins.

"Ah," said King Henry. "And is it your hope to enrich your future husband, or to enrich yourself, so that you need not marry?"

Malyn did not shrink from the king's scrutiny, or from his frank question.

"I hope my future husband will praise me for my prudence, in choosing what will make me more secure."

"Then you must marry a moneylender!" the king retorted, making us all laugh.

Elizabeth Holland selected a heavy gold trencher from the table of gifts.

"Beware of getting fat as you age," was the king's remark. "Husbands prefer slender women." His tone was dismissive.

Elizabeth, insulted, looked back at the king, at his thick, big-bellied body, burly and fleshy, his plump cheeks, his long swollen legs.

"And wives prefer slender men," was all she said, but in a cutting tone that made the king leap at once to his feet, so quickly and so athletically that one could almost forget how heavy he was.

He glowered at Elizabeth, then summoned one of the attendant chamber gentlemen.

"See that this woman and her trencher are returned to Lambeth. And that she is banished from court!" he said loudly. In a moment she was taken away.

In the uncomfortable silence that followed, the king, looking angry, muttered, "Better a soft bed than a hard harlot," but this time no one laughed.

"Well, she is Lord Norfolk's harlot, is she not? It offends me that he should send her here, his old, used-up whore!"

I wished with all my strength, at that moment, that I had never come to the palace. That I could slip away, quietly and unseen. The others around me were ill at ease, shuffling their feet, looking down at their laps, fingering their chosen gifts.

I was the only one who had not made my choice. The king was watching me. Was he still angry? I could not read his features. I sat where I was, tense and anxious.

But he was coming toward me, his tread light. When he spoke his voice was soft.

"And you, dear lady? What will be your choice?" I looked up at him, standing before me, dazzling in his sparkling coat, his light blue eyes enigmatic, questioning. Once again I felt many pairs of eyes on me.

"Your Majesty," I managed to say, "I am awed by your generosity. So many beautiful things to choose from, and all from your bounty."

He nodded in satisfaction, a smile on his thin pale lips.

"But I must choose the monkey. I must free him."

"Well said, Catherine," was his soft reply. "Well said."

He went to the table and, lifting the gilded cage, brought it to me and laid it at my feet. The monkey tilted his head back and lifted his small face to regard me gravely, sadly, as it seemed to me.

"He is a marmoset, from Brazil. He is the only one who survived. Thirty were captured, but the others perished on the voyage home."

I bent down to put my hand on the gilded bars of the cage. The creature slowly put its own small hand opposite mine.

"Catherine! Don't let that horrid thing bite you!"

It was Charyn's scolding voice.

"I don't think he will."

Even through the bars I could feel the warmth of the small hand, with its delicate fingers and pink palm. Then, without warning, the creature seemed to smile, baring its teeth. Was it a smile, or a grimace?

I pulled my hand back—and the king grasped it in his far larger one.

He bent down to whisper in my ear. I could hear the dangling ornaments on his cap jangle as he did so. His breath against my cheek was hot—and so foul that I wanted to draw away from him.

"I would not have this little hand be hurt—not for anything," he whispered, squeezing my hand. Then he released it, and straightened up.

"Now, ladies, I must return to my papers." He clapped loudly, and his men of business came back into the room. One by one we curtseyed to King Henry and filed out, carrying our gifts. The marmoset had begun to screech. The king put his hands over his ears, and smiled at me, letting his gaze linger. Then he turned and went back toward the cabinet of polished wood, leaning against it comfortably, and reaching for the papers being handed to him.

Our interview had come to an end.

"Never! Never!" Charyn said forcefully once we were back in our coach, on our return to Lambeth.

"I would never even *think* of becoming the wife of that man!"

"Nor would I," put in cousin Margaret, "though he is terribly rich. And I suppose he could command any of us to do anything. He is the king."

"He is terrifying," Alice said, her voice thin. She began to cough.

"I don't suppose we will have to make that decision, whether to marry him or not," said Malyn, with a sly glance at me, "though he did seem to favor you, Catherine."

I chuckled. "He will think of me as the monkey lady, if he remembers me at all." The gilded cage was at my feet. The marmoset had curled itself into a ball and was asleep, though how it could sleep with the jolting and jouncing of the coach I couldn't imagine.

"No! Never!" Charyn was repeating. "I would rather cut my own throat than share the bed of that fat dying old man." She shuddered.

"You won't have to, will you?" was Margaret's dry comment. "You have your lordling, Lord Morley's boy."

"Yes," said Charyn loftily, smoothing her satin skirt. "And I shall do my best to see that we are wed as soon as possible."

Though I made light of what Malyn said about King Henry's showing me particular favor, I was well aware that he had indeed singled me out for his special notice. His whispered words, his squeezing of my hand, his praise ("Well said"), his lingering glance were all eloquent. And there was something more, though I had no idea what to make of it. On first glimpsing me he had seemed startled, taken aback. Why?

There were other moments when I noticed him looking at me—looks I found disturbing: a slight wrinkling of his brow, a vague air of unease that seemed to descend over his features and then disappear as quickly as it came. Something about me troubled him, breaking in on his jocular, disarming manner. Yet he seemed pleased that I had chosen the marmoset as my gift, and he hadn't whispered in any other ear but mine, or taken any other hand.

I decided to call the little monkey Jonah, after the prophet in the Bible who was saved from drowning at sea. He became a great favorite among the women of Grandma Agnes's household—after I assured them that he did not bite and that his annoying habit of tearing off their headdresses and loosening their hair could be controlled. His cage had to be kept clean and his daily platters of apples and nuts supplied (if I did not attend to this he screeched horribly) but as long as he was cared for he made a very affectionate companion. I became very fond of him, and sometimes took him with me, carrying him under my arm or draped over my shoulders, when I went about through the house.

I thought of taking him with me when Uncle Thomas sent for me not long after my visit to the palace, but then decided not to risk uncle's disapproval. I found Uncle Thomas in Grandma

Agnes's private closet, his mood for once hospitable and his manner almost welcoming. With him were Grandma Agnes, looking equally agreeable, and my uncle William Cotton, who came forward to embrace me as I entered, and two others, one a priest and the other a soberly dressed man, a landowner by his appearance, with several books under his arm and a sheaf of papers in his hands.

"Now then, niece Catherine," Uncle Thomas began, "we have something to tell you. The king has been asking after you. Ever since you and the others went to the palace he has been wanting to know everything about you."

"Tell her what he said to you," Grandma Agnes prompted.

Uncle Thomas turned to me.

"'By all that is holy,' His Majesty said, 'if only I had seen this girl before Crum began these damnable talks with the Clevans!' Those were his words. And I said, 'It is not too late, sire.'"

"But I—" I began, then closed my mouth. If I understood Uncle Thomas correctly, he was telling me that King Henry might prefer me to the mysterious Anna of Cleves. I was pledged to Francis, but Francis had made it clear that our handfasted pledge need not hold me back from becoming the king's mistress. Or his wife.

I felt dizzy.

"Come, sit here, girl," Grandma Agnes was saying, patting the cushioned bench beside her. Obediently I went to sit down.

"Give her some wine!" she called out. "She looks pale."

"Perhaps we have not appreciated you up to now, Catherine," she said, speaking in a voice I had never before heard her use. Not stern, not demanding, not shrill. An almost motherly voice.

"There are so many girls living under my roof," she went on, "I have so many granddaughters and grandnieces, wards and orphans and babes left on my doorstep—" She waved her hand as if to dismiss them all. "I cannot see every one clearly. I cannot appreciate each one. They are a swarm, nothing more."

As she spoke I drank thirstily from the goblet of wine that was brought to me.

"If we have neglected you, I regret it. I assure you, Lambeth will be made a much more pleasant place for you from now on. I know your father does not provide very generously for you—"

"Where is father?" I asked, holding out my goblet to the servant who stood by, who hastened to fill it.

"Shouldn't father be here, to hear what you are telling me?"

Grandma Agnes looked uncomfortable.

"Thomas—" she began.

"He is in the North Country. He has been appointed Keeper of the Subsidies for Yorkshire and the Borders." Uncle Thomas spoke brusquely, hurriedly.

"But he was hoping to be made second under-cellarer to the new queen!" I said. "He expected the appointment!"

"The Lord Privy Seal does not wish it," was Uncle Thomas's response, spoken in a low, resentful tone.

"Lord Cromwell!"

"He ordered your father to Huddleston last week. He will take up his duties there as soon as possible."

Damnable Lord Cromwell! He was thwarting us at every turn. We Howards, whose descent was as far above his as the sky is above the earth, as I had often heard Uncle Thomas say.

"I see by the scowl on your pretty face that you share our view of the Lord Privy Seal," Grandma Agnes said, her tone acid. "He harms and thwarts our family's interests at every opportunity. You, on the other hand, may have the good fortune to advance our interests."

"Uncle Thomas, can you not ask the king to give father the position he wants?" I asked bravely.

"Perhaps not," came his answer, "but you could. And while making your request, you could feed his fancy, charm him further, nurture his love."

"Take the monkey with you," Grandma Agnes added. "He likes it that you chose the monkey from among all the gifts he offered. Will you do it?"

I felt no hesitation.

"If you think it would help father, yes."

"Before you go, I must tell you that the talks with the men of law from Cleves have run into difficulties." Uncle Thomas looked pleased. "Our own man of law here believes that Anna entered into a marriage contract with another man, and is still bound by that contract. And our theologians maintain that there are worrisome differences in doctrine between the Lutheran belief of Cleves and our English church as reformed by Parliament. Unless these differences can be removed, the Lady Anna cannot marry King Henry. She must conform to our ways in all things."

Both the lawyer and the priest were clearly eager to speak, but Uncle Thomas held up his hand to silence them.

"So it appears that the king may not be able to marry the lady Lord Cromwell has chosen for him after all."

Both Uncle Thomas and Grandma Agnes were smiling at me, expecting me to be pleased at all I had been hearing. Yet something held me back, some nagging sense that all was not as it seemed. Something unspoken hung in the air. I was uneasy. I looked at Uncle William, who had remained silent through everything that had been said, hoping for—what? Reassurance perhaps—or even a welcome touch of humor. But his kind face was grave.

"It is a lot for you to take in, all at once," he said. "But you must see the advantage to our family. Think of it! We Howards, who were disgraced by the scandals of Queen Anne, the daughter of a Howard mother, may now be cleansed of that taint by having another Howard gain the royal favor. Of course you would hardly be the first," he went on, half musing to himself. "There was your mother, your beautiful, beautiful mother, Jocasta—"

"William!" My grandmother's voice was sharp.

Uncle William was flustered.

"Yes, of course. I forgot. I should not have mentioned her. I'm sorry."

There it was again. My mother's name mentioned, her existence acknowledged, then a silence imposed. I looked from Grandma Agnes to Uncle William to Uncle Thomas, whose dark face was turned away.

"Father will not tell me what happened to my mother. No one is ever allowed to mention her name or recall her memory. I loved her. What can she have done that was so terrible? And how did she die? I must know."

After a time Grandma Agnes spoke.

"If Catherine is going to see the king, it might be well to tell her what she wants to know."

Uncle Thomas shook his head and looked sour. Uncle William sighed, then, after a moment, got to his feet.

"Come with me, Catherine. Let us go out into the garden where we can breathe the fresh air and smell the first of the lilacs. Let me tell you a story."

A chill breeze was blowing, I had to ask one of the grooms to bring me a shawl. I sat on a stone bench under a cherry tree that was just coming into bud. Uncle William stood nearby. From our patch of lawn and garden we could see the wherries coming up and down the river, with now and then a barge or a towed flatboat heaped with barrels and chests.

I watched Uncle William, waiting for him to begin.

"Imagine, Catherine," he said at length, "that your lovely mother was just about the age you are now. She had only been married to your father for a year or so. All the men of the court envied your father, because Jocasta was so beautiful, so lively and charming. I suppose I was a little in love with her myself. She had the grace of a butterfly, a face like a flower, she could make people laugh and she also had a generous heart. She didn't belong in a royal court, courts are sordid places, full of decadence and selfish pleasures. I know, I have served King Henry and his father before him since I was a boy.

"Jocasta saw through the pretense and sugared rivalries. She was too gentle a spirit to survive amid the clawing for power, the destructiveness of life lived in the shadow of a king. She deserved better.

"It was no wonder King Henry fell in love with her. But she was married to your father, and she was fond of him, partly because he was such an inept courtier. He fumbled and bumbled and could not seem to grasp how to rise in the hierarchy of power. Not for him the sordidness and decadence of the others. People laughed at him. His own stepmother was ashamed of him—she still is. He was not worldly, or greedy, he took no pleasure in others' pain.

"Yet though Jocasta was fond of Edmund, she truly loved the king. In his younger years he was every woman's perfect gentle knight, or so my wife—your aunt—always told me. Handsome, dashing, charming, a champion in the lists, a musician who wrote songs to his beloved and sang them in his strong, true voice.

"And though the king was married, his union with Queen Catherine was a tragedy. She was a noble character, to be sure, a valiant woman with the strength and valor of her mother, the great Isabella of Castile. We all saw it in her, and admired her for it. But Henry did not love her. He loved Jocasta, and the queen knew it. She also knew, by that time, that she could never give the king a son to succeed him. All her babies but one had died, and that one, as you know, was a girl, Princess Mary.

"The king took Jocasta to live in the Maidens' Bower, where he kept his mistresses. Edmund did not object, he knew it would do no good, and besides, King Henry gave him an estate and made him royal lieutenant for Sark, which more than satisfied him, even though it meant that he would be far from home for long stretches of time.

"As King Henry's mistress, Jocasta brought shame on our family. It could not have been otherwise. Yet secretly all the women envied her, for her beauty and for being loved by the king. Before long she knew she was carrying the king's child, and he was overjoyed. He felt sure she would have a son, and he meant to make that son his heir. He confided to his closest friends that he hoped Queen Catherine would either fall ill and die or decide to take the veil, leaving him free to marry. He was sure a way could be found to free Jocasta from Edmund.

"When her time was near Henry sent his beloved into the country, to the convent of St. Frideswide. He sent Mary Lascelles with her, to attend her. He hired a skilled midwife, Anys Cockerell, to deliver her child. Nothing was wanting in the birth chamber, Mary Lascelles saw to that."

Uncle William paused, unable to go on. I saw that he was overcome with sorrow and I thought, yes, it was as he said, he must have loved her. After a time he continued his tale, his voice hoarse with emotion.

"When word reached King Henry that she had died he gave forth such a howl as I had never heard from any creature, animal or human. He shut himself away for three days, eating nothing, speaking to no one. The physicians were worried about him, they had no idea why he was acting as he did.

"Then, at last, he emerged from his seclusion. He was haggard and white-faced. I had never seen him so ravaged. He staggered like a wounded deer. No one dared to speak to him, he raged in his sorrow. Finally he told those few of us who were closest to him what had happened. Jocasta and the baby had both died. He ordered the midwife to be hunted and executed, but she was never found. Mary Lascelles pleaded for her life and he forgave her, because he knew Jocasta had been fond of her."

He reached into an inner pocket of his doublet and brought out a velvet pouch. He handed it to me.

"I have kept this ever since she died. It was with the few possessions of hers that Mary Lascelles returned to the family. She was wearing it all through her labor, Mary said. I want you to have it."

Moved by his words, and the emotion in his voice, I opened the pouch and took out a golden pendant. The design was simple: three hearts entwined.

"The king wears a brooch of this same design," Uncle William said. "I know he still grieves for his lost love. He visits her grave. She is buried in a private chapel at Greyfriars here in London. The duke would not permit her body or the body of her son to be buried in the Howard family tomb in Norfolk."

He shook his head. "She was the best of us all, your mother. And yet she was shunned, even in death."

For a time we were silent, watching the boats come and go. The sun had sunk lower as Uncle William told his tale, and the wind off the river had grown colder.

"I look like her, don't I," I said finally.

Uncle William nodded. "Very much like her. And the light in your eyes, your laughter, your grace—it is as if she had been reborn."

"When the king first saw me, that day when the eight of us went to the palace, he was startled, dismayed by the sight of me. I knew then there was some reason."

"He sees her in you. Part of him imagines that she has come to life again in you."

"But he must have known, all these years, that she had a daughter."

"Of course. Yet he had no wish to see you, or even know whether or not you survived your childhood. It was all much too painful, the thought that Jocasta's child by Edmund might be living, while his boy died."

Uncle William sat down beside me and put his arm around me. "You are shivering. We must go back inside."

"No, please, uncle. Let's just sit quietly here awhile."

"Of course, if you need to, dear child." He stroked my hair. "I wish you could have been spared all this. But you had to know. Otherwise the king's interest in you would make no sense."

How long we sat there I don't remember, but I heard the bells ringing in the church tower as we got up to leave, and my feet felt heavy as we walked together out of the fragrant garden, the sound of the chiming bells still echoing in my ears.

Quarrels erupted at Lambeth that spring, violent quarrels that left many injured. Two of Grandma Agnes's household sergeants challenged a French dueling master to a contest of arms; one was killed, the other badly wounded. Two servants fought over a kitchen maid; both bled in the courtyard until a surgeon was found to bind up their wounds. (The kitchen maid jumped into the river and was never seen again.) Every time Uncle Thomas went to the royal court, it seemed, his guardsmen had words with the king's gentlemen, and swords were drawn.

But the quarrel that concerned me most nearly began when twenty of Lord Cromwell's serving men were set upon just at nightfall by men sent from our Lambeth household. The melee that resulted went on for an hour or more, and when it was over twelve men were dead and a score of others—among them my Francis—lay bleeding.

It was his arm, his sword arm, that had to be bound up with linen bandages. He had a cut over one eye, and a tooth came loose, but it was his head that hurt him most. He lay on the bed in our cupboard, full of the physick Joan gave him to dull his pain, halfway between sleep and waking. Edward Waldegrave, who had fought alongside Francis, had a deep wound in his side and tossed and moaned with fever for many days.

Joan and I were kept busy watching over them both. I was still coming to terms with all that I had learned in recent days, and it left me in a state of puzzlement.

Nothing was as I had thought it to be: I had thought I was married to Francis, now I discovered that I was a favorite of the king, and my marriage did not matter. I had thought my mother died of disease or in an accident; now I discovered that she had been the king's great love and had died bearing his son. I had believed I was my mother's only child; now I discovered that I had had a brother—briefly—who if he had lived, could have become King of England.

I pondered it all, as I put fresh bandages on Francis's arm and cleaned the cut over his eye. He slept a lot, and I slept too, lying beside him—until called into service to attend Grandma Agnes or meet with a dressmaker for a fitting on one of the many new gowns she ordered for me.

One afternoon I went to Greyfriars, to visit my mother's tomb. Uncle William had told me where to find it in the mendicant church, tucked in a corner in a private chapel, easily overlooked by visitors or worshippers. The stone that marked the tomb had no name, only a cross, and beneath it three entwined hearts, and the word "Beloved." I stood beside it, saying a prayer for my mother's soul and the soul of the brother I never knew.

I lingered there, in the cool of the church, lost in thought, until the two serving girls I had brought with me began to fidget and whisper to one another, and I realized it was time to go.

That evening I stayed awhile with Francis, sitting on the bed beside him. He was drowsy as usual from his medicine. He reached for my hand.

"Where did you go?" he asked me.

"I had an errand in London," I said. "For the duchess."

"Oh." Something in his tone told me he didn't believe me. But I did not want to tell him where I had gone, that I had been visiting my mother's grave, that I now knew a great deal about her that I had never known before. The knowledge was still too fresh, too new to me. I would tell Francis eventually, of course. But not just yet.

A distance had grown between us, ever since I learned of the king's avid interest in me. It was as if the king himself had come between us, cleaving our bound hands, severing our precious bond. The force of his presence in our lives shattered the future I had dreamed of—a future I thought Francis had been dreaming of as well. But I now saw that what mattered most to Francis was the king's patronage, his favor. I began to fear that Francis would give up almost anything—even me—to attain and keep that royal favor.

It was as if the craving for high court office was a kind of infection. My father had it. All the men of business had it, Lord Cromwell most of all. Even Uncle Thomas had it, for much as he liked to say that the Howards were above the old royal line of the Plantagenets, and that his descent was of an older and higher lineage than the Tudors, in truth he too fought for preeminence in the royal household, and was bitterly jealous of the lowborn Lord Cromwell because Cromwell possessed the one thing that eluded Uncle Thomas: power.

There were more quarrels as the days passed, more melees. We heard of injured men, men who died of wounds. The stables at

Lambeth became an arsenal, filled with weapons for the Howard men to use against their enemies. There was much boasting about how many of Cromwell's men had been hurt. The conflict widened, from duels of honor to disputes over precedence to battles arising out of wagers. No wagering was more keen than that over Anna of Cleves: would she or would she not become King Henry's next wife? Cromwell's men bet on Anna, the Howard servitors and partisans bet that another woman, possibly a girl of English birth, would be the one chosen.

And who would that girl be?

"Get that filthy creature out of here!"

The marmoset jumped gleefully from bed to bench to cabinet and back to the bed again, uttering short shrill cries and grunts and now and then shrieking so loudly that I had to cover my ears.

Francis, enraged, reached in vain for Jonah's gold collar with his uninjured arm, and swore at him.

"Get him away, I say!"

"He's only playing. He won't hurt anything."

"He stinks. He has fleas. He looks like a demon from hell—and sounds like one too."

I kept hoping that Francis would get used to Jonah, even become fond of him as many in the household were. But he obstinately resisted—in part, I felt sure, because he knew Jonah had been the king's gift to me, and was jealous.

His arm was healing, slowly. He resumed his duties, though without his usual quick pace and efficiency. There were times when I saw him lying on a bench in one of the dim corridors, taking a quick nap, and I knew that his arm was hurting him and his spirits were low. He was often snappish and fretful, even with me. But it was Jonah who brought out the worst of his temper. He shouted at the little monkey, glowering at him and threatening him.

Once when I went to our cupboard to see how Francis was I found him cursing Jonah. Just as I came in he picked up his tankard of ale and threw it at the scampering little beast. Jonah screamed, Francis bellowed in frustration and I was alarmed. Had the tankard hit the monkey?

But he was gone. The last I saw of him were his two hind legs, flying out behind him as he ran off and disappeared. I went looking for him but my search was fruitless.

That night I wept, thinking I would never see Jonah again. I couldn't sleep. I got out of bed and went to the window. Then I heard it—a soft whimpering sound. It had to be Jonah, outside in the courtyard.

Quickly I wrapped a cloak around my shoulders and made my way along the corridors and down the staircases to the kitchens, then out the wide doors that led to the courtyard, in the direction of the brewhouse and stables. I was intent on finding Jonah, I was incautious. There had been midnight brawls between Cromwell's men and Grandma Agnes's servants; I knew this, but I disregarded the risk. Finding Jonah was what mattered.

Listening for the whimpering I had heard earlier, I heard instead the shuffling of feet. Then I saw a light swinging in an arc: a lantern. The night watchman. Or was it? The next thing I knew I heard grunts, then cries—and I felt a hand grabbing at my arm.

Screaming, I turned and started to run, but there were men blocking my way. Tall, broad-shouldered men, looming up around me in the dark. I saw the glint of a knife, held in a meaty hand, as the lantern-light swung to and fro. I struggled, crying out. I tried to wrench myself out of the rough arms that encircled me.

Then I heard a familiar voice, as an even stronger arm was thrown around my shoulders.

"Catherine!"

He freed me from those who pulled and grabbed at me, and swept me past them to safety. Henry Manox had come back into my life.

SIX

HENRY Manox! I stared at him, while panting for breath, relieved at my rescue but completely baffled by my rescuer.

He reached for me, there in the cellar where we had taken refuge, and tried to kiss me. I pushed him away.

"By the short hairs of the Virgin, Catherine!" His strong, musical voice boomed out.

I stepped back. The light in the room was very dim, but I could clearly see his familiar face, the dark hair, dark moustache and beard—all with more grey than the last time I had seen him—the bright, darting brown eyes and full lips. Lips I had once found such pleasure in kissing.

"You might at least let me kiss you, as thanks for saving you from Cromwell's miscreants!"

"Thank you, Henry. Now what are you doing here at Lambeth?"

"The duchess summoned me to her service here."

"To teach music?"

"To be your secretary."

"What? I have never had a secretary, nor do I need one."

Henry grinned. "We must not question the wishes of our elders and superiors." He swept a mock bow. "She believes you have need of me. Though as I recall, the last time she saw us together I was not writing letters for you." He moved toward me again but I kept my distance.

"She can be forgetful." I was only too aware of what had happened with Henry in the duchess's chapel, of the way he had been able to excite me, of his urgent kisses. . . . Yet I was also well aware that even then our passion had grown stale, and that Henry had become demanding and difficult. I had been only too glad to leave Horsham and Henry behind. I had thought I would never see him again.

But I realized that life in my grandmother's household was unpredictable. She was indeed forgetful. She had lapses. Quite possibly she had no memory of what had gone on between Henry Manox and me, or of her wrath at our secret meetings, our embraces. Quite possibly Henry's father, her neighbor, had approached her and asked her to employ Henry in her household—and in her forgetful state, she had agreed. But what made her think I needed a secretary?

"She may be forgetful," Henry was saying, "but I am not." His voice took on a harsh edge. "I remember well that you denied me— your maidenhead."

I began to feel alarmed once again. We were in a small room, the only way out was down an unlit corridor, or back into the courtyard where the miscreants lurked. I had no candle or lantern. What if Henry decided that having rescued me, he had the right to make love to me? I used the only defense I could think of.

"I kept my maidenhead—for someone more worthy."

I could tell that my retort stung.

"And who is that, pray? I asked the duchess whether you were betrothed, and she said no."

"We are handfasted," I said—and then wished I hadn't. It was, after all, our secret.

"And you bed him?"

"Gladly. Willingly."

He glared at me, silent, angry.

At length he said, "You were prettier when you were younger. Next time you are in danger, call for your lover to save you." With that he strode off down the dark corridor, leaving me to find my way back, through the darkened kitchens, to the upstairs salons.

The next time I went to see the king I took Jonah with me, as Grandma Agnes had advised. Having been missing for two days he had found his way back to me, though I noticed that he kept his distance from Francis.

King Henry received me in a beautiful large room with intricately patterned wooden wainscoting and rich Turkey carpets in tones of red and gold. He sat in a Flanders chair, dressed less magnificently than he had been when I went to see him with my seven companions. He wore a fair linen shirt wrought with red silk and a velvet jerkin, velvet breeches edged with satin, white hose and soft red slippers. His hose were held in place around his knees by handsome garters studded with amethysts. On each hand were several garnet and amethyst rings.

I could not help but admire the elegance of the room, the king's finery, the carved ceiling. Everywhere I looked there was beauty. And in front of the king, on a low table, was yet another beautiful object: a miniature palace, intricately carved in wood, its turrets and crenellated battlements in perfect proportion, flags flying from its towers and miniature statues in its gardens.

"Your Majesty," I said as I was shown into the room. I began to kneel in reverence but the king dismissed the gesture with a wave of his hand.

"Come, Catherine. Look at this. Is it not exquisite? This, I am delighted to say, is my new palace. I am going to call it Nonsuch, for there is, I believe, no structure like it in all of Christendom."

Another Flanders chair was brought for me and I sat down, Jonah clinging to my neck and whimpering softly.

"How fascinating," was all I could manage to say. "Even in miniature it is a work of art."

"I designed it myself. It took me nearly a year. Of course there were builders to advise me, but the overall design is my own. Work has already begun. A whole village was torn down to make room for the palace."

"What became of the villagers?" I asked in alarm.

The king waved his hand once again. "They went elsewhere, I suppose. What is that to you?"

I opened my mouth to answer, then shut it again. I did not want to appear argumentative. But I could not help thinking, had the king really destroyed the homes and gardens and livestock of an entire village community? And done so quite heartlessly?

"Do you know what day the work on the new palace was begun?" He looked at me expectantly, his face alight with pleasure. "Of course you don't. How could you? It was the day my son reached the age of six months. And almost thirty years to the day since I came to the throne. I tell you, Catherine, this palace will outshine every other royal residence in Christendom!"

"I look forward to seeing it—when it is complete. How soon do you imagine that will be?"

He shrugged. "It depends."

"On what?"

"On whether or not we have to go to war against the imperialists, and the French, and most of the Italians!" was his impatient answer. "If I listened to Crum, I'd be terrified that the whole of Europe is about to descend on our island, cannon and catapults and all! He doesn't want me to build Nonsuch—but if I listened to him, I'd never do anything bold, anything worth doing! No one would fear me, or this realm either. I tell you, Catherine, a king dares not live timidly!" He slapped his thigh.

I could not help smiling. He was so wrapped up in his plans, so full of passion and energy—like a much younger man. Like Francis at his most energetic, only Francis was always more careful, more measured, in what he undertook.

"What do you think, madam?" the king asked me suddenly.

"I? Why, sire, I cannot form an opinion about such grand matters. I am far too ignorant."

"You are too modest. I want to know what you think."

I sighed. How to answer such a question, from the king himself, in such a setting? But I saw that I had to try.

"Sire, I will do my best. It seems to me that since you have been king for thirty years, you have great experience to draw from. And if you will pardon me for saying so, you have the strength and force of a much younger man. It must be that experience, and that strength, that lead you to make great plans, devise great palaces. How could you let anyone advise you to go against your nature?"

"Aha!" he cried loudly. "Spoken like a Howard! A true Howard, not your ugly uncle Tom! A true Howard, your grandfather, the old duke. Now, there was a bold commander. He would have swept Crum aside with one swing of his lance. I hope your tutors have taught you about your grandfather, Catherine."

I remembered a portrait at Lambeth, somewhat indistinct and darkened with age, of a resolute man who resembled father. I had been told that this was "the old duke," my grandfather.

"A little. I have seen his portrait."

The king nodded, and looked thoughtful. "He fought for my father at Bosworth Field. And for me, when I was young, and won a great victory over the Scots at Flodden. He was a worthy and valorous knight."

During the silence that fell, Jonah began to whimper. I soothed him and stroked him. It was a surprisingly comfortable silence. The king liked to talk on and on. But when he paused, I felt no awkwardness between us. In time I was bold enough to start to speak again.

"Your Majesty, I wonder if I might ask you, on my father's behalf—"

"Ah, yes. Your father."

"Your Majesty, he desires a post in the household of—of—your queen that is to be."

"Yes, and so do a thousand others," the king said, slapping his knees and grimacing and getting to his feet. I was reminded, watching him, that despite what I had thought earlier about his youthfulness, his enthusiasm and energy, his body was beginning to fail him.

"May I tell father that you are considering him?"

"Tell him what you like. But nothing will be decided until the lady is chosen. And that must wait."

Our eyes met. Once again, as on our earlier meeting, I saw a look, not of shock this time, but of recognition. He saw my mother in me.

"I will tell him that he is not entirely out of your thoughts. Along with a thousand others."

The king reached out and touched Jonah's back, gently. Jonah let out a small cry.

"Perhaps the monkey would like the post of major-domo. Or he could be Pantler for Nuts and Apples."

A valet entered just then, bowed, and waited to be acknowledged.

"Yes, what is it?" the king said irritably.

"Your Majesty, Lord Cromwell sends me to inform you that the Lutheran bishops from Cleves await you."

King Henry swore under his breath.

"Damnable Lutherans! Quarrelsome, mumpish, high-sounding old pedants! A bunch of dour old maids in clerk's gowns, that's what they are! Correcting my Greek! Mine! I knew my Greek when they were babes in arms . . ."

Jonah shrieked, and leapt out of my grasp. He ran toward the wall and began climbing up the tapestry.

Horrified, I tried to grab him but he only climbed higher. I was afraid he would ruin the precious stitchery, and that the king would be furious with me.

"Your Majesty, please forgive Jonah, he goes wild sometimes. Oh! Your beautiful tapestry!"

But King Henry was laughing.

"Never mind, I have dozens more in the storerooms at Baynard's Castle. Remind me to take you there sometime, Catherine. You would love the chests of gowns, old gowns, from long ago. Some that were—in your family—"

Jonah clambered nimbly down and dropped to the floor, then ran up onto my lap again.

"He knows who his mistress is, doesn't he?" the king said absentmindedly.

"Bring him to see me again, won't you. I'm so glad you like my Nonsuch. There is so much more to tell you, I have only just begun. The thing is designed to rival King Francis's finest palace, you see—"

Once again the valet made his presence known, by discreetly shuffling his feet and quietly coughing.

"Yes, yes, I haven't forgotten."

The king turned to me. "Will you come again, Catherine my dear?"

"If Your Majesty wishes it."

"I do. I do indeed. Now I must go—and debate whether worshippers ought to receive both bread and wine during the mass, or only bread—whether priests ought to marry—whether Christ had a human nature or a divine nature—ah! We must reach agreement on all these things, you see, or I cannot marry Cleves. I mean, the lady from Cleves."

"Surely our Lord Christ had both a human and a divine nature." I spoke without thinking.

"Thank you, Catherine. That will be our first point of debate. I will cite you as my source. Let me see, I shall cite Jerome of Alexandria, Gregory of Nazianzen, and Catherine of Lambeth. My three principal authorities." He grinned, then clapped his hands loudly. Immediately two servants appeared.

"My doublet! The new one with the French sleeves! And bring me a pisspot, before I burst!"

I took my departure, promising to return, confident that I had provided the king with diversion and pleasure. As I left the room half a dozen servants came rushing in, carrying a splendid doublet of red silk and maroon velvet, a thick gold chain studded with rubies as large as hen's eggs, and a large white bowl.

Henry Manox was a nuisance to me from the moment he appeared in my antechamber, accompanied by a servant carrying writing materials, scrolls, and two large ceramic inkwells bearing the Howard crest. He was peevish and rude, demanding and cross. He made mistakes in the few letters and documents I required of him. He spilled ink on my old carved wooden desk—an heirloom, lent to me by Grandma Agnes, who was rapidly becoming my benefactress in all things.

Not only did she decree that I was to have a secretary, she told the household steward that I was to be given my own separate suite of rooms, with a bedchamber and an antechamber for the secretary's use. I was also to be driven to the palace whenever the king summoned me, and in case he summoned me to Hampton Court or Greenwich, I was to be taken there by barge immediately. My least wish was to be gratified. If I was in conflict with anyone I was to be given the advantage.

When I walked by, heads turned. Whispers began. Officials who had never before even glanced at me now approached me, asking if there was anything they could do for me. Gifts began arriving, and letters begging for my help. Letters reached me, pleading for me to have unjust legal decisions overturned, or to supply the needs of poor widows. I was asked again and again for alms.

I had become someone of significance in the Lambeth establishment. I was talked about. Attention was drawn to me. My cousins were envious: envious of the fine new wardrobe Grandma Agnes provided, the clothes much richer and more becoming than Charyn's, envious of the attention I was receiving, above all envious of the interest the king was showing in me—which was, of course, the reason for all the special treatment and attention.

But Francis cautioned me that any sudden prominence I might attain could just as suddenly and swiftly come to an end.

"That is the way of it at court," he said blandly. "People achieve notoriety, or the illusion of importance, only to be toppled rapidly from their height. Slippery places, courts."

"I thought you were pleased that the king is showing me favor."

"I am—only from all I am hearing from the chamber gentlemen, his attention to you is likely to be shortlived. They are saying that the king will have to agree to marry the lady from Cleves, even though he doesn't want to."

"What of the disputes over matters of faith?"

"They will be put aside."

"Do you know this for certain, Francis?"

"No—but the wagering makes it appear likely. The odds in the privy chamber favor the Lady Anna."

I bristled.

"So my fortune is to be determined by a cast of the dice."

He laughed drily. "Hardly that. Your fortune—and England's fortune—rests with the strength of armies and alliances. If our king marries the lady from Cleves, the fighting men of Cleves—and of other Protestant forces—will protect us from the French and the imperialists. Or so Lord Cromwell hopes. The wagering is of minor importance, except to those who win or lose."

I grew weary of hearing these speculations. I could not understand them, not really; I could follow the logic of what was said, up to a point, when I heard Francis and others talking of England's future, and the likelihood of war. But it all seemed like a giant house of cards, fragile and flimsy. What if the Emperor Charles should die? Or what if King Henry should die, as had nearly happened only recently? What if the immense and fearsome armies of the Mohammedans should invade our lands, and sweep all before them? Surely it would not matter then who the king married. The soldiers of Cleves could not prevail against the forces of Suleiman the Magnificent.

All was risk and hazard, or so it seemed to me, all was fortune and luck. No matter how clever or how cautious we tried to be, we could be swiftly toppled from whatever height we attained.

My tutor had told me of the goddess Fortuna, worshipped by the Romans—or was it the Greeks? At any rate, the goddess was all-powerful, and no human effort could sway her. The ancients believed that she decided whether we lived or died, whether we attained our goals or failed miserably.

It is a sin to worship pagan idols, I know, but if asked to name the mightiest force in the world, I would be inclined to say it was

Fortune, for even the Lord God cannot seem to preserve us all from harm, and our fates are not written in the Bible, but weighed out in Fortune's scales.

When Henry Manox came to Lambeth as my secretary, Francis changed. He disliked having Henry near me, and treated him with icy disdain. Francis was a gentleman's son, while Henry's father was a mere landed knight, with no title or wealth. What was more, Francis had mastered the art of courtesy, while Henry could be boorish and unmannerly.

"I dislike having that churl near you," Francis said loudly, in Henry's hearing. "Can you not persuade the duchess to remove him?"

"Girlish little popinjay!" Henry snarled back. "I could knock you over with one of these inkwells."

The rivalry between them made me uneasy, especially since I had told Henry that Francis and I were handfasted, and had bragged that we were lovers. It was not long before the two men came to blows, and Henry threatened to tell the duchess of our secret bond. Francis, ever practical, bribed Henry to keep what he knew to himself. But the hostile rivalry continued, and Francis was never the same again.

He did not see me or speak to me for days at a time. He was irritable and easily upset. His smooth, even-tempered manner was gone, replaced by ill humor and an air of silent reproach.

Things were not easy for me. I belonged to Francis, yet I could no longer take comfort in his company. And though Henry's presence made me tense, it was also undeniably exciting. Of course I did not tell him that, or admit that I enjoyed the disturbing thrill and tingle that ran along my spine when he came near me. I did not tell him, but I'm sure he knew all the same. We both felt the disquiet of emotion.

Henry had a raucous temper, he thrived on discord. He had little to do as my secretary. He was bored and restless. He sought out the brawlers sent at night by Lord Cromwell to challenge the Lambeth men. He fought—and having fought, he drank.

And being drunk, he sometimes sought me out. I hid from him as best I could, sometimes taking refuge among the servants in the scullery when nowhere else seemed to offer safety. One night, however, Henry found me there, quivering with fear, and before I could escape him he lunged at me. One of the scullery boys threw me a knife before running off and I yelled at Henry that if he didn't leave me alone I would stab him.

He laughed. He was twice my size and no doubt many times my strength. Yet somehow I found the courage to point the knife at his crotch and stand my ground. I saw that he was reeling, he could not stand straight. A shout from the corridor distracted him, and in that moment I darted out into another room where pots of liquid were boiling over open fires.

With a roar Henry followed me, but by the time he confronted me again I had wrapped a cloth around my hand and snatched up one of the pots. As he came at me I hurled the boiling liquid at him, then hurled the pot itself and ran. I could hear his shrieks of pain and rage as I made my way to the upper floor and Grandma Agnes's apartments.

I took refuge among her guards, who shielded me when Henry, scalded and dripping and furious, came lumbering in. Grandma Agnes had gone to bed but was roused by the commotion. Before long she appeared in her furred black dressing down and demanded to know what was going on. I went up to her and knelt at her feet.

"He's drunken," I gasped. "He came after me. Please, I beg you, grandmother, send him away!"

It did not take Grandma Agnes long to see that I needed her protection from the sputtering, menacing Henry Manox. She had her guardsmen remove him and assured me that he would not be allowed to bother me again. I prayed that she would not, in some future forgetful state, bring him back to Lambeth or reappoint him my secretary.

He was gone—but his vengeance remained. Only two days after Henry's drunken assault on me, Francis and I were enjoying one of our infrequent evenings in the cupboard. I had told him everything that had happened, and he was holding me very tightly as we lay together, stroking my face and hair, kissing me gently. I was beginning to relax, letting my eyes close as he moved his hand down to cup my breast and then began to loosen my bodice.

All at once the quiet was shattered. He heard the key turn in the rusty lock—the door of the cupboard flew open—and there stood Grandma Agnes, whip in hand, with Mary Lascelles just behind her.

"So! This is how you repay my attentions, my trust! By being more of a whore than your mother ever was!"

She began laying about her with the whip, as I shrieked and Francis leapt up out of bed and did his best to shield his face from her vigorous assaults.

"Speak, whore! Are you pregnant by this Irish cur?"

"No, grandmother, no," I pleaded, tears running down my face.

"You let this man spoil you—the king will never want you now!"

I managed to roll off the bed, but not before the cruel whip had cut me on the neck and arm and shoulder.

Francis swore and ducked, and in a moment when the duchess was raining all her blows on me, he fled out the open door, knocking down Mary Lascelles and several others who had gathered in the corridor as he ran.

I collapsed onto the floor, the ripe smell of the rushes strong in my nostrils.

"Get up, whore!"

Shaking, I got to my feet, my clothes awry, blood dripping from my neck and arm.

Grandma Agnes flung her whip away and strode toward me. She slapped my face. Turning back toward where Mary Lascelles was rising from the floor, she told her to shut the door and guard it.

"Now then, Catherine, what am I to do with you, eh? Look at me when I speak to you!"

I raised my head, suddenly very aware of the sharp sting of pain where the whip had lashed me. I could see little, tears blurred my vision. I was dimly aware of the terrifying presence of my angry grandmother.

"I should have known better than to think Jocasta's daughter could be anything but another harlot," she was murmuring, half to herself. "I let Tom persuade me. Tom loves whores, little ones, big ones . . . he cares not. He sends his used-up whores to the king!"

She threw up her hands in a gesture of futility. Then she walked to the door and flung it open.

"Come in here, woman," she said to Mary Lascelles. "Give me that letter!"

Mary reached into a pocket of her gown and drew out a folded square. She handed it to Grandma Agnes who thrust it at me.

"Here. Read for yourself what I have had to read. What has made me sick with anger. I found it this morning in my chapel pew. Your discarded lover Henry Manox left it there for me to find."

I wiped my eyes and running nose as best I could, then took the letter and read it. In a few bitter words it condemned me in ugly, blunt language for being Francis Dereham's harlot and for boasting that Francis and I were married. There was more. Henry claimed that while at Horsham and Lambeth I had had many lovers, that I was the worst of all the girls for whoring and lying, thieving and stealing honest women's husbands.

I did not read every word. I crumpled the letter and threw it down. Grandma Agnes watched me, stony-faced. Then with a heavy sigh she rose and left the room. As she went out she said to Mary Lascelles, "Lock her in. Let her starve. If she screams, gag her." Turning to me, she added, "And be thankful I don't have you whipped and sent to a dungeon for your part in all this chambering and wantonness!"

"Grandma! Grandma!" I shouted frantically, again and again, as the door swung shut and the voices from the corridor outside began to fade away.

"Grandma, don't leave me!" Cruel as she had been, and unmerciful, it was far worse to be abandoned, left to starve. It was worse than any nightmare. I screamed, again and again. But no one came to my aid. Not Francis, not my father, who was far away, not my cousins or Uncle William.

I was alone. I was getting hungry. And in the windowless cupboard, the candles were guttering and soon I would be left in the dark.

I wept. I screamed. I shouted for help until my throat was hoarse. Had there been a window in the small room I might have jumped from it, ending my suffering.

After a day and a night without food my stomach hurt terribly, cramping pains grew worse with every slowly passing hour. I gripped my belly and writhed in misery, dizzy and feeling now cold, now hot and suffering the wretchedness of looseness in my bowels.

There was a tankard of ale beside the bed, and a half-full pitcher that Francis and I had not drunk. I drank thirstily, only to find that the liquor made my stomach pains worse than ever, and gave me pains in the head as well. I could find no relief. I writhed on the bed, on the floor, listening for the slightest comforting sound on the other side of the door—whispering, breathing—but hearing only the rats scuffling in the wainscoting and the moan of the wind as it blew around the ancient walls.

I shut my eyes, hoping for the release of sleep, but sleep brought only nightmares and I awakened to greater pain than before.

I found that I could discern day from night, and that there was just enough light during the day to reveal the objects in the room, which were in any case quite familiar to me.

It occurred to me that my one hope might lie in a written plea of forgiveness. Clutching my stomach and groaning with pain, I managed to take paper and pen and compose a heartfelt note to Grandma Agnes. I wrote simply that despite what the accusing letter had said, I was not guilty of having many lovers, that I did not lie or steal (which, I'm sorry to say, was not strictly true), nor did I tempt married men into adultery. Francis and I were handfasted, I admitted, but we were loyal to one another and I had not broken my vow to him.

"I beg you, Grandma Agnes, for the sake of Christian charity, forgive me!"

I scribbled "Catherine Howard" at the bottom of the note and pushed it under the door. Then I prayed that someone would find it and take it to the duchess.

Hours passed. Nothing happened. I had a terrible thirst. I began imagining things. That I was standing underneath a waterfall, open-mouthed, drinking my fill. That the ceiling opened and rain soaked me, delicious rain that fell on my parched lips and tongue. I imagined that through some miracle my grandmother had had a change of heart and that she came to me and said that she forgave me. She even said that she had been at fault in not taking better care of me, watching out for me and preventing me from going astray. In my dream we sat down together to a bounteous meal with plenty of wine and I knew I would never thirst again. And best of all, in my dream I imagined that I heard a key turning in the lock. Freedom!

Then light poured into the room and I realized I had not been imagining after all. The key had turned in the lock. There was a young priest standing by the bed, a grimace of distaste on his smooth face, averting his eyes from the sight of me.

"Father!" I cried out. "Father, please help me!" I saw that he had brought bread and soup and a pitcher of watered wine, which I grabbed out of his hands and drained. Only after I had drunk the soup as well and stuffed my mouth with bread did I begin to recover my modesty. Realizing that I was wearing only my undergarments and one petticoat—all my other clothing was stained and ruined— and that I had not been able to wash or dress my hair for several days, I did my best to put myself in some kind of order. But the father had gone out of the room, no doubt to escape the stench.

I called to him, and he said that he had been sent to hear my confession. Hoping that this was a sign the duchess's anger had lessened, I made my confession and received the sacrament. Afterwards, for the first time in days, I was allowed to wash and put on clean clothes and fresh rushes were strewn over the floor. My stomach still hurt, and I felt twinges of nausea from eating too much and too fast, but I was immensely heartened at my reprieve, and as soon as I lay down on the bed I was asleep.

It was Joan who came the following morning to tell me that I was wanted in the duchess's apartments. She knew of the suffering that I had undergone. She brought me a gown with a high-necked bodice.

"You want to hide your scars," she cautioned me. "You don't want to remind her that you deserved her whip."

"But I didn't deserve it!" I insisted. Joan merely rolled her eyes.

"She thinks girls are treated too leniently now," Joan said as she helped me dress. "She's always saying that when she was a girl, her father had her whipped until she bled. And that was for mild offenses!

"They say her sister, the old duke's first wife, was shut away in a dungeon for years and then poisoned!"

The duchess kept me waiting most of the morning before I was summoned into her bedchamber. She scrutinized my appearance. She showed no sign that her anger toward me had softened. My hopeful imaginings were no more than that—mere imaginings, born of thirst and hunger and illness.

"I want you to know, Catherine"—she said my name with scorn—"that the only reason you are here, I repeat, the *only reason*, is that the king commands you to accompany him on a trip to view his new palace of Nonsuch. Or rather, to view the place where his new palace will one day be. Were it not for his orders, you would still be shut away. You have betrayed my trust, not once but twice. I can never trust you—or abide you—again."

Inwardly I thanked all the saints and angels, forgetting, in my great relief, that saints were frowned on by our English church and angels regarded somewhat dubiously, as belonging to what Father Dawes called Romish superstition. Nevertheless I was very thankful. The king had saved me!

"The king knows nothing of your trespass with Master Dereham," Grandma Agnes was saying. "He must never know of it, else we shall all perish!"

"Where is Francis?" I dared to ask. "Have you been starving him too?"

"Hush! Don't say such things! No one has been starved. Master Dereham has gone. Back to Ireland, I have no doubt. Where, I have learned, he has a wife and two children!"

"No! It can't be!"

"Francis Dereham bore false witness when he swore to be your husband. You were never truly handfasted. It was all a lie."

I wrenched the silver ring Francis had given me off my finger and threw it in the fire. I felt anger, sorrow, bitterness welling up within me. My eyes were full of tears.

"It can't be," I said again and again, softly, while shaking my head.

"And he had no rich relative. That was a lie too. Everything he possessed, he stole."

It had never occurred to me that Francis was a liar, pretending to be something he was not. I took him at his word. I thought the love he pretended to feel for me, the tenderness he showed me, was real.

"Is it not possible that what you have learned is nothing but slander, spread by his enemies out of spite and envy?"

"No, Catherine. It is the truth. But it would seem that fate favors you nonetheless. Or at least the king favors you. Tomorrow you go with him to see Nonsuch. Now, go and make yourself ready."

I went to my apartments and found Jonah there, chattering and shrieking. I had been worried about him but saw right away that in my absence he had not wanted for food or care. I let him run up and down my arms and tear off my headdress and make as much noise as he liked, I was so overjoyed to see him.

But Francis! I felt certain I would never see Francis again.

I cursed him, I raged against his falseness, his vile cunning, taking advantage of my trust the way he had. I felt aggrieved, deeply wronged. But then my tears began to flow, and I could not stop them. My dream had been destroyed, the man I had adored was gone, and I would never love anyone as I loved him.

I reached for Jonah and tried to hug him to me, but he scrambled away, crying out derisively, as if mocking me. I had never been more miserable, not even when my stomach pains were at their worst. Those were only pains of the body; what I felt at that moment were the deeper pains of the heart. I had been betrayed, beaten, nearly starved—and now I had lost the one who meant more to me than anyone.

I sank down onto my bed, my face pressed into the soft pillows, and gave way to despair.

SEVEN

WHAT ho!" King Henry called out to me in his light tenor, rubbing his hands together. There was a joyful lilt in his voice, and his stride, as he approached my carriage, was buoyant.

"We are off to Nonsuch then," he said as he handed me down out of the carriage. "But first I must ask you, Catherine, are you fond of quince marmalade?"

"I am, Your Majesty."

"As am I," he confided comically, then called out, "Master Thurlsby! An extra pot of quince marmalade for the lady, if you please!" To me he added, "Mr. Thurlsby is my grocer."

The palace courtyard was aswarm with servants, preparing for our outing. Packs were being fastened onto horses, carts loaded with furnishings, rugs and hangings, baskets and chests. The king led me to a large cart that held barrels, jars and a variety of other containers. A muscular man in a corduroy weskit, the sleeves of his shirt rolled to the elbows, presided over the loading of the vehicle.

"Thurlsby! What's that you've got there? Cheese and ale, I know. And extra quince marmalade—"

"Here, Your Majesty," the grocer said, pointing to a wide-mouthed jar. "Quails from Calais, and dotterels killed this morning. New loaves and cold pasties and custard tarts."

"And plenty of ale!"

"Of course, Your Majesty. Plenty of ale."

"I shall have to ride in a carriage, I'm afraid," the king said to me. "My poor leg will not let me mount a horse at present. But for you I have provided a fine mare. She keeps a goodly pace but has a gentle disposition.

"Archyn! Where is the mare for Mistress Catherine?"

The king's chief groom came toward us leading a high-stepping brown mare, sleek and beautifully combed, her lower legs bound and her tail braided. On her back was a handsome saddle fringed with red silk and gold tassels. The stirrups gleamed with parcel-gilt and the saddle head was copper, curved and shaped in a fanciful design.

"What a fine mount! And so elegantly appointed!"

I loved to ride, and could hardly wait to get into the saddle.

"She belonged to my late queen," Henry told me. "Jane was a splendid rider."

I patted the mare's soft nose. She snuffled and tossed her head gently, eyeing me.

"I've also brought a leash of falcons, if we should want to hunt. And there are bows for the deer."

One by one the carts were drawn into a line, archers and halberdiers formed an escort, and before long we were under way, trundling along the high road toward Cuddington.

I was relieved to be offered my own mount instead of having to ride with the king in his carriage. The little mare stepped lightly and sure-footedly along, responding to my tugs on the reins and my soft-voiced commands. She had been trained well, and was a pleasure to ride.

I was relieved, chiefly, because my emotions were still very raw from hearing the grievous truth about Francis. I was in a state of sad disenchantment, I could not keep the tears from my eyes every time I thought of him, and of the lies he had told me. I knew that I ought to feel glad to be rid of him, for no one would willingly want a deceiver in her life. Yet my sorrow weighed on me, and I could not cast it aside, any more than I could forget the sound of Francis's voice or the grace of his lithe, supple body or the beauty of his smooth-skinned face and long-lashed eyes.

He had captivated me, and part of me, I knew, would always long to be his captive again, no matter what lies he had told or what wrongs he had done me.

The high road was crowded at first but as we went along the travelers thinned out and before long the royal train of carts and carriages was passing through lush green farmland, with streams and ponds and tall hedges just coming into bloom. Fat cattle cropped the grass, goatherds tended their flocks and a variety of birds flew above and around us, chirping and calling and squabbling with one another in a noisy flutter of wings.

Presently we stopped to refresh ourselves, and a groom brought me ale and cheese and a custard tart.

"From His Majesty," the groom said as he helped me dismount and spread the food and drink on a table for me. "He begs to be forgiven for not joining you, but his leg pains him."

"Tell him thank you and I hope his leg improves."

I fell on the food eagerly, as I had not eaten anything earlier in the day. But when I remounted and we resumed our slow journey, I began to feel sleepy and wished we were at our destination.

At last we came to a large grassy open area, filled with what looked to me, at first, like rubble. We stopped, and servants began unloading the carts and erecting tents, the entire operation smoothly and efficiently done, as if it had all been done many times before.

Presently the groom came to me again.

"His Majesty awaits you outside his tent," I was told. The groom helped me remount and guided me to a large tent with a peaked roof, gold tassels hanging from its edges. The king, mounted and looking fit, awaited me there.

"Now then, Catherine, are you ready for your tour of Nonsuch?"

"But there is nothing here besides rubble!" I could not help saying.

"That rubble, as you call it, is the palace in embryo. Every stone will have its place—in good time. Some of the stones, the smaller, humbler ones, come from the cottages of the village that was here until quite recently, the village of Cuddington. All the structures were torn down, but the best of the stones were preserved, as you see. They will be put to a much nobler use before long."

We rode on through the high grass. Now and then my horse stumbled over a stone. There were workmen digging, measuring, loading rocks into barrows. Sharp-voiced overseers called out orders. An air of brisk progress hung over the scene.

We rode to the highest point in the building site, from which we could look down and survey it all.

"When I went to France in my youth," the king mused, "the French King Francis was building a grand chateau, such as had never before been seen in his realm. It was called Chambord. It took him many years to build—it may not be finished yet, for all I know—but he told me that when it was complete, it would have four hundred and forty rooms. Imagine! Four hundred and forty. And not small rooms either, but large, grand ones, full of light.

"I swore then that one day I too would have an immense palace, with at least as many rooms, a palace more grand and opulent than

Chambord. I imagined that I would live there, with my loving wife beside me, our children surrounding us, until we grew old and yielded our bones to the earth. After we were gone, the palace would be our memorial in ages to come."

I had the feeling that he was speaking more to himself than to me. He pointed out where the two large main courtyards of the palace would be, and told me of his plan to decorate the inner courtyard in a way never attempted before.

"There will be sculptures there, enormous sculptures, that appear to be leaping out of the walls. Yes! Leaping through the very walls, can you envision it? All around these immense figures will be gold, gold that shines like fire when struck by the sun. Ah! I tell you, Catherine, it will be a most remarkable and unique place, my Nonsuch."

His excitement shone on his face, he was so caught up in his dream. As before, when full of plans and projects, the years fell away and he seemed a much younger man. An attractive man.

We rode here and there amid the rubble-strewn grounds, the king showing me where the royal apartments would be, the hunting parks and banqueting house, the large gardens full of statuary and fountains that spewed forth water in long arcs.

"And here, in the center of it all, will be my tower. My safe place. My tower of protection, where no danger can reach me. Five stories high, the tower will be, shining with gold, a gleaming turret visible for miles around."

We dined in the royal tent, lit by dozens of wax candles, the inner walls hung with tapestries, the royal musicians playing for our enjoyment. Roast venison and baked swan were cooked as skillfully as if we had been dining at Lambeth; cream of almond and sugared fruits tempted me to overeat—and I did not resist the temptation. The king consumed trencher after trencher of meats and jellies, breads and pastries, tarts and cakes. The meal went on and on, the wine flowed freely and when at last King Henry had had his fill, his talk flowed freely as well.

"Did you know, Catherine," he began as we settled ourselves on a soft Turkey carpet before two burning braziers, "that when I was a boy I had to run for my life?"

"No, sire."

He nodded. "I did indeed. I was only a little thing, five or six years old. London was in a state of turmoil. People were running through the streets, shouting that the Cornishmen were coming, trying to flee the city as quickly as they could. My father and brother were doing their best to keep order, I suppose, and prevent all the soldiers from running away. At any rate they were not with mother and me.

"I remember mother taking my hand and saying, 'Now then, Henry, you are going to be a brave boy and protect me.' I promised her I would. I had a small sword, though I had never used it. I thought I could use it if I had to, if it meant keeping mother safe.

"We were only a short distance from the Tower. We ran, together, through the crowded street and reached Coldharbour Gate safely. An old guardsman let us in.

"Once inside we managed to climb the stairs to the top of the White Tower, and entered the ancient keep. There was food there, and a barrel of rainwater, I remember. We knew we would have enough to sustain ourselves for many days. And I felt safe, there in the keep. No one could harm us as long as we remained in the safe heart of the strong old fortress.

"We heard guns going off and I thought the Cornishmen had breached the walls. I was afraid they might find us and kill us. But I took comfort from the thick old walls, the battlements that had withstood sieges and rebellions for centuries, ever since the time of William the Norman more than four hundred years before.

"I did not cry. I stood guard over mother, to keep her safe.

"The Cornish rebels were in fact outside the city, at an

encampment on Blackheath. It took many days, but finally my father led his army against them. And they were not only defeated, they were struck down by a plague and nearly all of them died. Mother and I were safe.

"Ever since then," he went on after a pause, "I have looked to the Tower as my bastion of protection. But the new tower at Nonsuch, once it is completed, will be stronger and more enduring than the old Norman keep. It will be my place of refuge, and my son's, and my wife's. It will endure down the generations as the strongest tower in the land. That is my hope—and my dream."

He looked into my eyes. There was no mistaking the meaning of his steady gaze. I was a part of his dream. I was certain of it. His broad, paunchy face was close to mine, his blue eyes small and squinting in the candlelight, the stench of his breath overpowering.

"Catherine," he said, reaching for my hand.

I drew myself up, so that I was just out of reach.

"I trust your tower will stand forever, and never fail to protect you, Your Majesty. You honor me in sharing with me your plans for this place, and your childhood memories. I only wish I had more to offer in return."

"You offer your company. I enjoy it greatly."

"May I ask your permission to retire now? I am very tired."

He looked crestfallen, and for a moment I felt sorry for him. But the moment passed and he called for a groom to take me to my tent. Before I could get to my feet he reached again for my hand and pulled it to his lips.

"My dear Catherine," he said, squeezing my hand and then releasing it, "sleep well."

We spent four days at the building site, watching the laborers at their tasks, Henry conferring with the builders in charge, discussing where and how large the chapel ought to be and whether the palace would require stabling for four hundred or five hundred horses. The king asked my opinion again and again, and seemed to listen to all that I had to say.

"How big should the nursery be, do you think, Catherine? Do you think six chambers will be adequate?"

"Does Your Majesty hope for six children by the lady who will be your wife?"

He smiled indulgently. "If the Lord wills it. It would seem He is providing me with a fruitful young wife. Why not assume that she will give me six fine sons?"

Again and again he was hinting—indeed more than hinting—by his words, his looks, his affectionate smiles—that I was much in his thoughts as either wife or mistress. I disliked the teasing, I have always preferred straightforward speech—unless of course there are reasons for discretion. I did my best to be agreeable, while not encouraging his hints and oblique references.

On the third day of our stay I brought up the important subject (important to me) of my father, and his hopes for a court appointment.

The king's response was impatient.

"Nothing has changed since the last time you asked me to favor your father with a court post," he said. "I told you I would keep your father in mind."

"Along with a thousand others, I believe you said."

"And now it is two thousand," he snapped. "The decision about who will be the next queen must be made before long. The closer that decision comes, the more I am pestered about the new queen's household—how large will it be, who will hold the principal offices, and so on. Even here, far from Whitehall, my secretary receives constant requests for posts."

I saw that if I was insistent I would only make the king more irritable. I drew back, and did not argue further.

"Then I will just have to tell my father that he must continue to be patient. And may I add your good wishes?"

"If you must. But I caution you, these eager candidates for offices have a way of misinterpreting good wishes as promises of future posts."

I was quiet. Presently the king announced that he felt the need to try out one of his new falcons, and left me, rather abruptly. I felt a chill arise between us, and did not understand why.

I napped, I went for a ride on my lovely brown mare. When evening came, and the king had not returned, I brought out a piece of embroidery work and contented myself for an hour or two with sewing, while the royal musicians played for me. At last I went to bed, mildly concerned that I had done something to cause the king displeasure. Had I done the wrong thing in raising the subject of my father? And if so, had I made it less likely that he would eventually be appointed to the new queen's household?

The following morning, however, the king seemed to have returned to his accustomed brisk, cheerful self. I could not detect any signs of his former irritation. Puzzled, I took his lead and did my best to act as though there had been no interruption in our smooth, pleasant relations.

Saying that his sore leg was much improved, the king suggested that we go walking, and I was happy to agree. Taking his thick walking stick, and leading the way, we started out, with one of the royal physicians and several grooms and the king's secretary Brian Tuke following at a discreet distance. King Henry limped very noticeably, and I saw that he grasped the gold knob of his stick so firmly that it shook under his weight, but he did manage to walk for half an hour or so, pausing now and then to rest.

I kept pace with him, patient with his slow progress and frequent stops. We talked a little as we went along, but it was not until we reached a wide pond fringed with drooping willows that we sat in the shade and talked at our ease.

The king sighed and set down his walking stick.

"I received word yesterday that the doctors of theology from Cleves have ceased to create difficulties for us. Crum informs me that the Lady Anna will be able to worship according to our rites—which means that there are no further impediments to our future marriage."

I heard the dull thud of resignation in his voice.

"Then you will marry her?"

Another royal sigh. "Not if I can find a reason not to." He looked at me fondly.

"You are my best reason, Catherine. I have grown quite foolishly attached to you."

"As you were to my mother," I said boldly.

"Yes. You are very like her, you know." He stroked my cheek. "The same beautiful auburn hair, the same smiling face and amusing manner. And, I hope, the same loving heart."

I said nothing. After a long silence, during which my head was spinning, the king spoke again.

"I want to find a reason not to marry the Lady Anna, but it must be a reason that will satisfy Lord Cromwell. And just now Lord Cromwell is sounding the alarm for war—and a marriage alliance with Cleves. You see my dilemma."

That summer, the summer of the year 1539, the drumbeat of war grew louder and louder. The trained bands and militiamen gathered and armed themselves, preparing to defend England from attack. Uncle Thomas summoned hundreds of soldiers to Lambeth and housed them in tents and outbuildings on the manor grounds, where they mustered and practiced their drills to the booming of drums and the blare of trumpets. We heard that fortresses all across southern England were being strengthened and castles fortified. And whenever we traveled along a high road, we encountered guardsmen, armed knights, strings of horses bought or simply taken from men of substance for the king's use in war, plus endless trains of carts carrying barrels of gunpowder and tents and supplies for the soldiers.

All the talk within my grandmother's household was of the defense works being hastily erected around the capital, and all along the southern coast and on the border with Scotland. We were told that thousands of men were needed to form new trained bands, and many of Grandma Agnes's strongest, most fit young servants left her employ to join the growing militias.

I saw little of the king during this crucial time, as he was visiting his bastions and supervising the repair of fortresses and the construction of bulwarks and blockhouses. He ordered plaques to be mounted on the walls of his castles, warning invaders of the perils of challenging England's might. "Henry the Eighth," the plaques read, "Invincible King of England, France and Ireland, Builded Me Here in Defense of the Republic to the Terror of His Enemies." A stout warning indeed, though what were needed, it was whispered, were more cannon, not more warning signs.

For an immense invasion fleet was said to be nearly ready to sail, a fleet of Spanish and French and even Venetian ships assembling in the harbors of the northern lowlands, intended to carry thousands of soldiers and mercenaries to our Channel coast. Storms arose to prevent the fleet from sailing—providential storms, divine aid sent to defend us. Yet as each storm abated, the watchers along the coastline peered into the mist and fog, certain that they would see the first flags and turrets of the enemy fleet any day.

The fear and activity reached a pitch in midsummer, and then, when no fleet appeared off our shores and no invaders had come down from the north, the war preparations slackened. But by then I was preoccupied by another concern, one much deeper and closer to home.

For my father, weary of his struggles and disappointments over money and increasingly harassed by moneylenders and tradesmen, had fled to Uncle William's house at Oxenheath, and was very ill.

As soon as I learned of his illness I went to be with him, only to discover, somewhat to my surprise, that no other family members were at his bedside. He had been abandoned by everyone, even his unpleasant wife, my stepmother Margaret.

"Poor man," Uncle William said as we sat at father's bedside, where he lay asleep, his breathing ragged and his forehead creased as if in worry. "He came to me a few days ago, asking me to hide him. He said his creditors were after him, and that he didn't feel at all well. Then he collapsed, and I put him to bed and called my physician to see to him."

"Is it his kidney stones?"

Uncle William nodded. "That, and fatigue. The physician says his body is just tired out, worn out. He has been sleeping most of the time since he arrived. He must be dreaming, because he talks in his sleep. I can't make out the words."

"Why is there no one else here?"

Uncle William made a wry face. "Have you not noticed, Catherine, that only the rich attract relatives to their deathbeds?"

I felt a catch in my throat. I hardly dared ask, yet needed to know.

"Is he dying then?"

Uncle William nodded. "The priest has been here. He has been shriven."

I reached for father's hand. It felt light, and very dry. As though it was drying up, or fading away. Such a dear, familiar hand, the fingers thin and curling under, the nails not entirely clean, or well trimmed. I began to cry. How would I go on without him?

"I will stay here with him, Uncle William, if you want to get some sleep."

He nodded and left.

I squeezed father's hand, but he didn't respond. His breaths became rasping, harsh. He began to cough. I was afraid he would choke. I tried to help him sit up, but he wrenched himself away and flopped back down, away from me, on his side.

"Father, it's Catherine."

At the sound of my name he struggled to lie flat again. In a moment he opened his eyes, squinting.

"Catherine," he said, and reached for me. The look in his eyes was so forlorn, so pitiable, that my tears flowed freely.

"Dearest father," was all I could say. "Dearest dearest father."

He made an indistinct sound.

"What, father? Do you want anything?" I looked around. Was he cold? Hungry? What could I give him? What could I do for him?

"Beaten—down—by—life," he managed to say. "No—good— trying—any—more."

The effort to speak tired him, and he took deep breaths, his eyes closed.

"Please don't give up, father. Please. For my sake."

He shook his head.

"No—good—any—more."

He smiled, a weak smile, but full of love. Then he slept. After a time I lay down beside him, and slept too. Later I was awakened by Uncle William.

"He's gone to be with the Lord, Catherine." He put his arms around me.

"Don't leave me, father. Don't leave me!" I cried, desolate.

My father's funeral was brief and without dignity or grandeur.

Few Howards were in attendance. I was embarrassed for him, my emotions in upheaval. I grieved, for both my parents, the mother I had barely known and the father I had so dearly loved. I was all that was left of them both. And now I was an orphan.

Great draughts of calming poppy broth helped me through the following weeks, while my grief gradually began to lessen. I had suffered two blows: first the betrayal and disappearance of Francis, and then the loss of my father. I was idle, adrift. I felt lumpish and glum, moping through my days, resentful of my relations who had not paid tribute to my father in death—for although he was entombed in the Howard family vault, his body was enclosed with many others and his name was carved in small letters, easy to overlook. The great Howards were magnificently memorialized; an insignificant Howard like my father was accorded barely any honor or distinction at all.

Meanwhile the long-drawn-out drama of King Henry's choice of a wife was ending. After insisting that a dozen other princesses be considered, he at last gave in to Lord Cromwell's insistent urgings and agreed to pledge himself to the Lady Anna of Cleves.

To avert war, to assure England's triumph over enemies whose enormous fleet might yet appear, it was necessary that he submit to a marriage that made him deeply uneasy. And so, Uncle Thomas told me, the king signed the marriage contract.

His brief flirtation with me was over. Anna of Cleves would become his wife. Fortune had decreed it.

"But King Henry may yet choose you as his mistress," Uncle Thomas told me. "He wants you near him, at the royal court. He insists that if he must marry the Lady Anna, you must be among her maids of honor. Unless this is assured, he will not agree to the marriage. Are you willing to serve the new queen as her maid of honor? I would not advise you to refuse."

It seemed inevitable to me, in that moment, that I should do as the king wished. As my uncle clearly wished. I agreed.

We began right away to prepare for the new queen's arrival. There was a great deal to do, and I realized, as I set about my duties, that it was good for me to be occupied. I had little time to dwell on my losses, my grievances. I was kept busy, kept moving from one part of the royal palace to another, occupied with many different tasks.

My promotion from Grandma Agnes's household to the royal court meant that I had a great deal to learn. Whitehall was vast, Hampton Court and Greenwich smaller but challenging, with their baffling interconnected corridors and confusing staircases, their warrens of chambers and antechambers. I felt that it would take time for me to find my way with certainty through the royal residences. And I knew that there would soon be another residence: Nonsuch. I was privileged to have seen it, as it were, through the king's eyes, before it was even built.

A special envoy, Herr Olisleger, was sent from the Clevan court to organize the Lady Anna's household. He was a short, stout, self-important man of forty, dressed in the outlandish, outmoded garments the Clevans seemed to prefer. He spoke little English and had to communicate with King Henry's officials and household officers in Latin—and they were overheard to complain, Herr Olisleger's Latin was hard for them to understand, as it was heavily accented and pronounced in the German manner.

Nonetheless plans were made and many officials and servants appointed—one hundred and twenty-six in all. I could not help but feel a pang as these officials were chosen, wishing that my father, healthy and feeling gratified, had been among them. I was to be one of a dozen maids of honor, Charyn another, my cousin Malyn another. We were to be under the care and direction of a Clevan matron called Mère Lowe, which, we were told, meant "Mama Lion" in the Clevan dialect. Many Clevan ladies were said to be coming to England along with the Lady Anna, and her two sisters, Sybilla and Amelia, and her mother who, it was rumored, had been opposed to Anna's marrying King Henry.

The late Queen Jane's suite of apartments was renovated for the new queen's use, and we were told that as maids of honor we would have two large rooms as our own, plus a smaller one for our wardrobe chests and baskets, and to serve as a sitting room during the day.

Furnishings began arriving, familiar beds and hangings, paintings and silver and napery sent from Cleves to make the Lady Anna's apartments more welcoming to her. We thought them hideous, but did not say so openly. We speculated among ourselves about whether the new queen's manners and behavior would be as odd and unwelcome as her furnishings.

And what of the Clevan maids of honor and ladies in waiting? What would they be like? Would they be gracious and accommodating, or unmannerly and domineering?

These were minor matters, we knew, compared to the importance of the alliance between our two realms, and the chain of further alliances that would result from the bond sealed by the coming marriage. All that truly mattered was what Lord Cromwell told Uncle Thomas, a tale that was quickly passed throughout the royal court. It was said that when the Emperor Charles learned that our king had at last chosen the Lady Anna as his bride, he howled in fury, and shouted at his councilors that a breach had been made in the walls of the mighty Hapsburg fortress, and that before long the fortress itself might tumble into ruin.

EIGHT

AFTER months of preparation we were nearly ready to receive Lady Anna into her new home. The late Queen Jane's apartments were now spoken of as Queen Anne's suite, and the glaziers had removed all the medallions bearing the initials H and J, for Henry and Jane, and replaced them with new ones honoring H and A, Henry and Anna.

New liveries had been sewn for the grooms and footmen and maids—even the three laundresses sent from Cleves to prepare linens and bedding had new gowns and aprons. The steward of the household, Herr Hoghesten, was installed in his own chambers and the chief cook, Master Schulenberg, was satisfied, or nearly satisfied, with the kitchens and larders and the assigning of places at the newly arranged queen's table.

We maids of honor, along with the ladies in waiting and the privy chamber women, were given places of respect at the long table, below the steward and the chamberlain Herr Olisleger and Lady Anna's physician Dr. Cornelius but above the lesser servants, the chamberer and cupbearer and the three chaplains who were expected to arrive from Cleves any day. Mère Lowe, or as we called her, Mama Lion, a tall, strong-looking woman who wound her long grey hair around her head in a bizarre fashion, was in charge of us; we had grown accustomed to hearing her loud, low-pitched voice ordering us to do this or that or correcting us when we made mistakes. Charyn and I were quick and efficient, and rarely displeased her. Malyn, however, grew nervous and confused when in her presence and was often reprimanded.

"But I can't understand her!" Malyn complained to us, exasperated and worried. "Why can't she learn to speak English properly! It will be much worse when the German women get here," was her frequent complaint. "They will all babble away in that peculiar language of theirs, Dutch or German or whatever it is, and we won't be able to follow a word they're saying."

I had already learned a little of the Clevans' language—I could hardly help learning it, I heard it all day every day—and could not sympathize with Malyn's distress.

"You just have thick ears," Charyn told Malyn unkindly. "You need to clean out your thick ears and listen harder."

By September the last of the obstacles in the marriage negotiations had been worked through, Lady Anna's small dowry had been put in the hands of the royal bankers for safekeeping, and the marriage treaty itself was drawn up.

King Henry signed it, after being repeatedly assured that his Clevan bride was lovely to look at, sweet natured and of good character.

"Her mother has raised her strictly," Mama Lion told us—with Herr Olisleger serving as interpreter. "She would never dare to do wrong or disobey. She is modest and quiet—not like you English girls with your loud voices and your wandering here and there. Not like you with your joking and teasing."

We did joke about the Clevans, behind their backs, and especially about Mama Lion with her heavy, foot-stomping walk and her severe braided hair and commanding low voice, almost the voice of a man rather than a woman. Herr Olisleger too was mocked and ridiculed (the English grooms mimicked him very amusingly), as were the head cook and the few Clevan guardsmen and the footmen, who gave themselves airs and thought themselves superior to their English counterparts.

At least there were no quarrels, or fights between the men of Cleves and our English household members. I hoped that when Lady Anna arrived with her many servants, there would be harmony among us all. With the formal marriage treaty signed, she was due to arrive very soon, leaving the castle of Duren where she had been living and going aboard ship for the crossing at Harderwijk on the Zuider Zee.

She was expected very soon—but in October the harsh weather set in and the sea was too rough to risk the journey. One storm after another delayed her, and while she delayed, King Henry became impatient and worried, bad-tempered, and then ill.

As always when he worried, his stomach pained him and he took cold. Rain spoiled his sport, the harsh medicines his physicians gave him sent him to the place of easement continually and he was unhappy and bored.

He sent for me.

"I am always ready to serve you, Your Majesty," I said as I was ushered into the presence of the king by Anthony Denny, his lean, suave body servant and privy chamber gentleman.

"He is not at his best, Mistress Catherine," Master Denny murmured as we entered the room. "I trust you have a fresh pomander with you."

"Perhaps I shall need more than one," was my rejoinder as we exchanged a fleeting smile. Anthony Denny, I had noticed, was the most benevolent and accommodating of King Henry's servants, and was becoming the one he relied on most often to attend to his personal needs. Master Denny was calm and well disposed. I had never seen him act otherwise.

As soon as the king saw me, with Jonah draped around my shoulders, his face brightened. But my own face fell. The king was seated on his close stool, and the stink was intolerable. I reached for my pomander and held it under my nose.

"He trusts you," Master Anthony whispered. "This is an honor he rarely confers. He trusts few people, especially women."

"Come closer, Catherine, and sit near me. Bring the little beast."

I obeyed, though the smell threatened to make me retch.

"They are purging me," King Henry said. "Dr. Butts and the others. This Cornelius fellow, the German. He's given me some physick so strong that I have to sit on the stool all day."

Offensive as the situation was, even after Master Denny brought in a screen to shield the king and give him privacy, I could not help feeling sympathy for the sufferer. I remembered how my father lamented the effects of the medicine he took to purge his kidney stones, and how it made him wet his bed and offend my stepmother.

"Tell me a story and make me laugh, Catherine. I am in sore need of laughter."

I told him Lord Cromwell's tale about the Emperor Charles and how furious he was about King Henry's betrothal to Lady Anna. I lengthened it and added more to it, so that the king was amused for quite a while. He then asked me to bring Jonah to him—but Jonah was too quick. He jumped down off my shoulders and went behind the screen quite on his own. The king called and clapped and encouraged Jonah to come to him and have his head scratched.

"I've decided I'm not going to show Lady Anna the building site of Nonsuch," King Henry said at length.

"Oh? And why is that?"

"Because I only want to share it with you."

I chuckled. "You don't want to make her jealous."

"She won't know."

He sighed. "And how is her household progressing? Are all the preparations complete?"

"For the most part, yes. But there are still complaints about Herr Olisleger and Mama Lion—I mean Mère Lowe. They cannot make themselves understood very well."

"About what?"

"Many things. Recently there has been some question about Lady Anna's travel. Herr Olisleger is in a conflict with one of Your Majesty's ship masters, Richard Couche. Master Couche speaks no Latin, and Herr Olisleger speaks almost no English, except to say, 'Pardon me' and 'If my lord pleases.'"

The king groaned in exasperation.

"Must I solve every dispute!"

He sent me to the new queen's apartments with Father Dawes, who lost no time in realizing that the disagreement concerned which route Lady Anna and her escort ought to take when they left Cleves for England. As Father Dawes explained to me, there were two routes she might take on her journey. She might come by sea through the Zuider Zee and along the coast, then crossing to the mouth of the Thames and going on upriver to the capital. Or she could take the much slower but safer land route from Dusseldorf through the imperial lowlands to Calais, embarking from there to make the crossing.

"Master Couche prefers the sea route, but Herr Olisleger says that Lady Anna's mother, the Dowager Duchess Maria, has sent him word that she is strongly opposed to it. She says Lady Anna is afraid of drowning. And she might freeze or become ill while on the rough seas. Also the harsh sea air would mar her complexion."

The disagreement was explained to the king, who shouted and threw up his hands in exasperation.

"Must I debate with the old mother now! First the theologians, then the diplomats and lawyers, and now the old mother of the bride! It is too much!"

He had recovered from his indisposition, and was no longer taking the purgative, but his temper had worsened. I brought him my favorite calming drink, poppy broth, in hopes that it would help him to compose himself. But he took on the quarrel with Herr Olisleger himself—his Latin was fluent—and we maids of honor could hear the angry words going back and forth between the king and the Clevan chamberlain. The queen's apartments were very near the king's; what was said in King Henry's sitting room could be heard in the queen's bedchamber and private closet.

The turmoil seemed to go on for days. A map of the coastline was brought, and endlessly argued over. The king insisted loudly that his ships would blockade the coastline if necessary to ensure Lady Anna's safety, and that he would send his own flagship, the *Great Harry*, to protect her. In the end, quoting Virgil, he accused Herr Olisleger of exaggerating something of little importance.

"The mountain groans in labor, and out comes a silly mouse," he pronounced in solemn Latin, adding, "No more of this quibbling. The girl will do as I say—if she wants to marry me. She will travel by sea!"

But it did not end there.

On a day of bleak early November rain, a carriage arrived at Whitehall and seven weary travelers alighted onto the muddy courtyard.

It was the Dowager Duchess of Cleves and six of her attendants. We maids of honor hurried to make the newcomers comfortable, while Herr Olisleger rushed to find the king.

"So this is the infamous palace of the infamous king who kills his wives!" the duchess remarked acidly, her voice strident. "And now he wants to kill another one! My daughter!"

So insulting were her words that her chaplain—her interpreter—was reluctant to translate them. But I was able to puzzle out their meaning clearly enough. The dowager duchess was a large, scowling, fleshy woman, her plain face deeply lined, with broad shoulders and big hands and feet. When she opened her mouth her pink gums were bare of teeth, and she whistled when she talked. Her gown of a deep plum color shrouded her body rather than flattered it, and her headdress, in the spaniel-eared Clevan style, did not entirely cover her untidily arranged grey hair. A faint stale odor clung to her; when she passed near me I smelled mold and onions and a whiff of lilac scent.

Mama Lion quickly gave orders and the Clevan ladies were taken to comfortable rooms in the queen's suite and a cold collation was prepared for them. But the Dowager Duchess Maria was not satisfied until she was presented to the king, whose mood darkened when he was told of the presence of his unwanted guests.

Still, he invited the duchess and her ladies into the throne room where he awaited them, arrayed in a splendid blue velvet doublet winking with gems. Lord Cromwell stood near at hand, along with the mariner Richard Couche and an array of officials. We maids of honor were present to attend to the guests should any need arise.

The ladies entered with a loud clacking of shoes—the Clevans, it seemed, did not believe in wearing soft slippers indoors. The king frowned at the noise, but kept his face set in a forced smile.

The duchess gave only the shallowest of curtseys before addressing the king, in very halting English.

"You wish to marry my daughter, ja? But you also wish to kill her!" Her heavily accented English was extremely difficult to understand.

"I assure you, madam," King Henry interrupted, "that my only wish is for the safety and protection of your daughter, who is, after all, going to be the mother of my children."

"You make her go over the sea! You make her drown!"

"Not when she is traveling with me, dear lady." At Henry's signal the ship master Couche came forward, with a bow to the duchess and a deferential touch of his cap.

"I know the waters of the Zuider Zee. I have sailed them. No one has ever drowned who sailed with me."

"But the cold! But the storm!"

"We will keep Lady Anna and her servants, all her precious cargo, safe and warm in her cabin."

"But her beautiful face! It is ruined by the sea! So dry, so full of cracks! So dark, like a black duck!"

The duchess put her large hands up to her own ravaged, wrinkled cheeks to show what she meant. I saw the king shudder.

"Madam," Lord Cromwell interjected, "if you will allow me, I know an apothecary who is wonderful with all manner of unguents and creams—"

"No!" The duchess stamped her foot, making a resounding clatter. "No! I forbid it! She goes in her gold carriage, not in a ship! Not until her gold carriage comes to Calais, the English town! Then she sails quickly quickly across the small water."

And with that she folded her arms and prepared to stand her ground.

King Henry rose and approached the frowning Dowager Duchess of Cleves, the frozen smile still on his lips.

"Dear lady," he said cordially, bending down so as not to tower over the Duchess Maria, "you honor my court by journeying all this way to tell me your thoughts. I am grateful. We are to become one family, are we not? Our blood will mingle in the veins of our descendants, will it not?"

She looked up at him suspiciously, then murmured, "Ja."

"We must begin by doing our best to please one another then, to reason together."

"What is this, 'reason together'?" She looked over at Herr Olisleger, who shrugged, then at the steward Hoghesten. But he only raised his eyes to the ceiling.

"Come, I will show you," King Henry said, offering his arm to the duchess and leading her toward a window embrasure, apart from the rest of us, where cushioned benches offered a comfortable retreat.

"Crum! Denny!" he called out as they walked, "bring us a table, and some of that soothing poppy broth!"

I admired King Henry's efforts to cope with the blustering Dowager Duchess Maria, but in the end he was unsuccessful. She got her way. He conceded, and agreed that his bride would travel from Dusseldorf to Calais by land, and then make the short crossing to Deal.

And I, and the other maids of honor, would travel with her. In order to do that, we would make the journey to Cleves.

I had never before made a journey of any distance—no farther than the distance from my father's estate to Horsham, and then to Lambeth and London. Now I was to cross the sea and sail many miles north to the cold lands, that strange, low flooded place where, it was said, there was so much water that boats sailed through the fields and towers had sails that turned lazily in the wind. A poor and benighted place, but above all, cold.

We had woolen petticoats, and gowns with thick padded bodices, fur-trimmed cloaks and fur-lined gloves. We wrapped woolen scarves around our heads and over our ears. Yet despite all this, as our ship, the *Eagle Royal*, ploughed through the rough seas on our way northward, we longed for warm hearths and sunshine.

Rain and storms followed the *Eagle Royal* for many days, tossing her up and down ceaselessly and flooding her deck with icy, sloshing water that dripped down into our cramped cabin and made us miserable. We were ill, we could eat nothing. In our misery we became quarrelsome, and cursed Lady Anna and each other.

I found myself in agreement with the Dowager Duchess Maria: a quick crossing to Calais, followed by a land journey northward to Dusseldorf would have been far preferable to our watery purgatory. Only we did not have time for that; we had to reach Cleves as quickly as possible, in order to escort Lady Anna to England before the end of the year.

When our cabin became too foul to bear I found the courage to attempt to go up on deck. Clambering up the slippery ladderlike steps was hard enough, dressed as I was in many layers of wool and fur. But when I managed to step out onto the windswept deck, and saw the high billowing waves coming toward the ship, crested with white foam, and felt the freezing water seeping through my boots and chilling my ankles, I did not wait to go back down the steps and rejoin the other girls.

How could anyone live in so savage a climate, I wondered. Perhaps the dowager duchess had been right. Perhaps the danger of the sea journey would claim us all, as she feared it would claim Anna; either we would drown, or freeze, or become deathly ill. Or, if nothing worse befell us, we would still arrive at our destination with dry, cracked complexions, as dark as a black duck.

It was a great relief to arrive, thinner and weaker but safe, on dry land at last. Only it was far from dry, for the rain persisted and the castle where we were taken, Schwanenberg, was barely heated and we shivered through every ceremony of greeting, every night of troubled sleep and every meal.

As we might have expected, we were most curious to see Lady

Anna, that mysterious being we had been hearing about for so many months.

Like her mother, she was tall and strapping, with a rather small bosom and broad shoulders. Her hair was a dark blond, her eyes more hazel than blue and her nose rather large and not well shaped. She pursed her thin lips when she saw us, and narrowed her eyes. Did she like what she saw? I could hardly tell, but I did not sense any warmth or welcome in her manner. It occurred to me that she might be shy, or perhaps half-frozen and that once she became acquainted with us or became unthawed she might prove to be friendly. I tried to think the best of her.

We each went up to our future queen and curtseyed, and as I drew nearer to make my show of reverence I was dismayed to see that Lady Anna's face was pitted with the marks of the pox. Lightly pitted, to be sure; many at our court were far more severely scarred. But pitted nonetheless. Had King Henry been told of this, I wondered. Or would he have to discover it for himself?

And over the first few days that we were at Schwanenberg I discovered something else: that when she was crossed, or displeased, Anna's usual rather bland expression could change very quickly, her face becoming hard and clenched.

I saw it when we had just finished dining, all of us—Lady Anna and her women attendants, the household steward, those of us from England and a few guests who spoke English—sitting at a long table, the food still abundant before us and our bellies very full. A liveried servant approached Lady Anna. A very old man and woman walked slowly into the room behind him, arm in arm, their eyes downcast.

"With pardon, Your Ladyship—or should I now say, Your Highness—I beg your indulgence for these poor folk," the servant said in the Clevan dialect. I understood some of what he said, and the rest was translated for me by the man seated on my right, a nobleman from Frisia whose mother was English.

Anna frowned, but did not refuse.

"Your Highness, I beg you to have pity on this poor man and his wife. He has nothing to buy food or provide shelter. He and his wife are of great age, as you can see, and he has been the victim of one of Your Highness's guardsmen, who tricked him and took all his savings. He has sold all of his possessions, even his bed, to buy food. Now he has nothing left. Can you not provide for him, since it was your guardsman who wronged him?"

I watched Lady Anna's face as the request was made, and saw there the transformation from irritation to annoyance to hostility. Her jaw was tight, her eyes narrowed.

"Why must you always do this to me, Buren, just when we have dined, when you know I will feel least likely to refuse! It is not right!"

She did not look at the two old people, but glared at the servant, who was far from young himself. She sniffed and sighed in exasperation, then swore—an oath the nobleman from Frisia did not translate.

"Very well, Buren, give them a few coins if you must. But take them away!"

"May I give them the food that remains on the table?"

"You may not! What would I have to feed my dogs?"

The poor man and his wife murmured their thanks and followed the servant back out of the room, leaving us openmouthed. By us I mean we English. The Clevans appeared to take Lady Anna's dismissiveness and lack of generosity for granted. Still, I hoped she would show some redeeming qualities to make up for her uncharitableness; after all, each of us has both faults and virtues.

She brightened when we taught her to play cards, especially the English game called "cent" or hundred. She liked to gamble, she liked risk. Her face grew animated when she won and she seemed to relish the feel of coins in her hand. I taught her to say the English words "I won" and she repeated them with childlike pleasure.

We English maids of honor were given the task of helping to plan Lady Anna's traveling wardrobe. Her chamberers laid out the garments she possessed for us to choose from. There were several dozen gowns, mostly black. It was explained to me that Lady Anna was still in mourning for her late father, who had died the previous year.

"But the English court is not in mourning," I managed to convey, in my halting French, to a helpful French pastry cook who served as interpreter. "Bright colors are preferred there, crimson and tawny and peach and lilac. And shiny, light silks and bawdkins."

There was, just then, a craze for all things new at the English court. Fashions changed quickly. New styles—French sleeves, bell-shaped skirts, embroidered petticoats, the list was endless—set off an instant demand for copies. Seamstresses and dressmakers were kept busy far into the night preparing fresh garments for both women and men.

Looking at Lady Anna's dour black worsted gowns and black velvet partlets, with only a touch of russet or purple trim to relieve their somberness, made me realize that what was needed was a whole new wardrobe.

I cannot say, looking back on those cold weeks in Schwanenberg, that I actually liked Lady Anna, for in truth I did not. But I felt sorry for her. She had no idea how to prepare herself to meet the very critical English courtiers, or how sadly lacking in youth and liveliness she would appear to them. She would look twice her age, I thought, in her own dark, shapeless gowns.

I set about to change that, insofar as I could. A silkwoman was sent for, and half a dozen seamstresses. I wished for Master Spiershon, or for a clever Frenchwoman who knew what was being worn at the court of King Francis. But time was limited. The silkwoman was able to provide lengths of brocade and gleaming bawdkins, cloth of silver and brilliant velvets, ribbons and trims. Each of us—myself and Charyn and Malyn—sacrificed our own most attractive gowns (trusting that they would be replaced) to donate more yards of cloth and trims and even a few jeweled buttons.

Lady Anna put on her new garments and walked in them in front of her pier glass. Her legs were long, she walked with great strides, like a man. When I tried to persuade her to try on a saucy French hood, to replace the style she was accustomed to that was quite unflattering, she balked. But I could tell that she liked all the attention she was receiving, and I saw how she picked up the skirts of her new gowns and swished them back and forth in front of the pier glass, enjoying the play of light on the shiny fabrics and the beauty of their colors.

I saw that I had pleased her.

"Kom," she said to me when we were departing from Schwanenberg, our large traveling party with its escort of soldiers, its carts of provisions, spare horses, chests and trunks. "Kom wit me." She smiled and pointed to herself, then to the coach in which she was to ride. "We speak, ja?" She wanted me to ride with her, and I agreed.

I had been teaching her a little English—she knew no language beside her own—and she wanted to learn more. I climbed into the coach, a large wooden vehicle with thick wheels and a sturdy undercarriage, covered entirely in cloth of gold.

It was a clumsy thing, and rattled terribly as we went along the rutted roads. I imagined how King Henry would laugh when he saw it. But it shone in the fitful wintry sunshine, and announced the high birth of its occupant, leaving the peasants who lined the roadway quite awestruck.

Here was the golden coach of Lady Anna of Cleves, it seemed to say. The lady who will soon be Queen of England.

• • •

All the way to Calais, far to the south, we spoke, Lady Anna and I, and by the time we arrived at the gates of the walled town Lady Anna had learned quite a bit of English and I quite a bit of the Clevan dialect. She was able to address the English in Calais in their own tongue, relying on a written message we had created together. She pronounced most of the words correctly enough to be understood, and when she finished the brief speech, she was loudly acclaimed.

A grand banquet was given in her honor on the day after our arrival, with three courses of thirty-three dishes each. So great was the feasting and entertainment offered to Anna that servants had to be sent across the water from Whitehall to help out. The banqueting hall was crowded, with steaming platters carried in from the kitchens in an endless stream. Wine was poured, flagons of ale drained, fantastic shapes formed from marchpane brought to the long tables.

Curtains screened the serving tables from the immense hall. I had been sent to request more sugar-bread for Lady Anna from one of the servers maintaining the tables, and had just parted the curtain when I heard a ripping sound.

I looked—and there was a sandy-haired, blue-eyed, freckled man with an embarrassed smile on his face, standing behind one of the tables. He had torn his maroon velvet doublet on a protruding sharp-edged board, and was examining the gaping hole the board had made.

"By the teats of the Virgin!"

Seeing me, he regretted his outburst. "Pardon, mistress," he hastened to add. "I—"

"Yes, I see. You need help."

I was adept with a needle and thread, in my years at Horsham I had patched my own garments over and over again, and sometimes helped the other girls with their embroidery. I sent a valet to find my sewing box and in the meantime, talked with the charming sandy-haired man, who had the most delightful smile.

"Tom Culpeper," he said, his friendly face open, unguarded.

"My mother's name was Culpeper, before she became a Howard," I told him, pleased at the thought that we might be related—though hoping the family links were not too close. "My grandfather was Sir Richard Culpeper of Hollingbourne. I am Catherine Howard. My father was once Controller of Calais."

"We are cousins then. And you are the kindest of cousins to offer me your help."

"I have just come with Lady Anna and her party from Dusseldorf."

"You are of her household then."

I nodded, then added, "Ja, I am her maid of honor" in my best Clevan speech.

He laughed, a most pleasant laugh. Then, lowering his voice, he asked, "And now that you have taken her measure, what think you? Is she meet to be the king's wife? Is she comely? I have not yet seen her."

"I must be loyal," I whispered.

"No, you must be truthful," he whispered back.

Just then the valet arrived with my sewing things and I set about to repair the gaping hole in the rich soft velvet.

All around us servants were coming and going, weaving in and out of the crowd around the serving tables. There was a clatter of silver and the jabber and murmur of talk. Yet as I bent to take my first stitches all the disturbance seemed to melt away, all the sound retreated. It was as if we were alone.

"Promise me you won't poke a hole in my chest," I heard Tom say. "I must be fit for the jousting."

"In this cold?"

"In the cold, rain or shine, we joust tomorrow, in honor of Lady Anna."

I looked up at him briefly, and our eyes met. I found it hard to lower my eyes to my sewing.

"I hope you will do well, and unhorse many rivals." I could hear the emotion in my voice.

"I will—if you will give me some token of yours—to wear on my sleeve."

Impulsively I untied my silk stomacher and, ripping away a piece of the silk, folded it and handed it to Tom. He kissed it and tucked it away.

I went on with my sewing, my head close to his chest, my stitches far less small and neat than usual. I felt unsettled, all my composure shattered. I tried to concentrate on mending the rip in Tom's doublet. I tried my best.

"There," I said at last. "That ought to do, for now."

He looked down at my handiwork.

"Neatly done. But I am still waiting to hear about Lady Anna."

"Very well then. Help me find a platter of sugar-bread."

He looked puzzled but did as I asked. When we had found the sugar-bread I said "Follow me" and led Tom out through the curtains into the grand hall. We made our way to where Lady Anna sat, surrounded by her ladies. She smiled at my approach.

Tom placed the platter of sweet bread before her with a murmur of "Your Ladyship."

"Who is this handsome one?" she asked me in Clevan.

"One of King Henry's gentlemen," I said in reply. "He will compete in the lists tomorrow."

Bowing, Tom withdrew—but not before he had smiled at me and murmured, "Until tomorrow, Mistress Catherine."

I took my seat at the table, and reached for a slice of the sweet bread. But I could only eat a bite or two. I had no appetite. My head swam. All I could think of was, I will see him tomorrow, I will see him tomorrow. I could not wait for the day to end.

When Tom rode out onto the muddy jousting field on the following day, rain clouds darkened the sky and soon it began to pour.

"Surely they can't mean to hold the joust in this weather," I said to Malyn, who was sitting next to me. We were shivering, our cloaks folded about us. We sat under a tentlike awning, along with hundreds of others waiting for the jousting to begin, all of whom, I felt sure, were cold and uncomfortable.

"They must," Malyn told me. "Lady Anna wants to watch English jousting. They have nothing like it in Cleves."

"But why not put it off until tomorrow?" I was concerned about Tom. What if his horse slipped and fell in the mud, and landed on top of him? It had happened to King Henry once, I knew; while jousting in the rain, his warhorse had stumbled and fallen on him. He had lost all sense for many hours.

"She may have to make the crossing to Deal tomorrow," Malyn said. "She could go any day—just as soon as the tides are favorable. So the jousting must go on."

I looked up at the sky. It seemed to be growing darker by the minute. But the heralds were riding onto the tiltyard, and announcing the first challengers. We cheered for the combatants as they rode onto the muddy ground, their horses' hooves throwing up mud clots to stain their brilliantly colored caparisons. There were twenty jousters. I could not tell which one was Tom.

With the first passes it was evident that the contest would be a dirty, confused jumble of men and horses. The thunder of hoofbeats was muffled by the sloshing of puddles, instead of the splintering of thick oaken lances we watched lance after lance slide off the wet mail and fall harmlessly into the ooze below. Horses faltered, falling to their knees in the mire. Collisions left jousters shaking their befuddled heads in confusion.

"Why don't they stop it?" I cried. "Why doesn't someone stop it!"

But Lady Anna, sitting not far from us, was clapping her hands in pleasure. How could the sorry entertainment be stopped, when it was clearly offering her such delight?

Then came the moment I had been dreading. Two weary jousters, lances weaving unsteadily as they rode through the muck toward one another, collided in an explosion of wood and metal, their longsuffering mounts whinnying in pain and fear. Both horses fell—and only one rider managed to get to his feet, covered in mud, and stagger away.

The other lay where he fell, motionless.

Lady Anna was laughing and cheering, but others looked on in shock and worry. Grooms came forward to stand around the injured rider, stooping over him, talking to one another. Still he lay where he was.

Minutes passed. Rain began to fall, hard rain that pelted noisily off every surface. I could not stand the suspense any longer. I got to my feet and made my way onto the tilting ground, knowing full well that no women were ever allowed there. No one stopped me, however, as I made my way, sloshing through the rain and mud, to where the unknown man lay as if lifeless.

As I approached, one of the grooms lifted the fallen man's helm. Despite the dirt on his cheeks, and darkening his hair, I could tell who it was: Tom Culpeper.

NINE

DAY after day we waited, there in Calais, for the storms to abate and the tides to be favorable. Lady Anna fretted, she was used to riding and vigorous walking and did not like being confined in the crowded walled town with little to do but play cards with her ladies.

There were no more jousts. Apart from the injuries to the jousters, the horses suffered greatly, and well-trained chargers were costly to replace. We prayed daily for a swift, fair crossing, but each new dawn brought rain and storms, and we prepared ourselves for yet another delay.

For me, however, the rainy dawns brought hope—and renewed delight. For Tom had revived, his injured leg and arm were healing, and he and I were growing closer and closer the more time we spent together.

For the first few days he was confined to bed. I visited him and brought him comfits, and he urged me to stay on, saying that my companionship made him feel better. We talked about our Culpeper relatives, he told me of his childhood spent in the royal court, first as a page to King Henry and later as a groom and then a gentleman of the privy chamber. The court had been his life, he said. He knew its ways, its pitfalls. He had seen many a man rise high only to tumble back fatally.

I told Tom of what had happened between Francis and me at Lambeth, of my painful disillusionment when he abandoned me and I discovered the truth about him.

"At least you are not bound to him, as you thought. You are free."

"As long as the king makes no claim on me, yes." I told him of King Henry's hints to me when we were together, of his sharing his vision of the palace of Nonsuch with me, and saying he would not tell Lady Anna about it.

"Clearly he favors me—but he has not kissed me, or spoken words of love to me."

Tom looked thoughtful. "That is unlike him."

Time passed quickly and very happily when we were together. I felt as if I had known him for a long time, not just a few days. He did not overpower me, as Henry Manox had, nor beguile and deceive me, as Francis had. Tom's open, trusting friendliness and affection were gentle and genuine, and it was easy for me to give him my openness and trust in return. Gradually, easily, our mutual liking and sharing turned to love.

How and when it happened I couldn't have said. But after a week of knowing Tom I felt I knew everything about him, and never wanted to be apart from him again.

What a hard thing it is to write of love! Easy enough to describe the burning brand of lust, or the yearning of infatuation, that yearning that can never be assuaged. But love! There is only the word, and the knowing of it.

Tom was soon recovered enough to carry out his duties, which were light, the king not being present in Calais, but only a few of his officials. I did my best to amuse Lady Anna, teaching her new card games and helping her to improve her English. The gentlefolk and well-to-do burghers and merchants of the town were invited to meet Lady Anna, and we arranged these gatherings, and sometimes brought in musicians to play while we danced—though Anna had been brought up to believe that dancing was sinful, and did not join in. Her diversions were few indeed. She did not like to read, her embroidery work was poor. Religious devotions took very little of her time.

She needs children to look after, I thought to myself. They will fill her hours soon enough.

Children were much in my thoughts during those precious weeks in Calais, children and my future with Tom. He had been betrothed as a child—to a little girl who died of plague before they could marry. Twice more he had come close to becoming pledged to a woman, but both times the two families had been unable to agree on the woman's dowry, and in any case Tom had had misgivings.

"Just like King Henry, feeling such worry about Lady Anna," he confided.

"Now that you have seen her, what do you think?" I asked him. "Will she make King Henry a suitable wife?"

He looked chagrined. "She is certainly no beauty. Ungainly, pockmarked, bad-tempered. Disapproving. What was Lord Cromwell thinking?"

"He did not meet her, don't forget."

"He should have."

"All that matters, really, is the alliance between England and Cleves, and the soldiers. The armies."

But Tom only shook his head.

Finally the sun came out and Tom and I climbed the highest

tower of the fortifications and walked along the battlements. The marshes spread out before us on all sides, green and lush and filled with wildlife.

"There's good hunting, good shooting, out there," Tom said, taking my hand. "Quail and bittern, snipe and dotterels."

"And fish, don't forget. And crabs, and wild duck." We whiled away an hour, there on the battlements, talking mostly of inconsequential things. Then Tom turned and looked at me, and kissed me, and I thought, I have never, ever known such happiness.

"These weeks with you have been the best weeks of my life," Tom told me as we embraced. "Tell me, Catherine, shall I go to your uncle Thomas, and ask for your hand in marriage?"

I did not have to ponder the question. Only one answer was possible.

"Yes, dear Tom. Sweet little fool," I said.

We stayed where we were for another long, happy hour, wrapped in each other's arms, watching the shadows lengthen across the marshes, and the birds dipping and rising in their flight.

We made the crossing a few days before the end of the year, with an escort of fifty ships and much celebration. When we set sail the skies were clear. By the time we landed at the English coastal town of Deal, however, in the dark of a wintry evening, hail was spitting down and a harsh wind was blowing in our faces. Before we could get to shelter we were all soaked and dripping. The Dowager Duchess of Cleves had come to Deal to meet her daughter, and Lady Anna rushed to embrace her as soon as she saw her, falling into her arms and weeping as if she had been a lost child at last reunited with her beloved mama. We rested at Dover Castle, then went on to Canterbury, Lady Anna traveling in her cloth of gold coach.

Tom was not with the others in the escort, he and I had agreed that he would return to London at once to speak to Uncle Thomas. Bursting with happiness, I confided to Charyn and Malyn that Tom was going to ask Uncle Thomas for my hand in marriage. Malyn embraced me but Charyn was skeptical.

"The duke is not about to betrothe you in such haste," she said. "Not when he knows you have become the king's favorite." She was scathing. I knew that she was envious. I hoped she was wrong.

On our way to the capital we stopped in Canterbury, reaching the town just at dusk. Cheering crowds of townspeople lit the future queen's way with blazing torches, while great guns were fired and Archbishop Cranmer made an eloquent speech. Lady Anna was in demand, everyone was curious to see her. Though the hour was late, we maids of honor were told to prepare Lady Anna's temporary quarters to receive guests. Fifty burghers' wives, dressed in their best, filed through and more would have come had we not announced that the future queen was tired and needed her sleep.

We pushed on, through more foul weather, to Sittingbourne and then to Rochester, in each town encountering large crowds that cheered and clapped, the townspeople doing their best to catch a glimpse of the honored newcomer from Cleves. Beggars, out of work laborers, wounded soldiers without captains or pay: these joined the eager crowds, in large numbers.

"Why so many poor folk?" Anna wanted to know. I explained that because King Henry had dissolved the monasteries and sold off their lands, the poor had nowhere to go for alms.

"Even the monks—the monks that were—now have to beg, though some have made their way in the world."

Lady Anna looked sour. "Too many beggars," I heard her say. "England is a country of beggars!"

But her sharp reaction seemed to pass, and she was becoming eager to meet her bridegroom. It was arranged that they would meet for the first time, very publicly, at Blackheath amid crowds and a thunder of guns, trumpets and pageantry. Until then we would remain at Rochester, where entertainments would be offered each day.

On New Year's Day the entertainment was bull baiting, which I have always thought to be a cruel sport. We were in a spacious chamber of the bishop's palace. Most of Lady Anna's women were there, some at the windows, looking out at the bull baiting below, others of us sitting at a table playing cards. Lady Anna's mother, the Dowager Duchess Maria, sat by herself observing all that went on in the room. A dozen ladies from the town of Rochester had come to see Lady Anna, and Charyn and I had just escorted them out.

Anna herself was at a window, watching an enraged bull gore the fierce dogs that were savaging him and toss them in the dirt. I could not bear to watch.

All at once there was a commotion in the corridor outside, and then—greatly to our surprise—six men came into the room. I felt a chill of fear, for they were in disguise, their faces hooded, their bodies cloaked in yards of multicolored wool. They were laughing and shouting as men do when far gone in drink, and their merriment had a rough edge.

My first instinct was to move closer to Lady Anna, to protect her. After all the beggars and shabby poor we had encountered on our recent progress, my first thought was that these men might be bandits, come to rob Lady Anna of her jewelry or to kidnap her and demand a ransom from the king.

Before I could say or do anything further, one of the six men— the tallest and stoutest—came boldly up to Lady Anna, and throwing back his hood, bent down and kissed her cheek.

Shocked, she drew back.

"Milady," he said and held out a velvet pouch. She took it, murmuring thanks, and looked at him, her expression more puzzled than fearful.

He gazed back—and then, watching him, I saw the most remarkable series of expressions on his face as shock turned to amazement and then to disgust, as if he had bitten into a piece of rotten meat and had an immediate urge to spit it out.

He mumbled something to Lady Anna—I could not make out his words—and then, for the first time, noticed me, standing nearby. Now his face was all confusion.

"Catherine!" he muttered, then swiftly turned and left the room, the other men rapidly following him.

Only a moment had elapsed since the men first entered the chamber. I did not know what to make of what I had just seen. But Lady Anna, though somewhat bewildered, soon went back to watching the bull baiting, the velvet pouch still clutched in her hand. Cheering came from beyond the window and I realized that the contest between the bull and the dogs was reaching its gory climax. Meanwhile the maids of honor and chamberers were giggling and chattering about the disguised men.

Then without warning the men returned, only this time five of them were in disguise and the sixth—the king—was dressed in royal magnificence.

Immediately we all fell to our knees. The king approached the gaping Anna, suddenly stupefied and pale, and reaching out to her where she knelt, raised her to her feet and led her into an antechamber. Very soon he came out again, alone, and once again he looked at me—appalled, his face ashen—before turning and leaving the room.

All was silence in the chamber save for the tortured, low-pitched screams of the bull, in his death throes.

"May all the devils of hell draw her soul to hell!" read the brief message I received later that afternoon, brought by Sir Anthony

Denny. "She is nothing like what I was promised, and I would rather die than marry her!" I read it quickly, then stuffed it in the pocket of my gown.

With the message was a basket.

"What is it?" Malyn asked. "Open it! Who sent it?"

"Not now," I said, handing the basket back to Master Denny and asking him to keep it until after supper.

"Alas, I cannot, Mistress Catherine. The king commands me back to court as soon as I have delivered his gift to you."

Murmurs in the room—and Malyn's repeated demand that I open the basket.

I carried the basket into the antechamber, Malyn following me, only to find Lady Anna there, with her mother. Lady Anna seemed much distressed.

"Pardon me, Your Ladyship," I said and prepared to leave.

"Wait! What is that?"

"I do not know. It just arrived."

"For you?"

Before I could lie and say I had no idea who it was for, Malyn spoke up.

"It is for Catherine, from the king's chamber gentleman, Sir Anthony Denny."

"Open it!" was Lady Anna's command.

I lifted the lid and took out the soft linen that protected the contents of the basket—which, to my amazement, was a gift. A gift of such splendor it could only have been meant for Lady Anna. Soft, lustrous sables, sewn with rubies.

Quickly I put the lid back on the basket.

"Let us see!" Lady Anna cried.

"Yes, let us see what the king has sent you, Mistress Catherine," the Duchess Maria echoed, her tone caustic.

"I believe Master Denny has made a mistake. Surely those

beautiful sables were meant for you, Lady Anna." And I handed her the basket, with a glare at Malyn to give her warning not to say a word.

Lady Anna took out the soft furs and handled them, holding them up to her cheeks, her eyes bright with pleasure.

"So!" she exclaimed, getting to her feet and wrapping the furs around her neck. "He loves me, though he did not stay with me. He ran away from me." She laughed. "A strange man, your King Henry! A strange man, my husband!"

I showed no one the note the king had sent me, but read it again and again, pondering what it could mean, for England and for me.

King Henry had told me he would rather die than marry Lady Anna—yet the wedding was to take place in three days, and the bride was trying on her wedding gown again and again, tugging at it to adjust the fit, admiring herself in front of the pier glass, trying out ways to wear her hair. When not wearing her wedding gown she wore her sables (which were really mine) and hummed to herself contentedly.

She talked of the coming wedding frequently, referring with pride to the king as "my husband," as if she were married to him already.

Her mother hovered nearby, watchful and distrustful. Whenever I came near she glared at me, her eyes seemed to bore through me. I pretended not to notice.

A tense day passed, and on the following day Uncle Thomas came to see me.

We were alone. He made certain no one could overhear us, then spoke bluntly and rapidly.

"You are aware that Thomas Culpeper has come to me to ask for your hand, are you not?"

"Yes, uncle."

"Do you wish to marry him?"

"More than anything."

"I thought as much. But I expect you to put the family's interests first, before your own."

I tried to fight off the heavy weight of disappointment. Was he going to refuse his permission?

"In what way?"

"You must allow the king to make you his mistress. You must arouse his fancy, entice his lust. He will enrich you—he will enrich all of us. Cromwell's dominion will falter. Indeed it has already begun to falter, for the king is balking at marrying the plain-faced woman from Cleves." Only he did not say "woman," he used a fouler term.

"He has been telling every servingman in his household how ugly she is, how he cannot abide the thought of bedding her. How she looks like her mother, that old witch, whom he detests. I tell you, Catherine, he is quite stupefied at the thought of taking this creature as his bride.

"He mislikes her exceedingly—her brown complexion, her pockmarked cheeks, her strident voice, her lumpy nose, her ugly breasts—"

"He did not see her breasts."

"He did not need to see them, all bare and dangling, to know that they would not please him in bed.

"She is not womanly," he said. "He mislikes her, it is just so. No more, no less."

A silence fell, Uncle Thomas was looking at me expectantly. I walked to the hearth, where a fire was blazing. I held out my hands to its warmth.

"Lady Anna expects the wedding to be held as arranged. She expects to meet the king in splendid array, amid pageantry, with many Londoners looking on, and then to marry him the next day. Will he simply be absent?"

"He has been closeted with Cranmer, who is advising him on a way to free himself from the marriage contract he is so desperate to avoid. Lady Anna was betrothed to the Duke of Lorraine's son for many years. Cranmer thinks he can persuade half a dozen doctors of canon law to come forward and object to the king's marriage. They will say it is contrary to law, that she was bound by a precontract. Therefore she was not free to become betrothed to King Henry."

"She will be very sad—and then, I suspect, very angry."

"She dares not defy canon law."

"So I am forbidden to marry Tom, and Lady Anna will be prevented from marrying King Henry."

Uncle Thomas laughed again. "Just so. But there is a difference. Lady Anna will never be able to marry the king, while you, if you are patient, will surely be able to marry Thomas Culpeper."

I searched his face. Was he serious?

"How so?"

Uncle Thomas shrugged. "I know the king very well indeed. His fancies do not last. If you become his mistress, he will eventually discard you and find a younger one, or a more submissive one. Or, far better, he will die."

"But it is treason to imagine the death of the king!" I said, horrified.

But Uncle Thomas only smirked. "Then most men of this court are guilty of treason. Everyone knows he cannot live much longer. His leg swells, he chokes, he cannot breathe—we have all witnessed him when in the grip of his grievous affliction. We have seen it again and again. Death lies in wait for him, and the waiting cannot be long now."

I wanted to shut my ears to this ugly talk. I sensed cruelty in it, and another sinister quality for which I had no name.

Suddenly the fire felt too hot. I moved away, toward where Uncle Thomas was sprawled in a chair, gripping its arms tightly, his thin fingers splayed.

"Just do not resist him," he was saying. "Let him make you his amour, his sweetheart. As he did your cousin Anne Boleyn, and her sister before her. It will not be for long, I promise you. Best of all, let him make you pregnant with his child. His son. Prince Edward is weak, he is assailed by illness like his father. He could well die at any time. Your son could become the next king. Just think what glory would come to me—I mean to our family—then. You would be known as Mother of the King's Son. Your blood—Howard blood—would be mingled with the royal line forever."

But even as he spoke I knew I wanted no part of the role he was describing for me. I had no ambition whatever to be the mother of the next king. I was not like my cousin Anne Boleyn, who had—so it was said—enticed the king and made him love her even though he was married to a fine loyal wife. Nor was I like my cousin Mary Boleyn, who had been willing to serve the king's lust for years and who had been provided with a husband in a false and hypocritical way. I sought no advancement, for myself or my family. I had no desire for power or high position—though I confess I did enjoy the fine clothes and fine food, all the comforts I had been enjoying for the past several years. I had known what it was to do without; I much preferred to have the things that those in positions of power enjoyed.

In truth, I told myself, all I really wanted was Tom. I told my uncle so, I wanted Tom more than anything.

"But don't you see, girl, you can have your Tom. Only wait until the king discards you—or dies."

Wait. Just as death waited. And in the meantime, let the king make me his amour. As he did my cousin Anne and her sister. Bear him a son, as my mother Jocasta had. Let other women, women who had preserved their virtue and their reputations, look down on me and shun me. Let me be despised, sneered at.

Or worse. What if the king should become angry with me and order me to my death?

I felt repelled by what I had been hearing. It was foreign to me. Suddenly I needed to escape from the stiflingly hot room, into the cool of the outdoors, where a light rain was falling.

"Very well, Uncle Thomas. I will—think on what you have said."

"You will obey me, Catherine." How ominous his words were! How frightening!

"Now you may go."

I fled from the stifling room, overcome by a need to breathe cool air and get away from my fearsome uncle. I did not hurry back to Lady Anna's suite, knowing what I would find there: a scene of joyous preparation for a wedding that I now knew would never take place. Instead I lost myself in the maze of corridors and staircases, decaying unused rooms and quiet courtyards that made up the venerable bishop's palace, seeking a respite from my troubled thoughts and finding none.

Lady Anna set off in her gold carriage for London. She and those of us in her household were to be lodged at Suffolk House in the Strand, from there she would ride in procession for her formal meeting with the king and, on the following day, to her wedding.

But as soon as we reached Suffolk House we were met by a sputtering, angry Lord Cromwell who had been waiting for several hours and could hardly contain his consternation.

He greeted Lady Anna with a deep bow.

"Your Ladyship, I beg your indulgence but I must tell you that the king is infirm and cannot attend the ceremonies to be held at

Blackheath. He sends his regrets. Unfortunately, I must hasten back to the palace." And he bowed again, clearly intending to leave immediately.

"That is all?" was Lady Anna's startled retort, delivered in a harsher voice than I had ever heard her use.

"What is going on? What is the matter with the king?" Duchess Maria demanded, almost at the same moment.

Lord Cromwell hesitated.

"I shall have to send further word to you from the palace," he said curtly, then lowered his head and made his exit.

"But why? What is happening? I must know." Lady Anna looked around the unfamiliar room, a beautifully appointed sitting room, ample and gracious, with tall windows and rich oak wainscoting.

"Olisleger!" she called, and when the chamberlain came forward, she told him to go to the palace at once and discover all he could about the state of the king's health.

"He suffers from pains in his leg," I put forward. "He may be very ill. We must pray for his recovery, which ought to be our chief concern."

All eyes were turned on me, especially the suspicious eyes of Duchess Maria.

"It is not for you to tell me what is my chief concern," Lady Anna snapped. "I am about to be married! My wedding! That is my chief concern!"

And a very selfish one too, I told myself.

"If Your Ladyship pleases, I can go to the palace and find out what I can from my uncle, and the privy chamber gentlemen."

"Yes yes, go at once."

I was only too glad to be relieved of the strain of Lady Anna's alarm and that of her servants. I was sure that I knew what lay behind Lord Cromwell's curt announcement, and the cause of his distress. King Henry had decided not to marry Lady Anna.

No doubt he would be sending her back to Cleves. I did not envy her.

When I arrived at the palace I sought out Tom. I had been aching to see him. I was told I would find him in attendance on the king, who was in his private library.

He slipped away and met me, taking me in his arms and crushing me to him. How safe and happy I felt, in his warm strong arms! All my worries fell away. Nothing could touch me or hurt me, I felt, as long as Tom was there to protect me.

"My darling wife to be! My sweetheart! It seems a year since we were together!"

Arm in arm we found our way to a servants' chamber and communed there quietly, just glad to be together.

"I guess you know that your uncle said no," Tom told me after a time.

"He came to tell me. He was harsh with me. He said I had to try to entice the king into making me his mistress. That I owed it to the family to do whatever the king might ask of me."

Tom shook his head. "I would never want to share you with another man—even the king." After a moment he added, "Do you think he loves you?"

"He is fond of me. He enjoys me. But there is no passion between us, none at all. And I see no lust in his eyes, as I used to see in Henry Manox's eyes. None. Yet it appears he has decided not to marry Lady Anna. Could it possibly be because of his fondness for me?"

"I wish I knew," was Tom's reply. "He has been shut in with the archbishop and the law doctors for hours, there in his library," Tom said. "I could not help but overhear what they were discussing, all about prior contracts and whether or not Lady Anna's advisers were wrong to tell her she could become King Henry's wife. They were mumbling their Latin to one another, on and on, until I thought they would drop from weariness. I know I almost did. But then you came—just in time to save me."

He kissed me on the cheek.

"What are we to do, Tom? How can I bear to be without you? Uncle Thomas tried to convince me that it would only be for a short time. That I could let the king give me the favor of his love until he tires of me, or until—"

"Until he dies. No one believes he can live much longer. If he marries Lady Anna the honeymoon alone may kill him!"

Tom knew how to make me laugh.

"Until the Lord takes him, I was going to say. Then, afterwards, you and I can marry, except that I will be dishonored. No one in your family would ever speak to me. Our children would bear the stigma of my dishonored state, just as I have borne the stigma of my mother's dishonor. I would not wish that for you, or for our children. I think if I became the king's mistress and then was cast aside, I would want to shut myself away in a nunnery, or go and live in some wild place, far from people and towns—"

"I wouldn't let you do that. I would come looking for you. I would never rest until I found you."

We held each other then, more tightly than ever, as if by clinging to each other we could forestall the worst of what we feared.

Two days later Master Denny brought me another message. I slipped it into the pocket of my gown and did not read it until I was alone.

Catherine, dearest little friend of my heart,
Though I would rather die, I find that I must,
despite all my efforts, marry Lady Anna. I cannot
do this dread thing without you there to be my

friend and comfort. You must promise me this—
send word of your answer—in haste,
Henry R.

I read and reread the message. "Dearest little friend of my heart," he had written. A tender salutation indeed, but not, surely, the greeting of a man in love. He needed me, that much was clear. What harm would it do to give him what he was asking?

I gave Master Denny a message to take back to the king, to say that, assuming Lady Anna gave me permission, I would attend her at the wedding. I would give King Henry as much comfort as I could offer.

On the wedding morning we were up before dawn, all of us helping to prepare Lady Anna for the day she had been waiting for. Her dismay at the king's change of plans, and the cancellation of the grand ceremony on Blackheath, seemed fleeting. All that mattered was that the wedding would go forward, even though it had been delayed.

Her wedding gown of cloth of gold, embroidered with clusters of pearls, was provided by the king, and was a match to his own garments of cloth of gold garnished with silver. She seemed quite overawed by the splendor of it all, especially the jeweled coronet she wore over her long thick blond hair, which we had brushed until it shone. She stood before her pier glass admiring herself, turning from side to side so that the diamonds sparkled in the early morning light. Then we went into the small room where Archbishop Cranmer was waiting, along with Lady Anna's mother and two of her favorite Clevan ladies in waiting. I was allowed to attend; I had asked permission and Lady Anna, animated and full of happy anticipation, did not refuse me.

When the king came in to join us, the first thing he did was to look around for me. When he saw me he smiled, and I smiled back, nodding encouragingly. Then he joined his bride and stood before the archbishop. He pointedly avoided looking at Lady Anna, though she watched his face eagerly.

The ceremonial words were spoken, the hands of the bride and groom clasped, rings exchanged and promises made. I heard the king pledge himself to Lady Anna, his voice wavering as he spoke, knowing full well how he really felt. "May all the devils of hell draw her soul to hell," he had written. I prayed that the king and his wife, his queen, would prove to be a blessing to one another, despite all that augured against it.

TEN

"LOATHSOME!"

The shout echoed throughout the king's suite, startling the servants and causing those of us in the queen's apartments nearby to perk up our ears.

"I tell you she is absolutely loathsome!"

It was unmistakably King Henry's loud, rich voice—and he was unmistakably referring to his wife.

Malyn and Charyn and I stopped winding Queen Anna's lengths of gold and silver trim and looked at one another. I could hear Jonah, in his cage, whimpering. The quiet in the queen's suite remained unbroken for several minutes. We listened for more shouting, but heard none.

The meaning of the king's explosive outburst became clear soon enough. Servants in the privy chamber told servants in the kitchens what they had overheard, and the kitchen servants passed the word on to Queen Anna's chamberers, who whispered the news to some of us.

King Henry, having spent his wedding night with his bride, had confided the worst to his closest advisers and friends. She was repellent. He was horrified.

Not only could he not bear to make love to her, he said, but he suspected that she was not a virgin. Her sagging breasts were too full, her belly too rounded to be the breasts and belly of an untouched maid. He could hardly bear to touch her. He was prepared to swear on oath that whoever had taken her virginity, he was not the one.

He was going to talk to his physician Dr. Chambers about the awful situation and then he was going to do his penance, crawling the length of the royal chapel on his knees, all the way to the cross on the altar, while confessing his sins and asking for forgiveness.

In his role as privy chamber gentleman Tom could not help overhearing the king's conversations with his advisers, and he confirmed the below-stairs gossip that had reached us. He told us more than we cared to know about the king's revulsion at his queen's deformed flesh, her hanging breasts and flabby arms and legs. About her womanly parts King Henry claimed to know nothing, for he had not gone near them.

All the talk would have been titillating, at least to some in the household, if it were not so grave. For the marriage had been made, not only to forge a political alliance, but to strengthen the succession, and no one ever forgot that.

We all watched the new queen's belly. Would it swell with a prince? Would the king be able to overcome his revulsion for long enough to make her pregnant?

The queen herself seemed surprisingly untroubled. When asked if she expected to become a mother soon, she simply shook her head.

"No, I am not with child," she said complacently, smoothing the skirt of her satin gown.

"But how can that be," Malyn pressed her, "when the king shares your bed each night?"

Anna smiled. "It is as God wills."

"But did not the Lord command Adam and Eve to be fruitful and multiply?" another of the maids asked.

"I am fruitful. I am a healthy woman," Anna said stubbornly. And when pressed further, all she would say was that the king kissed her each night and said goodnight, then kissed her again in the morning and bade her farewell.

"Nothing more?"

She shook her head.

"Then you must intrigue him, tease him. Make him lust after you."

"Do not say such language to me! I am a pure Christian woman, not a harlot!"

So it went, the wintry days lengthening into weeks, the queen's belly remaining slack and loose instead of growing rounder and more prominent. We waited for some sort of resolution of the odd situation: a marriage that was not a marriage in the fullest sense, the succession resting on the uncertain health of the weak little Prince Edward who was not likely to have a brother.

And still Uncle Thomas was hoping that King Henry would make me his mistress. He did not. Instead, he confided in me.

"They plague me, oh how they all plague me, Catherine!" King Henry said when he summoned me to his private closet where he mixed his herbal remedies. I brought Jonah along, knowing how he enjoyed the little creature.

"They are like the fleas on that monkey, swarming, biting, tugging at my very flesh, all the place-seekers and petitioners, the rising young men and the panting, desperate old men, the fathers of ripe daughters who imagine I can be swayed by the offer of firm young flesh! Even my councilors, yes even old Tunstal, the wisest of them, only wants what is best for Tunstal, and not what is best for our common good, our common realm."

"And Lord Cromwell?" I asked, rather daringly. "Is he too a flea?"

"He is the king of fleas. He has sucked much of my blood over the years." His tone was bitter. "And he has forced me into a cankered union with—your mistress Anna."

I was silent, waiting for him to go on. Jonah left my lap and jumped into his.

Presently the king looked over at me, while stroking Jonah's head and running his fingers down his back. "She has begun to become piggish and stubborn. She does not do my bidding, as she promised to. Her mother goads her into willfulness. Ah!" He threw up his hands. "How I hate that old witch, the dowager duchess! I have ordered her to go back to Cleves, but she refuses. She says the seas are too rough—"

"Perhaps she fears the ruin of her lovely complexion, as she once feared the ruin of Anna's," I said, and the king laughed heartily.

"Why not send her as your envoy to the lands beyond the sea? To the place where Jonah came from?" I asked whimsically. Jonah had jumped off the king's lap and was climbing on the shelves that held jars and pots, books, a heavy inkwell, folded papers and a rusty knife, its hilt gleaming with gems.

"Or to the gates of hell," the king muttered, reaching for his herb pots and his mortar and pestle.

"Just thinking of the duchess makes my head ache," he added, dipping a small silver spoon into several of the pots and sprinkling spoonfuls of what looked like withered grass into the mortar bowl. "This is my best headache remedy. First marjoram and rue," he said, pulverizing the herbs, "then a few rose petals, then some sage, and finally lavender, to soothe and calm me and make me sleep." As he mixed the concoction he seemed to grow more relaxed. I found that the strong scent in the air was making me sleepy.

A thought occurred to me.

"Your Majesty, may I ask whether you mix this potion for yourself at night, before you go to bed?"

"Yes, often. Why do you ask?"

"At the risk of offending you—"

"Speak, girl!"

"Could this potion cause such a stupor that—it prevents you from—from—carrying out your husbandly tasks?" I could not bring myself to use a crudity, as the servants so often did.

"Do you mean, am I so sleepy that I do not make love to my wife?"

"Yes. You see, we—that is, many in the household—are hoping that Queen Anna will have children—a son, or more than one."

"No one is more concerned about the succession than I am. I have talked to Dr. Chambers and Dr. Butts about it. Half my chamber gentlemen have jokingly offered to carry out my husbandly office for me. I know what is being said. But the plain fact is, I cannot bring myself to touch that repellant woman. I can hardly bear the sight of her, if I look at her I see her mother and I want to retch."

As if at the mention of vomit Jonah emitted a small scream.

"Is there nothing that can be done?"

He poured wine into a flagon and added some of the herbal mixture, stirring it, then drinking it. When he had downed it all he rose and joined me on the bench where I had been sitting. He took my face in his two hands. His breath was overpowering.

"Dear Catherine, if I entrust a great secret to you, can I rely on you to keep it to yourself?"

He released my face, but continued to look steadily into my eyes. His eyes were pale blue and beautiful, even though surrounded by pouches of flesh. No wonder he had been so very handsome, so very attractive to women, when young.

"Yes, Your Majesty."

"It has become clear to me, as I ponder my predicament, that most likely I am not in fact married to the queen."

Startled, I waited to hear him say more.

"Right before the wedding, when Cranmer and his doctors of canon law, and Cromwell and his experts all were trying to find some reason why Anna was not free to marry, they failed. They believed that although she had been betrothed to the Duke of Lorraine's son, the betrothal was made null by church authorities in Cleves. Are you understanding what I'm saying?"

"I think so, yes, Your Majesty."

"Aha! They were wrong! They did not look into it carefully enough. But I have sent two of my own advocates to Cleves, to request the document that nullified the betrothal. And do you know—no such document could be found! Because no such document ever existed! It was all a lie, a ruse. The Clevan diplomats thought we would never doubt their word."

"Does Anna know this?"

"I can't imagine that she does."

Jonah had jumped to the floor and was making scratching sounds in the rushes.

"So you are saying that your wedding to Anna was no wedding at all."

"Indeed. In fact, I believe that it is providential that I cannot bring myself to lie with her. The Lord has made her loathsome to me, because if I did lie with her, our union would be an unholy thing."

"I see."

"But I am waiting for the right time to reveal all this to my councilors—those fleas—and to the entire court, indeed to Christendom. For there will be such an uproar, such wailing and gnashing of teeth—"

"But you will be free of the torment this has all been to you. I'm very glad for you."

He kissed me then, taking me completely by surprise and quite overwhelming me with the awful taste of his mouth, his wet lips, the reek of his breath. The kiss took my own breath away.

"Dearest Catherine," he said as I struggled to catch my breath. "I knew I could trust you. Sometimes I think you are the only one I can trust."

"I—I don't know what to say, Your Majesty."

"Say that you will consider becoming my consort, just as soon as I can disentangle all the knots they have tied around me."

Dumbfounded, my head swimming, I fought for clarity.

"I must ponder this."

"Ponder all you like. Only be sure to ponder with your uncle Norfolk. Hateful man! He will be only too glad to know what has passed between us. Only remember—do not tell him anything I have confided to you about the lies of the Clevan diplomats. That must wait until I am ready to announce the truth to the court and the world."

"Very well."

The king smiled benevolently, and took my hand in both of his.

"You are very dear to me, you and your monkey. I want you both beside me for the rest of my days."

Tom! My dear, dear Tom! Whatever would he say? How would he advise me? For we had to decide together what my answer to the king would be. Tom was my husband-to-be; even if I married the king, I would afterwards marry Tom. The king's life would soon end, and at that point my true happiness would begin. I had to believe that, or I would have been in despair.

When I told him all that the king had said to me, Tom listened patiently. He was thoughtful, considered. There was nothing hotheaded or rash about Tom, in that way he was completely unlike Henry Manox or Francis, both of whom had been overly quick to react to anything that seemed to threaten them.

He hugged me to him, kissing me again and again. Then he released me and, smiling, looked into my eyes, taking my hands in his.

"My dearest Catherine, nothing will ever change how much I love you, how much I will always love you."

"Tom!" He brought tears to my eyes.

"But I think we both realize that you cannot refuse the king's request. It is not merely a request, it is a command. He needs and desires you, therefore you must obey. He is treacherous: one moment charming and benign, the next moment cruel. Those of us in the privy chamber have seen him change suddenly, we know his moods. If you should refuse him, nothing could protect you from his wrath.

"And then there is your uncle. I think you know what he might do if he thought you were going against the Howard interests."

I nodded, sadly. Uncle Thomas's harshness toward those who crossed him was legendary. And I had told Tom about my grandmother's cruelty as well, when she whipped me and shut me in the dark day after day without food or drink. Left me to die.

"There is much to be thankful for in this, Catherine. Just think! How very much better that he wants you for his wife than for his mistress! A wife is honored, a mistress is scorned by her family— indeed, she all but loses her family. You will be Queen Catherine! I shall have to bow down to you, we all will."

And he got down on his knees and bowed low, until his head nearly touched the floor. Then he rose again, grinning.

"You will be very grand, above us all," he went on. "You will put up with his demands and be an ornament to his life. And all the time you will think, he's old, he's going to die. And then I will be free."

I tried to smile, though worry still nagged at me.

"Tom? You won't leave me, will you? You'll stay nearby."

"Right at your fingertips, Catherine. Right there in the privy chamber—or wherever else he may send me. I must obey him, just as you must."

"Please, please, never leave me."

He took me in his arms once again, murmuring words of comfort. "It will only be a little while, sweetheart. Not long at all. Soon we will be together, pledged to one another forever, and then I will never leave you again."

Everything changed for me that spring, the spring of the year 1540. Anna was still queen, she still appeared content with her marriage. But King Henry no longer came to her bed every night, he spent many of his evenings with me. And not a few of his nights as well, though at first only those closest to him knew that.

Our physical lovemaking was awkward. His enormous weight and bulk crushed me and when he was on top of me, grunting and straining, it was all I could do to breathe, he was so heavy. I am a very small woman. I could not help dreading his onslaughts. I prayed to be able to endure him. And often, when he struggled to attain his pleasure, the struggle was lengthy. At times he failed. And even when he succeeded—or appeared to succeed—I felt that something had gone wrong. His lovemaking was nothing like what I had known with other men. It cost him too much in effort, and when the effort was ended, there was often nothing to indicate that he had succeeded in spilling his seed inside me. Or, at most, there were only a few drops of sticky wetness left behind.

It was all I could do to keep breathing, as I have said, and to endure his reeking breath and crushing bulk. I tried to think of Tom, and to tell myself that my trials would not last long.

I had given my consent to wed him, once he freed himself from what he called his "entanglements." He behaved as though he was a bachelor again, and a very rich one, spending money on me daily and spoiling me with his lavish attentions.

Bishop Gardiner, who had long been opposed to King Henry's marriage to Anna, and even more opposed to Lord Cromwell and his overweening power, made ready an entire wing of his palace for the king's use and mine. I had apartments there, all my old belongings were moved there from Lambeth, and all my new belongings—the sumptuous new gowns the king had made for me, the chests of jewels he presented to me, Jonah's large new cage, as tall as a man and nearly as wide, the musicians the king sent to entertain me—all arrived in the courtyard of Bishop Gardiner's residence, and not at my grandmother's great mansion.

The king had yet to reveal what he had discovered about the impediment to his marriage to Anna, to reveal, that is, that in actuality he was not married at all. He told me he would disclose this fact to his advisers at the right time. But I began to wonder when the right time would come, since in the queen's household all the talk was of her coronation—a coronation that everyone said would soon take place, and Queen Anna herself was said to be full of excitement over the spectacle of her crowning.

I confess that I was tired of all the waiting and confusion—and besides, at Bishop Gardiner's palace I had less opportunity to see Tom, and seeing Tom was very important to me—more important than anything. So I concocted a ruse. I gave a false impression. I did not exactly lie, but I did create an illusion meant to hasten my marriage to the king.

I began complaining of feeling ill, I said that my stomach hurt and that my clothes were suddenly too tight. I stuffed handkerchiefs in my underwear to make my breasts look heavier than usual. I remarked to the chamberers in Queen Anna's household that I had not received my monthly flux for some time, knowing that they would immediately spread the word that I was with child.

Now all eyes were on my belly, especially Grandma Agnes's critical stare. She came to the bishop's palace and regarded me from all angles.

"Well then, is it true?"

I pretended not to understand her question. I was a good dissembler.

"Has the king given you a child?"

"I know not."

She bristled. But her anger no longer frightened me. I was the betrothed of the king.

"Come, girl, you are no innocent! Are you with child or are you not?"

"I suppose we shall know well enough by harvest time."

She stepped toward me, as if to slap me, but I stood my ground, stiffened my spine and glared up at her.

She hesitated, then with a smirk and a shrug she turned and left me. I was not certain whether she heard my parting words.

"Before long you will have to ask my permission to leave my presence!"

Summer arrived and I kept up my ruse. As I hoped, King Henry wanted to believe that I was carrying his child, and began clearing the "entanglements" that stood in the way of our wedding.

The first obstacle was Lord Cromwell. Suddenly and without warning, without even a trial, he was arrested and taken to the Tower, accused of treason and heresy. The fell hand of the king had been raised against him, and he was shown no mercy. While he languished in his prison, Queen Anna was removed from court, sent to the palace of Richmond. Once there she was told that her marriage to King Henry would soon be declared invalid, which must have come as a great shock to her, and an even greater shock to her mother, who, I had no doubt, was outraged.

Meanwhile I was preparing for my own wedding to come. The queen's apartments, so recently renovated and made ready for Anna, were now made ready for me. And the members of my large household were chosen, one by one, from my lord chamberlain to my master of the horse to my chaplains and maids of honor, my yeomen and footmen and grooms, to the sumptermen who would carry my litter and the cooks, scullery boys and clerks who would govern the preparation and serving of my food.

I pretended to have difficulty in choosing all these servants and officials, plagued as I was by pains in my stomach and dizziness and the increasing tightness of my clothes. I kept up the pretense as long as I could, aided by the heat (which really was quite oppressive) and all the confusion surrounding the king's sudden, decisive decrees. In a few fateful weeks he had swept his most powerful official from court to prison and removed his queen as well: everyone wondered who would be next, and how soon the next blow would fall.

I am happy to say that King Henry was lenient with Anna, who was made to understand that although she would no longer be queen, she would be welcome to stay on in England with the respectful title of "Sister to the King," and her own fine houses and a generous income. Her mother, however, was required to return to Cleves, and to stay there indefinitely.

To King Henry's great satisfaction, a convocation of more than two hundred clergymen met in July to ponder the serious matter of whether or not the royal marriage was indeed a valid one. And to hardly anyone's surprise, they decided, after much debate and haranguing, that it was not valid. That the king and Anna had been living in sin for many months, and that the king was free to marry any suitable partner he chose.

The king could hardly wait to marry me, he seemed as eager as a boy, not a mature man, stout and potbellied, with white hairs in his beard and a balding pate. Five seamstresses worked day and night to complete my wedding gown, which was by far the most costly and elegant garment I had ever put on. It was made in the French style, with yards of flowing silver bawdkin falling in luxuriant folds over a kirtle of cloth of gold. My headdress framed my face in sparkling diamonds, at my throat was a beautiful necklace of diamonds, rubies and pearls, with a great pendant diamond as large as a walnut.

When I tried on all my finery on the day before the wedding, standing before the large pier glass in the queen's suite at Hampton Court, the seamstresses fussing around me, it all felt foreign to me. I was not this splendidly attired young woman, about to become Queen of England. I was Catherine Howard, short and smiling, who liked to make people laugh and whose nose was too big. As Charyn used to tell me, I was the runt of the Howard litter, who could not be allowed to breed and who would never marry.

Now I was marrying in splendor, to the most highborn man in the realm.

And I would have given anything not to be going ahead with it. What if I ran away, this very night? Where would I go? How far could I run before the king's agents came after me and found me?

But of course I could not go. I could not leave Tom.

Wild thoughts flitted through my unsettled head as I stood staring at my reflection. What would the future bring? Would I become a widow soon, as I fervently hoped? Would I be able to do all that was required of me as queen? Would my husband's subjects accept me, and pay homage to me, or would they mutter against me and shout insults at me as they had my cousin Anne Boleyn?

I could not sleep at all, the night before the wedding. In the morning I was bleary-eyed and pale, my hands shook and my stomach rebelled. I could not eat or drink. I allowed my chamberers to adorn me, brushing out my long auburn hair so that it fell in waves down my back, dressing me in my beautiful gown, fastening the sparkling necklace around my neck, the huge pendant walnut so heavy it seemed to drag my head down.

When I was ready I took Uncle William's arm and let him lead me into the chapel. His kind, reassuring presence steadied me. But when King Henry entered the chapel, magnificent despite his girth in silver and white, jeweled rings on every finger, a massive necklace of emeralds spilling down his chest and a jeweled cap covering his balding head, I began to tremble. For just behind the king came his privy chamber gentlemen, with Tom prominent among them.

When I saw Tom I began to cry, quietly, and Uncle William bent down to kiss my cheek, at the same time wiping my tears with his glove.

"Be brave, Catherine," he whispered. "The family is watching."

And they were. Glancing around the small chapel I saw Uncle Thomas, looking very proud and smug, and Grandma Agnes, white-haired and wraith thin, and many of my cousins, aunts and uncles, even my stepmother Margaret. How I wished, in that moment, that my father had been beside me, instead of Uncle William. My dear father! Oh, how I missed him in that moment!

The ceremony was brief, the words went past my ears in a blur of sound. Standing next to the immense king, so very much taller and wider than I, a foolish happy smile on his broad face, I repeated my vows as carefully and accurately as I could, aware that my small voice shook with every word.

• • •

A few days after our wedding, King Henry took me to the site of his future palace of Nonsuch once again. We toured the grounds, noting where work had progressed. There were no buildings in place as yet, only the wooden scaffolding where some of them would one day stand. He had given orders that the high tower be completed first, and it was under way, though far from being finished. Masons were laying the stonework when we rode by, sweat pouring from their naked backs as they suffered under the hot sun.

"It won't be long now, Catherine. Soon my tower will rise, and I will be able to come here to take refuge from my enemies. The northmen are preparing to rebel against me, my councilors say, just as they did four summers ago. If they come this far south, we'll wait for them here, you and I."

"I think we may need a few guardsmen. And perhaps a culverin or two."

"Nonsuch will be well defended, I assure you. It will be the largest and strongest fortress in England one day.

"This is my dream, Catherine," he went on after a time, in a lower tone. "This place, with you beside me. In you my dear love has come back to me, you know. My blessed one. My Jocasta. In you her sad loss will be redeemed, when you bear me a son. A boy to replace the one she lost, all those years ago."

"I—I'm no longer certain that there is a child within me," I confessed. "It may have passed from me."

The king frowned. "When?"

"I am not certain, I just—no longer feel ill, and my belly has not swollen—"

"Perhaps it was simply a woman's fancy."

"Or perhaps a misbegotten babe."

Suddenly the king blanched, a look of utter terror crossed his features.

"Don't say such things! Only the devil sends misbegotten babies, deformed things with two heads or no arms or legs—" He shuddered. "When I was married to the first Queen Catherine, she presented me with one deformed dead babe after another. And all because our marriage was flawed. Your cousin Anne was cursed in the same way, and could not give me a healthy son. Only Queen Jane was able to do that, because there was no shadow over our marriage, no sin. You, my dear little wife, will give me sons because we are truly wed, with no sin to overshadow us, no impediments to cloud our union. It will be as God wills. In you my dream will at last come true."

His faith in the future, his confidence in the purity and sinlessness of our marriage struck me to the heart—and filled me with guilt. I had only pretended to be pregnant. I had deceived everyone. And the greater deception was that my marriage to King Henry was just as flawed as his marriage to Anna had been. She had had a precontract with the Duke of Lorraine's son, I had been handfasted to Francis Dereham. If the king was right, and only valid marriages were blessed with sons, then ours was doomed.

I pondered this on the way back to Whitehall, concerned about all that had happened and the unknown future, fearful lest I give birth to a deformed child and the king become suspicious about my past.

In the worst heat of that sweltering August word came from the rural manor of Shaddesburgh that Prince Edward was gravely ill. King Henry abandoned his planned hunting trip and rode to Shaddesburgh at once, taking Dr. Chambers and Dr. Butts with him and insisting that I go along as well, which I was only too glad to do. I had not seen the young prince, who was only rarely brought to court, and was concerned about him.

We rode through scenes of destruction; dead and dying cattle littered the sere pastures, withered crops blighted the fields, and the plague was said to be widespread nearly everywhere. I prayed that Prince Edward had not been struck with the plague, for it did not spare children and if stricken, the weakest of them died within days.

We found the little prince in his gilded cradle, surrounded by nurses and rockers. He was not yet three years old, but he looked much younger, lying curled into a ball, his eyes shut, his delicate face white. The servants knelt to honor the king, who hurried to peer down at his son, feeling his small head with his own large hand.

"He burns with fever!" King Henry exclaimed, "yet his face is white, not red. How can this be!" He turned to Dr. Butts and ordered that a specific potion be given to the prince to counteract his fever, then demanded of the servants whether an apothecary had been summoned.

"A wise woman from the village was brought to attend the prince as soon as he fell ill," the steward told King Henry. "She made him drink what she prepared."

"By all the saints! She's killed him!"

The two royal physicians lost no time in treating the prince, ordering the servants to bring cool wet cloths to wrap around his body, moving him to the coolest part of the manor—the cellars—and making certain he was given cold rich cow's milk and cider to drink.

We stayed at the manor for three days, and by the close of the third day little Edward's cheeks were not so pale and his wide blue eyes were regarding us gravely. Those three days were an agony for my husband. (I must now accustom myself to writing of him that way, as my husband, though it has never ceased to feel odd to me.) He spent hours sitting uncomfortably by his son's cradle, stroking him and talking to him, praying, conferring with the two physicians and with an apothecary brought from the nearest town. Through it all he needed to have me nearby, and I too sat beside the prince's cradle, praying and watching for the least sign of improvement in his condition.

"He resembles his mother," Henry remarked during our long vigil. "He has her brow and nose. I hope he will inherit her calm, gentle spirit. And her loyalty—I admired her loyalty above all.

"You are like her in that way, Catherine," he resumed after a pause. "As I have told you so often, I can trust your loyalty." He shook his head. "Not like the dastardly Crum—and the others. So many others." The Lord Privy Seal had been executed on our wedding day. Others had followed him to the scaffold.

He stood—and grimaced. I could tell that his leg was giving him pain. I smiled sympathetically.

"Dear Catherine, I do so hope that we will have a son before long. Another Harry, like me, what do you say? A healthy, strong boy. A champion at the tilt, as I used to be–"

The little prince stirred, reaching out with his hands, clasping and unclasping them. The king gave him one of his own large fingers to hold.

"I had a little son once, many years ago. Catherine's son. We named him Henry, but we called him Harry—while he lived." He shook his head in sad remembrance. "We held tournaments in his honor, he had a grand christening—I seem to remember that he did—but he lived such a short time! Then the Lord took him."

"I am praying that you will never have such a disappointment again," I offered, not knowing what else to say.

"If all goes as I hope, your prayers will be answered."

We left Shaddesburgh with hope that Prince Edward would continue to recover from his fever, and with the promise from the royal physicians that messengers would be sent daily to the traveling court, wherever we were, with news of the prince's health. Then my husband, who had been fretting at being cooped up with no exercise, went hunting.

And I, fretting inwardly over my own very private concerns, sent a messenger of my own—to my household at Whitehall, to ask that Joan Bulmer be dispatched to join us, as swiftly as possible, as I had need of her.

ELEVEN

WHEN my friend Joan joined our traveling court my husband was away at a hunting lodge deep in the forest, and I was staying at a comfortable manor house half a day's ride away. The king had taken many in our household with him, and expected to be gone for several days.

"Dear Joan!" I burst out when she was shown into my bedchamber. "I am so very glad to see you!"

She knelt, then rose at my signal and looked at me quizzically. "And why is that, pray, Your Highness, when you have seen me so recently? I am one of your chamberers, after all. And you have not been away from the palace very long."

We sat together companionably, I on the edge of my bed, Joan on a soft cushion.

"I have no one else to talk to—about certain things. And you are very knowledgeable."

She continued to regard me with her level gaze.

"First, I must tell you that I am not with child, and never really thought that I was."

She nodded. "I knew you were dissembling. Your face did not fill out, your cheeks didn't become plumper as they would have had you been telling the truth. Also you lacked the glow of the woman with child. I know those signs—and I saw immediately that you lacked them."

"I hope no one else saw through my deception—Grandma Agnes for instance."

Joan guffawed. "She is the master dissembler! She would have applauded you."

I confided to Joan all that had gone on between Tom and me. I told her that we wanted to marry, but that the king's proposal to me—in reality a command—had taken precedence. But that we hoped to wed in the future.

"After Prince Edward becomes king, you mean."

I nodded. Clever Joan had avoided mentioning the unmentionable—the king's eventual death.

"You did what you had to do. And now you are married to a man with a severe affliction. Those legs of his! With such awful weeping sores. I have heard the laundresses complain that they cannot wash the smell of the pus from his hose. Is it true he rubs his sores with an ointment he makes from powdered pearls?"

I nodded. "I have watched him prepare it. Mixing potions and ointments is something he really enjoys. He shuts himself up in his closet, and spreads out his pots of herbs and flasks of fluids, and carefully prepares each tonic and physick. He has studied the works of the alchemists, actually he seems quite learned."

"Nonsense. He seems learned to you, because you know nothing. He imagines that he knows more than the apothecaries, but I assure you, Catherine, he does not. His own potions may be the death of him!" I flinched, hearing her speak those forbidden words.

I moved closer to Joan, and, keeping my voice low, I told her about how Prince Edward had recently been taken ill.

"He was pale as ashes, when we first saw him. Such a little thing! All curled up, hardly breathing. The king was beside himself with worry. He stayed by the prince's cradle for hours each day, until he appeared to be getting better."

"Was it a fever?" Joan wanted to know.

"Yes. Thank heaven he was not struck with plague. But Joan! He looks to me like such a weak child, not at all what you would expect a son of King Henry to look like. I thought he would be large and sturdy, with strong limbs and a clamorous disposition. Instead he was small and fragile. He looked up at us with such mournful eyes the day we left him. As if to say, don't leave me, I will only be sick again.

"I believe the boy nearly died when he was first born, though the midwives and physicians were sworn to tell no one. I only found out because my cousin was attending one of the midwives."

Joan went on to tell me more about the prince's birth, how he had had to be pulled out feet first and how his face was blue and it took him a long time to begin to cry the way a newborn should. She had heard that Queen Jane had developed a fever right away, and pains and swelling in her head and her arms. She had been bled many times, Joan said, but the bleeding did not ease the fever, which only became worse until it killed her, only days after giving birth. Gradually we came around to the subject of the prince's fragile health once more.

"King Henry fears that no son of his can survive," I told Joan. "He relies on me most urgently to give him more sons. I must not disappoint him. But Joan!" Now I became more urgent. "How can we create a child, when he—has such difficulties! You know so much about how babies are made, and what we women must do to avoid them. I need your help. I need you to teach me what to do to ensure that I become pregnant."

Joan laughed. "No one has ever come to me with that problem before!" But she quickly became serious again.

"Tell me about his difficulties."

"So often he seems—unable to complete the act of love. This has happened more and more since the little prince's grave illness. He tries again and again, so very urgently that his face turns scarlet and I'm afraid he will burst. He quite wears himself out with his efforts—and once in a while he succeeds. But most of the time he fails. And then he gets angry, and humiliated too, I can tell. And he is afraid, so very afraid."

"Afraid of what, exactly?"

"His greatest fear, I have discovered, is the fear that God is punishing him for some sin. He believes that his weakness, his inability, may be a curse from God."

"I see."

"I believe he thought, when he married me, that with a very young and healthy woman as his wife he could succeed in overcoming the curse—especially a woman whose mother he loved so very much in his youth. There are times, late at night, when he has drunk a good deal of wine, that I am sure his memory betrays him. He thinks I am my mother. I am told I resemble her."

Joan shook her head. "This is too much! You are asking for my help with a knotty tangle of problems." As she spoke I thought of how my husband, before our marriage, had referred to his entanglements, the web of obstacles that lay in his way to prevent him from marrying me.

"You are married to a deluded old man, all but incapable in body, ill, who knows he may die at any time—and beyond this, an old man who believes himself to be cursed! There is no physick to heal such a man! Only a miracle could do that." She grew quiet, continuing to shake her head. But after a moment she began again, as I hoped she would.

"Still, there are tonics to restore a man's potency. I can prepare one. But you will have to convince the king to drink it."

On into the fall our progress continued, with the hot rainless days following one another and the sad devastation of the countryside continuing. My husband hunted with vigor, pursuing deer and boar and waterfowl of many kinds. Nearly every town of any size held a banquet in my honor, to welcome me as their new queen consort. I learned to comport myself with dignity, to straighten my back and hold my head high as I entered the banqueting hall, dressed in my costly finery and with a fortune in jewels at my neck and wrists. It pleased my husband to see how I was admired, how the women came forward to feel the stuff of my skirts and the men became tongue-tied and ill at ease when I came among them.

And they all, men and women alike, stared at my belly, as I was only too aware.

Tom and the other privy chamber gentlemen were present to assist at these banquets, undertaking small tasks and large, standing behind the king's bench and mine, escorting local officials in and out of the hall, overseeing the passage of platters of meat and fish, vegetables and custards from the kitchens to the dining chamber.

I watched for a signal from Tom, or for the briefest of notes, pressed into my hand during the meal, to indicate when and where we might be able to meet and exchange a few words and a kiss—or sometimes more. The later the hour, the more likely we were to find a way to be together, for my husband ate and drank until he was almost insensible, and after such a heavy meal and so great a quantity of wine he began to fall asleep and had to be helped to bed. He had no awareness of what I did or where I went.

I felt torn—between wanting to be with Tom and needing to continue my nightly habit of pouring some of Joan's tonic into my husband's bedside wine—which I invariably did late at night, after the banquet's end.

Was the tonic having any effect? Sometimes I thought it was, but for the most part the king continued to struggle in the vain attempt to spill his seed inside me.

Toward the end of September we were staying at the manor of Morefield. It was late at night. My husband had been playing cards with Lord Delaney and some of his gentlemen. They were still playing when I retired, and as I did each night, I poured a little of the tonic into the flagon of wine by our bedside.

My husband surprised me by coming into the bedchamber suddenly, with several of his hunting dogs at his heels.

He saw what I was doing.

With a howl he limped toward me and knocked the flagon to the floor.

"What are you about, woman?"

The dogs began lapping at the spilled wine. Shouting "No!" the king slapped them on their haunches and sent them whining out of the room.

"I asked you, what are you about? What were you doing?"

I sighed and hung my head.

"I was putting a potion into your wine, Your Majesty."

"Yes? And what kind of potion?" He was glowering.

"It was—a tonic. To—increase your desire."

"A love philter? What need do I have of a love philter?"

"Not that, it is a potion that increases your ability to—to complete the act of love."

"By the teats of the Virgin!" he cried. "So you are not satisfied? Are you insatiable then? You want me to lie with you every hour of the day and night!"

I was trembling with fear.

"My lord and my love," I managed to say, "please understand. It was not for my sake that I put the potion into your wine, it was for yours."

"Ah." He raised his eyebrows. He understood—or at least I thought he did. I was greatly relieved, for having to talk of this issue between us was intensely embarrassing to me. I did not know how much talk he would tolerate. He saw how frightened I was and patted me reassuringly.

"Yes, I see. You and I are both hoping for the same thing, that you will soon feel yourself with child."

The incident passed, and my husband continued to take his nightly dose of Joan's tonic. Perhaps he thought he was humoring me—or perhaps he was in earnest, and truly hoped that it might have a good effect.

I decided that it was time to talk to Dr. Chambers.

He came in response to my summons. He was a very old man, much older than the king, and his wrinkled face was always dour. Yet on this afternoon he looked, for once, quite pleased and expectant.

"Am I to hope that Your Highness has good news? Have you summoned me because your monthly flux has ceased?" He searched my face, no doubt looking for the fullness Joan had not been able to detect there.

"Dr. Chambers," I began, feeling more than a little uncertain what words to use, "I am concerned that I—that His Majesty and I—have not yet created a child together."

"But if you are not with child, why have you summoned me?"

"I hope that if I confide in you, you may be able to advise us."

The doctor looked stern.

"I advise you to be fertile, madam."

I was quite taken aback, not only by the physician's frankness, but by his reprimand. And his assumption that any deficiency lay with me rather than with my husband.

"You should be talking to a wise woman, or a midwife," Dr. Chambers went on. "Women know how to heal other women."

"But I need no healing!" I exclaimed.

"Of course you do. You must. And I may as well tell you," he added, "that everyone thinks so." He stressed "everyone" in such a way that I knew he meant to include the king.

I was dumbfounded. It had never occurred to me that while I was assuming our deficiency was due to the king's inability, he was assuming the reverse.

"But I—" I began.

Dr. Chambers silenced me.

"There is no need to say more. You must seek healing for your infertile womb. The king has proved his own soundness, his manly capability, many times. He has had children by others. You are barren! Barren!"

No one had spoken to me in this way since I became queen. What gave Dr. Chambers the right to become my accuser? For that is how his scathing words felt.

After I sent him away I kept thinking of what he had said. I was barren! And he was right. I had never been with child. With Francis and Tom I had always been careful to use the preventatives Joan had taught us at Horsham. With the king I used none. But in fairness, I had to at least consider the possibility that I might, in fact, be barren. My first thought, on considering that terrible possibility, was that I would never be able to have children with Tom, once we were married. My second thought, however, was a more immediately frightening one: that the king would discard me. Or would he do worse? Would he blame me, as the bearer of a divine curse? And would he then have me executed, as he had my cousin Anne?

● ● ●

We journeyed back to London just as the leaves were turning to rich reds and yellows and the air was cool and crisp. Peasants in the villages we passed through brought us apples, I remember, and the sweet taste of them was a pleasure to me. I tried my best to savor the pleasures of those days, and to keep my spirits buoyant, knowing how the king disliked it when I showed even the least sign of dejection. I tried to look forward to seeing Jonah again—I had not thought it wise to take him along on progress—and to rejoining my full household. But I could not help worrying. I was failing in my chief task as queen. I could not help but bear the stigma of my failure. And I had to find a way to overcome it, and soon.

On All Hallows' Eve I noticed my husband limping more heavily than usual, and grimacing with each step. The following morning he did not get out of bed, but lay where he was, the stink of his sore leg strong about him.

"Shall I call for Dr. Chambers and Dr. Butts?" I asked him.

He waved his hand no, and sent me away. He did not speak, his breath was rasping in his throat.

I did not want to anger him, so I left the room but alerted Master Denny who went in at once to do what he could for him.

Hour after hour his condition worsened (Master Denny kept me informed) until by late afternoon the physicians were sent for. Soon the entire court knew that my husband was once again suffering from a painful eruption from his ulcer, and prayers were being said every hour in the palace chapel for his recovery.

Somewhat to my surprise, Master Denny came to tell me, on the following day, that my husband had ordered me to leave Whitehall for Greenwich.

"He wants you to travel downriver on your barge," I was told. "Enjoy your journey. Invite your favorite companions. Feast yourselves!"

"But how can I do that when he is here suffering?"

Master Denny leaned lower to talk to me quietly. "He doesn't want you to see him in his suffering state. He wants to spare you the sight of all that."

"But I have never asked to be spared. He has my sympathy." And it was true. Though it was also true, I must confess, that my hopes were raised—my hopes that my marriage to the king would soon turn to widowhood.

As queen I had my own barge, a brightly painted, beflagged vessel rowed by twenty-six bargemen. There were twenty other servants to spread rushes on the deck and scent them with rosemary and clean the small interior chambers, laundresses to wash the curtains that provided privacy and cooks to prepare the modest collations I was expected to offer to my guests. I had hardly ever had an opportunity to even go aboard my barge, let alone ride in it for an extended trip, but it seemed that now was the moment. Besides, I thought—uncharitably, given my husband's condition— besides, I could take Tom with me.

"I don't believe Your Highness has traveled aboard your barge before," I heard a rasping voice say. Lady Rochford had come up behind me, unseen, and now was talking to me, having curtseyed rapidly.

Lady Rochford had been thrust on me as one of my ladies in waiting—a command from the king. I would not have chosen her to be a part of my household, not only because she was too closely related to my disgraced cousin Anne (she was the widow of Anne's brother, my disgraced and executed cousin George Boleyn) but because she irritated me. She sidled. She wheedled. She insinuated. There was nothing straightforward about Jane Rochford, and besides, she was unattractive and old. Nearer forty than thirty years old. She was tall and bony and wore her hair in three unbecoming curly clumps, poorly covered by her headdress.

I gave her a begrudging glance.

"I assure you, I can make your first voyage aboard your barge a very pleasant one."

I glared at her. "Nothing in life is pleasant to me as long as my husband is in pain."

"Of course, Your Highness. A most commendable sentiment."

But not one you would share, I thought. When your husband George was accused of incest with his sister Anne (an accusation long thought to be false), it was your testimony that condemned him. How you must have hated him! Or did you testify against him in order to avoid being executed yourself? In either case, you were heartless and selfish.

"But I am certain the king would want you not to worry over him unduly. He would not want you to be in anguish, but to be distracted by a pleasant river journey, among friends."

I certainly did not consider Lady Rochford a friend. But perhaps she could be useful to me.

"And are you familiar with this vessel? If I were to go downriver to Greenwich, and even beyond, could you take charge of the servants and make certain everything would go smoothly?"

"Yes, Your Highness." She smiled an oily smile, showing her darkened teeth.

"Very well then. We will leave tomorrow."

Apart from the servants and bargemen, only Joan and Tom and Lady Rochford came with me on our excursion. We did not go directly to Greenwich, but moored wherever we chose along the way, taking on fresh provisions, stopping when the tides were strong or the skies poured down rain—most welcome rain, after the long drought.

Tom and I reveled in being together; we had not been able to enjoy one another without fear of discovery since our weeks in Calais. We did not have to hide our feelings from Joan, for she knew of our love, I had confided in her. And as for Lady Rochford, she seemed to understand without being told that Tom and I were eager to be together. To the bargemen and servants, Tom was nothing more or less than the king's privy chamber gentleman, sent on the barge in order to ensure the safety and wellbeing of the queen. At least I hoped that that was what they assumed.

When we reached Greenwich we did not stop there, going on as far as we could downriver until the currents and tides were too strong, then we turned back and the oarsmen rowed us upriver, by slow stages, all the way to Hampton Court. A small private chamber in the center of the vessel enclosed us each night, and I found myself wishing we could spend every night there, so happy were our hours in the small bed, lying in each other's arms.

To recall those nights fills me with joy even now, remembering how Tom held me, covered me with kisses, whispered soft words in my ear. He was a passionate lover, giving himself up heart and soul to sharing his body with me. But he was playful as well, we snuggled and snuffled like happy children even as we became aroused and amorous. He always helped me to lay aside my dark thoughts and worries. And he told me I did the same for him. We lost ourselves in each other, as lovers, and we shared ourselves, as loving friends. My dearest, dearest Tom, how precious you were to me then!

But all too soon we were informed that the king's swollen leg was improving, and that he was asking for me. The barge took us back to Whitehall, and I had to hurry ashore.

In the Advent season it seemed to me that, far from acting like a man who had just had a brush with mortality, my husband sprang back to life and health quickly and with more vigor than in the past. He went riding each morning, ignoring the frost that hung from the eaves and the wintry wind. He called for the musicians to play after supper each night and tried, for the first time since our wedding, to dance—though he tired quickly and his leg began to throb and he soon had to sit down again.

He was full of plans for the Christmas festivities. He designed a pageant car and wrote a masque he called "The Seven Virtues" for me and my ladies to perform in. I was cast as Fruitfulness, Malyn as Graciousness, Joan as Truth, Charyn as Honor, Alice as Fidelity, Catherine Tylney as Generosity and—when another of my maids of honor fell ill, Lady Rochford took her place as Mercy.

The seven of us, clad in shining garments of cloth of gold, took our places on an artificial mountain glittering as if sprinkled with diamonds. We each recited verses—written by the king—in praise of our particular quality, then descended to dance with seven gentlemen representing Chivalry, Nobility, Integrity, Courage, Steadfastness, Loyalty and Strength. The pageant, though it was a great deal like others I had witnessed, was very well received, and my husband, as its author, bowed again and again to his cheering courtiers.

Every day he gave me new gifts: a stunning necklace of twenty-seven matched diamonds interwoven with clusters of rubies, a diamond and ruby brooch said to be worth a fortune, a jeweled muffler with sables, sewn with thirty-eight large rubies and hundreds of smaller stones. The muffler, he said, was to replace the one he had given to me and I had given to Anna, on the day he first glimpsed her.

"She was never meant to have it," he said, chiding me. "It was for you."

But my husband's overflowing generosity did not stop there. For in that Advent season he made over to me all the castles and manors that had belonged to Queen Jane—a legacy beyond price—and in addition, all of the late Lord Cromwell's lands, and others besides.

To say that I was now mistress of a large fortune would be a foolish understatement; with those gifts my husband made me a very wealthy woman, one of the wealthiest in the land, I was told by envious officers in my household. I never saw a reckoning of value of the properties that became mine, but I am certain that, had I seen such a reckoning, I would have been astonished.

But the king's most significant gift to me by far was a marvelous bed, a bed like no other I had ever seen or even imagined. It was made so cleverly that it appeared to be crafted entirely of pearl, and it glowed softly, as if giving off a shadowy iridescent light.

Master Denny told me in confidence that my husband had brought a master artisan all the way from Paris to work on the remarkable creation, and that he had been working in secret for months to ensure that my bed would be finished by Christmas.

Never had the king been so lavish in his gifts to me—and never, gossip said, had I been less worthy of his generosity. Dr. Chambers, it seemed, had been indiscreet; in order to prevent people from suspecting that my husband might be incapable of fathering a child, the physician had been saying quite openly that I was barren. There were titters from the crowd when I portrayed Fruitfulness in the masque of "The Seven Virtues," and now I realized why. The irony of a barren woman representing Fruitfulness! No wonder they laughed.

I did my best to brazen out the humiliation of it, glaring at those who chortled and ridiculed me, holding my head erect and acting as if I was indifferent to all the unkind gossip. But inwardly my vanity was wounded, and I was afraid. For when the king presented me with the beautiful pearl bed, he took me into another chamber fitted out as a nursery, with exquisite tapestries on the walls and a cupboard full of lace-trimmed infant clothing and—at the center of the room—a glowing pearl cradle.

"For our son," the king said pleasantly, "who I have no doubt will arrive in the new year." His words were not menacing, but I was left in no doubt as to their underlying meaning. I was expected to fulfill my task. My urgent, primary, one and only task. And if I did not, well, who could say what fate awaited me?

On New Year's Day we had a surprise. Lady Anna, the king's beloved sister, as she was officially known, came in her cloth-of-gold-covered carriage from Richmond to visit us.

She brought only one maidservant with her, and a tall, lanky footman who seemed to anticipate her every need. He was instantly in place to help her down from her carriage. He dogged her footsteps. He gave orders to the carriage driver and to our grooms—rather presumptuously, I thought. And once Anna had been welcomed and brought into my suite, he stayed near her, always within reach, watching for her least need or request.

I was pleasantly surprised at the change I saw in Anna. She was softer, more flatteringly dressed than in the past in a peach-colored gown, and she had exchanged the spaniel-eared Clevan headdress for a face-framing French hood of the kind I favored. She looked, I realized, more English. And why not? She had been in England for a year, and by all accounts was well regarded by the country folk who lived near her palace. When I first saw her in Cleves she had been uncharitable, now, however, she chattered away to us about the alms she gave daily to the beggars and poor discharged soldiers who came to her gate.

It was still true that she could not by any means be called pretty—Charyn would have been merciless in appraising her few charms and reducing them to cinders. Nor was she appealingly feminine. She was too tall and ungainly, her shoulders too broad, her gait too striding, and worst of all, her complexion had not improved. But she no longer pursed her lips in disapproval, or clenched her face. She seemed more open, more ready to be herself. It was a welcome change.

And yet, as I soon realized, she had not come on a sociable visit. She had come to gloat.

"What then, Catherine! No babies yet?" she trilled. Her English pronunciation had improved, though her accent was still strong.

"What has happened! Does the king decide he does not like you after all? My dear mama said he would grow tired of you. Perhaps he goes to search for a different wife!" She laughed at her own joke. "Perhaps he goes to Cleves to look for one!"

"We have not yet been blessed with children, Anna," I said evenly. "They will come when the Lord sends them." I turned the conversation to the weather, the state of the roads, the recent Christmas festivities and our masque. But Anna seemed bored by all these topics.

"Do you still have your monkey?" she wanted to know.

"Yes, Jonah is well and flourishing."

Anna tittered. "Perhaps he will be your only son. That monkey!"

The king joined us, leaning on his cane as he came into the room. He was overly polite, as if he felt he had to compensate Anna for an injury done her. And indeed that was precisely the case: he had injured her. He had changed the entire course of her life by his rejection of her. But looking at her as she had become after living among us for a year, I could only conclude that the change had been for the better.

"What about a game of cent?" he said, and at once Anna's face brightened. I remembered how she liked to play cards, how engrossed she became in the petty losses and victories of the game. How she loved risk, and found it at the card table.

We played on into the afternoon, while Anna's maidservant sat inconspicuously in a corner and her footman hovered behind her bench. I had the satisfaction of winning—a satisfaction I would not have sought had Anna not made such cutting remarks about our lack of a child. Anna was miserable. King Henry offered to give her the money to pay what she owed to me, a small sum which she accepted gratefully. Then she said, "I have heard you have a pearl bed. I want to see this."

I saw no reason not to show off my beautiful bed, and, after the king excused himself and kissed Anna's hand, I led her into my bedchamber. There stood the beautiful symbol of our union, glowing in the wan fading sunshine of late afternoon. Anna went up to the bed and ran her hand along its surface. She moved her head from side to side, watching the play of faint iridescence.

"Such a bed to make deep love in," she said. "To make babies in. I am sorry you do not do this."

She was not sorry at all, her mouth turned up at the corners. She looked at me out of the corner of her eye, watching for my reaction. But I only jingled the coins in the pocket of my gown. My winnings from the card games. I smiled back at her, and said nothing.

A few days later Anna's footman asked to see me. My chamberlain brought him to me, giving me a quizzical look as if to say, who is this and what can he want?

I looked him up and down. He was quite tall, and gangly, very thin with long dangling arms and legs. He wore Anna's livery but his bony wrists protruded from the sleeves. His boots were scuffed and in need of a polish. His coarse black hair hung loose to his collar, falling over his forehead into his eyes. He did not meet my gaze, but looked down, shamefaced—or was his manner furtive? I couldn't tell.

"Who are you, boy?" the chamberlain asked. The footman handed him a folded paper.

"For you, Your Highness," my chamberlain said, handing me the note. I unfolded it and read.

To her gracious Majesty Queen Catherine,

Greetings to Your Majesty from my palace at Richmond and may all the blessings of Providence be yours. I hope you will look kindly on my former footman Englebert who is seeking a position in your royal household. He is without employment and I cannot afford to add him to my already crowded household. I have too many servants from Cleves. They keep coming to me looking for places and I cannot refuse them. They are fleeing the soldiers of the Emperor who are attacking us.

I would be grateful if you could find a place for Englebert who is a devoted and excellent servant. Please do this as a favor to me,

Wishing Your Majesty every blessing,
Anna, beloved sister of King Henry

"So, you wish to join my household," I said to the footman, who nodded vigorously. "Do you speak English?" I could not remember whether he had spoken English or Clevan when at our court.

He nodded again.

"How well?"

He shrugged.

A taciturn footman is not at all a bad thing, I tend to think, but this man seemed mute.

"Speak to me then!"

"Your Majesty," Englebert said in flawless English, bowing low, "I am at your service. If you take me on, I shall endeavor to give you satisfaction in all things."

TWELVE

THAT winter I awoke each morning in the great pearl bed, with my husband already up and dressed and gone. He continued to be a font of energy, riding, hawking, meeting with his councilors and with a new group of builders who he set to work enlarging Hampton Court and building a new palace, St. James's, where the leper hospital used to be.

His list of new constructions was a long one. He ordered a new closet for Windsor Castle, new kitchens for Anna at Richmond—she had begged for these—a new gallery at Eltham and another at Whitehall, a new tiltyard at Whitehall and a vast new enclosed tennis court as well, and new leads for all the palace roofs. He rubbed his hands together with glee when telling me all that his laborers were doing, and all that he meant to have done in future. When the royal stables burned to the ground—a source of great sorrow to my husband, who loved his horses—he built vast new stables where the royal mews had been, with barns to hold the horses' fodder and housing for the grooms and stable boys.

So eager was the king to have these works completed that he ordered the laborers to stay at their tasks day and night, working by candlelight in the sunless hours. He took great pleasure in inspecting the progress of his undertakings, hiring more and more designers and craftsmen and visiting the work sites again and again, often taking friends and officials with him and sometimes combining a tour of inspection with the pleasures of banqueting and even hunting, when the weather was not too foul.

I expected to be taken along on these excursions, but he did not invite me, and when I asked to be included he made excuses for leaving me behind.

"You must not tire yourself, sweetheart," he said, or "I would not want you to take cold." I was sure he was hoping that I would soon conceive a child, if I had not done so already, and wanted me to stay quietly indoors, without exerting myself or exposing myself to the outdoor air, in order to ensure that I would not lose the babe in my womb.

When word reached him that a huge double cannon he had ordered from a German foundry had finally arrived, he celebrated by taking a number of ladies of the court to see the monstrous thing as it was brought ashore. As usual I was not included in the party, but I heard from Master Denny how when the king first saw the ordnance he cried, "Oh! I like it marvelous well! I shall put it in my tower at Nonsuch!" and all the ladies clapped and cheered. He called for wine and comfits to celebrate, and had his gunners load and fire the great cannon until all the ladies were nearly deaf from the explosions.

One lady in the party drew particular attention: Anna. I did not know whether my husband had invited her or whether she had simply discovered that he was going to the docks to see the new cannon and decided to join the group, confident that she would be welcome. But her presence led, inevitably, to gossip. It was whispered that my husband might be having second thoughts about Anna, wondering whether he might have been too hasty in declaring their marriage null. Dr. Chambers's opinion about my being barren was still lively conversation, I was sure, while no physician had ever ventured such an opinion about Anna.

Even within my own household I was beginning to hear disloyal voices. Charyn, appointed to be among my ladies in waiting—and very mortified to find herself in such a subservient position to me, the girl she had once called an inferior whelp—approached me one day.

"Are you to have no coronation then, Catherine?" she asked. "You have been the king's wife now for many months. Why is it he has not had you crowned queen?"

"I imagine he will order it, when he thinks the time is right," I said, trying to keep my voice mild—and trying not to look at Charyn's waist, which was expanding. She had married Lord Morley's son and was expecting a child in the spring.

"I don't believe coronation robes have been ordered," Charyn went on. "But then, it may be that the king is waiting until you have had your first child."

Others among my ladies who were strict Protestants whispered that I was lax in my religious observance and far from sober enough in my conduct to be queen. My lightness of spirit, my joking manner were held against me, as signs of the devil at work in me. I was unworthy to be the mother of the next king, they told one another (as Joan and Lady Rochford and others were quick to inform me).

I was advised to purge my household of such critics, but I did not, fearing that anyone I sent away might spread much worse gossip about me from a desire for revenge.

I did tire of hearing about my husband's excursions in the company of ladies, however—excursions which always excluded me. I became vexed and worried when I discovered that among the ladies he invited was Madge Shelton, a beautiful, dimpled woman who had been his mistress in the past, when his marriage to my cousin Anne had been troubled and the court was full of gossip— as it was now—about how he might be thinking about ridding himself of Anne and marrying someone else.

The next time he organized a party of ladies to go aboard his flagship the *Great Harry*, with a promised banquet to follow on shipboard, I resolved to be a part of the festivities. I ordered my barge to be made ready, and when my husband and his many lady guests arrived at the river pier, I was already aboard my barge and the oarsmen were ready to row.

I had my own group of women supporters on board with me: Joan and Malyn, Lady Rochford and Catherine Tylney and some others I felt I could trust to be staunchly loyal to me. The number, I am sorry to say, was disconcertingly small.

My plan was to follow the immense flagship when she set sail. I knew she would not travel far, only a short distance past the lower docks and on downriver. I consulted my pilot concerning the tides and calculated that the barge could keep pace with the flagship for at least a few miles, depending on the strength of the winds.

The *Great Harry* set forth, and my barge followed. From both vessels came the faint gabble and murmur of female voices carried on the breeze. Then I heard a loud male voice.

"Aha! Catherine! A race! A race!"

It was my husband, waving and challenging us to a contest. Knowing it would be futile, I nevertheless spurred my oarsmen on, while shouts and yells went back and forth between the two vessels. We kept pace for as long as we could, but before long the wind rose, favoring the flagship—which was in any case much faster than my poky barge—and we were left far behind. But at least I had made an effort, and my oarsmen cheered, making my spirits soar. My loyal women and my oarsmen—and, I was sure, a few of my guardsmen as well—were on my side. They admired my daring, my boldness. I felt certain of it. I saw how they looked at me, smiling and nodding, when I disembarked. I knew.

Just at that time the court seemed at loose ends, lacking in direction and—despite the king's strong presence—lacking leadership. Quarrels erupted, proud words were spoken in anger, leading to blows. Grudges were held, threats made. Factions formed, only to dissolve suddenly. It was as if the courtiers were running here and there, back and forth, now taking momentary pleasure in adorning themselves with the latest fads in gowns and doublets, now abandoning them, now championing certain favorites, now casting them aside. Old wounds festered, new wounds were created—and in the midst of it all, the king seemed to dart from one building site to another, elusive, his motives unreadable.

He announced that it was time for me to make my first official entry into London as queen, though what prompted him I could not tell. I would not be part of a procession through the streets, but instead would travel through the town by river, aboard the king's barge, with my husband at my side, in all our finery. There would be a cannonade from the Tower, the king told me, and all along the riverside, colorful displays of flags and painted ensigns and mottoes would proclaim my welcome.

The City guilds were alerted, and the citizens were given an incentive to turn out to acclaim me; they were told that wine would pour from all the fountains and conduits and that food in abundance would be provided on the day of the royal entry.

The day arrived, overcast and with a hint of rain in the air. We went aboard the barge and took our places, standing in the bow where we would be seen to greatest advantage. The king's barge was much larger and more grand than mine, splendidly gilded and decorated and rowed by seventy-five strapping oarsmen. Pennants flew from every corner of the vessel's canopy, and silken streamers floated in the rather cool spring air. I wore a gown of glimmering silver embroidered with clusters of pearls, and my neck, wrists and fingers sparkled with gems. The king looked at me approvingly as we began our journey, as if to say, yes, you'll do. But he did not take my hand, or make me laugh, and his manner, though regal, was subdued.

The barge shot London Bridge and then was joined by dozens of other brightly decorated barges, with the mayor and livery companies aboard. Hundreds of smaller boats carrying Londoners of all ranks crowded around our barge, some with choristers serenading us, some with musicians, others with well-wishers who threw flowers into our vessel and shouted words of welcome.

Suddenly the Tower guns began to boom forth, a deafening sound that went on and on, getting louder the farther downriver we went.

"Is that your double cannon I hear?" I asked my husband, but he only gave me a quick smile and then turned away, distracted. For it was just then that we began to hear the clamorous voices shouting insults.

"Bitch! We will have none other than Queen Anna!"

"Devil's harlot! Bring back our rightful queen!"

To my horror, someone in a small boat threw an object into our barge that landed at my feet. It was a dead rat.

The insulting cries continued, while others shouted "Good Queen Catherine" and "Queen Catherine forever!"

Meanwhile more things were thrown at us—or rather at me—

and I shrieked when a pile of bloody entrails nearly struck me, splattering filth on my gown.

King Henry quickly pulled me under the barge's canopy and shielded me, shouting orders to the guardsmen to "attack the filthy churls" with their pikes.

"Seize them! Take them to the Tower!" he ordered, though the harassers were too quick and too nimble. They turned their small boats swiftly and rowed away, and there was no catching them.

Servants hurried to remove the offending things flung onto the deck of our barge—not only entrails but bloody cloths, fish scales and bones, the head of a cat. I covered my eyes. I didn't want to see any more.

"By all the saints! I have a woeful people to govern! It was an unlucky day when I was crowned! But I will chasten them, I will chasten them until they beg for mercy! I will make them suffer!"

It was a full hour before my husband was able to master his anger, and even longer before he stopped sputtering curses and threats and managed to eat his supper. We returned to the palace, having received the ceremonial welcome from the Lord Mayor and the City guilds. There were no more insulting words or flung objects, though for the remainder of our barge journey I remained alert to insolent outcries and kept looking around me, watching for rats and offal.

I was badly shaken by the incident on the river. I could not eat at all, and had to drink a good deal of calming poppy broth before I could go to bed and try—in vain—to sleep. I kept thinking about what Charyn had said weeks earlier, asking me if I was to have no coronation. I thought of the empty pearl cradle, of the harsh judgments of the strict Protestants who condemned me for lacking in sober conduct. I thought of the beautiful Madge Shelton, sailing away aboard the *Great Harry* with my husband, and of the somewhat improved Anna—improved in appearance but not in manner. Was she to dog my footsteps with her gloating and her unkind teasing banter?

Finally, toward morning, I managed to fall into an uneasy drowse, with the great bulk of my snoring husband by my side.

It was to be the last night we slept side by side for many days.

The day after my official welcome into the capital my husband gave orders to his privy chamber gentlemen that the door of his bedchamber was to be closed to me. And kept closed until he told them otherwise.

Tom brought me the news.

"He is irked," Tom told me. "You know his quicksilver moods, full of happiness and generosity one moment and thundering with anger the next."

"But why?"

Tom shook his head. "None of us knows why. He is uneasy in his mind. So many things trouble him. His leg hurts. The northerners are rebelling again. His favorite horse is spavined. He imagines that one of the yeomen of the bedchamber found a dagger hidden in his bed. He was wrong, to be sure. It was no dagger, but only a short stave, though what it was doing in his bed I cannot imagine."

"He is angry with me for seeming to be barren. Though he is surely the one who deserves the blame."

We were silent for a time. "Can nothing be done?" Tom asked.

"Joan has given me every remedy she knows of to administer to the king. Nothing seems to help him. Dr. Chambers blames me for the problem, as everyone knows. I cannot ask him for help."

Tom was thoughtful for a moment. "It is said Queen Jane had a relic, a tear of the holy Virgin, that she wore around her waist. It brought her her child."

216

"What became of the relic?"

"No one knows. Perhaps it was buried with her. Or perhaps she gave it to Archbishop Cranmer when he blessed her as she lay dying. She was a kind woman. She would have wanted others to have what had been precious to her. Though they say she was quite mad in her last days, with her fever."

Tom took my hand and pulled me into a corner of the staircase, after listening for footsteps. No one was near. He kissed me and held me close, until we heard someone coming up the stairs.

"I will do my best to find out what became of the relic," he whispered as he left me. "Think of me, dearest. And remember what I said about the privy chamber."

The surgeons were at work, doing their best to heal my ailing husband. Once again his leg had flared up (how tedious these repeated inflammations had become to me!), and Dr. Chambers and Dr. Butts had called in half a dozen surgeons to minister to him. Knowing how he disliked having me see him when in agony and danger from his inflamed sore, I wanted to believe that the king had barred his bedchamber door to me because of his illness. Yet I knew that his order to me to stay away had come before he fell ill, several days before. So he was, as I suspected, angry with me. Punishing me, knowing full well that by barring me from his presence he was frightening me as well.

The surgeons were skillful, Tom told me. They lanced the pus-filled sores and probed them with hot irons to counteract the infections. They burned away the inflamed flesh and drained blood from a nearby vein and sewed up the wounds their painful ministrations left behind.

"They set no store at all by his ointment with the powdered pearls," Tom told me. "They explained to him that it had made his leg much worse. You can imagine how he liked being told that! They brought leeches to suck out the poisons and he yelped with fright at the very sight of them, though I do think that, of all the remedies, the leeches help the most."

Once again, in a grotesque way, our hopes were raised, for even the surgeons, Tom said, were shaking their heads and admitting to one another in low tones that the king could not live. Soon, I hoped, my brief uncomfortable time as queen consort would be over, and I could retire from court and, after perhaps a year of mourning, marry Tom.

But my husband, in fear of his life, sent to the French court for an apothecary he had heard of who was said to work wonders. We all awaited the arrival of this remarkable man, who was known only as S, with a great deal of interest. Intriguing newcomers were always welcome in any case, but in this instance, the mysterious S was said to be bringing with him a wonder-working remedy that would make the king well. Indeed he had the reputation of being able not only to restore health but to make the patient so strong and healthy that he or she would never be ill again.

By the time S made his appearance, the king was in a very serious state indeed, fighting for breath, crying out in pain—piteous cries, Tom said, like a wounded animal—and so swollen and bloated he was all but unrecognizable. Tom told me how the Frenchman wasted no time in bringing forth from a velvet chest a golden vessel filled with the powerful medicine. He called it the mithridate, and said that it was a secret mixture of some seventy ingredients, including dried mummy and powdered snails, poppy juice and a piece of the flesh of a hanged man. It was an ancient remedy that had been used for centuries. Apothecaries had kept it secret since the time of the Roman emperors.

It was as if the entire court held its breath, waiting to see whether the mithridate would restore the king to health. Hours passed—and then I heard the sound of running feet in the corridor outside my apartments. A buzz of voices, muffled cries, and then the word was passed to me: the king had not died, but was breathing a little more easily. By evening he was said to be regaining a little of his strength, and on through the night there were more bits of news coming from the royal privy chamber, all of it positive.

Positive, that is, for the king. Negative for Tom and me. I told my chamberers that the tears I shed were tears of relief, of joy. But in truth I was sadly disappointed, even though I knew a relapse was always possible, no matter how amazing the French apothecary was, or how remarkable his potion.

I was to be crowned, after all. My husband had announced it, the entire court had been informed and soon, very soon, the heralds would proclaim the forthcoming coronation in towns large and small throughout the land.

I, Catherine Howard, queen consort, would receive the venerable crown from the hands of Archbishop Cranmer, amid the solemnity of Westminster, with all the peers of the realm in attendance.

The king had commanded it, and so it would be carried out, at Whitsuntide, on the second day of June.

"But surely not," Grandma Agnes cautioned me, rushing to my bedchamber as soon as she heard the news, and barely remembering to curtsey. "Not at Whitsun. It would be bad luck. Your cousin Anne was crowned at Whitsun, and nothing but ill fortune followed."

"Perhaps my good fortune will cancel out her misfortunes."

"It would take more good fortune than any one woman could have in a lifetime to cancel Anne's bad luck," she said vehemently. "Besides, whatever you do reflects on us all. The Howard name must be honored in all things, especially now that we have come into our own. Most of the royal offices are held by our family now."

"Thanks to me," I said bluntly.

"Thanks to your dead mother, you mean. You are only her shadow, her echo in the king's mind."

"And heart."

Grandma Agnes shook her head. "Has he a heart? If so, it is a shrunken, withered thing." I thought this an odd sentiment, coming from my grandmother, the woman who had carried a whip when chastising us at Horsham and Lambeth. The woman who had struck me and starved me.

I dismissed her, much to her displeasure, and called for the tailor Master Spiershon and his seamstresses. I required new gowns and robes for my coronation, and they were being sewn and fitted, which took a good deal of my time.

The king's decision to order my coronation had come suddenly, as had so many other events that spring. While recovering from his illness, he once again allowed me into his privy chamber, and the first time he saw me, he seemed delighted. As it happened, I was wearing a bodice of thick double Milanese velvet, which made me look heavier than I was, and my stomacher was loose—purely for comfort's sake. Also I wore at my waist the relic Tom had found for me, the small silver reliquary with the tear of the Virgin, hanging from a silver chain.

"Catherine! Sweetheart! How happy you have made me this day!"

I realized at once that he imagined, from my bulk and loose stomacher, that I was carrying a child—and I decided immediately not to correct him. It was not impossible, after all, merely unlikely. He had not entirely stopped trying to make love to me, right up until his decision to bar me from his privy chamber and the long frightening week of his illness.

He asked about the reliquary hanging at my waist, and I told him it had belonged to Queen Jane, and that it had brought her the good fortune of giving birth to Prince Edward.

"Yes! Of course," he cried. "Now it has brought you—that is, it has brought us—good fortune as well. Ah, Catherine, I have been waiting for this day! And now we must have you crowned."

The chosen day of my coronation, June the second, was only weeks away and there was a great deal to do in the meantime. I had to have a splendid gown for my procession through the streets of the capital, when I would be acclaimed by the people, a white gown for my entry into the Tower, robes of purple velvet for my entry into Westminster on coronation day, a magnificent gown for the coronation feast—not to mention new petticoats and underclothes. My coronation regalia and jewels had to be brought from the Jewel House in the Tower, not only the venerable crown but the jeweled circlet I would wear when entering the Tower and the heavy scepter I would carry, and the royal heirlooms the king wanted me to wear, including his mother's necklaces and his grandmother's long loop of pearls.

I was quite overwhelmed by all that I had to learn and all that there was to do. The coronation ritual was long and had many parts. I had to memorize where to go and what to do in each long section of the ceremony, as there would be no one to prompt me or guide me on the coronation day itself. I kept being interrupted by the women of my chamber, who, like me, had to have new gowns and who were to take part in the coronation itself. They fussed about their gowns, and worried over their assigned tasks and roles. Charyn demanded that I give her precedence over the others, and there was much squabbling and bickering.

But as it turned out, the commotion in my apartments was as nothing compared to the disputes that arose among the peers. My Howard relations demanded that they be given the premier roles in the coronation ceremony—which caused all the others to complain and make demands of their own, and to threaten not to participate at all. Some were bold enough to say that I was unworthy to be queen. Tom repeated some of the harsh words he overheard when the fractious nobles were quarreling among themselves.

"This king changes wives as often as other men change their hose and doublet," Lord Morley said. "Why should we take part in a solemnity that will not endure above a year?"

"We did not crown the last one," Lord Abergavenny remarked with a sniff. "Why should we crown this one?"

Even those who were eager to take part in the ceremony were disgruntled over the way it was to be carried out, and fought with one another over who had the privilege of supporting my right hand when I carried the scepter, and who would be given the honor of carrying my crown.

The northern lords were in revolt, and refused to take part in the coronation at all. On hearing this my husband, fed up with all the petty wrangling, shouted that he was surrounded by jackals and stomped off, limping, to inspect his new tiltyard.

In the end he lost patience with the entire undertaking, convinced as he became that the choice of Whitsun was indeed inviting bad luck, because Queen Anne had been crowned then. His master of the works brought news that repairs were needed at Westminster and in the White Tower, and that they could not possibly be completed by the second of June. But what weighed on him most, I suspect, was his growing fear that the Londoners would not rejoice when my open litter passed through the narrow streets on the day of my coronation procession. Like the insolent few who had harassed us when the royal barge passed along the river, there would be Londoners who would cry out insults, throw offal, and perhaps even attack me.

He confided his worries to me as we lay together in the ample pearl bed.

"I fear the crowds might agitate you too much, sweetheart, especially now, when you are in a delicate state. Who knows what frightening things they might do?"

"I am told that the Londoners mocked Queen Anne when she rode through the streets in her litter, and called out insults. And she was carrying her child at the time." It was true. My cousin Anne had been crowned when she was pregnant with her one and only surviving child, the Princess Elizabeth.

"They did—and she bore it well enough. She was one who always gave as good as she got. But look what happened! She did not have a son, only a daughter!"

The coronation was cancelled, and the royal household was told to prepare for a great summer progress to the north country, where the king hoped to meet with King James of Scotland and reassert his power and authority over the rebels once and for all.

Uncle William was about to leave us. The king was sending him to the French court, to be his ambassador there. It was time, my husband thought, to strengthen old alliances that were tottering and build new ones. Sending the queen's uncle was a sign of special favor.

Before Uncle William left he came to see me. He embraced me and kissed the top of my head. We sat together in a window embrasure.

My uncle looked older than when I had seen him last. His kind face was creased and lined, his grey hair sparse. He was still rosy-cheeked and benign, but there were pouches under his eyes and they were a more faded blue than in the past.

"What's this I hear? There is to be no coronation after all?"

I shook my head. "It would not have been a happy occasion, uncle. Half the peers were in revolt and the other half were fighting over who had the right to hold the train of my gown."

He smiled. "I thought it was the queen's ladies who always held the train."

"They were fighting too."

"Do you think it may happen in the fall? Your coronation, I mean."

"I don't know. The king is so changeable, no one can say what he will do from one minute to the next."

"It was ever thus with monarchs, so they say." He smiled again. "When is the baby coming?"

I looked at him, and could not hide the truth. I shook my head, trusting that I would not have to say the words, to confess that I was now certain I was not pregnant. My monthly flux had come as usual.

"But he believes—"

"I know."

He sighed and sat back against the cushions. "Ah Catherine, you are indeed in trouble. Your uncle Thomas is feeling the weight of the king's expectations. You have already had one miscarriage, so the court believes. Should this pregnancy not come to fruition—"

"I know. My husband's wrath would fall on Uncle Thomas, for being the one who brought me to court, put me in the way of his notice. He is so quick to blame! And then to punish."

All at once Uncle William sat upright, his face alert. "You must seize the moment, Catherine. You must! Heed what I say, for you must be serious about this, if about nothing else."

He reached over and took my small face in his two large hands.

"You *must* produce a child. If it cannot be the king's child, then let it be someone else's. What about your beloved, Tom Culpeper?

He has the king's high coloring, he is tall, though not as strong as our sovereign. Still, Tom's son could pass as the king's son. Tell me, Catherine, would Tom be willing to have a child with you, and tell the world it was the king's son?"

"We have talked about it. We have wondered what would happen if—"

"But you have never had to find out. Now, Lord willing, you need to hope for a desirable outcome. Otherwise . . ." He did not need to say what he was thinking, what we were both thinking.

"But you and Tom must be aware of the high risk you would be taking. If you were to be found out, if the king discovers that you are lovers, he will show you no mercy. And there would be no mercy for your child either, an unwanted bastard, proof of the queen's faithlessness—" He shook his head. "But if you go on as you are, your future is equally uncertain. The king believes you to be pregnant now. The child he believes you are carrying must be born. You cannot risk a second miscarriage, or he will believe what Dr. Chambers is saying, that you cannot bear a living child."

Now it was my turn to sigh. "Oh, Uncle William, if only I could go with you to France!"

"You will, one day, my dear. When you have done your duty and given the king children, children he has no doubt are his own. Think on that, look forward to the best outcome."

"Dear Uncle William."

We sat together quietly for a time, each thinking our own thoughts.

"I did not imagine, when you married the king, that you would ever have to risk his disapproval. I thought that his love for your mother would protect you, no matter what."

I got to my feet and looked out at the gardens, the fruit trees in bloom, the beds of pink and purple and blue flowers, the deep green lawns where gardeners were laboring in the hot sun. All the beauties of the spring were within my reach, indeed at my command, as queen. Yet I was married to an aging man who could no longer bring forth fruit, and whose heart, as Grandma Agnes said, was as withered as the weeds the gardeners were uprooting.

"I doubt whether anyone is safe from him. He grows more moody and irascible by the day, he seems almost to take pleasure in destroying people. Though at times he can show gentleness— toward his horses, for instance. I cannot solve the riddle of his mind."

"It is the riddle of his soul, Catherine. A dark place, the king's soul."

"Only a few days ago," I confided, "two archers of the royal guard were brought before him, accused of robbing his treasury. They were Uncle Thomas's men, who had been loyal to him for years. They were innocent of robbery, I'm sure of it. Their accusers were some of the late Lord Cromwell's men, still trying to take vengeance on the Howards for having opposed their master. I spoke up for them, but I could see by the glare in my husband's eyes that he had already made up his mind to have their blood. Both men were tortured and killed, cruelly and wrongfully."

"And you took a risk in defending them. It was a risk you ought not to have taken. You must learn prudence. Remember the old saying, 'Around the throne, thunder rolls.'"

I looked at my dear uncle. He was in earnest. I trusted him to give sound advice. But I felt myself trembling.

"You must do as I say, Catherine. This is a risk you must take. With Tom, if he will, or with another. Any man with fair hair and blue eyes, tall and strong. And do not delay! There must be a child in the pearl cradle by the first snowfall. If there is not, I cannot answer for your safety—or the succession!"

What he was urging me to do clearly involved grave risk. Yet what would happen if winter came, and the pearl cradle was still empty?

Would I end my days like my husband's discarded fourth wife Anna, reduced to being, like her, a beloved sister, sent away to a palace of my own, with my marriage declared null? Would I ever see Tom again?

My trembling increased as another, far graver thought struck me. What if I proved to be barren, just as Dr. Chambers said. Would the king's thunder roll, mighty and terrible, and would no place ever be safe for me again?

THIRTEEN

It was the largest traveling court anyone among the servants could ever remember, the vast assemblage of thousands that prepared to go northward with the king in that June of 1541.

At least five thousand horses were seized from the stables in and around the capital. Hundreds of carts were brought together in the palace courtyards and outbuildings to hold folding tents, provisions, chests of clothing and hangings and carpets, plate and linens, candles and lanterns—everything to create not only comfort but elegance while on our journey. For no town could hold us all, not while there were so many of us. The large moving court would take shelter in temporary structures, set up each evening and dismantled each morning in a flurry of activity. We were a moving town of tents.

Because the men of the northern shires had been in a state of disorder and resistance for months, with open revolt in some places and lawlessness nearly everywhere, we had to take armed knights and archers, halberdiers and pikemen and guardsmen, a thousand soldiers in all, along with their mounts and draft horses and chests of arms. The cannon went northward by ship, but the huge warhorses, twice the size of my mare and larger even than the horses in the tiltyard, required many carts just to carry their fodder and trappings, and the entire armed force had its drummers and trumpeters and heralds, its banner-carriers and grooms, cooks and farriers and laundresses and camp-followers whose nightly activities no one could ignore.

But what made this royal progress unlike any other was that my husband had determined to send not one but two traveling groups north: our horde many thousands strong, and a second set of laborers and servants and carts, horses and guards bound directly for York. These York-bound journeyers were to prepare what the king called a great lodging, a temporary royal residence where he would meet his young nephew James V of Scotland.

The king talked on and on about this meeting, how it would be the first of its kind ever, the kings of England and Scotland meeting in concord instead of in battle. How he looked forward to conversing with his nephew, and to embracing and conversing with his sister Margaret, James's mother, whom he had not seen in twenty-five years.

"Much can be accomplished," he told me. "We can come to an understanding. We can strengthen our family bonds." I knew that my husband was taking a chest of gold coins to present to his sister, who claimed she never had enough money and had even tried to flee the country in order to have an easier and more comfortable life, free of responsibility.

"She is nearly fifty-two years old," Henry said. "She needs her warm fire and her cushions. Perhaps James will let me bring her back south with me, to live in London. I think she would like that.

"Once before I arranged a meeting with a fellow-monarch," the king mused aloud. "Many years ago, when I was young and strong. A champion in the tiltyard."

"And the most handsome king in Christendom," I put in, smiling.

"More handsome than my brother-monarch King Francis, that was certain. Everyone said so. Though he had a devilish look about him, and the women liked him. We met in terrible weather, near the French coast. People called it the Field of Cloth of Gold for all the glitter and splendor of it. I had a tent all lined with gold. Quite magnificent. And I won all the prizes of arms.

"King Francis is an old man now, but we still compete. Oh, yes. Now we compete for the loyalty of other rulers, like my nephew. Ah! What a grand thing it would be if the three of us, myself and nephew James and old King Francis, could all meet at York! I could still beat the old man in the tiltyard. I'm sure I could!"

I indulged him, I always laughed at his lighthearted joking, whether it amused me or not. I was determined not to lose his favor again, never again to find myself shut out of his privy chamber. I did not want to risk his anger or even his mildest irritation. I needed to keep up the illusion that we were closer than ever, bound together by our hope for a son. And there were times when he was very affectionate toward me, kissing my cheek, patting me on the arm and hand, even patting my belly and humming to the baby he was sure I was carrying. He joked with the guardsmen and privy chamber gentlemen about how lusty I was, and how he enjoyed having me beside him in the pearl bed.

On the eve of our progress, it seemed to all at court that whatever had divided us had been put behind us, and that we would look forward to the birth of our child united in married happiness.

•   •   •

At last the immense train of horses and carts got under way, cannon booming a farewell salute and the lowering skies dripping rain. The carts and wagons trundled along the rutted road, our carriage, surrounded by archers and guardsmen, bounced through the thickening mud as showers became downpours and, toward evening, a storm broke and by the time the tents were struck everyone in the traveling party was drenched.

My husband, who earlier in the day had been filled with enthusiasm, now turned glum. He complained about his sore leg. He shouted at the valets who were hurriedly bringing in the furnishings of our dripping tent. He grumbled about his age, the rain, the long journey ahead.

The grooms could not manage to start fires in our braziers. We shivered under heaped blankets, after eating a cold supper, the king drinking a great deal of ale. Finally, hours later, we did our best to sleep.

But the following morning the rain continued. When our servants brought us food from the kitchen tents, their boots and clothing were muddy. Water trickled along the poorly covered floor of our tent and down the walls. Dry firewood was found, but not until late in the day. And by then the king's mood was foul indeed.

There was no going on while the storms and rains continued. We were stuck in sparsely populated countryside not far from London. And knowing full well that the fen country lay ahead of us, as the next stage in our journey, the decision was made to stay where we were, in order to avoid traveling through the flooded marsh.

We played cards, we read, we made music, but everything we did was half-hearted and unsatisfying. We could not go out of our tents lest we become mired in the sucking, stinking mud—thick, clinging dark brown mud that made an ugly slurping sound as the servants slogged through it.

Bored and confined, we became bad tempered. The king

remained in the large tent we had been sharing, and ordered a second one put up and furnished for me. I could hear him carousing and laughing with his privy chamber gentlemen, the noise becoming more raucous as the day went on. I saw him only at mass—he sometimes heard three masses a day in those tedious initial days of our journey. He did not come to my bed at night. I could not help but wonder whether, in secret, he was arranging to have other women brought to him in the dark hours. Tom assured me that he wasn't, but I worried anyway. Tom might not know everything that was going on, especially since, on some nights, he was spending a few hours with me.

I said that I was feeling ill, and as women with child were often ill, I was believed. Only a few of my women were allowed in my tent—Joan, and Catherine Tylney, and Lady Rochford, who quickly proved to be both discreet and skilled in the art of concealing midnight meetings. She told me that she had often done this for my cousin Anne, when she was one of Anne's ladies. Now she seemed more than willing to do the same for me, to be my go-between with Tom, who was in full agreement that I needed to become pregnant as quickly as possible.

My new footman Englebert was also allowed to come into my tent, to be the one to supply the braziers with dry firewood (not an easy thing to find in those wet days), to bring in food and drink from the tent kitchens. I have to say he was an excellent servant, quiet—indeed almost noiseless, save for the sucking sound of the mud as he approached the tent—respectful, his eyes downcast, his murmured words few. Anna had been right about him. I was glad she had sent him to me.

Heavy clouds moved across the windswept skies above us, dark clouds that brought more rain each day, until the ploughed fields were reduced to sucking mudpits and we began to wonder whether we would ever be able to resume our traveling. All my clothes were damp, there was no way to dry them. My food was damp as well, and often cold. Worst of all, my monthly flux arrived and I knew that I had not yet conceived a child. I continued to wear the relic of the holy tear of the Virgin around my waist, praying that it would work a miracle for me, but a second week passed and there was no sign that I was pregnant.

It was during these weeks of tedium that I received an unwelcome visit from Anna, who had come from her palace at Richmond to visit me. She brought with her the woman we had called Mama Lion, who had been in charge of us when I was in Anna's household as a maid of honor. There was another woman with her as well, a hard-faced, meanly dressed older woman with a bulbous nose and pitted skin and a truculent expression.

Englebert brought Anna and the others into my tent, muddy boots and all, and went to find some refreshment for them. Anna and her two companions curtseyed deeply to me, then seated themselves at my invitation.

"Such a rain!" Anna began. "And so cold, even in July. This is more like Cleves than England!" She smiled, a wan smile, not a bright or eager one. Perhaps, I thought, her journey from Richmond has tired her.

She looked at my belly. "How many months is it now?"

"No more than two," came the gruff voice of the unknown older woman. "If—"

"Yes, Else, we will come to that. Mère Lowe, the gifts, if you please."

From under her cloak Mama Lion brought out a small carved wooden chest with a gilt clasp and laid it on the table. "For you," she said curtly.

I thanked her and opened the chest. Inside were small blankets, elaborately embroidered with the Tudor rose, and a very small cloak of purple velvet trimmed in gold.

"For the prince," Anna said. "When do you expect him?" She looked at me sharply. "What do your midwives say?"

I thought quickly. "My husband has not chosen to make that announcement yet," I finally said. "And I have been ill—"

Before I knew what was happening the hard-faced woman thrust out her hand and nearly succeeded in touching my belly. I drew away quickly and went to the door flap of the tent, intending to call for the guardsmen.

"Do not take alarm," I heard Anna call out. "Else is a midwife. She is here to help you."

But I was already through the door flap and out in the rain, sloshing through the mud, headed for the king's tent. I dashed inside. My husband was sitting in the midst of his councilors, engrossed in conversation.

"Catherine!" he exclaimed. "What is it! You are flushed! You should be staying quietly in bed." And he began to give orders to Master Denny to take me back to my tent.

"If you please, Your Majesty, I cannot go back there."

"Why not?"

"Please, I must speak to you."

He frowned, but asked his councilors to leave us alone. They left, glancing at me with sour faces as they passed me.

"It's Anna," I said.

"Ah."

"She's come here. With a midwife. The midwife tried to touch me. I ran."

"She is envious! She wants to destroy our child!" He got to his feet and called out for Master Denny, who came quickly at his summons.

"Take the queen into the purveyor's tent and stay there with her. Don't let anyone else come near her. Send two guardsmen to escort the Lady Anna from the queen's tent and see that she does not return. And make sure anyone with her is removed as well. And Denny—"

"Yes, Your Majesty?"

"Tell them to be courteous, but firm."

"Yes, Your Majesty."

I felt safe with Master Denny, who took me to a tent stocked with sacks of grain and barrels of ale, beef carcasses and freshly killed rabbits and large jars of quince marmalade. We stayed there until he received a message from the king that I could return to my tent; Anna, he said, would not bother me again.

The rain did not stop, and the king, irritated and discouraged, was prepared to give the order for everything to be packed up into the carts again and returned to the capital. The progress, with its elaborate climax in York when the two kings were to meet, was to be called off.

But then Uncle Thomas rode in, wet and covered in the grime of the road and the sodden marsh, and told us that he and his scouts had found a way to traverse the fen country without the risk of accident. He described the route in detail, and was persuasive. He had indeed found a way through. The king did not respond at first, but after a time gave in—with a grimace of dissatisfaction— and the next day our progress northward resumed.

By the time we reached the outskirts of Lincoln my husband was in better spirits. Nothing pleased him more than a disguising, and he put on a jacket and hose of Lincoln green, a jaunty hat with a green feather, and had his gentlemen put emerald green buckles on his shoes. I was told to dress myself from head to toe in green as well, and thus arrayed we went to greet the citizens.

Every house in the town, it seemed, was hung with colorful cloths and carpets. Choristers in bright garments sang for us, town officials in all their robes and chains of office made speeches in Latin and English, and we processed along the streets with heralds announcing us and soldiers and gentlefolk surrounding us. Two great warhorses, their magnificent caparisons flashing with gold, were led before us while the sword of state proclaimed the king's authority.

Only a few short years earlier, Lincoln had been in rebellion. Now the town appeared to be loyal to the last man, and I heard no voices raised in mockery or defiance as we passed along between crowds of cheering citizens. It was hard to believe that so very recently, hundreds of rebels were hanged, their bodies left to rot along these same streets, the severed heads of those who had defied the royal authority set on spikes and put on display for all the townspeople to see.

The speeches we heard spoke of concord and harmony between the crown and the king's subjects, of loyalty and steadfastness. When we reached the towering ancient cathedral, and knelt to kiss the crucifix, I prayed that nothing would occur to disrupt that loyalty—and prayed as well that I would be able to find a way to tell my husband that I was not pregnant any longer.

For I could no longer maintain the deception. He had believed me to be carrying a child in April. Now it was August and I did not have the rounding belly, the full cheeks, the expanding breasts of a pregnant woman. I had to tell him, once again, that I had lost the child. That I had miscarried. But how was I to do this without arousing my husband's anger?

I decided to wait until he was in his best humor, after a successful hunt.

As we went on northward the royal huntsmen were alert for good hunting sites. Near Hatfield they gathered hundreds of stags and does for the king to shoot, and he spent a day killing many of them. At the same time birds were shot in the nearby marshes, and fishermen swept the ponds for pike and bream. Many of the day's prizes were cleaned and roasted on the spit at once, and a banquet was prepared. The king and I welcomed hundreds of villagers and townspeople living in the vicinity, and offered them a bounteous meal. It went on for hours, with all of us eating and drinking our fill. Afterwards my husband was more than content. He had had a very good and pleasurable day.

Then just at dusk his contentment was shattered when a messenger arrived with news from the building site of Nonsuch. He had left orders with all his workmen that they should send him word of the progress on each building project during our journey. All the reports he had received had so far been satisfactory. Now he heard of a disaster.

The tall tower at Nonsuch, the tower he had spoken of with such feeling as his future refuge, his shelter, had collapsed. Five workmen had been killed and a number of others injured. No repair seemed possible.

On reading the message the king called at once for his astrologer, a thick-set, rather awkward man, clumsy in his movements, with tumbled, uncombed black hair and a mournful mouth.

"The stars are unfavorable, Your Majesty," the astrologer announced. "This is a day of disaster and loss. The collapse of the tower is an omen. I fear there is worse to come."

The king was crestfallen.

"Will my progress end in failure then?"

"It may—unless countervailing influences arise. I cannot say at present. This I can say: you face possible adversity until the end of the year."

"Or possible good fortune—am I right?"

The astrologer lifted an eyebrow. "Prediction is difficult. But today is a day of disaster and loss."

The king waved the man away. "I could have told you that. Now leave me—before I predict disaster for you!"

I decided that my moment had come to tell the king I was not carrying a child.

"Your Majesty," I began, interrupting his grumbling about how the astrologer was a weasel, always squirming out of making a definite prediction for the future, "I fear the tower's collapse may indeed be an omen. A tragedy has occurred."

"What tragedy?"

"As Your Majesty knows, I was very much alarmed by Anna's sudden visit recently. When her midwife all but attacked me—"

"Yes, yes. I trust she has not returned."

"No, Your Majesty. But ever since that frightening attack I have had pains in my belly. I did not want to alarm you, so I have kept this affliction to myself. Today my pains became worse, and when I visited the house of easement I bled. I fear—I have lost our child."

He looked stricken. My words had clearly touched him to the quick.

"Is there no remedy?"

"I fear not."

"But Catherine—" He did not say more, yet his wretched expression told me all. I had wounded him beyond imagining.

"But I wanted to show you off to King James. I wanted him to see that I would soon have another son. That my lineage is secure. It will not fail."

"And so it will not, sire. Your first queen, Queen Catherine, lost many children in her womb, and yet she bore you a living child."

"A daughter, not a son," he said softly.

"My cousin Anne miscarried more than once, did she not, yet she too bore you a living child."

"Another daughter," even more softly.

"And my mother? Was her child not a son?"

He shook his head. "I know not."

"I believe it was a boy. My mother's family produced many sons.

More sons than daughters, Uncle William says. My heart tells me her child was a boy. Just as my heart tells me that the next time, you and I will have a strong son. I am young and healthy. There is plenty of time. Perhaps on this progress, as our pleasures increase, and we feel the support of Your Majesty's subjects, I will conceive another child."

He looked at me, his face drawn and weary, the face of an old man.

"Or perhaps Dr. Chambers is right," he said at length. "Perhaps you are barren." And he turned his face away.

Eighty archers with drawn bows escorted us on our entry into Pontefract, and all the bells of the town rang in celebration. The sun shone brightly on us, flowers and greenery decorated the narrow streets and above all loomed the grey bulk of Pontefract Castle, forbidding in its strength, its thick walls a reminder that the king was sovereign and no rebels dared oppose him.

I had my women dress me in a gown of crimson velvet for our procession into the town, and the king was garbed in a purple velvet doublet furred with ermine. I did my best to accept the loud acclaim of the onlookers graciously, nodding and smiling as I had grown accustomed to doing. Once or twice I saw the king looking over at me and watching to see what impression I was making. But his look was critical, he was judging me rather than encouraging me as in the past, and that made me very uneasy.

I knew that he was heartsore over the loss of our child. I did not doubt that he believed what I told him about losing the child, just as he believed without question that I had been pregnant. It was only his pain that was making him distant, I told myself. He wasn't so much angry at me as he was angry at his fate. His old fear, the fear of being cursed by God, seemed to return. He lost the buoyancy of spirit that had been so strong in him. He seemed tired and listless. When the mayor of the town presented him with the sword and mace, symbols of submission, he accepted them with murmured thanks and a leaden smile, and did not acknowledge me or even glance at me, though I stood right next to him.

As soon as the procession and the other formalities were at an end, the king went off to hunt, and I was escorted into the castle, where an apartment had been prepared for me.

My husband had told me earlier that the castle held sad memories for him, because his bastard son, Henry Fitzroy, had lived there during much of his childhood.

"A fine, well-meaning boy," he mused. "Not very tall or good-looking, not a very good athlete, though I did try to train him for the tilt. But a boy who tried to please me, and would have made a satisfactory king, had he lived long enough."

I knew of Henry Fitzroy, born to the king's mistress Bessie Blount. He had died young, but no one seemed to know how he died; there was a rumor that my cousin Anne had had him killed, not wanting him to be given preference over the son she hoped to have. He had died not long after her execution, and had been given an obscure burial.

No wonder the king has gone to hunt, I thought. The less time he spends in the castle the better for his mood.

That evening Lady Rochford appeared at my side, suddenly and noiselessly.

"All is arranged," she whispered. "There is a gate. The gatekeeper has been rewarded. He will be there at midnight. Englebert will bring him to you."

"He" was of course Tom. I felt a thrill of excitement, knowing I would be with him soon.

Lady Rochford had been busy. Ever since the start of our progress she had made sure to discover hidden places where Tom could meet me, in secret. She had recruited Englebert to help her make our secret meetings come about.

We had met a dozen times and more, sometimes for only an hour, sometimes longer. To reward Lady Rochford, and to ensure her loyalty and her silence, I had given her several of my many estates. Englebert had been generously rewarded as well. It was a beneficial arrangement, all around.

Just after midnight I heard a quiet knock on my bedchamber door. I opened it and let Tom in. He took me in his arms at once and held me close to him. It had been so long since our last meeting. I clung to him, unwilling to let go. I clung to him like a lost child who has found her strong, loving father at last. He was my rock, my shelter. My safe place. The king had had his high tower, until it collapsed—I had Tom. I had not realized, until that moment, just how much I needed Tom and relied on him. I had not realized how frightened I had become.

The castle was a warren of small chambers connected by narrow winding corridors. I led Tom to a room prepared for us by Lady Rochford. A log fire burned brightly in the stone hearth, twigs snapping and sparks flying upward into the darkness of the ancient chimney. Candles glowed and flickered, shadows were cast on the walls as we reclined on a pile of soft cushions and blankets, resting on the straw of a mattress.

I knew well enough that our time together had to be limited, yet I sought to forget time entirely as we lay together, disturbed by nothing but the occasional sound of a log collapsing in the hearth, sending out showers of dancing lights. Our passion ebbed and flowed in patterns that had become wonderfully familiar between us. We knew each other's bodies so well, we fitted together so perfectly. Tom was everything Henry was not; his breath was sweet, his hands were gentle as they roved over my skin. The look in his eyes was loving. He was slim, limber, his movements quick and strong. And he was mine, without any doubt or misgivings. He was mine, forever and for always.

"I thought I saw the watchman tonight," Tom mused as I lay in his arms after our lovemaking. "Just as the gatekeeper was letting me in. I hope he didn't recognize me."

I felt a slight stir of concern.

"Did he challenge you?" I asked.

"No. But he did shine his lantern toward me, before passing on. And I thought I saw him hesitate, just for a moment."

He kissed my forehead. "I don't want to worry you, dearest. But I thought I ought to mention it."

"My own Tom, dearer to me than life," I wrote a few nights later, my hand shaking and the candle before me guttering in the wind, "I cannot bear to be without you. I miss you, my own, my sweet little fool. I am unwell, have you the sickness also? Shall we take a physick together, and lie abed until we are in health again? Oh how I wish you were here with me this night! If only, sweet little fool, you were beside me as I write this, guiding my pen. My heart is apt to die, I miss you so much. Send me word how you do, and tell me when I shall see you again. Do not fail to do this or I faint.

Yours as long as life endures, Catherine the Queen"

I folded the letter and sealed it, and called in Englebert to take it to Master Culpeper, who had gone with the king to Hull to visit the new fortifications he was building there. I knew that Tom would only be away for a few days, a week at most. But even that brief separation seemed an age to me.

Now that I had told the king that I was no longer carrying his child, I was beset by fears. I had begun to dread the future. When I married King Henry I had believed that our marriage would be brief, that my husband would soon die and I would marry Tom. But my husband was proving to be remarkably strong—stronger than the disease in his leg which had so often brought him to the brink of death but had not been able to kill him. I now wondered whether he might live for many years, long enough to marry again and again, until he found a wife who was fertile and could give him the sturdy sons he longed for.

If that happened, there would be no place for me. Unless I was treated as Anna had been treated, with leniency and generosity. For I had to admit that my husband had been generous with Anna. Perhaps, if he found another woman, and became hopeful again, he would treat me well.

While I pondered these deeply worrisome thoughts, Englebert stood quietly before me, waiting to do my bidding. Finally I handed him the folded letter.

"Take this to Master Culpeper," I said, "who is with the king at Hull."

Without looking at me Englebert gave a brief nod and took the letter from me, putting it in a leather pouch. Then he left me.

I went to the window. The night sky was black, there was no moon. Grey-black clouds blotted out the stars. I thought of Tom, wondering whether, at this moment, he was also looking out into the night and thinking of me. Wondering when I would see him again, and feel myself safe in his enfolding arms. As I stood there, I heard the clopping of hooves in the courtyard below. Then the horse broke into a gallop. It was Englebert, I felt sure, taking my message to my love.

FOURTEEN

IT was while the king was away at Hull, and Tom with him, that one of the grooms brought me a visitor. I was still at Pontefract Castle, my nerves on edge and my worries expanding. I was not eating much or sleeping well. I was counting the hours until Tom returned.

Then I saw the carefully groomed, slim man who was following the servant into my chamber. A man with light brown wavy hair, smooth skin, clear, light blue eyes with long lashes . . .

"Francis!"

Stunned at first by the sight of him, I was speechless. But instinctively I reached for the nearest piece of furniture, a heavy oak table, and grasped it firmly for support, as the servant went out of the room, leaving us alone.

Francis bowed deeply. "Your Majesty," he said, his voice grave.

In that moment I realized, to my horror, that he still had the power to unnerve me, to draw me to him. His blandly handsome face, his fine soft skin, the thick lashes that swept across his clear blue eyes . . . I had to force myself to remember that this was the man who had so craftily deceived me. The married man with two children who had become my handfasted husband. Who had taken my naïve girlish trust, and used me abominably ill . . .

But I was no longer that naïve girl. I straightened my spine and lifted my head, letting go of the oaken table, and faced him squarely.

I thought I saw him flinch, ever so slightly, under my gaze.

"What do you want?"

He reached into his doublet and pulled out a leather pouch. From it he extracted a folded letter.

As I watched him I held my breath. It was the pouch I had given to Englebert, and the letter—was my letter to Tom. I was certain of it as Francis unfolded it and held it before me. There was my writing. There were my words, expressing my desperate, urgent love and need. And my signature, Catherine the Queen.

"I have not yet shown this to King Henry," Francis said, "but I'm certain he would be interested to see it."

I felt faint. I could not catch my breath.

"You would not do that. You could not."

"Do what you can, take what you need, act as you must. That has always been my motto."

For a moment it was all I could do to breathe. I swayed on my feet, but did not fall. Once again I reached for the table to steady me.

I dared not call for help. No one must see the letter in Francis's hand. Even if I managed to snatch it and destroy it, still there was Francis himself. No doubt he had copied the letter, or memorized it. It was Francis himself who was the danger to me—the danger of exposure, of the king's terrible wrath. How could I get rid of Francis? If I were a man, if I had a sword—

"You see, Your Highness, it is this way. You have taken me into your confidence—unwillingly, to be sure. You are going to have to trust me to keep secret what I know: that you have a lover, that his name is Thomas Culpeper, and, of course, that you had another lover before him, namely me, Francis Dereham. And no doubt there have been others."

"There are no others!" I shouted. "And you are guilty of threatening the queen! You! A base liar, an exploiter of innocent women! An adulterer and thief!"

He held up his hand. "What I am is of no concern. All you and I have to talk about, Catherine, is whether or not we can strike a bargain, given all that I have found out."

I loathed him then, I loathed him far more intensely than I had ever loved him. I wanted to kill him, cool, crafty, underhanded repulsive creature that he was. And I knew that Tom would want to do the same. If only Tom were here! I thought. But then I thought again. No, not Tom. I would not want Tom hurt or blamed. I would do anything to spare Tom.

"What sort of bargain?" I asked, trying to keep the tremor out of my voice.

"All I want, Catherine, is to be your secretary, as Henry Manox once was."

"What!"

"Yes. I want to be your secretary. Your rather well-paid secretary. My aim is not to reveal your many sins to your husband—or the sins of your paramour Master Culpeper. After all, my own past, and your part in it, must also be kept secret from the king—for my own sake. We both have a great deal to hide. We are partners, whether we wish to be or not."

"I am no partner of yours."

"You were once. You were only too pleased to be called my wife."

My stomach churned. I feared I might throw up. "Never say those words again," I managed to say. "If you do, I swear, I will not let you live."

Francis only chuckled. "But Catherine, you once boasted that we were husband and wife. You showed off the ring I gave you to your friends. Even your grandmother once saw us together, quite intimately. And your women, your chamberers, know that Master Culpeper visits you at night. I myself have seen him coming and going, late on a midnight."

"It was you! You are the watchman Tom saw! The watchman with the lantern!"

His grin told me that I was right. But then the grin disappeared. He became menacing.

"Our bargain, Catherine. What is it to be?"

My initial shock and fear was beginning to recede. I was starting to grasp the situation I was in, and to realize that Francis, repugnant wretch that he was, was in considerable danger himself.

"And what if I should go to my husband, right now, under the protection of the guard—who are just outside the door, in the corridor—and tell him that you tried to force yourself on me? That any lie you may tell, or any forged letter you may show him, is worthless! He loves me. He will believe me."

"Ah, no, Catherine. He would want to believe you. But deep down he knows that a man of his age, yoked to a wife young enough to be his granddaughter—such a man must expect to be cuckolded sooner or later. Especially by a wife whose mother was a whore."

I flew at him then, but he was stronger than I was. He pinned my arms to my sides until, squirming and swearing, I could resist no longer. Still holding on to me, he sat me down on a bench beside a table.

"Now! I am your secretary, is that understood?"

"First I demand that you tell me how you got the letter."

"Your foolish footman was careless. I was keeping watch outside the castle when I saw him come out and go to the stables. I knew he must be on an important errand, to leave at such a late hour of night. I followed him, of course. He was alone. He stopped at a tavern. While he was getting drunk I went through his possessions, looking for money. I found the letter instead."

"He does not know that you have it, then?"

"I imagine he believes he dropped it, or lost it. He was quite drunk when I saw him last." Francis chuckled to himself. "He did not see me following him. He could hardly blame me for its loss."

I sighed. Suddenly I felt extremely tired. I could not fight Francis any longer. I could barely summon any anger toward him, only aversion. He was like some creeping thing, a spider or a snake, to be crushed. But I did not have the energy to crush it just then.

"I am your secretary," he said again. "From now on. In return you will order your steward to give me the income from, shall we say, six of your manors? I know you have many estates." But it was clear to me that he had no idea just how much land I possessed, or how rich I had become, thanks to the king's bounty. I pretended to be shocked.

"Six!" I exclaimed. "But that is far too much."

"Very well then, tell your steward to give me the income from three of your manors."

"If I must," I said wearily.

"I shall draw up an agreement between us. It will be my first official document as your secretary. You will sign it—I know I can recognize your signature—and I will keep it in a safe place, in case I need it in the future."

"I want my letter back."

But Francis only chuckled again, and I felt such renewed loathing at the sound that I had to cover my ears.

•   •   •

I could hardly bear to have Francis anywhere near me, yet he clung to me like a limpet from the time he became my secretary on. Joan and Catherine Tylney, who knew all about my old relations with Francis and had heard me proudly say that we were husband and wife, and then had stood by me when Francis left Lambeth and I learned that he had deceived me, could hardly believe that I had taken him back into my household. They may have guessed the truth—that he had forced me to take him back by threatening to reveal all that he knew of my past. But if they did indeed guess, they said nothing, and I did not take them into my confidence.

Our royal progress had in any case reached its final stage, the visit to York and the all-important meeting of King Henry and his nephew King James.

For the past two months and more, work had continued on the new northern palace, a renovated abbey near the town of York, restored and much enlarged so as to house our own vast traveling party and the household, soldiery and servants of the Scots king. Broken walls were mended, dilapidated interior chambers renovated, painted and decorated in palatial style. Cartloads of tapestries, gold plate, candelabra and table ornaments, linens and napery, bedding and even fine paintings were put in place, new stables were erected and new kitchens added to the old. When complete, the new structure was strongly fortified, and the cannon brought from the south by ship were hauled into place.

As I observed, the king never forgot that York had been the center of the rebellion five years earlier. When rebellion flared again, I heard him say over and over, he meant to be prepared. He did not want his nephew and all those who would accompany him to find themselves in danger.

We settled in to the new royal lodging, only to find that the apartments intended for our use were not yet completed. Once again we stayed in tents, erected in the gardens. At least, my husband said, the lodgings prepared for his nephew were ready, even if ours were a disappointment.

"Never mind," he remarked as he kissed me and retired to bed— alone—"next year when we return to the north country everything will be in readiness to welcome us. Perhaps I shall arrange to have you crowned at York, if all goes as I hope."

"As Your Majesty wishes," I answered, though with a sinking heart. I would not be able to endure another year, I thought. Not another year of the king's caprices, his sudden enthusiasms and equally sudden fits of moodiness and gloom. I could not wait that long to escape from my role as queen, a role that was becoming a rat's nest of worries, worries growing greater by the day.

The rebuilt stables were stocked with swift post horses ready to carry messages between York and King James's palace at Berwick. My husband sent a message as soon as we arrived, to say that we were settling in and to inquire when the Scots party would be coming. Then we did our best to make ourselves at home.

Much to the king's relief the citizens of York proved to be as submissive and peaceable as those of Lincoln had been. Thousands of former rebels came to kneel before him and ask for his forgiveness. They swore to him that if only he would be a good lord to them, and bear them no malice for their former misdeeds, they would pray for him—and for me and Prince Edward as well. The king received these humble acts of submission in good spirits, and though he told his guardsmen to be on the watch for troublemakers and malcontents, and to take careful note of any lawlessness, there was no sign of any trouble.

Instead we found that the citizens of York had gone to great expense to make their town worthy to receive us, with elaborate banqueting and pageants in the decorated streets, banners and flags waving, and speeches of welcome from the mayor and aldermen. I heard no grumbling or mockery as we passed the noisy crowds, only the twang of northern accents and cries of "When will you give us another prince?"

It was mid-September when we arrived in York, and the chill nights and cool days of fall kept me in my fur-trimmed nightdresses and fur-lined cloaks. When a storm broke at the start of our second week in the town, and no message had arrived from King James, my husband began to worry that bad weather might hinder his nephew's plans to come south. As so often when worried, he went tramping in the hills and hunting, leaving me to occupy myself in my tent.

But my tent had become the last place I wanted to be. Spending the long hours of my idle day with Francis, who simply would not leave my side, was tedious in the extreme, and the tedium was only made worse by Tom's displeasure at having Francis near me so much of the time.

"Why don't you just have him stay in an antechamber until needed?" Tom wanted to know. "Or if you must, give him a small tent of his own?"

I could hardly explain why not, I did not want Tom to know of Francis's hold over me. As it was, the two men were at odds, every time Tom came near me I worried that they might come to blows. I told Tom only that the king, who knew nothing of my former relations with Francis, had given him the post as my secretary and that I had not had any choice but to accept him.

Days passed, the skies stayed cloudy and the Scots did not come. Nor was there any message from Berwick. It began to look as though all my husband's expense and effort had been for naught. He was offended—and disappointed. His anger flared when reports were brought to him of Scots war parties coming across the border in murderous raids and burning the fields and barns of the English.

"So this is how my hospitality is rewarded! With killing and destruction! Assaults on my subjects! My nephew offends me by ignoring my invitation. Even my sister stays away!" the king shouted. "Well then, I'll send my soldiers to burn their fields and murder their folk in revenge! Three hurts for one!"

"There is talk," I heard Uncle Thomas say gruffly. "While you have been away these three months, there has been much talk. Some of it must have reached the ears of the Scots."

Uncle Thomas had left our progress a month earlier and ridden south to London. Now he had returned, looking and sounding somber. We sat at supper, the king and I and Uncle Thomas and the few royal advisers who had come north with us. I noticed that my uncle did not look at me, or address me. He had been morose and oddly silent during the meal. I assumed he was tired from his journey, but as the platters were cleared away and he began to speak I sensed a darker mood descending. He had somber matters to convey.

"Once again the Reformers among us are speaking out."

"Not those dreadful theologians from Cleves," my husband said. "I have had quite enough of them."

"No. It is the moralists, the ones who say your court is a cesspit of wickedness."

The king raised his one eyebrow. "I have been denounced as wicked ever since I was a lad, since I first came to the throne. There are always purists who denounce sin, no matter how venial. And I am no saint."

Uncle Thomas paused. When he spoke he sounded unusually tentative.

"It is not your sin they speak of, Your Majesty."

The king looked at him, frowning. "Whose then?"

He shrugged. "The camp followers, for a start."

The king threw up his hands. "All armies have whores! If they didn't, the men would rape all the honest women within reach!"

Uncle Thomas persisted, but in a lower tone.

"Your court is said to be polluted by lust. I am only repeating what is being said. There is wantonness."

"Who is spreading these lies?"

"Those who fear a return to the old ways, the old teachings. Before you became head of the church. They fear what they call the laxity of the papists. They favor the more extreme teachings of the Genevan, John Calvin. They desire further reform in our church. And, as always, they desire power for themselves. They wish to destroy the influence of my family. The Howard family."

King Henry slapped the table. "I am no papist! And I will tell anyone who listens that there will be no running back to the pope in this realm! The laxity of the papists indeed! Not while I am sovereign here! And as for the Howards—" His gesture indicated tolerance.

"If I may speak more openly, Your Majesty," my uncle went on, "it is being said that King James did not come to meet you here in York because he has heard your court is impure. The Scots disliked your putting aside the lady from Cleves. They dislike your present marriage even more—indeed they are bold enough to say that your wife is childless because the Lord has sealed her womb. It is His judgment against the wickedness of your court."

At his words I gasped and crossed myself. At the same moment my husband gave forth a roar of outrage and tottered to his feet— he had drunk a good deal of ale and was unsteady.

"You dare to repeat such slander in my presence!"

"It is necessary that you should know what is being said. I would be remiss if I did not tell you. None of your other councilors are brave enough, it would seem."

The others at the table murmured uneasily at this sharp exchange.

The king glared at Uncle Thomas.

"Just who is saying this?"

"It is not only one—there are many. And their numbers are growing. But I have heard the name of a certain man, John Lascelles, a bush preacher. His is an unusually loud voice of disapproval. He denounces your court."

"John Lascelles, John Lascelles. Who is this John Lascelles? I never heard of him. One moon-mad lunatic preacher!"

"He speaks for many. There are murmurs of criticism even among the most thoughtful and sensible of your subjects. They wonder why you don't put a stop to the waywardness of your household."

"Enough!" the king shouted, slapping the table once again and making his flagon of ale bounce. "I will hear no more of this, from you or anyone else! There are always troublemakers spreading tales at court, especially when I am not there to shut their mouths. When I return to London this babble of scandal will cease. As for my nephew, I believe it is the bad weather, and nothing else, that has prevented him from coming to meet me as he promised. There will be other summers, other progresses. Or mayhap he will come to London for a visit. Yes, I think that would be even better." The king grinned at the thought.

"Let him come south, when the chill winds of Scotland drive him to seek a warmer clime. By then, Lord willing, I will have a new son to show him, and make him envy me even more than he already does!"

The tents were folded and loaded onto carts, our furnishings packed and our provisions gathered for the journey southward. The great lodging my husband had created for his meeting with King

James would soon be deserted. The gardens were already blighted by the nightly frosts and harsh winds, faint cracks had appeared in the newly mended walls—badly mended, as it seemed. The fires had gone out in the hearths and under the immense cauldrons in the renovated kitchens. And in the stables, chaff and straw blew about in the wind, with only the warm yeasty smell of the horses so recently installed there remaining behind.

My women were packing my things. But my cousin Catherine Tylney, I noticed, was hurriedly putting her own clothing and other possessions into a large chest and two smaller baskets.

"Why such a rush?" I asked her. "We will not be starting our journey until noontime tomorrow."

She looked flustered. "Your Majesty," she said, "Uncle Thomas has ordered me to leave your household today and go south with him and his party."

Something told me that this order had to do with the unpleasant talebearing he had disclosed at supper.

"Did he say why? Is it possible he has arranged a match for you?" We both knew that wasn't likely, but it was the most optimistic possibility.

"He hasn't said so."

"But you will be returning to my household as soon as we arrive at Hampton Court, will you not?"

"I cannot say what is in Uncle Thomas's mind." It was unlike my cousin to be evasive. Her tone and manner worried me. Her brow was wrinkled in worry.

"Very well then, Cousin Catherine." I left her to her packing and sent one of my grooms to find another of my Howard relations, Richard Singleton, a more distant cousin who was among my husband's yeomen of the chamber. The groom had some difficulty finding him, but eventually returned, to report that, like Catherine Tylney, Richard had been ordered by Uncle Thomas to pack his things at once and leave the king's suite to return to the south with him.

I asked Lady Rochford to take a message to Tom, to tell him I needed to talk to him.

We met just at dusk. The courtyard was full of carts and wagons, carriages and barrows. Men moved briskly among the vehicles, carrying heavy sacks of provisions, coffers and trunks. I heard shouts of irritation, barked orders, as the last of the light waned and torches were being lit so that the work of loading could go on into the late hours.

"I cannot be away long," Tom cautioned me. "The king is pressing us to hurry. He is eager to be back at his southern court."

I told Tom about my uncle's disturbing revelations and about the king's angry response. I confided that I was feeling very uneasy, especially after learning that Uncle Thomas had ordered both my maid of honor and my distant cousin Richard to leave my household and travel with him.

"And two of the king's chamber gentlemen also," Tom put in. "Both are Howard relations. Also I overheard that your uncle William is going to be recalled from France."

"Why?"

"I don't know. But it would seem that the Howards are closing ranks."

"Why would Uncle Thomas do that?"

Tom shrugged. "Fear, most likely. The threat of a challenge to his power. It is the way of the court, is it not? Those who have power must constantly guard it against the assaults of those who would take it from them. It was the same when Lord Cromwell was brought to ruin. Your uncle Thomas withdrew his servants from Lord Cromwell's household, then the assault on his authority began. Within a month he was in the Tower, awaiting execution."

He was right. I remembered how, at the time Lord Cromwell

was about to be deprived of his offices, a number of my relatives and in-laws who were members of the Lord Privy Seal's household were ordered to leave and given posts in the royal household. My uncle had been gathering his family around him, as he appeared to be doing now.

And then there was Englebert. Just as we were preparing to leave York and begin our homeward journey, he vanished. No one saw him go, or noticed when he left or in which direction he went. It annoyed me that he would leave my service without a word, especially after he had been such an attentive and reliable servant. It occurred to me that he might not have left at all, but rather that he might have suffered an accident or worse. There were vagabonds and robbers in the countryside, no one could ever be completely safe. And Englebert had enjoyed riding alone, as he had when I had sent him to Hull. He disdained the protection of guardsmen. I wondered, was it possible he had come to harm? I had no way of finding out. I had to let his disappearance remain a mystery—and a disturbing one.

We set out for the south, our long train of carts and wagons moving slowly, hampered by roads in poor repair and windblown trees that fell in our path, by streams that overflowed their banks and turned the roads into quagmires. On we slogged, impatient at the constant delays, fretting at the discomforts we seemed to meet at every turn. My own discontent was greatly increased by the fact that I saw Tom so rarely, and so fleetingly. I watched for him, constantly hoping to see his tall, lithe form riding past or to observe him when he and other gentlemen of the privy chamber accompanied the king to my tent in the evening. I longed to be alone with him, even for an hour—and we did manage to be alone together, twice, thanks to Lady Rochford's clever arrangements. But we dared not try for more than that.

We dared not try—because Francis was always there, watching

what I did and said. His hovering presence made Tom irritable—and the last thing I wanted was for the two men to quarrel, arousing my husband's suspicions. So I went without Tom's cherished company for most of our long journey southward, until at last we arrived at Hampton Court in the last week of October, weary and bedraggled, greatly in need of rest and better news.

But there was to be no rest. For almost at once we learned that once again, Prince Edward was very ill.

"What now!" my husband exclaimed, his face a knot of anxious wrinkles. He had just received word that the citizens of both Lincoln and York, those cheering, pacific subjects who had seemed to welcome us with such good will when we were among them, were once again in revolt. He was still reeling from the shock and deep disappointment that his planned meeting with his royal nephew had not happened. And now, wounded and angry, he was dealt an even more severe blow. For the physicians were saying that the prince lay near death from a quartan fever.

Prince Edward had been brought to Nonsuch, to a newly completed wing of the vast palace which was slowly rising (apart from the collapsed tower) and promising to be a magnificent structure. We set out from Hampton Court at once, traveling the short distance to the new palace quickly. We found Dr. Butts and Dr. Chambers watching over the prince, with his nurses and the others in his household in attendance in an outer chamber. The chief apothecary, Thomas Alsop, occupied a chamber of his own where his assistants were at work preparing potions and syrups.

At my first sight of the boy I realized that he was much more ill than he had been the last time I saw him. He was so still he was almost corpse-like. There was only his rasping cough to indicate that he still lived. Thin and weak-looking, with dark circles under his closed eyes, he lay inert, sweating heavily, in the grip of the fever.

"He has been bled twice," Dr. Chambers told the king. "But the surgeon would not bleed him a third time because it was the day of the new moon and besides that, the air was too cold. As soon as the moon waxes, and the weather warms, he will be bled again."

"There is no doubt it is a quartan fever then?" my husband demanded.

"No doubt. The heat rises within him every third day, and lingers through a fourth. See how his nails have no color. How his body swells—and sweats. The crisis comes and goes, but there is no lessening of it, except by bleeding."

I remembered very well how the prince had looked when ill the previous year. How small and fragile he had seemed. Even now he appeared to be very small, though his fourth birthday had just been celebrated.

"Can you not apply a poultice? I have made many such myself, as you know well, to be used on my legs. They are effective."

"But not against fever. For fever there is only bleeding—and prayer."

"Bleeding did not save my wife," I heard the king say in an undertone, speaking more to himself than to the physician. "My good wife. The one who gave me a son."

A weak son, I wanted to say but did not. And of course I did not want the prince to be too weak to survive.

We stayed by the prince's bedside, sleeping in his bedchamber and taking our meals near him. The king conferred often with the apothecary and his assistants, giving them advice, checking and approving every remedy they concocted. He paced up and down the bedchamber, impatient to see the results of the treatment the prince had been given.

On the third day of our stay the surgeon came. The moon was

waxing, he announced, and he could bleed Edward again. He opened a vein and the prince's blood dripped slowly into a bowl. Yet still the fever increased. Hour by hour his small body grew more red and hot, his cheeks fairly burning to the touch. The physicians were anxious, and the king was fairly beside himself with frustration and worry.

"By all the saints!" he cried out, "Can nothing be done?"

A long silence spread through the room. Then I heard a timid voice say, "There is a wise woman."

It was one of the prince's nurses, a gentle young girl.

"Speak up, girl!" the king said irritably. "What wise woman?"

"She comes from Cuddington." Cuddington I knew to be the village that had been destroyed in order for Nonsuch to rise.

"Yes—and what of her?"

"She—she has the healing power."

The king looked at the girl, his eyes narrow, his gaze shrewd.

"Have you seen her perform healings?"

"If you please, Your Majesty, she healed many who were stricken of the plague."

"And you know this for a certainty."

"Yes, Your Majesty. She healed my mother and my two young sisters."

"Well, she can do no harm. Bring her here."

"She is here already, Your Majesty. She has been waiting to be of service."

My husband looked at Dr. Chambers.

"Why did no one tell me this!"

The physician shook his head. "We put no faith in such witchcraft, sire. Only proven remedies are effective—"

But the king only pushed the old man aside.

"Bring her in!" he said to the girl, who went out of the room and soon returned with a much older woman, stout and grey-haired but vigorous in her movements, and with a face of surprising youthfulness. Her skin was smooth, her forehead unlined. There was a radiance about her. She carried a basket, which she handed to the girl. Then the newcomer curtseyed deeply to the king, and again to me.

"Can you heal my son!" The king's words were a demand, not a question.

The wise woman smiled, a luminous smile.

"Yes, sire." Taking her basket, she drew from it an earthen pot. She removed the cap and bent over the prince's small bed.

At this Dr. Butts stepped forward.

"Your Majesty, you cannot let this—this leech—do harm to your son! I pray you, dismiss her at once!"

King Henry silenced him.

"Go on," he said to the wise woman, who proceeded to take some of the contents of the pot on her fingers and smear it over the prince's body. The stench of the substance was terrible. I drew away and put my pomander to my nose.

"What is that you are using?" King Henry asked.

"First I roast a fat cat. Then I stuff it with bear and hedgehog fat and herbs."

"What herbs?"

She began to reel off a long list of names, from rue and rosemary to other plants unfamiliar to me.

"The compound is from an old herbal that has been in my family since the days of King Henry—the fifth King Henry. I have never known it to fail."

The physicians began to protest again and this time the king sent them out of the room.

Three times over the next few hours the compound was spread over the prince's corpse-like body, until he began to wriggle and shake himself and then, to our astonishment, he slowly sat up.

261

The wise woman nodded. "Yes," she said quietly. "The fever is leaving him."

Under the direction of his benefactor, the prince was bathed, then dressed in warm flannel, and then given supper.

The physicians were brought in to observe the remarkable change in their patient.

"I would never have believed it," Dr. Chambers said, shaking his head. "The apothecary must be given the formula for that stinking grease."

"For that life-giving balm, you mean, don't you?" was my tart retort. I had not forgiven Dr. Chambers for the way he had treated me when I confided in him, or for telling the entire court that I was barren.

But the physician ignored my remark, and went into the apothecary's chamber without taking any notice of me.

My husband came over to me and put his arm around me, a gesture he had not made in some time. He was clearly overcome with relief and joy at the prince's great improvement.

"Ah, Catherine! What a near thing! My boy! My dear boy! He does seem so much better, does he not?"

"Indeed he does," I said with a smile. "He has his father's strength."

We stayed at Nonsuch another day and a night, until it seemed certain that the prince would recover completely. Then, after giving the wise woman a fat purse of gold coins and thanking her with fervent courtesy, my husband and I climbed into our waiting carriage for the return to Hampton Court.

FIFTEEN

IT was the time of autumn that I liked best, that unsure end of the season when the weather varies day by day and the gold and auburn leaves are everywhere underfoot and a few warm days linger on. I was glad to be back in my apartments at Hampton Court, with their view of the river and its mists. I could see the barges coming up from London, discharging their passengers and taking on new ones. I had no wish to be among them. I had had more than enough of traveling, now it was time to settle in and wait in peace for the winter season to come, with its cheering holidays and its cold blasts.

It was as I sat watching out my window, Jonah scampering nearby, that I caught a glimpse of a familiar tall rotund man, coming ashore from a wherry and striding toward the river stairs. It was Uncle William, returned from France. I had not expected him. I was overjoyed to see him.

"Dearest Catherine!" His greeting was warm as ever, his smile wide and comforting. I led him into my bedchamber where I knew we would not be disturbed.

"Do you think we could have some of your good calming poppy broth?" he asked as we seated ourselves comfortably near the warm fire. "I feel the need of a soothing posset. I don't know whether the news has reached you yet, but I was caught in a very bad storm—the worst I've ever encountered—coming back from France."

"But how terrible!" Pausing just long enough to ask my chamberer for the poppy broth, I fixed my attention on my uncle, who was describing the crippling of his vessel in the high waves and fierce winds.

"We didn't sink, though it seemed for a time as though we would. The vessel was badly damaged. I confess to you, Catherine, I was lucky to escape alive. Unfortunately, everything I had with me—most of my possessions, other than the furnishings of Oxenheath—was lost. Even some of my treasured family heirlooms."

He took a long breath and, in expelling it, seemed to shrink down, as if in unburdening himself about the loss of his possessions he had lost something of his girth.

The broth arrived and we both sipped it, anticipating its calming effect.

"At least you survived. That is all that matters."

He nodded. "Of course, only—"

"Only what?"

"The terror of it all lingers. Some of the fear has stayed with me, maybe because I'm old." He grinned. "Old and fat—but lucky."

"Like Jonah here," I said, picking up the monkey. "You know I named him after Jonah in the Bible, who was lucky too."

"Thrown into the sea during a terrible storm, as I recall—but then rescued by a whale. I saw no whales while enduring that alarming crossing."

As we sat together, sipping our broth, I saw a further change come over Uncle William. His look was, as always, benign, but tinged with concern.

"I fear there is another storm coming, Catherine," he said after a time. "And I must be the one to tell you about it."

I stopped petting Jonah and put him down.

Uncle William licked his lips and set down his cup of broth. He took a deep breath.

"The king has left Hampton Court, Catherine. He left last night, in haste and in secret. He went to London to meet with his councilors." He paused, then took another breath and went on. "I'm very much afraid, my dearest girl, that the king is about to set you aside."

I felt my knees turn to water. I thought I was going to faint. I reached out to Uncle William, who took my hand in his two strong warm hands, which felt slightly moist.

"You must be brave, and listen carefully to what I am going to tell you. Can you do that?"

My head felt muzzy. I could not think clearly.

"I will try." My words were so soft I could hardly hear them.

"That's my girl. This is what you must understand, Catherine. We Howards are under assault. All of us. I was summoned back from France because our family is being attacked on all sides. I have been accused of stealing funds from the royal treasury. Your uncle Thomas is accused of conspiring against the throne, and concealing treason. Your grandmother is accused of treason, of stealing valuable papers and burning them. And you—you are being made the center of it all, I'm sorry to say."

"I?"

He nodded gravely.

"Because I am Jocasta's daughter."

"No, dear. Because you are—to use Archbishop Cranmer's words—unchaste."

I began to cry then. There was no help for it. I could not even try to conceal from Uncle William what was well known to Grandma Agnes and no doubt to Uncle Thomas and Uncle William as well. That Francis had been my lover and Henry Manox my would-be seducer, my partner in lechery.

After a few moments I managed to wipe my eyes and look into Uncle William's kind face once again.

"But I never allowed Henry Manox to take my maidenhead," I said softly. "And I was handfasted to Francis Dereham. We were husband and wife. At least I believed we were."

"Your crime, Catherine, was in concealing what you have just confessed to me. Your unchastity made you unfit to become queen. Also your untruthfulness about it. You betrayed the king every day that you continued to conceal your past."

I pulled my hand out of Uncle William's grasp and buried my head in my hands. I could bear no more.

I felt him pat me on the shoulder, meaning to comfort me.

"Drink your poppy broth," he said. "I will be back later to talk to you further."

I did not know what to do. As soon as Uncle William left me, I rushed, panic-stricken, into the corridor outside my apartments. But there were guardsmen there, a dozen or more, and they blocked my path. I was told, firmly but courteously, that it was the king's command that I keep to my own rooms.

My women had disappeared. Even the boy who came in to bring my firewood did not come as he usually did. Where was Joan? Where was Lady Rochford? And all my other maids of honor and ladies? I looked out of my bedchamber window at the river, and saw the royal barge, moored near the river stairs.

Had my husband returned? Could I appeal to him for mercy?

I watched the barge, but saw no one enter or leave it. I was hungry. How was I to eat if there were no servants to bring me food from the kitchens?

I found some apples one of the servants had left behind, and fell on them hungrily. I tried to sleep, but could not. I was far too worried. When would Uncle William return? Where were my women? As if to echo the turmoil I was feeling, the skies began to darken and soon a dismal rain began to fall.

Toward evening I heard the outer doors of my apartments open noisily and men's voices ringing out. Without the least ceremony one of the king's cofferers, Sir Stephen Dyer, accompanied by Master Denny and half a dozen liveried servants came into my bedchamber.

"Catherine Howard! Surrender your jewels!" the cofferer called out, making me jump.

"I believe I can locate the lady's jewel cases," Master Denny said. I noticed he did not refer to me as "Her Highness." As I watched, Master Denny, who knew my chambers well, went right to the chests and coffers that held my jewels, and, having obtained the keys, began to unlock and empty them into cloth sacks the cofferer held open.

It was done quickly, and with no regard for the lovely casks and velvet mountings of the priceless jewels my husband had lavished on me. All my diamonds, my ropes of pearls, my earrings and pendants were tumbled into the sacks, one on top of another.

My pendants—

There was one pendant I needed to save.

I went to a large wardrobe and opened one of its two broad wooden doors.

"Shut that door at once!" the cofferer shouted.

"But I need a handkerchief," I demurred, looking over at Master Denny.

He hesitated, then nodded. I reached into the wardrobe and pulled open a small drawer. The drawer where I kept my most precious possessions. My father's gold toothpick, a rose Tom had given me, pressed between the pages of a small leatherbound book of poems, and Jocasta's pendant, with three hearts intertwined, hanging from a thin gold chain. I slipped the pendant into the pocket of my gown and quickly pulled an embroidered handkerchief from a nearby drawer. Then I closed the wardrobe and sat down, wiping my cheeks with the handkerchief.

The emptying of my jewel coffers went forward, until every gleaming bit of finery I possessed had been put into the bulging sacks and taken away.

The fires in the hearths had nearly gone out.

"Master Denny!" I called. "Master Denny, can you please send me some firewood?"

"Only if the king orders it," he replied, adding, in a milder tone, "I'm sorry."

It was not Uncle William who came to see me late that evening, but Uncle Thomas and Archbishop Cranmer.

My scowling uncle, arrayed in furred robes and with a thick gold chain of office around his neck, barely glanced at me. The archbishop, who I had scarcely seen since my marriage ceremony, wore his clerical robes. He was an ill-favored man but soft-spoken; his small eyes, set close together, contained no anger or malice that I could detect.

"As Earl Marshal of this kingdom and ranking peer of the realm," Uncle Thomas announced, "I am here to examine you and to report to the king the answers you give to the very serious charges brought against you in the royal council. You should know that two of your lovers, Henry Manox and Francis Dereham, have

been thoroughly examined"—here he gave me a brief glance—
"and have admitted to the most shameful and treasonous acts. You
were a willing participant in these acts. Do you admit this?"

"I am innocent."

"Filthy whore! Lying cunt! Admit your guilt or you will be
stretched on the rack along with your lovers!"

I was shaking. I tried not to imagine Henry Manox and Francis
screaming as their limbs were stretched and twisted. Of course
they would have admitted anything when in such unbearable pain.
I squeezed my eyes tight shut, as if to keep out the terrible images
that came into my head unbidden.

"My husband would never allow me to be hurt," I managed to
say.

"You think not! You cannot imagine his rage when he learned
that you had betrayed him, lied to him, dishonored him again and
again! He cursed you at the top of his lungs! He called for his
sword. He wanted to kill you himself!"

"But it was you, uncle, who told me to capture the king's fancy if
I could—even though you knew full well that I was handfasted to
Francis Dereham!" My knees were weak, but my voice was becoming
stronger. "There is no shame or treason in that! And as for Henry
Manox, I swear on the cross of Our Lord that I never lay with him,
though he did force me to reveal to him my nakedness. Grandma
Agnes knew of this. She witnessed it."

Uncle Thomas began to swear at me again, but the archbishop
raised his hand to interrupt him.

"Do you then confess, Catherine," he said in his strong, magisterial
voice, "that you believed yourself wed to Francis Dereham, by the
ancient rite of handfasting, and that knowing this, you married King
Henry, committing the sin and crime of bigamy?"

"At Uncle Thomas's bidding, and under the king's command,
yes."

"And are you willing to confess to the same in writing?"

"If my uncle and my grandmother will confess to their part in the deceit, yes."

Uncle Thomas stepped toward me as if to strike me, shouting "Brazen strumpet! Foul daughter of a fouler mother! Jezebel! You dare to accuse your own relations of taking part in your lecherous scheming! Lying trollop!"

The archbishop stepped deftly between us. His face registered no emotion. He remained calm.

"You are the liar, Uncle Thomas! You are the guilty one! I never wanted to be the king's wife! Never!"

"Be careful what you say, Catherine," the archbishop cautioned me calmly. "Not all truths are welcome." He spoke in an undertone to my uncle, who after giving me a contemptuous look, swept out of the room.

"Now then, come and sit at this desk, Catherine, and write out all that you have told me. I don't want to give you false hope, but I believe there may be a way for you to cease being the king's wife and still retain your honor—or at least some shreds of it. I would not want to see a young girl like yourself racked and tortured, much less facing the executioner like your cousin Anne Boleyn, when all she really did was love a young man and pledge herself to him."

"I want my uncle and my grandmother to confess that they all but forced me to marry the king."

"I have no doubt the royal council will call them to account for their actions."

I was not satisfied, but I did not have the strength or energy to insist. I certainly did not want to encounter Uncle Thomas again. I sat at the desk as the archbishop asked, and began to record my relations with Henry Manox and Francis Dereham, leaving out nothing. Writing was not easy for me, I formed my letters slowly and clumsily. But at last I finished and gave my confession to the archbishop to read.

"Yes, that is sufficient," he said when he had puzzled his way through my statement. "Now I would advise you to write a little more. Plead for the king to be merciful to you. Ask him to consider how young you were when your music master tried to seduce you. Say that Francis Dereham deceived you, and led you astray. And be sure to say that you loved Master Dereham and were faithful to him—as faithful as the true wife you believed yourself to be."

I did as he asked, and produced a satisfactory confession. By this time it was after midnight. I was very tired.

"You see, Catherine," the archbishop said as he folded my document and put it into the inner pocket of his robe, "I believe you and Master Dereham had a precontract. That meant that when you married the king, the royal marriage was not a valid one."

"Just as when Anna of Cleves had a precontract with the Duke of Lorraine's son."

"Precisely so. I believe that the king would be overjoyed to be able to say your marriage to him was null. Then he would not have to punish you. You see, when your uncle told you that the king was furious, and called for his sword to slay you, that was only part of the truth. I was there, I saw what he said and did when he learned of your relations with Master Manox and Master Dereham. He wept, Catherine. That strong, fierce bull of a man actually wept for sorrow. He wept like a heartbroken child, he loves you so much. I believe he could find it in his heart to forgive you, once he knows of this precontract.

"You must pray for forgiveness," he went on, "and for divine mercy. You must be shriven. You must appear penitent, not defiant. It may well be true that your uncle and grandmother and others in your family encouraged you to inspire the king's lust, and even to satisfy it—all the while knowing full well that you were not chaste.

But it is not for you to accuse them, it is for God to judge them according to their deeds."

He left me after giving me his blessing, and I got undressed quickly and went to bed in my cold bedchamber, with no supper and no one to attend me. Before I got into bed I knelt and confessed my sins and prayed for forgiveness, asking the Lord to bless my husband and those who accused me, to spare me the rack and the pains of hell and above all, to keep Tom safe.

"Catherine!"

I thought I heard someone whisper my name. The candle by my bedside had gone out, and the room was dark, as I had no fire.

The whisper came again. "Catherine!"

I sat up and looked into the darkness. Faint moonlight illuminated the windows. With a start I saw a man's form outlined against the lighter glow. A large man.

"Who is it?"

"It's Uncle William, Catherine. I could not come any earlier. They are questioning me. I only managed to get away by bribing the guards. I wanted to warn you. Your lovers have confessed."

"I know. Uncle Thomas and the archbishop were here for hours. I wrote out my confession. But the archbishop says the king wants to spare me. He may be able to put me aside as he did the lady Anna, because I was handfasted to Francis Dereham."

"Yes, I believe he could do that, if he chose. Just as he can pardon me—not that I am guilty of any crime. But I am frightened, Catherine. For myself as well as for you."

I got out of bed and found my gown, which I had laid across a bench. I took my mother's pendant from the pocket.

"Can you find a way to get this pendant to the king, and say that I sent it?" I held out the pendant and Uncle William took it from me. His hand was cold.

"This will touch him to the quick. I will do my best to have it taken to him. Good fortune to you, dear Catherine," I heard him murmur as he slipped out of the room.

"And to you, Uncle William. May the Lord protect us both."

In the morning I was awakened by a scraping noise in the hearth. A lad was making a fire for me. Firewood was piled in the box, and as I waited, relieved, for the room to warm up more servants were brought in: two chamberers, a groom, and three of my ladies—Joan, Mary Sidford, and—much to my surprise, my cousin Charyn.

"Archbishop Cranmer has appointed us to serve you, Lady Catherine," Joan said. "We may not call you Your Highness any more. Malyn wanted to join us but the duke forbade it. Charyn has asked if she could take her place."

"Thank you all," I said, and held out my hand to the women, who curtseyed and, one by one, took my hand and kissed it.

"Charyn," I began when she knelt before me—but then I saw that she had begun to cry.

"I want to serve you, Catherine," she said. "Please forget all the unkind things I have said in the past. I was your friend when we were children. Let me be your friend again."

We embraced then, and my own eyes filled with tears. It was some time before I was able to dress and compose myself and sit down to the good meal that was brought to me, with my ladies around me and a warm fire crackling in the hearth.

But there was much worse to come.

A few days after this, four men entered my apartments and, without saluting me or acknowledging me, placed a bench before me and told me to sit down. After the four men came a dozen soldiers. My ladies were ordered into an antechamber. Two of the men sat at a table and wrote down everything that was said, their pens scratching across the paper before them. From time to time they looked up at me, frowning, and then began to write again.

A third man drew a folded paper from his doublet, unfolded it and began to read from it. "'My own Tom, dearer to me than life,'" he began, and I felt my stomach clench. "'I cannot bear to be without you. I miss you, my own, my sweet little fool.' And so on. Catherine Howard, did you write this letter? I caution you, the recipient of the letter has already confessed to being your lover during your marriage to the king. Now, I ask you again, did you write this letter?"

All I could think of to say was, "I want Archbishop Cranmer."

"The archbishop cannot help you now. Answer my question!"

I hung my head. "I believe you already know the answer."

"The king demands your answer!" he shouted. "You must say the words. You must also confess in *writing* to adultery with Thomas Culpeper while married to the king. You must confess to treason!"

The terrible words resounded in my ears. You must confess to treason. You must confess to treason. The room spun. I felt myself droop on the bench. Then I felt arms supporting me—ungently.

"Where did you get my letter?" I whispered when I had begun to recover myself. I was not able to speak aloud.

"From the torturer. He found it on the person of Francis Dereham. The wretch Dereham meant to bargain with it. To assure the condemnation of Culpeper, in hopes of saving his own life."

"But not mine," I said softly. Then a thought struck me. "That letter does not prove anything against me."

"But when your sweet little fool Tom was tortured, he confessed to being your lover. His confession is more than enough to convict you. And then there is the confession of Lady Rochford."

Once again I felt my stomach constrict.

"She told us much about your meetings with your lover Culpeper. She said you forced her to serve as your go-between, to seek out private places for your loathsome treasonous meetings with your lover. That you met him again and again, at Lincoln and at Pontefract, and—"

"Yes, yes."

"Do you confess to having met your lover at these places? Do you confess to having lain with him adulterously, to the peril of the succession?"

"I will confess to Archbishop Cranmer."

My interrogator pounded on the bench I sat on with his fist, making me jump. "You will confess to me! Here! Now! Or your women will be tortured, as your lovers were!"

"No! No!"

"Take the women to the Tower," he said, his voice cold. "She will not confess."

But I did confess, of course. I could not bear to think of my women stretched on the rack, made to suffer unbearable pangs, just because Tom and I loved each other. I confessed, and the pens scratched across the paper.

I confessed to treason.

My women were questioned, mercilessly and at length, but in the end they were returned to my apartments, unharmed but terrified. And in fear of being threatened again.

I lay awake all that night, in the dimness of my bedchamber, thinking of Tom. Where was he? Had he lived through his ordeal? Was he thinking of me? Or was he undergoing such torment that he could not think at all, but only suffer, in agony, the wretchedness of despair?

●　　●　　●

When Archbishop Cranmer came to me again, I searched his face for any sign that might tell me my fate. I had confessed to treason. Would I be racked? Would I suffer a traitor's death?

But he looked as he always did, mild and unruffled.

"Have you brought me news?" I asked anxiously.

He composed himself further before replying. I could tell he was choosing his words with care.

"There has been a change in the king," he began. "He is withdrawn and melancholy. He broods. He speaks often of the fall of the tower at Nonsuch—an omen, he says. It symbolized the loss of your unborn babes, and he rants on about how they may not have been his, about how you deceived him. But in his disordered mind the tower's fall foretells much more loss to come. He imagines that he will lose his kingdom, perhaps even his life."

"Yes but what of me? What of my fate?"

"That's what I am trying to tell you. He is confused. He talks about you, his disloyal wife, but he calls you Jocasta. He says Jocasta has betrayed him. He suffers so over this betrayal. He weeps, he threatens. He even drags out his old sword and sweeps it back and forth, as if to repel an enemy. But it is all about her, not you.

"And another thing. He has begun to wear a chain around his neck, with quite a plain pendant hanging from it. He wears it constantly. Though it is hardly of any value, quite unlike the immense gems and pearls he is accustomed to wearing. This is a simple ornament, with three hearts entwined."

I cried out with delight. Uncle William had managed to deliver Jocasta's pendant to the king! And he was wearing it, as a token of his love. That meant his heart was softening. Surely it did.

The archbishop looked at me quizzically. Perhaps he thought me as distracted in mind as my husband. However, he went on with what he was telling me.

"I have been sent to tell you that from now on you will be

housed at Syon. You will have three chambers for yourself and four ladies in waiting. Twelve servants may accompany you, but the rest of your household will be dismissed. You may take such furnishings and hangings as befit a gentlewoman—but no cloth of estate. You have forfeited your honor. You are no longer queen."

He cleared his throat, then drew a paper from his robe and began to read.

"Your wardrobe is forfeit to the crown, save for six French hoods, six pairs of sleeves, six gowns of mean stuff, six kirtles of satin damask and velvet. Six pairs of slippers, two woolen petticoats, one woolen cloak, two cloaks of velvet and damask."

The list went on and on. Nothing, it seemed, had been left out: not underclothes, not fans, or gloves, or trims, or lengths of lace. Even the number of carts I was to be allowed, and the number of cart horses and grooms, was prescribed.

But all that mattered to me was that the king was showing me mercy. I was not to be sent to the Tower, but to a respectable place of reasonable comfort, with servants and a gentlewoman's wardrobe and furnishings adequate to my needs. He still cared for my comfort. He still loved me—and forgave me. It must be true. It must.

On the following morning, filled with this immeasurably consoling thought, I took my seat in the wagon, Joan and Mary Sidford and Charyn beside me, and set off for Syon House, my woolen cloak drawn about me and the chest that held my remaining possessions close at hand.

SIXTEEN

EXCEPT for my ceaseless worry about Tom, I settled in to life at Syon House with relative content. The terrible strain of the recent past had been lifted from me. I was under the protection of the king's mercy. I was safe.

I was no longer queen, and the life I had once dreamed of, a life in which I became the king's widow, and then married my beloved, was gone forever. I tried not to think of that shattered dream, as I lay on my straw mattress covered with my dogswain blanket. I tried not to remember the soft comfortable bed I had enjoyed as queen, the great glowing pearl bed in which the next king was to have been conceived. All the beautiful, costly things that had so recently surrounded me had been swept away, and in some ways my state was not unlike what I had known at Horsham, when I first went to live in Grandma Agnes's establishment to learn courtly manners and accomplishments and to be groomed for marriage.

Those days seemed to belong, not only to a distant past, but to a different life. It was hard to realize that only a handful of years had passed since I left my father's house for Horsham. If only I had known what life held in store for me, would I have run back to my father's house and never left it? I would have been spared much worry, much sorrow. But I would never have known Tom, and felt love.

I tried to wean myself from such thoughts, as the days went by quietly and November gave way to December and the Advent season. Joan taught me to weave, and I occupied myself with soft colorful yarns. I played cards with my women. I read my Bible, I played with Jonah. I fed the birds that came to the windows of my rooms, and when the December snows fell, I took in the weakest of the birds and put them in a cage near the warmth of the hearth so that they could recover.

Small things calmed me, simple pleasures helped me to put aside the worst of my nagging thoughts. But when I dreamed, I could not suppress the ghastly images that came before me. Of Henry Manox and Francis, bleeding, their bones cracking, screaming in pain. Of Tom, lying injured and helpless and in need of me. Calling out to me. Of my father, my dear dead father, sitting beside me and talking—talking endlessly, constantly, and always about himself. Talking on and on so that he could not hear me when I begged for his help.

"Better a soft bed than a hard harlot." My husband's old saying ran in my head, foolish and meaningless. That other saying—so recently uttered by Francis—haunted me as well: "Do what you can, take what you need, act as you must." Had that been my motto, during my years at court? If so, I had much to repent.

Of one thing I felt more and more certain—that my barrenness was a gift, the act of a merciful Providence. Had I borne a child—Tom's child—the succession would have been tainted, polluted.

I began to realize as never before that the succession to the throne was something sacred, to be revered. It had been entrusted to me, as queen. And I had failed to preserve it inviolate.

I was to blame. I confessed my shortcomings, and felt better. But when I looked into my pier glass I was startled to see that, in among the rich red-brown strands of my hair, threads of silver had begun to appear. I was far too young to have an old woman's silver hair. I knew that. Nevertheless there they were, the few telltale strands, reminders that I had lived with guilt and fear too long. My body had begun to yield up its strength and youth.

I told Charyn to take the pier glass away, and I covered the unwelcome strands with one of my French hoods, edged in gold. I put on the best of my modest gowns and ordered my fiddler to play while I danced with Mary Sidford. For a time, I was able to banish my dark mood.

It was not until Grandma Agnes came to see me that my mood darkened once again, and my worries rose.

Charyn led her into the largest of my rooms. She was greatly changed. Her once proud, straight-backed figure had become the hunched form of an old woman. The look in her eyes, once so superior and defiant, had become wary and fearful. She walked with difficulty and leaned on a cane—and on Charyn, who helped her to a pillow-covered seat.

"Grandma!" was all I could say as she seated herself, slowly and painfully. "What have they done to you!"

I noticed that her lips twitched, she blinked quickly and often. All her arrogance was gone. When she looked up at me, it was with the tired, pleading eyes of weary old age.

"Catherine," she began, her voice rasping and grating, "help me."

I never expected to hear those words from my grandmother. It took me a moment to react.

"What must I do?"

"Throw yourself on the king's mercy. Deny all, confess all, do what you must. But do not let him throw you to the wolves, or we all perish!"

She told me, speaking slowly and somewhat haltingly, her every breath an effort, that I was the hope of the Howard family. I, the dishonored, adulterous wife of the vengeful king, held the family honor in my hands.

"You will be spared," she said. "Cranmer has asked me to take you back to live with me. When you leave here, you will come to Lambeth." She shook her head. "Only it is not the Lambeth you knew. It has been stripped of its beauties, shorn of its riches. They have taken everything, Catherine. Everything in my strongboxes! My jewels, my manors." Her indignation flared, briefly, then all at once she sank into her enfeebled state once again.

She looked around the room warily, then beckoned me to come closer.

"I had eight hundred pounds, Catherine. I hid it in my corselet. I thought they would never find it. I meant to give it to you. I thought you could bribe your guards. But they found it! They searched me closely, Catherine, so closely. They took the money. And then—"

"What? What did they do to you, grandma?"

She blinked quickly. She did not look at me, but at the rushes under her feet.

"They showed me that dreadful device." I knew that she meant the rack, the instrument of torture. "They lifted me up and laid me down on it. I screamed, I was in terror. I was sure they would stretch me and break me. Then they said to me, tell us which papers you burned. I told them everything. I admitted that I had burned some letters. I told them where the rest of my money was hidden. I told them all that they wanted to know, and more. They lifted me off the terrible device and I fell on my knees, begging for mercy, praying for the king's health, saying everything I could think of. And all the time weeping such bitter tears."

"Brutes!" I cried out. "Cruel brutes, to treat you so."

"It may go worse for me," she half-whispered. "Unless you can obtain mercy for yourself, for us all."

She went on to tell me, pausing often to catch her breath, that everyone in our family was being questioned, many of them tortured, many others imprisoned.

"Your uncle William is in the Tower," she said curtly, and at this news my tears fell freely. "My nephew the Great Chamberlain, at least nineteen of your cousins, my servants and pensioners, even John Spiershon, our tailor, and others who have supplied and provisioned our household."

"And Master Culpeper? What news of him?"

She paused, pursing her lips. "Your lover is condemned."

I fell forward, and knew nothing more.

When I awoke I was on my bed, with my women around me, looking down at me.

"Is she gone?"

"Yes," they each said. "She told us to tell you to beware of Lady Anna. She is your worst enemy. She sent you her footman—to be her spy. She sent him to the royal council, to tell them everything he had heard and seen while you and the king were on progress."

So that was why Englebert had disappeared so suddenly, I thought. I should have realized how odd it was that Anna should send her servant to me. How foolish and blind I was!

"She hopes King Henry will make her his queen again."

"Yes, of course she does. How little she knows him." It was my one satisfaction, the certain knowledge that no matter what else happened, the king would never again take Lady Anna to be his wife.

To see Grandma Agnes in such a sorry condition, her pride broken, her strong spirit reduced to fearfulness, was a blow to me. But to know that Tom had been condemned was a hundred times worse. Each time I thought of him a shudder passed through my body, and I grew short of breath. I tried not to think of what must be, that he must suffer horribly, and be hanged. That all his sweetness must pass from the earth forever, never to be known again. That I would yearn for him, and would go on yearning for him, for as long as I lived.

When I learned that Tom was condemned something within me gave way. I was not the same after that. I seemed to lose part of myself. I ceased to think of my future. I no longer could imagine a day, a far-off day, when all the horrors of recent weeks would be behind me and a new life would unfold.

I grew listless—yet at the same time small irritations galled me more than ever and I was curt with my servants, treating them ill, not at all as they deserved, for they were good and faithful to me. They tried to tempt me to eat, as I was becoming thin. They did their best to bring me cheer.

I no longer asked them to tell me what news they heard of the court, for all the news was grim. Still, some part of me wanted to know what was going on, and Joan, who always seemed to find out, brought us all word that the court was as silent and gloomy as anyone had ever seen it. There was no gaiety, no Advent celebrations were being held. Feasting and revelry were forbidden. The king shut himself away, or attempted to go walking, only to find that his leg hurt too much and he had to return to the palace. Hunting was bleak in winter, there was little sport to be had. Throughout the court, a mood of sullenness lay like a shroud. Or so Joan's informants told her.

Late in December a large group of lords came to Syon. I was brought before them, and was told that all my Howard relations had been found guilty of failing to disclose treasonous acts—my acts. They had all been committed to the Tower, their goods forfeit to the crown. Their lives were forfeit to the king's judgment, whether to be condemned or to be spared. In the meantime they would languish in prison. All except Uncle Thomas, whose evidence against his relations had been found useful, and whose pleas for royal clemency had been heard.

Hearing that Uncle Thomas had been spared, while Uncle William was still suffering in the Tower, I sank into lower spirits than ever. For days it has seemed as though I could no longer eat or sleep or even find the strength to dress myself. I mourn. I can barely lift my pen. I can—

Tower Green

February 1542

My cousin Catherine having entrusted to me her written account of her life at court, I feel I must complete it. She did not ask me to—indeed the only thing she asked me to do was to feed the birds she kept by the hearth at Syon and to take care of Jonah, her beloved marmoset.

I have not her eloquence. I can only set down, while it is fresh in memory, what happened during the last days of her life, as faithfully as I can. This, then, is what I heard and saw.

It was a bitterly cold morning, the thirteenth day of February. An unlucky day. A day when the stars were aligned unfavorably, as the king's astrologer told the captain of the guardsmen who told a halberdier who knew Joan well. Joan then told me, though in a low voice so that Catherine did not hear what she said.

It was early in the morning, the scaffold had been erected on the Green. The three of us, myself and Joan Bulmer and Mary Sidford, were being kept with Catherine in an interior room, with guardsmen present as Catherine had twice tried to escape and had struggled to get away when first brought to the Tower by barge. She had been erratic, beside herself with anguish one moment and exploding into laughter the next. I think she was half out of her mind with grief and terror.

She was wearing her high slippers, the ones that made her appear taller. They made her stumble at times. In her moods of foolishness she pranced in them, laughing at the absurdity of it all, that she should be so young, and about to die.

They had come for her three days earlier at Syon, and told her she was to be taken to the Tower. She said no! She wasn't ready, they must come back another day. I think she truly believed, until that moment, that she would be spared. Her grandmother had told her so. She wanted to believe it. "There are signs," she had said to me. "There are signs that I will be preserved. The king wears my mother's pendant around his neck."

All I knew was that when the Lord Privy Seal and members of the council came to Syon, they did not come to show mercy, but to carry out the king's orders. They were unsparing. And so when Catherine said she wasn't ready to be removed, there was a dreadful scene. She struggled, she refused to let them take her. They seized her and dragged her, shouting and shrieking, to her barge. The three of us were told to come as well, and we did as we were told. That was three days ago.

Ever since then she had been at times distant, lost in thought, and at times terrified. She had had a dreadful shock when we were traveling downriver on her barge, on our way to Traitor's Gate. The barge had passed under London Bridge, as it must, and there, impaled on spikes, were the severed heads of Tom Culpeper and Francis Dereham.

She screamed when she saw them, and we could not quieten her. That night Joan had to give her a powerful drink to make her sleep—though even so, she woke up shouting, as she so often did. She had very bad dreams.

As we were waiting there in the inner room of the Tower, with the guardsmen watching us and especially watching Catherine, I could not help remembering the last time I stood on Tower Green in the early morning, on the day six years earlier when our cousin Anne Boleyn was led out to die.

I was standing next to Catherine on that day, she held my hand. All of us were near Uncle Thomas, with Grandma Agnes nearby, tall and proud. All our aunts and uncles and cousins stood together, so many of us, and I remembered hearing Uncle Thomas say "Kill the big whore!" as if to tell everyone he had no love for his niece Anne who had so dishonored our family. I had been far too timid to watch my cousin Anne die. I hid my eyes. But I remembered the sound of the executioner's blade as it swished through the air, and the sharper sound as it bit into flesh. A sound at once soft and blunt. As of a huntsman when he strikes a wounded deer with the heavy hilt of his knife, to kill it.

As we waited in the interior room, we were told that a large crowd had gathered on the Green. There would be no Howards among them, of that I felt certain. All the Howards were in prison. All but Uncle Thomas, and myself and Joan—

the two of us having been allowed our freedom so that we could serve Catherine.

She was sitting quietly, lost in thought, paying no heed to the activity around her. We had dressed her in a simple black velvet gown. We were told she was to wear no hood, and that we were to arrange her hair so that her neck was exposed. Her only ornament was the relic she always wore at her waist, a relic of a tear of the Virgin. In her plain black gown she looked pale, drained of color and vitality. Her eyes were dull. There were frown lines on her forehead. Her upswept hair was lusterless, with here and there a few strands of silver grey.

On the previous evening the Lord Privy Seal had come into her cell to tell her that she would die the next day. A chaplain was with him. She made her confession and then asked to see the block on which her head would be struck off. It was brought to her.

"Was this the block on which my cousin Anne's head was severed?" she asked in a surprisingly calm voice.

She was reminded that Anne's head was struck off by a sword.

She then asked to be shown how to place her head on it correctly, as she believed her cousin Anne had not got it right. Once again she was told that Anne had died by the sword, but she appeared not to hear.

She was shown how to kneel, facing the crowd, and the chaplain advised her to say her prayers as she knelt, so that she would be carried up to paradise when the blow fell.

This made her laugh. "And am I to go to paradise then?" she asked. "A sinner like me?"

But she paid attention, and practiced kneeling and laying her head down, and in a short time the block was taken away again.

We had been waiting, that morning, for at least an hour. I was tense with the waiting. My feet hurt. My mind wandered. We had been told that a number of executions were to take place. Catherine was to be the first to die. By noon, I thought to myself, it will all be over and I will be gone from this awful place. I hope I can be pardoned for having such an unworthy thought, but I believe anyone who has waited, as the three of us did that morning, for our mistress to be killed will understand. The waiting was unbearable—because the event for which we were waiting was unbearable.

Finally we were given the signal to follow the guardsmen out of the room. I picked up the cloths I was going to need, to wrap Catherine's head and body in. How sad it makes me to write this! And how sad I was on that day, one of the worst days of my life.

I watched Catherine, to make certain she did not struggle or resist. But she was calm. The outer door was opened and a blast of chill air struck us as we stepped onto the grass with its thick layer of frost. There were the people, so many of them. A large crowd, spilling out over the Green and down toward the river. Murmuring and jostling one another uneasily. So many people! So many faces. It was as if all London had come to the Tower that morning, to watch the blood flow and the lives end.

The Lord Mayor and aldermen in their long black robes were in their places. The chaplain was already on the scaffold, his head bowed and a Bible in his hands. The executioner too was in place, a big man with powerful legs, dressed in a dark jerkin and with a hood covering his face. His heavy axe rested against the stone wall.

I saw all this at a glance, and then Catherine stepped forward, slowly, and we followed her. As she approached the crowd there were taunts and jeers.

"Kill the wench! Kill her and be done with her!"

"Whore!"

"Traitor!"

Excited voices made a hubbub of sound. Catherine did not look at the crowd, she kept her eyes on the brittle grass under her feet. When she reached the steps that led to the scaffold she began to mount them, but stumbled. I reached out to help her but two guardsmen came forward and supported her as she went up.

The strangest thing, to me, was that as she took her place beside the thick wooden block and prepared to say her last words, she had no expression. She had always been so animated and full of life. Emotion flowed out of her. Now she had no emotion left. Or she had entered some state in which emotion had no place. I would have expected her to begin to cry, as she always had at important moments. But there were no tears. The only sign that she had any feeling was that, as she began to speak, her voice shook.

Archbishop Cranmer had taught her what she had to say, which was that she deserved her punishment because she had been a sinner all her life and had broken all of God's commandments. Her condemnation was just, because she had offended against the majesty of the king. She had put his authority and the kingdom in danger by her wanton acts.

I do not remember her words exactly, but I remember thinking that they were the archbishop's words, not hers. Had she spoken her own mind, the mind of the girl I had known so well since we were children, she would have said, I believe, that she had acted from her heart, and that if acting from one's heart was wrong, then she would take her punishment. But she did not think it was wrong.

Still, it matters not what I think, but only what she said.

Then the terrible moment came. I stiffened myself to endure it. I knew I must not flinch, or crumple at the sight, but I felt myself shaking. I heard Mary crying. Joan was silent, but she had turned her face away from the block. Catherine knelt in the way she had been shown, and laid her head down. I did not notice whether she prayed or not as she waited those last few seconds. I hope she did.

Then the executioner raised his axe, and grunted, and brought it down with a loud crunching sound.

A cry went up from many throats as Catherine's head fell from the block and her life blood spurted forth from her neck, staining the block and the planking, spilling down onto the grass. The smell of the blood was overwhelming. I had to take a step back, I could not help it. I tried not to look, but the sight before me, horrible though it was, drew me. Her body began to shake and twitch. Blood stained the black velvet gown.

I remembered what we had been instructed to do. We were to lift Catherine's head from where it fell and wrap it in the smaller of the two cloths I held. With shaking hands I unfolded the cloth and approached the block. Joan came with me but Mary, weeping uncontrollably, did not.

But almost at the same moment there were people rushing forward out of the crowd, dipping cloths of their own into the gushing blood, dipping their hands in it, thrusting forth cups and vessels to catch it. For the blood of an executed man or woman, as everyone knows, can cure sickness.

Joan's hands were quicker and stronger than mine. She reached into the midst of the mayhem and snatched Catherine's head by the red-brown hair, turned to crimson by her blood. I held out the cloth and Joan placed the head in it, mouth open, eyes open and staring. I have no doubt that as long as I live, I will never forget that dreadful, staring face.

Then we took the larger cloth and wrapped it around Catherine's body. Mary helped us. Together we carried our burden past the outstretched hands and the shouting voices, our way made easier by the soldiers who walked on both sides of us, to the nearby chapel of St. Peter, as we had been instructed. Catherine, we were told, would be buried there in the chapel, where cousin Anne was buried and no doubt many others.

Ignoring the blood on my hands and my gown, doing my best to ignore all that I had seen and heard on that awful morning, I knelt there in the chapel. I knelt there for a long time, and prayed as I had never in my life prayed before. For the soul of my cousin Catherine, and her beloved Tom, and for all those who are too full of life and love to do as they ought, or to act prudently. For all those who follow their hearts, foolishly, and to the end.

Charyn Lady Morley
Written on this thirteenth day of February in the Year of
Our Lord Fifteen Hundred and Forty-Two.

NOTE TO THE READER

Once again, dear reader, a caution and a reminder: *The Unfaithful Queen* is a historical entertainment, in which the authentic past and imaginative invention intertwine. Fictional events and circumstances, fictional characters and whimsical alterations of events and personalities are blended. Fresh interpretations of historical figures and their circumstances are offered, and traditional ones laid aside. I hope you have enjoyed this reimagining of the past.

Rats on
the Range

RATS ON THE RANGE

and Other Stories

JAMES MARSHALL

· Dial Books for Young Readers ·

New York

Published by
Dial Books for Young Readers
A Division of Penguin Books USA Inc.
375 Hudson Street
New York, New York 10014

Printed in the U.S.A.
First Edition
Typography by Jane Byers Bierhorst
1 3 5 7 9 10 8 6 4 2

Library of Congress Cataloging in Publication Data

Marshall, James, 1942–1992
Rats on the range and other stories
James Marshall.—1st ed.
p. cm.
Summary: In eight animal stories the reader
meets a rat family that vacations at a dude ranch,
a pig who takes lessons in table manners, a mouse who keeps
house for a tomcat, and a buzzard who leaves his money
to the Society for Stray Cats—or does he?
ISBN 0-8037-1384-3. ISBN 0-8037-1385-1 (lib. bdg.)
1. Children's stories, American. [1. Animals—Fiction.
2. Short stories.] I. Title.
PZ7.M35672Rar 1993 [Fic]—dc20 92-28918 CIP AC

"Buzzard's Will" is a playful
tribute to the comedic opera *Gianni Schicchi*
written by Gioachino Forzano, with
music by Giacomo Puccini.

CONTENTS

Miss Mouse

When Thomas J. Cat looked out his window and saw who was standing on his front doorstep, he couldn't believe his tired old eyes. It was a mouse. She was wearing a hat covered with daisies, in one hand she carried a small leather purse, and in the other a wicker suitcase tied up with string. Her skirt was a coarse wool, as it was the dead of winter.

"Dinnertime!" exclaimed Thomas to himself. "She's awfully small, but perhaps I can stretch it out with chopped carrots and celery."

The doorbell rang insistently.

"Yoo-hoo!" called out the mouse.

Thomas J. Cat threw on his bathrobe and opened the door a crack. If she sees I'm a tomcat, she'll scamper away, he thought. And I am much too old and sickly for a chase.

"Who is it?" he called out.

"My name is Miss Mouse," said the mouse. "I've come in response to your advertisement for a housekeeper. I have references."

She began to fumble about in her purse.

The tomcat hadn't the slightest idea what the mouse was talking about.

"This *is* 93 Hollow Road, is it not?" said Miss Mouse.

The tomcat was about to inform her that it was 89 Hollow Road, when he thought better of it.

"Er, yes indeed, 93, that's me," he said.

"May I come in?" said Miss Mouse. "It's chilly out here."

"By all means," said the tomcat, throwing open the door, but remaining behind it.

Miss Mouse stepped over the threshold.

"Why are you standing behind the door?" she said.

"Er," said the tomcat. "I'm ashamed of my appearance."

"I see," said Miss Mouse.

Then she looked about the tomcat's messy living room.

"My, my," she said. "I'll have to start in right away. That is, if I have the job. You won't regret it, I do good work."

The tomcat thought for a minute. Certainly he could use some straightening up around the house. In the past few years he'd really let things slide. And when all the work was finished, *then* he could eat the mouse—around snack time. And he wouldn't even have to pay her a penny.

"Excellent," said the tomcat. "The job is yours."

Miss Mouse inspected the pantry and the area under the sink.

"You have no detergents or cleansers!" she said. "I'll just pop around the corner to the market and buy some things. I'll need about twenty dollars."

The tomcat found a twenty-dollar bill in his robe pocket.

I was planning to spend this at the races, he thought.

Miss Mouse took the twenty.

"I'll be back in a jiffy. Perhaps you can make us a nice pot of tea?"

"By all means," said the tomcat, who'd never made tea in his life.

"And by the way," said Miss Mouse, "I know you're a tomcat, so you can come out from behind that door."

"How could you tell?" said the tom-cat.

"One knows these things," said Miss Mouse. "But I'm sure we'll get along just fine."

Miss Mouse firmly believed that kindness, industry, and generosity of spirit could tame the most ferocious of creatures.

She went out the front door.

"Perhaps I've made a mistake," said the tomcat. "What if she doesn't come back? Ah well, you just have to trust."

He went into the kitchen to try and rustle up some tea.

When Miss Mouse returned, carrying two shopping bags full of detergents and cleansers, she heard a pitiful groaning coming from the kitchen. The tomcat had badly burned his paws while making tea. He was rolling about the floor in considerable pain.

"Dear, oh dear," said Miss Mouse.

"We'll have to attend to this immediately. Fortunately I have a first aid kit in my suitcase."

"Hurry," said the tomcat. "I'm dying!"

Miss Mouse retrieved her first aid kit, applied some soothing ointment to the burned paws, and wrapped them with bandages.

"Snug," she said. "And now you must get into bed and do absolutely nothing. We don't want these paws to become infected. Let me help you to your room."

The tomcat leaned on Miss Mouse, and together they haltingly made their way to the bedroom.

"Holy cow!" cried Miss Mouse. "This is worse than the living room. It will take me *days* to clean."

"I'm somewhat disorganized," said the tomcat, slipping in between the gray sheets.

For the rest of the morning and most

of the afternoon, Miss Mouse worked in the living room.

"Tut, tut, tut," she said. "And cats have the reputation of being so clean and orderly."

She swept out a large ball of fur that had accumulated under the sofa.

At four o'clock the tomcat, who had been dozing and dreaming of all *sorts* of tasty things, was awakened by a gentle tap at his bedroom door.

"Come in," he said.

Miss Mouse came in struggling with a large tea tray piled high with sardine sandwiches and potato chips. There was even a mug of hot cocoa. She sat on the side of the bed and popped the sandwiches into the tomcat's open mouth. "Yum, yum," said the tomcat.

When snack time was over, the tomcat felt all plump and rosy.

"I think I'll go back to sleep now," he said.

"Oh no," said Miss Mouse. "I have to change these filthy bedclothes."

And she put the tomcat, all bundled up, on the back porch while she cleaned and tidied up the bedroom.

She was in the bedroom quite some time and the tomcat grew concerned and went to investigate.

The bedroom smelled of cleanser and room freshener and was as neat as a pin. Miss Mouse was sitting propped up on the bed and absorbed in a thick book.

"I found this on the top shelf in the closet," said Miss Mouse.

"It must have been left by the previous tenant," said the tomcat. "I don't read much myself."

"Well, it's wonderful," said Miss Mouse. "Just listen to this. . . ."

The tomcat sat beside the bed, and Miss Mouse began to read.

It was a story about a treasure ship with billowing sails, a swashbuckling hero, and wicked pirates. An hour later Miss Mouse finished reading.

"And the evil pirate Captain Black-heart was never seen again. The End."

The tomcat, whose pulse was racing, was enchanted.

"More!" he cried.

"We'll read another tomorrow," said Miss Mouse. "I must cook dinner. We're having a tuna casserole."

Days went by and Miss Mouse and the tomcat established a fixed and pleasant routine.

While the tomcat slept late, Miss Mouse tidied up the house, went shopping, and cooked. Every day just after snacks she read a story from the thick book. It was the tomcat's favorite hour. Miss Mouse read thrilling stories about dinosaurs, cowboys, and space explorers. And the tomcat could never get enough.

"Things are working out quite nicely, aren't they?" said Miss Mouse. "I hope you are pleased with my work."

"Indeed," said the tomcat.

But one day Miss Mouse discovered something that shook her to the core of her being. While straightening up once again the tomcat's cluttered bedroom, she spotted a newspaper that was open to the Home Section. It was a full page of recipes of various mouse dishes. Several of the recipes were circled in ink. Miss Mouse had to sit down and catch her breath.

"Really!" she said. "I see my philosophy of kindness and generosity of spirit has not paid off. A cat is still a cat."

She checked the newspaper again, just to be certain she hadn't overlooked something. Perhaps the tomcat was planning to substitute parsnips or potatoes for the mouse meat in the recipe. But no such luck. There in the tomcat's own shaky handwriting was a shocking notation beside this recipe:

MOUSE MOUSSE

Boil a large mouse, as large as you can catch.
Brown an onion.
Place in a blender, turn on to finely chopped,
   for five minutes.
Scoop out the mixture and place in a but-
   tered pie tin.
Place in the refrigerator overnight. Serves one.

"Yum, yum," the tomcat had written. "I'll have this one for my Easter dinner."

Miss Mouse consulted her calendar. Easter was several weeks away. If she used her wits, she would be able to stay in the snug tidy house a bit longer. On the day before Easter she would—sadly—leave.

The tomcat entered the room and Miss Mouse hurriedly hid the newspaper behind her.

"Shall we read another story?" she said.

"Excellent," said the tomcat. And he settled himself on the bed.

Miss Mouse opened the thick book, but she was disappointed to find that all the remaining stories were about love and romance—entirely unsuitable to be read to a tomcat who loved adventure.

He'll soon grow tired of them, and then there's no telling what he'll do, she thought.

"I'm waiting," said the tomcat.

Miss Mouse cleared her throat and pretended to read. "Once upon a time in a dark and smelly cave, there lived an evil dragon."

"Oh goody," said the tomcat. "This is going to be a hot one."

Miss Mouse continued to make up her story, all the while pretending to read from the book. It was all about a brave knight and how he defeated the evil dragon.

"This is the best of all," said the tomcat.

Weeks passed. Sometimes Miss Mouse told stories that were scary. The tomcat's fur stood on end. Sometimes the tales were creepy.

"Ooh," said the tomcat.

And every day Miss Mouse checked off the calendar.

On the day before Easter, while the tomcat was dozing, Miss Mouse packed up her wicker suitcase, wrote a hurried note, and tiptoed out of the house. At the corner of Cedar and Maple she caught a streetcar for the train station.

When the tomcat awoke, he was miffed at not finding Miss Mouse who always brought in his tea and then "read" him a story. But Miss Mouse was nowhere about. Pinned to the back of the sofa was the following note (in Miss M's neat little handwriting):

Dear Thomas J. Cat,
I know what you are planning to have for your Easter dinner. That is too much of a sacrifice for me to make. So I must save myself. I am leaving.

Yours truly,
Miss Mouse

P. S. There is a casserole in the refrigerator.

"Rats!" cried the tomcat. "She has left me! I wasn't *really* going to eat her!"

But in his heart of hearts he knew the opposite was true.

On the local train to Trenton Miss Mouse gazed out the rain-streaked window. She would pay a visit to her Aunt Tillie before looking for further employment.

"No cats this time," she said out loud, startling the passenger in the next seat.

In the following days the tomcat grew weaker and weaker. He'd gotten used to being waited on, and TV frozen dinners were no longer to his taste. And more to the point, he missed Miss Mouse's stories. (He even may have missed Miss Mouse herself, hard to say.) A day without one of Miss Mouse's stories was a day without sunshine. He tried to make up his own stories, but found it was not so easy to do. "Once upon a time . . ." was as far as he could get. He knew of course that Miss Mouse had been making up her stories for quite some time now. "She always held the book upside down," he said fondly.

To keep the stories in his memory the tomcat wrote them out in a notebook. As his paws were still weak and shaky, it took him several more days. Copying out the stories made him sad, and finally he fell into a swoon.

The doorbell rang, and the tomcat flew to open it. It was Miss Mouse.

"Had enough?" she said.

The tomcat was overjoyed to see her.

"Please come back," he said.

"Things will have to improve," said Miss Mouse. "You must give up eating mouse meat," she said. "And I want it in writing." And she thrust a legal document under his nose for him to sign.

"Anything," said the tomcat.

"Now let's have a nice hot dinner," said Miss Mouse, stepping into the kitchen.

"And then can we have a story?" asked the tomcat.

"Of course," said Miss Mouse.

And that is the end of the story of Miss Mouse and the tomcat. Except that perhaps you'd care to know that the tomcat sent off Miss Mouse's stories to one of the better publishers, who snapped them right up. And with the arrival of Miss Mouse's money from the publisher, they were able to live a far more comfortable life. They were even able to hire full-time help.

When Pig
Went to Heaven

When Miss Lola the new school-teacher came to town, Pig fell head-over-heels in love. Miss Lola was the pret-tiest, sweetest-smelling pig he'd ever met.

"She's the one," said Pig.

And he asked her for a date. Miss Lola, who was on the shy side, said no. Pig was heartbroken. But every day he sent flowers to the schoolhouse and put his poems in Miss Lola's mailbox. And Miss Lola agreed to a date.

"Next Saturday night at 6:30?" said Pig.

"Fine," said Miss Lola. "I like to eat early."

Pig was overjoyed.

On Thursday Pig stopped by the barber's to have the coarse hairs on his snout trimmed.

"Saturday night, eh?" said the barber. "Where are you taking her?"

"I'm not sure," said Pig.

"I hear Chez Marcel is the best restaurant in town," said the baker, who'd stopped in for his daily shave.

"Then Chez Marcel it is," said Pig.

"Chez Marcel is very fancy," said the barber. "You will have to wear a tie. And I hope your table manners are okay."

Now Pig had never been to a first-class restaurant. He always ate at Porker O'Shaunessy's Hamburger Haven down the road. And he was *always* there when the three-for-one special was on.

"Do you know about the little fork and the big fork?" said the barber.

"There are *two* forks?" asked Pig.

"The small fork is for appetizers or salads," said the butcher.

"I love salads," said Pig.

"Pay attention, Pig," said the baker. "And the bigger fork is for your main course."

"I see," said Pig, who was already confused.

"You will impress Miss Lola if you speak in French," said the barber. "Just a few words will do. Say *Bonjour* to Monsieur Marcel when you arrive (it means 'good day'), and when you are seated, ask for *La carte, s'il vous plaît* (which means 'the menu, if you please')."

"I know that," said Pig.

"I have an idea," said the barber. "Let's do a practice run. We'll pretend this is Chez Marcel."

A card table and two chairs were set up in the middle of the barbershop.

"Now go out and come back in," said the barber to Pig.

"What a great idea," said Pig.

He went outside and came back in.

"Hi, guys!" he said.

"NO, NO, NO!" said the baker. "You must say 'Bonjour, Monsieur Marcel.' "

"Bonjour, Monsieur Marcel," said Pig.

"I think he's got it!" said the barber.

"Now offer Miss Lola the nicest seat," said the baker.

"Miss Lola's not here," said Pig.

"We're *pretending!*" said the barber.

"Oh," said Pig.

All afternoon and most of the next day Pig was instructed in the art of good restaurant manners. With the exception of a few mistakes, Pig seemed to get the hang of it.

"Now comes the hard part," said the barber. "Making interesting and amusing conversation."

"Huh?" said Pig.

"Ladies prefer gentlemen who can keep them amused," explained the barber. "I'll pretend I'm Miss Lola."

And he sat down across from Pig and batted his eyelashes.

"Now say something amusing."

"Er," said Pig. "Do you like brussels sprouts?"

"Oh dear," said the barber. "We have more work to do."

For hours and hours Pig practiced making interesting and amusing conversation.

"Read any good books lately?" said Pig.

"I've just seen the most beautifully written play," said Pig.

"Would you care to hear one of my poems?" said Pig.

"No," said the barber. "Not that."

At 6:30 a taxi pulled up at Miss Lola's house. Miss Lola was ready and waiting and peeking out the window. Pig came to the door, handed Miss Lola a beautiful corsage, escorted her to the taxi, and they were off.

Monsieur Marcel himself greeted them at the door of his restaurant.

"Bonjour, Monsieur Marcel," said Pig.

Miss Lola was impressed.

And Monsieur Marcel gave them the best table in the house.

Pig put his napkin in his lap.

"La carte, s'il vous plaît," he said to the waiter. "That means 'the menu, if you please.'"

"I know," said the waiter.

"Oh Pig," said Miss Lola. "What a lovely place."

"Glad you like it," said Pig. "I come here quite often."

Miss Lola and Pig studied the menu.

"I'll start off with a crisp green salad," said Miss Lola. "And then I'll have the Chef's special."

"Me too," said Pig.

That was easy, he thought.

While dinner was being prepared, Pig tried to make interesting and amusing conversation. At first it was slow going.

"Read any good books lately?"

"Not really," said Miss Lola.

"I just saw the most beautifully written play," said Pig.

"What was it called?" asked Miss Lola.

"I forgot," said Pig.

"Do you have any more of your poems?" said Miss Lola.

Pig was delighted. And until dinner was served, he recited his poetry.

"Ooh," said Miss Lola.

The waiter brought the salads.

"Merci," said Pig.

He was delighted that things were going so well.

Then Pig noticed that Miss Lola had stuck her snout directly into her salad and was noisily munching away. There was a lot of slurping, grunting, and intake of air. Pig picked up his fork.

"I never use forks," said Miss Lola. "They're so silly."

"I agree," said Pig, who'd become adept at using a fork and wanted to show off.

Then Miss Lola dropped some of her lettuce on the floor, picked it up with a swoop, and popped it into her mouth. Other diners couldn't help but notice, and whispered among themselves.

"I'm thirsty," said Miss Lola.

Pig ordered a bottle of mineral water.

"Not the bubbly kind," he said.

When the mineral water was brought, Miss Lola said, "I'll do that." And she bit off the plastic cap.

Later Miss Lola ordered three desserts and devoured them in no time flat. She had gobs of whipped cream all over her snout and some in her ears.

"I liked the eclairs best," she said.

"Have another one," said Pig, who'd brought a lot of money and wasn't worried about the bill.

Miss Lola picked her teeth and burped so loudly that all conversation in the restaurant came to a halt.

At the door of the restaurant Monsieur Marcel said good-bye to them personally.

"Do come again, please," he said. "It's so gratifying to have customers who really know how to enjoy their food."

On the way home Pig asked the driver to pull over and stop.

Then he and Miss Lola got out and had a lovely mud bath in a ditch by the side of the road.

"You really know how to entertain a girl," said Miss Lola.

And Pig was in heaven.

When Pig
Took the Wheel

When Pig received his driver's license, folks about town shook in their boots.

"We're in for it now," said the barber who was standing outside his shop.

"They actually gave Pig a *license?*" asked the pharmacist. "That's insane!"

"What is the world coming to?" said the baker.

Just then they heard a terrific roar, the screeching of brakes, and the grinding of gears.

"Here comes Pig now," said the barber. "Run for your lives!"

They all hurried into the safety of the

barbershop and looked out the window. Around the corner came Pig. He was driving a bright yellow sports car and was leaving a tremendous amount of dust and exhaust behind him.

"Hotcha!" cried Pig to the three in the barbershop.

And he tore off down the street. "Birdbrain!" called out the barber.

A block away Pig narrowly missed hitting an old duck crossing the street.

"Imbecile!" screamed the old duck.

And Pig was gone.

"This town won't be safe as long as Pig is at the wheel," said the baker.

The barber and the pharmacist agreed. Pig was a serious danger to himself and to others.

"I've already given Pig ten speeding tickets," said the sheriff, who'd happened by. "He hasn't paid a single one of them—

just puts them in his glove compartment. If he doesn't pay them soon, he'll end up in the slammer."

"Good place for him," said the barber.

Later that afternoon as the Homer J. Catkins family was sitting down to tea, Pig drove up their driveway, roared past the side of the house, spun around on Homer Jr.'s basketball court, and zoomed back down the driveway.

"Hotcha!" he cried out as he disappeared down the street.

Mr. Catkins's nerves were totally shattered. "What if I'd been gardening by the side of the house? I might have gotten run over."

"And that Pig is such a bad influence on the young," said Mrs. Catkins.

"I want a sports car just like Pig's," said Homer Jr.

"You see," said Mrs. Catkins to her husband. "What did I tell you?"

At the weekly town meeting folks discussed the situation.

"Pig must be stopped," someone said.

Suddenly there came a tremendous roar from outside.

"We know who *that* is," the barber said.

Pig appeared at the door.

"We're glad you're here, Pig," said the chairperson. "This meeting has been called to discuss fast and reckless driving in town. Someone has been abusing his driving privileges and is endangering everyone."

"Shocking!" said Pig. "I *am* glad I came. These things must be stopped. It's unfair when one citizen takes advantage of the others. So selfish and inconsiderate."

"*Really,* Pig!" said the chairperson.

"We're talking about *you!*"

"Well!" said Pig. "Of all the nerve! I know my rights!"

And he stormed out.

"Pig just doesn't get it," the barber said.

The next day Pig was out on one of his joyrides about town. He was driving especially fast and recklessly, taking the corner of Maple and Elm on two wheels and scaring the same old duck half to death.

"They can't slow *me* down," said Pig. The barber, the baker, and the pharmacist stepped back into the safety of the barbershop.

"I hope Pig doesn't head south of town," said the pharmacist. "I just heard the high bridge is out over Gopher's Gulch. And it's a long way down."

"Sharp rocks and boulders," said the barber. "Someone should inform Pig."

Just then Pig roared by.

The barber and the pharmacist tried to flag him down.

Everyone is waving at me, thought Pig. They mustn't be mad anymore.

He waved back.

South of town Pig headed out to Gopher's Gulch to do some fishing. Folks along the way jumped up and down and waved their arms.

"Such nice, friendly types around here," said Pig.

He waved back.

"The high bridge . . ." someone cried, but the rest was drowned out by the roar of Pig's powerful machine. Pig was gone in a cloud of dust and exhaust.

Gopher's Gulch was just around the

next bend. Pig stepped on the accelerator. He was getting closer and closer. With tires screeching he rounded the bend and aimed for the bridge. He was going entirely too fast to read the signs:

BRIDGE OUT!
TURN BACK!
DANGER!

And he crashed right through the wooden barrier.

"Have you heard about Pig?" said the pharmacist.

"Oh no, he didn't!" cried the barber. "Poor, poor Pig. He just wouldn't change. Tell us all the sad details." And he got out his handkerchief and wiped away a tear.

"Oh, Pig's all right," said the pharmacist. "He crashed through the wooden barrier and shot over Gopher's Gulch—or almost. The sports car fell short of the other bank and got smashed on the sharp rocks."

"And Pig?" said the others.

"Pig grabbed onto a branch and was just dangling there until Sheriff Bob rescued him. He's shaken up—scraped his knees, I believe—and is in the hospital for observation."

"I hope he's learned his lesson," said the baker.

Then they heard the sound of what appeared to be a runaway lawn mower approaching the corner.

"At least we know it isn't Pig," said the pharmacist.

But it *was* Pig. He was riding an electric wheelchair. His knees were all bandaged up. And he was going much too fast.

The barber, the baker, and the pharmacist all shook their heads. "Hopeless," said the barber.

They were surprised, however, to see Pig pull up in front of the jailhouse, stop, and get out. Sheriff Bob was waiting at the door.

"Pig has turned himself in!" cried the barber. "We've just seen Pig's last ride."

"Too bad," said the others.

But Pig was out of the jailhouse in a jiffy. He'd paid all his tickets and turned over his license for good. In no time he was back in his wheelchair and zipping down Main Street—just as the old duck was about to cross.

"Hotcha!" called out Pig.

"Hotcha yourself!" screamed the old duck. "I'm leaving this town!"

And he did.

Mouse Party

Miss Mouse was tidying up in the kitchen when her friend the tomcat came in from a stroll.

"See anything interesting today?" said Miss Mouse.

"Maybe," said the tomcat, who loved to tease.

"What? What?" said Miss Mouse, who *hated* being teased. "What did you see?"

The tomcat sat down in his favorite easy chair, unfolded the newspaper, and pretended to read.

"If you don't tell me what you saw, you won't get a story," said Miss Mouse, who knew when to get tough.

"Well," said the tomcat. "It seems that a large family of mice has moved in several blocks away. I saw them carrying in furniture and boxes. And one of them was painting a name on the mailbox."

"Oh?" said Miss Mouse. "Perhaps I know them."

"They're called the Johnsons," said the tomcat. "A common enough name."

Miss Mouse decided she did not know any mice by the name of Johnson.

"I shall invite them to tea for tomorrow afternoon," said Miss Mouse, sitting down at her writing desk and scribbling a quick note.

"Hmm," said the tomcat.

He did not especially relish the idea of having a house full of mice—especially as he'd given up mouse meat. But he didn't want to spoil Miss Mouse's fun.

"Do as you like," he said.

"You'll join us of course," said Miss Mouse.

Maybe they won't miss one or two, thought the tomcat, who was feeling a relapse coming on.

"Not so fast," said Miss Mouse. "*I* know what you're thinking. You must promise to behave. Or else."

"Oh very well," grumbled the tomcat.

"What is the address?" said Miss Mouse, licking closed the envelope.

"Two hundred Hollow Road," said the tomcat.

Miss Mouse wrote the address on the envelope and handed it to the tomcat.

"Be so kind as to drop this off in the Johnsons' box," she said.

The tomcat took the envelope and sauntered out the door.

"I'm trusting you to behave," said Miss Mouse.

The next afternoon at five minutes to four Miss Mouse surveyed her tea table, which was piled high with cucumber and watercress sandwiches, scones, butter, and various jams. She had laid out her best china and silver and had put some roses from the backyard into a vase.

"Now go put on a tie," she said to the tomcat.

"Aww," said the tomcat.

"It's proper," said Miss Mouse.

And the tomcat obeyed.

At four on the dot a hot rod pulled up in front of the tomcat and Miss Mouse's house. There was a lot of shrieking and laughing and carrying on.

Miss Mouse ran to the window.

"Oh no!" she cried.

"Let the good times roll!" someone yelled.

And everyone got out of the hot rod.

"Oh my stars!" cried Miss Mouse, peeking through the curtain.

"What seems to be the trouble?" said the tomcat coming into the room and adjusting his tie.

"They're coming *here*!" cried Miss Mouse. "It's the Johnsons and—gulp—they're *rats*! Great big ugly rats!!"

"They did seem on the large side," said the tomcat.

The Johnsons came to the door, rang the bell, and yelled, "Open up! We're hungry!"

"Are they wearing ties?" said the tomcat.

"No," answered Miss Mouse. "They're shabbily dressed."

"I'll go change," said the tomcat.

The Johnsons rang the bell again and again.

It would be rude not to let them in, thought Miss Mouse. After all, I *did* invite them.

And she opened the door.

"Hi, honey!" said Mr. Johnson. "What took ya so long? Nice place ya got here. Let's eat."

Without bothering to introduce his wife and kids—and there were a lot of them— Mr. Johnson plopped down on the sofa and began helping himself to the sandwiches. Right away he broke one of Miss Mouse's china plates.

"Save some for me, ya big lug!" yelled Mrs. Johnson. "Don't make a rat of yourself!"

And finding that terribly amusing, they all laughed loudly. Little bits of cucumber and watercress sandwiches were spewed about the room. And one of the kids broke a teacup.

"What is this stuff?" he said, peering into the teapot. "Yucko."

Miss Mouse was outraged.

"I think you'd better leave," she said.

"Leave?" cried Mrs. Johnson. "We're gonna stay for dinner!"

Suddenly the tomcat stepped into the room.

The Johnsons' beedy little red eyes nearly popped out of their heads.

"Holy cow!" they cried. "She's got a bodyguard!"

And stumbling all over themselves they raced for the door, down the sidewalk, and into the hot rod. And they tore off.

Miss Mouse looked at the mess and sighed.

"I hope you've learned something," she said to the tomcat. "That was not a large family of mice, but a family of large *rats.* There *is* a difference!"

"So I see," said the tomcat.

And just to be sweet he made dinner that night and brought it to Miss Mouse in bed.

Fair-weather Pig

Have you heard about Pig?" asked the pharmacist.

"Oh no, what *now*?" said the barber, who'd come into the drugstore to get a prescription filled.

"He has a new job," said the pharmacist. "It's his fourth this month."

"It wasn't *always* Pig's fault that he kept getting fired," said the baker, who was buying toiletries. "Imagine hiring Pig to be an assistant chef! Monsieur Marcel had to close down for two whole days. There wasn't a morsel of food left in the kitchen."

"Then there was that job delivering groceries," said the pharmacist. "Same problem. None of the delivery orders got delivered. Pig had a picnic all by himself in the town square."

"And *then* he was hired to operate the merry-go-round in the park," said the baker. "But he couldn't resist shifting into high speed. Little kids had trouble staying on. The mayor fired Pig personally."

"This new job may work out," said the pharmacist. "No food about, no fast engines. Let's see how Pig's doing—it's about that time."

He switched on the television set above the cash register.

"And now for Mr. P and the weather," said the announcer.

"Oh my gosh," said the barber. "It's Pig. He's the new weather person."

"Hello," said Pig, looking directly at the camera. "Let's check the national weather."

With a long stick Pig pointed to the West Coast on the weather map.

"In Chicago it is hot and humid today."

"He's got it all wrong," said the barber. "He's pointing to San Francisco."

"Maybe Pig never studied geography," said the pharmacist.

"Pig quit school," said the baker. "Said he knew everything already."

"Shocking," said the pharmacist.

"My, my," said Pig. "What are these little white things doing all over the board? I'll just get rid of them."

And he removed all the snowflakes that were blanketing Texas.

"In that part of the country it will be clear and warm—I'm absolutely certain of it," said Pig.

"Oh dear," said the pharmacist. "Pig

isn't really cut out for this line of work. He's too imprecise."

"And now for the local weather," said Pig. "Get out your slickers, your umbrellas, and your rubber boots—it's gonna rain all week. I feel it in my bones."

The next day folks in town went to their jobs and schools wearing their rainy day clothes. As the day was sunny and hot, they all nearly melted. Many of them grumbled about the incompetent new weather person.

"The morning paper announced that he'd been fired," someone said.

"Have you heard about Pig?" said the baker a few days later.

"Yes," said the barber. "He was fired."

"Not that," said the baker. "Pig has a *new* job. Come have a look."

The barber hung up an "I'll be right

back" sign in his window and followed the baker. They were joined by the pharmacist. At Maple and Oak they came to Pig's little home on the hill. The place was crawling with little kids—climbing up the hill, squealing and zooming down the mud slide in front of Pig's house.

"That'll be another nickel," said Pig to one kid.

"Don't we ever get a free slide?" said the kid.

"Certainly not," said Pig. "This is a business."

"However did you think of it, Pig?" said the barber.

"Just one of my brainstorms," said Pig.

But the truth was that Pig had left the dishwater running when he'd gone to answer the phone and had forgotten all about it while he chattered away with Miss Lola. It was only when he felt his feet all wet that he realized what had happened. The sink had overflowed; dishwater had poured through the house, out the front door, and down Pig's hill—and had created the most magnificent mud slide in the county.

"You should be very proud, Pig," said the barber. "You have a fine business here."

Pig let his friends glide down the magnificent slide for half price. Then he helped himself to a ride.

"Hotcha!" he cried out.

And down he zoomed.

When Pig
Got Smart

When Pig's slippery slide went out of business (parents had not been amused with their kids coming home covered in mud from head to toe), Pig went out to look for other employment.

"I have lots of bills," Pig said to the barber.

"Have you had any nibbles for a job?" asked the barber.

"I saw a sign in the window of the candy shop for a salesperson," said Pig.

"Most unsuitable, Pig," said the baker, who was having his ears combed out. "You mustn't be around anything too tempting."

"You're right," said Pig.

"I've got it!" said the pharmacist. "It says here in the paper that the Board of Education is advertising for a truant officer. Seems that kids aren't showing up for school in record numbers."

"What's a truant officer?" said Pig.

"Someone who tracks down kids who are playing hooky," said the barber.

"It will just be like hide-and-seek," said Pig. "I'm sure I'd be good at it. I'll apply right away."

He hurried out of the barbershop and went off to be interviewed at the Board of Ed.

"No one else wants the job," whispered the Head of the Board to the other members. "We might as well give it to Pig."

The others agreed.

"The job is yours, Pig. Good luck."

Pig was overjoyed. It hadn't taken him long to find a job.

I just have the knack, he thought.

"Then it's all settled," said the Head of the Board. "You'll begin first thing tomorrow. Report to the Watson School at eight o'clock sharp."

"Beg pardon?" said Pig. "Do you mean eight A.M.? I'm a late sleeper. Eleven would suit me much better."

"Eight A.M.," said the Head, removing his glasses. "Of course if you don't *want* the job . . ."

"I'll be there at eight," said Pig.

That night Pig set his alarm clock for seven forty-five the next morning.

"I'll have to rush," said Pig. "But I'll get a bit more sleep."

At eight o'clock the next morning he appeared at the Watson School. He'd slept in his clothes, and they were all rumpled.

"The principal will see you now," said Miss Gomez, the secretary.

Pig knocked on the principal's door.

"Enter," said the principal. "Ah, Pig, your first day on the job. It's going to be a tough one."

"May I take two hours off for lunch?" said Pig.

"No," said the principal.

Gosh, thought Pig, this *is* going to be a tough job.

For several days Pig looked for kids playing hooky, but he couldn't find any. Then one day in the park he saw a young dog sitting on a bench, reading a book.

"Shouldn't you be in school?" said Pig.

"Nope," said the young dog, completely absorbed in his book.

"And why not?" said Pig.

"I know everything already," said the young dog, turning the page of his book.

"I see," said Pig.

He decided to be clever.

"Oh, yeah, Mr. Smarty?" he said. "So what is the capital of Miami?"

The young dog put down his book.

"Miami is a city," he said. "It is in the state of Florida. And the capital of Florida is Tallahassee."

"Oh," said Pig. "I knew that."

The young dog went back to his reading. But Pig had not given up.

"If you're so smart," he said, "what's seventy-two times twelve?"

"Eight hundred and sixty-four," said the young dog.

"How did you do that so quickly?" said Pig.

"Brains," said the young dog.

"Well, you can always learn something in school," said Pig. "You might become even smarter."

"Not today," said the young dog.

"And just why not?" said Pig.

"Because it's Saturday!" cried the young dog.

And he ran off howling with laughter.

"Have you heard about Pig?" asked the barber.

"Oh no, he got fired again?" said the pharmacist.

"Not exactly," said the barber. "Pig was so ashamed by all the things he didn't know that he's gone back to school."

"Well, maybe Pig is smarter than we thought," said the pharmacist.

Rats on
the Range

When the Waldo Rat family boarded the bus in New York City for the Far West, they were in pretty bad shape. Mrs. Rat was skinny and pale. Her tail was bandaged in three places where it had been stepped on by clumsy pedestrians. Waldo Rat's paws shook so badly that he could barely lift the tin suitcase up into the bus—the suitcase that contained all their worldly goods.

"I've lived here all my life," said Grannie Rat. "But I'm not sorry to be leaving. Life in the big city is just too strenuous. And the food has gotten simply inedible."

Little Floyd was not unhappy to be

leaving either. There were a lot of mean bullies in his neighborhood, and he was always having to defend himself.

Little Wanda, the baby, didn't know *what* to think.

"All aboard!" called out the bus driver.

The Rats settled into their seats for the long ride to the West and said good-bye to New York.

"We might come back for a visit," said Waldo. "If things improve."

Meanwhile, way out West, a yellow dog (a rat terrier to be precise) was sweeping out the bunkhouse at his ranch. To make extra money Tom Terrier and his wife had turned their property into a dude ranch—a place where city slickers could come to escape the big city, enjoy the fresh open air, and eat excellent, healthy meals. The Rats of New York were to be their first customers.

"We'll have to fatten them up," said Tom Terrier, giving his wife a look.

"I'll find something in my recipe book," said his wife, who knew perfectly well what that look signified.

Several days later the cross-country bus dropped the Rats at the gate of the dude ranch. They had not slept well on the trip, had deep circles under their eyes, and were nervous and jittery.

"Well, here we are!" sang out Waldo Rat in as cheerful a voice as he could manage. "What a lovely spot."

But it wasn't really so lovely—just flat rocky land, no trees, and only a few scruffy bushes.

"I'm going back to New York," said Mrs. Rat.

"Give it a chance," said her husband.

A cloud of dust appeared on the horizon, and they soon made out a jeep coming toward them.

"Welcome to the Bar T Ranch!" said Tom Terrier. "You must be the Rats."

Mrs. Rat all but fainted.

"Er," said Waldo. "In your letter you failed to mention you were a rat terrier."

"I'm a vegetarian," said Tom Terrier.

He was lying.

With some trepidation the Rats climbed into the jeep. As the next bus was not due for several days, they had no other choice. And they were tired and hungry.

Mrs. Tom Terrier welcomed them at the door of the ranch house.

"I'm a vegetarian," she said.

The Rats were delighted to have the bunkhouse to themselves.

"I wouldn't relish sleeping under the same roof as a rat terrier," said Grannie.

"They seem nice enough," said Mrs. Rat.

That night the Rats went to bed early, slept all night and into the next day. When they awoke, Mrs. Terrier had prepared a big country-style meal—Southern fried chicken, mashed potatoes, hot buttered biscuits. The Rats gobbled it all up, asked for seconds, and then asked for thirds.

"She uses too much salt," whispered Grannie.

Days went by and the Rats' health and nerves improved considerably. Tom noticed that they were putting on weight. And the horses noticed it as well. Every morning the Rats went for their ride around the corral. And every morning the horses got slower and slower—until they refused to budge.

"Those rats are eating us out of house

and home," said Mrs. Terrier to her husband. "We're not making any money."

"I'll think of something," said Tom Terrier, giving his wife one of those "You-know-what-I-mean" looks.

"Oh," said his wife.

But something occurred during the night that proved astounding. When Waldo Rat awoke, he noticed that his legs and feet were sticking out beyond the bedposts. The same was true with Grannie, Mrs. Rat, Floyd, and baby Wanda, who was huge. Mrs. Terrier's cooking and all the healthy air had really gone to work.

"We've grown!" cried Mr. Rat.

"So I see," said his wife. "It must have been all that home cooking."

When Tom Terrier saw the Rats coming in for breakfast, he nearly dropped dead. They were the biggest rats he'd ever seen.

"Good morning," said Waldo Rat. "We're hungry!"

"Coming right up," said Mrs. T., who went to the kitchen to rustle up some grub.

Tom Terrier couldn't help but feel that the Rats had grown even more while they were eating. Mr. Rat bumped his head on the door frame as he left the ranch house.

"They've gotten too big," said Tom to his wife. "We'll go broke if they stay."

"Their month is almost up," said his wife.

Waldo Rat came to the door.

"Good news," he said. "We've decided to stay another month. We're so happy here. Our health is much improved."

"So I see," said Tom Terrier.

There was no arguing with a six-foot rat. Tom said that he and his wife would be overjoyed to have the Rats stay on.

At dinner the Rats noticed that the portions were on the skimpy side.

"More candied yams, please," said Floyd.

But there weren't any more.

The next day Mrs. Terrier took the last of her savings and went into town for supplies.

"They're the biggest rats I've ever seen," she said to the grocer.

"You're joking," said the grocer.

"Six feet tall and then some," said Mrs. T.

"My, my," said the grocer. "I'd pay to see *that*!"

"Me too," said a shopper.

"Oh, really," said Mrs. T.

At first the Terriers had a hard time persuading the Rats to exhibit themselves.

"We don't want to be on display," said Grannie.

Her stomach began to grumble.

"Think of all those homecooked meals we'll be able to afford," said Mrs. T.

And the Rats agreed to do it.

That afternoon Tom Terrier removed the Bar T Ranch sign over the gate of the ranch and replaced it with "Prehistoric Rat Range—admission Fifty Cents." Folks from miles around came to have a look. The Rats were even persuaded to dress up in Western duds. And Grannie Rat became so stagestruck that she did a little dance for the customers.

Buzzard's Will

When old Buzzard Watkins appeared to be on his last legs, friends and relatives he hadn't seen in years came to pray at his bedside.

"Poor old Buzzard," said his nephew Clyde. "He was my favorite uncle."

"I'll cry for him for months and months," said Aunt Rose.

"For years and years!" said the barber, who'd been called in to give Buzzard a last shave.

"Poor Buzzard, poor poor Buzzard," cried everyone.

"Good riddance!" said Rooster Calhoun, who never liked Buzzard Watkins.

They lived across the road from each other and had never hit it off.

"What if he leaves you a little something in his will?" said the barber.

"I never thought of *that*!" said Rooster. "Do you think he might?"

"He has gobs of money," said Clyde the nephew. "You never can tell."

Old Buzzard opened his one good eye, looked about the room, heaved a deep sigh, and closed his eye.

"He's gone," said Aunt Rose.

"Where's that will?" cried Rooster Calhoun. "It must be somewhere here in the house!"

The friends and relatives dashed around opening drawers and chests, turning vases upside down. Chairs and side tables got knocked over. Papers flew about.

"It's not here!" said Aunt Rose. "It's just not here!"

"Wait a minute," said Rooster. "What's that sticking out from underneath the pillow?"

Rooster pulled out a scroll of paper.

"The will!" he cried.

And everyone huddled around him.

"I hope I get the house," said Clyde.

"Surely he'll leave me all the jewelry," said Aunt Rose. "He loved me so."

"I could use some money," said the barber. "After all, I shaved him for years."

Rooster Calhoun dropped the will and stared into space.

"Nobody here gets anything," he said. "Buzzard Watkins has left all his money, his house, and all his personal possessions to the Society for Stray Cats!"

"Why, that horrid old thing!" cried Aunt Rose. "How selfish of him!"

"He was probably feeling guilty for all his wicked ways," said Clyde.

"We've been robbed!" cried the others.

Rooster Calhoun scratched his beak and was lost in thought.

"Hush," said Aunt Rose. "Rooster Calhoun is thinking."

A silence fell on the room.

"I may have a solution," said Rooster. "But it will require your help."

"We'll help," said the others.

"What," said Rooster, "if there was another will, leaving *us* everything?"

"Impossible," said Clyde. "This one is dated yesterday."

"Nevertheless," said Rooster. "There *could* be a newer one."

"But Uncle Buzzard is *dead*," said Clyde. "He can't sign a new will."

"Don't worry," said Rooster. "I have a plan."

And old Buzzard Watkins was removed to the guest room.

That afternoon the lawyer Foxworth came to call.

"Poor Uncle Buzzard is on his last legs," said Clyde. "You'll hardly recognize him."

"Take me to him," said the lawyer Foxworth.

Clyde led the lawyer into Buzzard Watkins's bedroom. Around the bed the friends and relatives were on their knees praying. The lawyer could not get close to the bed.

"Look, Uncle Buzzard," said Clyde. "Here's lawyer Foxworth. You asked to see him, remember?"

From the bed there came a soft wheezing sound. Rooster Calhoun stuck out a shaky wing toward the lawyer.

"Not too close," he said. "It could be contagious."

"You wished to see me, Buzzard?" said the lawyer.

"Ah yes," said Rooster in his most gravelly Buzzard Watkins voice. "I've had a change of heart. I want to alter my will—in favor of everyone here."

"You're too kind!" cried out Aunt Rose.

The lawyer unrolled a blank piece of paper he'd brought along.

"Very well," he said. "You will dictate and I will write it all down."

"First of all," said Rooster, "I wish to leave something to dear Aunt Rose. She will receive my cuff links."

"Awk!" cried Aunt Rose, clutching her heart.

"To my nephew Clyde," continued Rooster, "I bequeath my riding boots and saddle."

"What!" cried Clyde.

"And to the others," said Rooster, "I leave one dollar apiece."

"What?!" cried the others.

But they could say no more. Tampering with a will is a serious offense and they could get into big trouble.

"That leaves the house and all the rest of the money," said the lawyer Foxworth.

"Ah yes," said Rooster. "I almost forgot. Those I leave to my beloved and cherished friend, Rooster Calhoun."

"Sign here," said the lawyer.

Rooster Calhoun made an "X" at the end of the will.

"You've been most helpful," he said to the lawyer. "Now if you'll leave me to my prayers."

"Of course," said lawyer Foxworth. And he left.

The friends and relatives were furious.

"You tricked us!" they cried.

"You will kindly leave my house this instant!" said Rooster Calhoun. "Or I'll have to summon the authorities."

With much grumbling the friends and relatives began to leave. Suddenly the door flew open, and there stood Buzzard Watkins.

"So!" cried Buzzard. "What a lot of scheming, conniving thieves I see before me!"

"But, but . . . ," said the others.

"I was only pretending!" said Buzzard. "Only pretending."

"Rats!" said Rooster.

And he stormed out.

"Rats!" said the others, following on his heels.

They knew they'd never get a single penny from old Buzzard now.

But no matter—Buzzard Watkins lived another fifteen years. And he did not leave his money to the Society for Stray Cats after all. He spent it all on himself. And what a fine time he had too.